COELIA
CONCORDIA
·THE LAST VESTAL VIRGIN OF ROME·

COELIA CONCORDIA

·THE LAST VESTAL VIRGIN OF ROME·

DEBRA MAY MACLEOD

AUTHOR'S NOTE

Many of the characters in this novel—including the title character—are based on real people. To help remind you of who's who and to distinguish between characters with similar names, I have included a dramatis personae, along with other helpful and interesting content, at the back of the book.

A few words about a word: Humans have a talent for turning an innocent word into something derogatory or sinister, and the word "pagan" is a shining example of that. The word itself is neutral and originated from the Latin *pagus* or *paganus*, likely referring to a person who lived in the countryside. It only seems to have taken on a pejorative meaning when Christian writers began to use it to describe non-Christians. Non-Christian Romans— those who believed in multiple gods—would not have referred to themselves as pagans. Since their religion was ancient and widely practiced, they may not have needed a special term to describe themselves. Perhaps they simply referred to themselves as those who worshipped the true gods or the gods of their ancestors. For the purposes of storytelling, however, I do require a special term. I have chosen to use the word pagan in this novel—as opposed to a word like polytheist—as I believe the understandability and modern reappropriation of the word supports the most natural reading experience.

For over a thousand years—since the founding of Rome in 753 BCE—the priestesses of Vesta kept the virgin goddess's perpetual fire burning in her temple. In reward for their thirty years of chaste service, the Vestal Virgins were revered. They lived lives of luxury, wielded political influence and exercised rights and privileges consistent with their esteemed place in Roman religion and society. Upon retirement—between 36 and 40 years of age—a Vestal was free to leave the Order as a wealthy, independent and well-connected woman. The Vestals rode in the triumphs of Caesar, saw statues erected in their honor, performed public rites, were entrusted with the state's vital documents, acted as political emissaries during times of crisis and brought a sense of constancy to Rome and her people as it moved from kingdom, to republic, to empire. Through times of famine and feast, of war and peace, the Vestals never wavered in their duty. They were the guardians of Rome, beloved and respected, for as long they kept Vesta's Eternal Flame burning in its sacred hearth, the gods of Rome would protect the Eternal City.

*This is the story of the last Vestal Virgin.
Her name was Coelia Concordia.*

CHAPTER I

Rome, 380 CE

"At the beginning of time, the world was dark and empty, but then emerged the earth, the sky, and the gods and goddesses. One of these gods, Prometheus, took the clay of the new earth and fashioned all the creatures that would move upon it, or fly above it, or swim in its waters. One of these things was" — the Vestal priestess Coelia Concordia poked a young novice in her shoulder, making her laugh — "*you*. Prometheus shaped mortal people to look like the gods, but he made us much smaller and not as beautiful. When his sculpture was finished, he asked Minerva, who the Greeks call Athena, to breathe life into it. She did, and the creature got up from the ground and began to move about with all the others. Prometheus then gave each creature its gifts—the birds were made to fly, the fish to swim, the lion to roar and the rabbit to run. But by the time Prometheus got to people, all the best gifts—speed, strength, vision, hearing— were gone. So he did something very mischievous. He gave his mortals something so powerful that only the immortal gods knew how to use it."

"Fire," said one of the novices.

Coelia regarded the four young faces that stood around the altar fire with her, the crackles of the sacred flames resounding within the encircling marble wall of the Temple of Vesta, and the smoke rising up to slip out the oculus in the domed roof. With their white-veiled heads and smooth complexions, she wondered whether she had looked so different as a young novice of the Vestal Order. But now in her thirties, she was nearing the end of her tenure. They were just beginning. She couldn't decide if she was envious or relieved.

"Fire," she affirmed. "When the people first saw fire, they were afraid, but Prometheus showed them its beauty and usefulness. Soon, the people learned to love fire so much that families built their homes around it, and Vesta—the purest of the goddesses—entered the flames to live among them and protect them. She warmed their bodies, cooked their food, and carved light out of the darkness so they could see things they couldn't see before—not just things at night, but also the spirits of their loved ones, so they could be comforted. When the people looked into the flames, they felt the presence of the goddess so keenly that their hearts nearly burst. So they all got together and decided to build a temple to honor her. But they couldn't all stay at the temple. They had to go home and keep their own fires going. So they decided to choose the smartest, most perfect daughters in their towns and cities to care for Vesta's sacred hearthfire." Coelia smiled at the novices. "That is you."

"But how did Vesta's fire come to Rome from Troy?" asked a girl named Florina.

"By quick thinking and tunnels," replied Coelia. "But that is a very big story, and a person should never begin a big story this close to lunch."

One of the bronze doors to the temple opened, and the Vestal priestesses Terentia and Proculeia entered for their watch.

"*Salvete*, little sisters," Terentia said to the novices, her high-born demeanor naturally commanding their attention. "Go to the kitchen. The cooks have a sweet surprise for you."

The girls squealed and exited the temple as a happy little herd while Proculeia placed a strip of kindling into the flames. "The high priestess is asking for you," she said to Coelia. "She wants to know how it went in Praeneste."

Coelia nodded and left the temple, descending the steps to find her new personal guard waiting at the bottom. He followed her dutifully as she crossed the short distance to the adjacent House of the Vestals, the luxury multistory residence of Rome's Vestal Virgins. As she reached the portico, one of the sentries opened a heavy chestnut door embellished with rosette carvings, and she entered the house, continuing on to the manicured central courtyard where she caught sight of the last of the novices disappearing into the kitchen. Suddenly sensing someone on her heels, she stopped and pivoted, her large eyes peeling wider at the sight of her guard and—of all things—three large black dogs trailing obediently behind him.

"You're not supposed to follow me in here, Brutus," she said. "Weren't you—"

"It's Brogos, Priestess." He brushed his long hair off his face, revealing the blue eyes of a Goth.

"You're not supposed to follow me in here, *Brogos*," she said. She gestured to the dogs. "You can't bring dogs in here. Weren't you briefed on protocol?"

"On what?"

"Oh, for the love of the gods," she muttered. "Go wait outside."

"On the street?" he asked.

The chief house slave, a scowly middle-aged Greek woman named Ptolema, emerged from behind a column in the statue-lined peristyle and snapped the long rag in her hand at the guard.

"Yes, on the street, you rancid barbarian," she said. "And stay there until someone tells you otherwise. Now get out! You and your mutts are getting mud on the tiles!" The guard slunk away, his dogs in tow, as Ptolema lowered herself to her knees with an exaggerated grunt of effort. "Damn fool," she grumbled, as she began to scrub the dirt off the fine tiles of the garden pathway.

"Where is Claudia?" Coelia asked her.

"In her office," Ptolema replied without looking up.

Coelia crossed the garden and entered the richly adorned, high-ceilinged *tablinum* of the *Vestalis Maxima* to find the high priestess Claudia hunched over her desk, writing a letter. Her expression was the same as it usually was these days. Severe. Tired. Worried. Although not that much older than Coelia, her position as head of the Vestal Order had prematurely aged her.

"*Salve,* Claudia," said Coelia. "*Laus Vestae.*"

"Praise the goddess," the chief Vestal replied in her chronically hoarse voice. "Did you get back last night or this morning?"

"Last night. I've been in the temple all morning with the novices."

"Better you than me," said Claudia. "They exhaust me these days." She stood to retrieve a wax tablet from a shelf, her statuesque height dominating Coelia's smaller frame. She sat back down and put her elbows on her desk. "How was Praeneste? Did you go to the Temple of Fortuna?"

Coelia sat across from her superior, declining a cup of hot chamomile and honey water from a house slave and pointing accusatorily to the still unlit fireplace. "Praeneste is the same as ever. The cooks put purple dye in the garum and charge ten times what it's worth, then everyone acts like it's the best thing they've ever tasted." She watched the slave start a fire and turned back to Claudia. "And yes, I went to the temple. I made the offering exactly as you instructed."

"Word for word?"

"Word for word."

"What about the Oracle?"

"She wasn't there," said Coelia. She pulled off her white veil and raked her fingers through the length of her dark brown hair, trying to work out a knot. "Since the attacks on the temple in Eleusis, she only comes twice a month. The exact dates are kept secret for her safety."

Claudia tapped her stylus on desk. "Damn." Her eyes fell on the letter she had read a hundred times over the past few days, the one from the elderly hierophant who oversaw the sacred Eleusinian rites in Greece:

The mob was led by Christian clergymen, and what they didn't destroy with their iron bars and stones, they desecrated. The Temple of Demeter and the statue of the goddess were defiled in ways I do not have the words or the heart to express. I fear a coming darkness.

The chief Vestal had received similar letters from colleagues describing the desecration of pagan temples in other areas, especially in the country: gangs running from temple to temple, stripping the sanctums of gold, smashing the altars, profaning what they could not ruin or steal and beating the pagan priests who tried to stop them. Thankfully, such violence hadn't spread to the pagan-majority Rome. Yet the Christian co-emperors—Theodosius, who ruled the Eastern Empire from Constantinople and his counterpart Gratian, who ruled the Western Empire from Mediolanum—had their own ways of trying to suppress worship of the gods. Not only did their edicts spread contempt for the pagan gods, they banned public sacrifice upon pain of property loss, at the very least. They also ordered the arbitrary closure of temples, confiscating the holy treasures within and sending them to the forge.

"Can I have a new guard?" asked Coelia. "This one is a fool."

"This one is cheap," said Claudia. The worry of money seized her, and her gaze floated upward from her desktop to the ceiling in troubled thought.

"This new edict," said Coelia, referring to the latest law enacted by the co-emperors. "It has nothing to do with Rome. Senator Perses told me it's directed toward heretics of their own religion. The emperors look past what we do, and the Senate is still pagan. Our funding is secure."

"It isn't the emperors I worry about," replied Claudia. "Damascus and Ambrosius will use this law to strike at us if they can."

Ambrosius. Coelia bristled at the name. The bishop of Mediolanum had for years been on the warpath to slander and shut down the Vestal Order, competition as it was for the monastery of Christian virgins that his sister belonged to. *Dishonorable. Wanton. Unchaste.* That is how the man spoke of Rome's most ancient and respected priesthood of women. No one was more responsible for the early lines on the high priestess's face than he.

"You should rest, Claudia," said Coelia.

The chief Vestal sifted through a pile of documents. "What is on your agenda today?" she asked.

"I have watch in the temple tonight. Right now, I have to go to the *ludus.* A gladiator school shut down in Capua, so the fighters have come to Rome looking for work. I need to hire—"

Claudia raised a hand, cutting Coelia off. "Find Antonia before you leave. I need her help with this month's accounting." She looked up from her desk, but only briefly, her voice taking on a tone of judgment. "And take Domitia with you to the ludus. If you must mix with gladiators, at least try to maintain some air of decorum."

Coelia stood. "I will try to keep my dress on," she quipped as she exited the office, feeling Claudia's stylus hit her on the back of the head on her way out.

Rome's largest gladiator training complex, the *Ludus Magnus,* was located a stone's throw away from the amphitheater. It was a facility that Coelia knew well, even better than the amphitheater itself. As the owner of a small gladiator school that contracted its space and services, she certainly spent more time and money at the ludus than at the stadium, especially lately. The cost of putting on the spectacles—the purchase of exotic animals for the beast hunts and the room, board and training of her roster of gladiators—was increasing every month, and not just for her, but for the owners of the other schools, too. Worse, it was all happening at a time when stadium attendance was steadily declining. The shows in the amphitheater just weren't what they used to be. Decent talent and good showmanship were getting harder and harder to procure.

Coelia sat next to Domitia in the stands that framed the ludus's open-sky training arena. As the shouts of men, the clashing of weapons and the clouds of kicked-up sand filled the air, she found herself suddenly envious of her fellow Vestal. Like most of the spectators in the stands, Domitia was just there for pleasure. All she had to do was sit back and watch the fighters train without a worry in the world. For Coelia, it was business. If she didn't snag a few of the better gladiators, her operation would be in even direr straits.

Her guard, Brogos, approached and sat next to her—he was supposed to stay standing behind her, but no matter—and pointed to one of the hundred or so gladiators in the arena. Some of them were seasoned veterans engaged in regular training, but most were potential new recruits.

"That bald *retiarius* over there," he said, "the one with the green net and bent trident. He has promise."

Coelia sat up straight and caught the attention of her *lanista*. He was meandering through the apprentice gladiators, assessing their strengths and weaknesses—there was much more of the latter than the former in this lot—and deciding which ones, if any, his Vestal boss should bid on.

"Kaunos," she shouted, and pointed to the bald retiarius. "What about him?"

The gladiator trainer followed her finger and stared at the potential fighter. He watched the man's form for a few moments, and then shook his head and kept wandering through the candidates.

Brogos huffed. "Kaunos is too bloody lazy to train them, that's the problem. What about that *murmillo* with the orange and blue shield? He's not bad."

"I'm up to my ears in murmillos. I need a *provocator* and a retiarius, in that order." Frustrated, Coelia waved at Kaunos. He jogged over. "What was wrong with the bald one?" she asked.

"His form is passable, but he's a half-wit, Priestess. One too many blows to the head."

"You can't work with him?"

"I am not Midas, *Domina*," he said. "I cannot turn brass to gold. There are none here worth investing in."

Coelia tensed as a figure—Senator Olympius, the owner of another troupe of gladiators—strolled over, catching the last of their conversation.

"Brass to gold," he reflected. "I have a business proposition for you, Priestess."

"I'm listening," allowed Coelia, although she already knew that whatever proposition came out of Olympius's mouth would not be to her benefit, at least not in the long term. She privately studied him: his black-haired slick appearance, his arrogance, his tight smirk that revealed pointed eye teeth when it expanded into an almost predatory smile. All of that made him unlikable, but it was his quality of unpredictability that made him dangerous. Anyone unwise or uninformed enough to do business with Olympius lived to regret it.

"Sell me your men," he said cordially. "I'll give you top *denarius*, though they're barely worth brass, and you can go back to spending your free time doing woman things—buying jewelry, brushing your hair." He jabbed a thumb toward the training arena. "Why invest in more gladiators when you can barely afford the ones you have?"

"You've heard the news, I see."

"What news?"

"Cassius from Arelatum. He's thinking of moving his ludus to Rome."

"Is he?" When the priestess didn't play along, he changed his strategy. "If you won't sell them to me, then why don't we combine our resources? Merge our schools. We have enough good men between us to do well enough."

Coelia chewed her lip. Gods, it was tempting. If it were anyone else, it would be an easy yes.

"I'll think about it," she lied.

Olympius spun around to stare into the training arena, putting his hands on his hips and his back to her. He mumbled an obscenity just loudly enough for her to hear. *There it is,* thought Coelia. *The speed at which he can turn when he doesn't get his way.* Before them, more gladiators took to the sand to train. None looked any more promising than the previous ones.

"Thank you for your time, Priestess," Olympius said without looking back at her. He moved off to sit farther down the row.

"He's such an ass," said Domitia.

"True, but he's right to be thinking ahead," replied Coelia. She certainly was, and always about the same thing: the unlikely yet ever-present threat that Emperor Gratian would revoke the state funding of the Vestal Order, including the stipends paid to each priestess.

While her sister Vestals were all patricians from wealthy families, Coelia's roots were plebeian. Her temple service was predicated on finances as much as faith, and it was her father—a man sickened by debt as much as disease—who had secured her future via the prestigious priesthood shortly before his death. She was fortunate he had fought so hard for her novitiate. The generous Vestal *stipendium castitas* and various perks of the Order, including the legacies left by benefactors and the right to own businesses and property, had afforded Coelia an independent upper-class lifestyle. It had done the same for her free-spending but devoted mother, who Coelia now funded. But regrettably, Coelia had made the same mistake as her father. She had left her mother in charge of managing their finances. And while they were not poor by any means, there had been enough monetary missteps to cause problems if Coelia's Vestal profits and privileges were to disappear. She had to make this gladiator school pay off.

"*Mehercule!*" shouted Brogos, springing to his feet and causing both Coelia and Domitia to jump. He sloughed off his red soldier's cloak and flung it to the side. Marching into the arena, he ripped the short sword out of the hand of one of the Vestal's apprentice gladiators. "Have you never maneuvered behind a shield, you idiot? You look like a plucked chicken, flapping your arms around and going nowhere! Do it like *this!*" With a flurry of precise violence, the Vestal's guard soon had not one, but two men lying on the sand, his sandal on the neck of one and the tip of the sword at the neck of the other. He faced the trainee whose sword he had taken—with his mouth agape, the man looked even more idiotic—and threw the weapon back at him. "It's simple, just do it like that!" Redirecting his anger to the Vestal's lanista, Brogos continued his tirade. "Kaunos, get your hands out of your fucking loincloth for once and get to work! What is she paying you for if you can't even teach them to move their bloody feet?"

The exasperated lanista flashed him an obscene hand gesture and kept assessing the batch of potential new recruits while Brogos returned to sit next to Coelia, exhaling angrily through flared nostrils.

"A discreet scolding," said Coelia. "Thank you for that, Brogos."

"You should fire that useless *caudex*," Brogos griped. He turned quickly to Coelia, spurred by opportunity. "Hire me instead. I can fight in the arena and help train the men."

Coelia faced him. "Have you ever fought in an arena before, Brogos?"

"I've fought on the battlefield. I was a *foederatus*. I served under General Arbogastes in Germania." He jutted his chin toward the arena. "I can hold a *gladius* and a shield better than any of these old women."

"I know you were in the army," said Coelia. "I also know you were dishonorably discharged, without a veteran's pension."

"What use is there for honor in the arena?" He looked at her seriously. "I'll never get ahead on a guard's salary. I can barely afford to feed my bloody dogs. This morning I had to beg for scraps from your slave Ptolema—an experience that was its own version of Hades, by the way—and she threatened to poison them if I asked again." He held out his arms. "The Fates have conspired to help us both. You will pay me a salary, my room and board, and a cut of—"

"Will I?"

"Yes. And I will make you—I'll make *both* of us—even more money."

"Sorry, Brogos. I can't afford to bet on long odds right now."

A whistle blew, and the violence in the training arena ceased. It was time for the gladiators' midday meal. Capitalizing on the break to stretch their legs and purchase refreshments from the circulating vendors, the spectators left their seats and began to socialize. One giggling group of them—young women come for the guilty pleasure of ogling Rome's biggest fantasies—drifted past Brogos like a colorful cloud of silk dresses and perfume, all flashing him suggestive smiles. Coelia recognized one among them: Anthea, the daughter of Senator Perses.

The young woman bowed politely to Coelia. "Priestess," she said. Her gaze quickly shifted to Brogos, and she winked at him.

The girl's coquetry prompted Coelia to rethink Brogos's proposition. The man's skill and brutality would bring in the male spectators, while the rest of him would bring in their wives and daughters. They filled the stands just as well, and they were a lot less critical. And as for the recruitment and training of her gladiators, the Goth's doggedness would force Kaunos to earn his payment or take his own pummelling for it.

Domitia read her friend's face and slapped Brogos on the back. "You're hired," she said.

CHAPTER II

A beautiful pink-sky dawn was just breaking when the Vestalis Maxima Claudia arrived at the steps of Vesta's temple, dressed on this particular morning in her ceremonial attire: a fine white *stola* and crimson-bordered white *suffibulum* veil, the formal headdress pinned in place at the breastbone by a gem-studded gold *fibula*. On her feet were the ritual shoes of the Vestal, shoes made from the wool of unbred sheep and designed for silence, so as not to interrupt even the softest snap of the flames during special rites or prayers. On the landing at the top of the steps waited a novice priestess, Sergia, dressed in a delicate white *tunica* with a gold belt. As her superior approached, the novice opened one of the embossed bronze doors of the temple.

Claudia entered the *Aedes Vestae*, the door closing behind her and the larger world contracting into the circular embrace of the sanctum's white marble encompassing wall. Near the center of the space, the holy fire of Vesta burned in a bronze firebowl atop a round laurel-draped marble altar, the goddess's divine breath rising as smoke to escape out the oculus in the domed roof. The goddess's fire had burned in this very spot for eleven centuries, since the time Romulus founded his city—Rome, the Eternal City, so-called because of its Eternal Flame.

The chief Vestal crossed the ornate tile floor to join the five priestesses who already stood around the sacred hearthfire—Coelia, Antonia, Domitia, Proculeia and Terentia—their palms up in prayer over the moving orange flames as the snaps of the fire, the voice of Vesta, reverberated within the sanctum. Claudia crumbled a round holy wafer into the fire. Made of salted flour, these sacred cakes had been used by the Vestal Virgins since the Order's earliest days to better commune with the goddess.

"Mother Vesta," said the chief Vestal, "guardian of Rome. We six, your virgin priestesses, make this offering on behalf of the emperors, the Senate and the people of Rome, in gratitude for the peace treaty between the Roman people and Gothic tribes of Germania." Next, she took a bowl of red wine from a niche in the marble wall, dipped a *simpulum* ladle into it and poured the red liquid into the flames. They flickered and rose higher. "*Vesta Sancta*, we make this libation in honor of the *pax deorum* between Rome and the immortal gods."

As Claudia set the simpulum back into the bowl of wine, Coelia placed six strips of polished oak branches into the fire in a criss-cross pattern. Each bore the name of a Vestal Virgin carved perfectly into the wood. She watched the letters S SAC COELIA CONCORDIA—*Holy Priestess Coelia Concordia*—disappear in the flames. When she looked up, Claudia was smiling. A rare sight.

"I have good news," said the chief Vestal. "Symmachus is to be given special honors in the Senate next month for his work with the peace treaty. He'll also be the next urban prefect of Rome."

The next most senior Vestal, the aristocratic Antonia, pursed her pretty lips in happy surprise and poked the flames with an iron stoker. "That means he'll be the leader of the Senate, too. A strong advocate in a high place."

Claudia nodded, the relief visible on her face. Symmachus had already served as *Pontifex Maximus*, chief priest of Rome, for years. Since the time of the first Caesars, it was a position held by the emperor, though the Christian co-emperors Theodosius and Gratian had refused the title and instead conferred it on the respected pagan senator. Now, they were showing their support for him in even greater ways. He would soon be the most powerful man in the city, with jurisdiction over everything from the courts to the grain supply.

The priestess Proculeia sprinkled frankincense into the fire, her slender hands moving with their characteristic quickness. "I told you not to worry about our stipend," she said to Coelia. "Symmachus has always cared for our Order."

Coelia scoffed. "Cared for? He roots through our business like a truffle hog."

"He has his reasons," defended Claudia. She sighed. "Coelia, come with me. You can help me update some files in the Regia."

Leaving the other Vestals to watch the fire or attend to their various duties, Claudia led Coelia out of the temple and across the Via Sacra, heading toward the nearby Regia. As ancient as the Temple of Vesta and rebuilt as many times, the traditional house of the early Roman kings had for centuries served as the headquarters of Rome's *Collegium Pontificum*, housing both the archives of the priesthoods and the city's most important historical records.

"The breakfast bread is probably out of the oven," Coelia hinted.

"Probably," Claudia replied, but did not change course.

The two Vestals entered the sacred civic structure, passing by a white-veined red marble altar dedicated to the war god Mars. On top sat a sword and shield that, legend had it, Mars himself had thrown down from the heavens. It was said that the weapons shook whenever Rome was in danger. The women briefly stopped to make an offering at an archaic ivory shrine to Ops, mother of Vesta: Vesta, whose virgin priestess, Rhea Silvia, had been chosen by divine Mars to bring Romulus—his son and Rome's founder—into the world.

The priestesses proceeded to the rear of the building where relics gave way to record-keeping. Floor-to-ceiling pigeonhole shelves stuffed with papyrus scrolls covered every wall, with writing tables arranged in neat rows along them. Two young priests of Jupiter were just packing up their wax tablets and *styli*, and they bid the Vestals courteous farewells as the slave Ptolema stood from a desk and approached, helping each woman in turn remove her ceremonial attire and strip down to the comfort of a simple white tunica and loosened hair.

"It is good news about the peace treaty and Symmachus," said Coelia, trying to broker her own peace with the irritated chief Vestal.

"You don't have to like him," replied Claudia, "but you do need to respect him."

"I do respect him."

"You do not."

"No, I don't," admitted Coelia. "He's intrusive and rude. He's that way with the orders in Tivoli and Bovillae, too, always accusing priestesses of wanting to leave before their tenure is over."

"He's trying to avoid the embarrassment of another Primigenia," said Claudia, referring to a priestess from the temple in Bovillae who had absconded, purportedly to follow a lover.

"Everyone wants to avoid that," Coelia replied. "Hounding the innocent won't help."

The high priestess put her hands on her hips and stood in front of a shelf packed with scrolls. Whatever confidence she had shown in the temple was suddenly gone. "Centuries of our history," she said, her eyes moving over the scrolls. "Centuries of our customs and religious rites. Our most important moments. Our most sacred ancient prayers." She took a step closer to the shelf and withdrew a scroll, unfurling the papyrus. "*Sacerdotem Vestalem, quae sacra faciat... ita te, Amata, capio.*" she read aloud.

"I remember the words," said Coelia. They were words from the rite of *Captio*, the formula spoken by the Pontifex Maximus when initiating a novice into the Vestal Order.

"The same words have been spoken here for over a thousand years," said Claudia. "Every Vestal Virgin who ever served the goddess in Rome, all of our sisters dead and gone, heard those words as a child." She slid the scroll back in its place and withdrew another, this one sending dust falling to the tile floor. "Here is the will of Augustus, which the Vestalis Maxima Occia read in the Senate House the day the emperor died. He speaks of the gifts he gave our temple and the rites the Senate entrusted to the Vestal Virgins in his honor." She re-filed the scroll, and moved to another wall overlaid with documents. "Here are the pontifical books that derive from Numa and Priestess Amata, Rome's first Pontifex Maximus and Vestalis Maxima, who dined with Romulus himself. Over here, the writings of Julius Caesar, Hadrian and Marcus Aurelius… and here is Cicero, Pliny and Virgil." She touched a scroll, and recited words by heart. "'To thy hands Troy entrusts her holy things and household gods.'"

"And Vesta's ever-bright, undying fire," added Coelia. She heard the high priestess sigh unsteadily and realized she was fighting off tears. She put a hand on her superior's shoulder. "Claudia, it will be all right."

"I don't approve of all your choices," said Claudia, "but you have always been a competent and dedicated priestess. I cannot fault you." She wiped her eyes. "But I know you plan to leave the Order at the end of your tenure, and that has made you look past what we are facing. If the bishops have their way" — Claudia gestured to the rows of scrolls — "every word ever written about the goddess, about all the gods, will be burned to ash. Every letter or memoir ever written by our sister Vestals… it will be like they never existed. Our holy relics will be thrown into the forge or paraded as conquered trash."

"It will never come to that."

Claudia leveled her gaze at Coelia. "Symmachus and those like him—Praetextatus, Junius and the others—they have protected us in ways that you will never know. All they ask in return is that we respect them and uphold the dignity of our service."

"I will be more respectful, Claudia. I promise."

The high priestess moved to a desk and sat. Ptolema, who had been listening quietly, placed a tray of hot honey water in front of her, and Claudia poured herself a cup. She sat back in her chair. "At least I was right to send you to the sanctuary in Praeneste," she said. "We can thank Fortuna for Symmachus's promotion." She took a sip, but flinched—it was still too hot—and blew into her cup. "Perhaps it will be all right after all."

"Of course it will," said Coelia, pushing down the pang of guilt, of apprehension, she felt at keeping the whole truth about that trip from her fretting superior. The Oracle had indeed been at the sanctuary. But it would do no good to tell the long beleaguered chief Vestal what she had prophesized.

CHAPTER III

Brogos hated the taste of fish and he hated the smell of it too, though there was no escaping the latter. Despite the sprawling size of the multilevel market adjacent to the Forum of Trajan, it seemed the putrid odor permeated out of every shop, every doorway and every basket in the cosmopolitan shopping district. The bustling commercial complex was a city unto itself, boasting scrubbed cobblestone, gilded bronze roofs, elaborate equestrian statuary and marble-faced walls as far as the eye could see... and yet no relief for the nose. Even smells that would normally please him—freshly baked bread, exotic fruit and various women's perfumes—could not compete with the fishy stench. He passed by a particularly pungent storefront selling sole, snorted in disgust, and spat on the street.

Seeming to materialize from thin air, a soldier growled at him. "You're not in Germania anymore," he said.

Brogos ignored him, instead trying to recall the directions that Priestess Coelia had given to Marcus's *taberna*. According to everyone at the ludus, Marcus was the best custom armor designer in the empire, a regular Vulcan. But Brogos had learned that a bad reputation was usually more truthful than a good one, so he would reserve judgment until he saw the man's work for himself. He looked around and spotted what he was searching for—a giant fountain with three levels sculpted as conch shells. Slipping through the crowd and dodging women shoppers—why did they never look where they were going?—he navigated his way through the throng, past the fountain, to find a young man with burns on all ten fingers carefully arranging an assortment of *gladii* on a display table in front of his shop.

Brogos lifted one of the short swords off the red cloth and inspected the intricate design engraved on the silver of the blade.

"Isn't this dainty," he said. "Was it your mother's?"

Marcus plucked the sword out of Brogos's hand. He polished the Goth's fingerprints off the blade and set it back on the table.

"Selling one of these to a rich man so he can chase his wife around the bed like an oversexed gladiator pays my rent for a month," he said. "Dainty turns a profit."

"Can't fault you there, brother," Brogos replied. "You're Marcus, I assume. I'm supposed to meet my boss lady here. She said I need armor with more—now, this is her word, mind you—*flair.*"

"She's already here," said Marcus. "Come with me."

He turned to lead Brogos into his shop, but hesitated at the three black dogs—they looked too fancy to be street dogs—on his heels.

"Yours?" he asked.

"Mine," replied Brogos. "This is Cosmos, he's the oldest. You can tell it's him because the tip of his tail is bent." He pointed to the next dog. "That's Sirius—see the scar on his ear?—and that's Orion. He's as perfect as they come."

Marcus nodded in a way that suggested he couldn't care less. "Leave them outside."

Brogos whistled, and the trio sat just outside the entrance to the shop as Marcus led their master inside. Coelia and the temple guard who had accompanied her to the market were there, the

Vestal perusing a row of shelves stacked with designer pieces of armor. While most were vanity pieces made for men who couldn't tie their sandals without puffing, several choice pieces were customized for working gladiators.

"*Salve, Patrona*," Brogos greeted.

Coelia stepped on a stool to reach a helmet on the top shelf and passed it down to Brogos. "Try this on."

Rounded with circular eye grates, the helmet was impressive yet fairly standard for a provocator gladiator like Brogos. He lifted it over his head of uncombed blond hair and tried unsuccessfully to put it on.

Coelia turned to Marcus. "See? He has the head of a bull."

"I hit like one, too," said Brogos, but no one acknowledged the quip. It was all business.

Marcus took the helmet from Brogos and set it on the floor. He lifted a loop of rope from where it hung on the wall and wrapped its length around the gladiator's head, measuring the circumference. "*Prodigiosus*," he sputtered. "You were right, Priestess. I'll have to make something special. It'll cost."

"I thought so," she said, lifting the hem of her white tunica and stepping down from the stool. She faced the guard. "You can go back to the temple. Brogos will take me home." Turning to her new gladiator, she said, "Let's go get something to eat. We need to strategize."

"Great, I'm starving. Some fresh bread and cheese—"

"The vendor in the square by Trajan's statue has the best goatfish in Rome. We'll have that."

"Perfect," Brogos replied unenthusiastically. "I haven't had a good goatfish in ages."

They meandered through the sunny market, down streets and along arcades filled with statues, having to stop several times as Vesta's faithful lowered themselves to their knees, soliciting the priestess for a blessing. She declined no one. Finally, they passed under a triumphal arch to enter the massive open square in the forum, at the far end of which stood a giant bronze statue of the emperor Trajan seated on a horse. Tourists pointed up at it before moving on to explore the adjoining basilica on their way to the famed column of Trajan. But for Coelia, it was the vendor near the base of the equestrian statue who was most worth seeing.

As they arrived and the smell grew unbearable, Brogos forced a smile onto his face. "Two of your best goatfish, brother."

"And make sure it's fresh cooked today," added Coelia. "I don't want your soggy scraps from yesterday."

The vendor feigned a wounded look. "Priestess, before I put each goatfish onto the fire, I look into its eyes and I ask it 'Are you good enough for Lady Coelia?' Only if the fish winks do I cook it for you. Otherwise" — he jabbed a thumb at the multitude of people in the forum — "I feed it to these fools."

"Mm-hmm," sounded Coelia. She accepted two rough terracotta bowls teeming with fish meat and headed toward a nearby bench as the vendor held his palm out to Brogos. Coelia spoke over her shoulder to him. "I pay for your armor, your lodging, your training and your meals at the ludus—and by the way, you might hit like a bull, but you eat like a pig—so you can buy two bowls of fish."

The gladiator pressed a coin into the fish-seller's palm. When the seller didn't withdraw his hand, Brogos added a second one.

"*Gratias ago*," said the vendor.

Brogos sat beside his employer on the sun-warmed marble bench and accepted his bowl of fish. Holding his breath, he dug his fingers into the white flaky meat and pushed it past his lips. It was... as awful as he expected. He looked at the Vestal and raised his eyebrows as she stuffed a huge handful of baked goatfish into her mouth.

"I have seen dying men on the battlefield with better manners," he said. "I pity your sister priestesses, having to dine with someone who eats like the Cyclopes."

The Vestal laughed, but kept chewing as Brogos's three dogs sat side by side in front of him. Their intense gazes alternated between their master and the bowl of fish in his hands, their three heads moving as if they were one beast.

"Cerberus is in the market today," said Coelia. She looked at Brogos. "You can't bring them everywhere. Leave them home."

"Ah, they're no trouble," he replied, ruffling one of the dog's ears. "Extra protection for you." He tossed each of the dogs a piece of his fish.

"If you're going to make us money in the arena, you need the crowd to care," said Coelia. "You need a name and a look that people will remember." She grew pensive. "What makes you unique?"

"I hit hard. I anticipate."

"That's weight and skill, but it's not unique. It's not a persona."

He cocked his head. "I was thinking maybe Alcaeus the Avenger or some version of Hercules." *Anthea would like that*, he thought. The young woman now attended almost all of his training sessions in the ludus, though he knew that would end when her parents found out.

Coelia crinkled her nose. "Boring. Everybody wants to be a hero. Be a villain. That's what brings in the crowds, and the gods know we need them. I only have a couple years left in my tenure at the temple, and then I plan to retire. I need to make as much money as possible before then."

"What will you do afterward?"

She pushed another piece of fish past her lips and spoke while chewing. "There is a seaside villa in Cumae that my family used to own. I lived there as a child, until my father died and I entered temple service. I want to buy it back. My mother and I will live there together. If I can make enough from my gladiators, and if I don't lose my Vestal stipend in the meantime, I'll be able to do it, and I won't even have to sell my house on the Esquiline."

"I thought all Vestals were rich."

"They usually are," said Coelia, "but I spent the first five years of temple service repaying my father's debts. On top of that, my family—the *Coelii*—have financed the *Epulum Jovis* since the time of the Republic, so I have to pay for that twice a year. It's a big banquet at the Temple of Jupiter on the Capitoline. And then there are extra civic duties I have as a Vestal. I'm supposed to donate to public works, like gardens and orphanages." She sniffed. "All of that is before my mother's expenditures, may the gods have mercy. Even so, serving the goddess has given me a good life. I don't know what would've happened to me and my mother otherwise." She turned to Brogos. "What will you do with your winnings?"

"Move to Egypt."

"Why Egypt?"

"Because I want to live in the desert. I hate the sea and I hate fish, and I want to live as far as possible from both." He shrugged. "I want to climb the pyramids. I want to raid the tomb of a pharaoh."

Coelia grunted in appreciation as she ate. "All those secret passageways and hidden treasures," she said. "Sneaky. I like it."

"I want to try real Egyptian beer," said Brogos. "Not that swill they make for the legions."

"Beer is disgusting," replied Coelia. "Claudia made us drink it at the chariot races once, after a brewer left his estate to our Order. Antonia couldn't even keep the stuff down, but her stomach is pure patrician."

"It's an acquired taste." Brogos frowned. "Are you sure you don't like Alcaeus the Avenger? Romans love a good revenge story."

"No, you have to be a villain. What about the Goth Avenger? Use what you are."

"Romans hate Goths."

"Precisely."

"They'll catapult me over the gates."

"No, they won't. The war is over. Anyway, you fought for Rome." She looked at him, suddenly curious. "What did you do in the army anyway?"

Brogos set his bowl on the bench and stood. "I'll show you."

As Coelia watched, Brogos took five large strides away from the bench, all three of his dogs keeping their black eyes fixed on him. He whistled and made a quick gesture with his right hand, at which point the dogs leapt to their feet in flawless unison and raced toward a young man who stood by a shrine to Mercury. The man spotted them and shrieked, clambering on top of the shrine and knocking over the offerings. Brogos whistled again and the dogs stopped in their tracks and sat on their haunches, pink tongues hanging out of black muzzles, their focused eyes locked on their owner, awaiting their next instruction. Those around the shrine burst into laughter as the man sheepishly crawled down. He retrieved the offerings from the ground and arranged them back on the shrine, glaring at Brogos but saying nothing. Brogos snapped his fingers, and the dogs rose as one to return to the bench. They sat side by side at Coelia's feet, their formation as straight as a line of legionary soldiers.

"But can they play dead?" asked Coelia.

"They can't play dead," Brogos smiled, "but they can kill."

"So that's what you did in the army? Managed the war dogs?"

"I trained them as sentries and took them into battle..."

"And?"

"That's how I got dishonorably discharged," he said. "General Arbogastes ordered me to strap oil lamps to them and send them into the enemy's camp to start it on fire. I couldn't do it. Can't blame the general for discharging me, though. We all have a job to do."

Coelia's thoughts briefly landed on the general, but then skipped to a vision of the three black dogs running through the orange flames. An idea came to her, and she laughed so suddenly that she inhaled a piece of fish. Coughing to clear her airway, she regarded Brogos's canine trio with eyes as calculating as theirs.

"It was there all along," she said. She dropped her empty bowl to the ground and lifted Brogos's bowl off the bench. She finished the rest of his portion before standing. "I have an idea for your armor," she said, and wiped her oily fingers on his tunica. "Let's go back and see Marcus."

CHAPTER IV

Baiae (five days by horse south of Rome)

I t had been a long war. A grimy, exhausting war full of extremes—extreme weather, extreme terrain, extreme bloodshed—and fought against an enemy so wild and blood-chilling that the Roman general Arbogastes felt certain he would never shake the image of their blazing eyes setting upon him while his fellow soldiers fell, died, all around. That vision formed a constant picture in his mind, like a haunting mosaic depicting every form of grotesque death imaginable.

But the war was over. The peace treaty said so. The bodies of slain Roman soldiers had either been dumped into collective funeral pits or left where they had fallen to rot or be ripped apart by vultures and scavenging wolves and wild boar. The corpse of the Roman emperor Valens—the Imperial predecessor of Theodosius—had fared no better. It had simply disappeared as the barbarians hacked everything in a Roman uniform to fleshy, bony bits.

Despite the morbid imagery in his mind, Arbo felt himself being lulled into something close to sleep. The rhythmic movement of his horse beneath him, combined with easy travel on good roads and a perfectly temperate day, was a formula for sleep. He stretched his spine, squeezed the reins and inhaled an invigorating breath of the clean air. He looked sideways at his riding companion, a younger man dressed in the same style of soldier's tunica and riding the same breed of standard-issue military horse. He, too, was drifting into sleep.

"Stilicho," barked Arbo, and laughed as his younger companion jerked awake. He gestured ahead. "We're almost there."

"Oh, good," remarked Stilicho. "Why enjoy Rome's taverns or brothels after years of war, when instead we can ride out to Baiae like two messenger boys for Gratian?"

"I released you from duty," said Arbo. "But you keep following me like a dog I once fed."

"You're too pretty to travel without an escort, General." Restless, Stilicho shifted in his saddle and glanced at the scroll box that hung from Arbo's saddlebag. "Who's the letter for, anyway?"

"How should I know? The emperor instructed me to give it to the custodian of the baths. It's probably for some idiot senator getting sponged and fellated by the Sirens on taxpayer coin."

Stilicho shrugged. "Doesn't sound like an idiot to me."

"We'll deliver it, and then we're free to do as we please," said Arbo. "Anyway, it gives us a chance to see how the finer half live while we're running for our fucking lives in Germania."

As they neared Baiae's monumental bath complex—a seaside resort famed for its decadent indulgence of the rich and powerful—Stilicho muttered under his breath. "*Futuo.*" He tongued the roof of his mouth, absorbing the grand scale of the port city's luxury district. Its terraced network of tall arches, domed bathhouses, manicured gardens, elegant statues and buildings, and massive thermal spas dominated the seaside in tiers of increasing extravagance and, no doubt, pleasure. "Have you ever been to a place like this?" he asked.

"Stop gawking," said the general. "You look like a bloody tourist."

"Sorry. Can't help it."

They kept riding until Arbo spotted a roadside shrine to Diana, goddess of wild beasts. Dried flowers surrounded the base of her statuette. At the sight of it, Arbo's mind played a memory. He was a young soldier who had not yet seen his sixteenth year, separated from his troop and wandering a foreign forest, within hours of succumbing to starvation, when a young injured deer had appeared directly in his path. It had taken the last of his strength to accomplish two noble feats—putting the animal out of its misery and putting food in his stomach. Meat had never tasted so good, raw and bloody as it was. He had wept at the taste, wept at his second chance at life, wept in gratitude for the goddess's boundless mercy.

He slowed his horse and dismounted, approaching the shrine to pray. But as he drew near, he could tell something was wrong. The statuette had been altered. The goddess's bow and arrow had been broken off, and a cross had been carved into her forehead. Words had been roughly cut into the wooden surface of the shrine: HUNC DAEMONEM IESUS CHRISTUS OCCIDIT. *Jesus Christ slew this demon.* Arbo lifted the statuette from the desecrated shrine and took it back to his horse, stuffing it in the saddlebag.

Guessing what had happened, Stilicho said nothing as his superior mounted his horse and they again began to ride.

His thoughts soon returning to the nearby town of Baiae, Arbo broke the silence. "They say this town was named after Baius, Odysseus's helmsman."

"Now who's the bloody tourist," said Stilicho.

The gibe performed as expected, and Arbo's mood lightened.

Reaching the main gate, they dismounted as a pair of guards arrived to inspect the horses and gear of the travelers. One of them rummaged with unnecessary zeal through Arbo's saddlebag and withdrew the scroll box. He opened it—there was really no reason to do so—and plucked out the papyrus scroll inside, his bullish demeanor now piqued by curiosity. The scroll bore the Imperial seal of Gratian, the emperor who ruled the conflict-ridden expanse of the Roman world alongside his co-emperor, Theodosius.

"Here on official business?" the guard asked Arbo.

"That's right."

"What is it regarding?"

Irked by the guard's condescending tone toward the general, Stilicho slipped between them and snatched the scroll box from the guard's hand. "Maybe you'd like to inspect our loincloths, too?"

The gate guard pressed his lips together in the kind of tight smile the veteran Arbo had seen countless times: the smile of someone with a little authority to exert over others and a lot to prove to himself. Yet while Arbo had long ago learned to shrug off the petty assaults of others, Stilicho hadn't. As the guard reached out to grab the scroll box back from him, Stilicho propelled the metal cylinder forward, directly into the guard's nose. The man cried out and put his hands to his face as blood coated his fingers.

The second guard, who had been busy inspecting Stilicho's gear, strode over to see what the ruckus was about. When he got a closer look at Arbo, he put a hand to his chest.

"General Arbogastes," he said, "I am legionary soldier Publius Mallius." When Arbo didn't show any signs of recognition, he held up his other hand. It was missing three fingers. "Discharged after a bit of bad luck on the Danube, sir."

"Ah, well there are worse parts you could've left behind in that swamp," replied Arbo. "Easy work now though, hey?"

"Sure is, sir." Ignoring his fellow guard—he was still moaning and trying to tamp the blood gushing from his broken nose—he spoke to a nearby young woman dressed in a vivid yellow dress. "Take General Arbogastes and his man to..." he looked expectantly at Arbo.

"The chief custodian," said the general.

The guard glanced at the weapons-laden belt around Arbo's waist, but said nothing. Even if it cost him his job, he would not disrespect the general by asking for his weapons. Sensing as much, Arbo unfastened his belt and relinquished it, signalling for Stilicho to do the same.

"Thank you, sir," said the guard, a touch of relief in his voice.

"You're welcome, legionary soldier Publius Mallius," replied the general, and saw the flash of pride on the former soldier's face.

Arbo and Stilicho followed the woman in the yellow dress into the lavish complex and through a long columned arcade that dripped with green vines, soon emerging into even more opulence. As they walked along, Arbo laughed inwardly at Stilicho's self-conscious preening. The younger man straightened his tunica and ran his fingers through his cropped hair, all while alternating his gaze between their escort's enticing backside, the brilliant structures around them and the serene blue waters of the bay in the near distance. Arbo understood the allure. After seeing nothing but red and brown—blood and dirt—for as long as they could remember, it was like a world of color had blown in on the warm sea breeze.

The woman led them through a flower garden and along a row of archways, the blue sky overhead giving way to painted ceiling frescos as they finally entered the shaded office of the custodian. He looked up from his desk, assessing the two soldiers. The older man had the height, light hair and blue eyes of a Frank. The more junior was also taller than the typical Roman, but darker complexioned than his colleague. The custodian rose from his desk to greet them, one hand reaching out to accept the Imperial scroll from the taller and lighter of the two, Arbo.

"*Salvete*, soldiers," he said.

"*Salve*," replied Arbo.

The custodian broke the emperor's red wax seal and unfurled the papyrus. He read quickly and curled it back up. "General Arbogastes, I presume?"

"That's right."

"Are you aware of this letter's contents, sir?"

"Its contents are not my business," said Arbo. "Only its transport."

The custodian nodded. "By order of Emperor Gratian, it is my duty to ensure that you are treated to the best our facility has to offer for a period of fourteen days." He smiled in the stunned silence that followed. "Allow me a moment to assign personal escorts," he said, and slipped into a back room.

Stilicho rocked on his heels. "Fourteen days," he whispered, enthralled. "I must be dreaming. Fourteen days of hot baths, gourmet food, good wine, laundered bedlinen and soft whores," he said, counting off the benefits with his fingers. "All with a view. And to think I almost didn't come with you."

Arbo raked his fingers through his short hair, irritated. "I can bathe at home. I haven't seen my pigeons in over two years."

"I know who you haven't seen in two years," said Stilicho. "And since she's still at the temple, you have to couple with something or you'll go mad. That's what happens if you don't empty your balls at least once a month. It all backs up—up your guts, up your neck, right up to your head—and stays trapped in your skull until you turn into a raving lunatic."

"Who told you that?"

"Why can't you just enjoy the emperor's generosity? You earned it. It was you who suppressed the Goths in Pannonia and Macedonia. Theodosius's officers couldn't do it."

Despite his characteristic humility, Arbo couldn't argue with that. But then again, Theodosius's officers had done what they could with the men they had. Mercenaries, deserters and farmers scared so shitless of fighting they cut off their own toes so they couldn't march.

"We both know this peace with the Goths won't last," he said. "And then there's Magnus Maximus, who is—"

"If peace is to be short, we should enjoy it while we can."

"I would prefer to enjoy it on my rooftop, repairing my dovecotes."

Stilicho sighed. "You're the boss."

Arbo eyed the young officer. Though Stilicho had the aspect of an aristocrat—good looks, strong features, wide shoulders— he had been born and raised in poverty. He hadn't tasted meat until he joined the army, and he certainly hadn't enjoyed a day's pampering in his life.

The custodian returned to the room with a woman on each arm, like beautiful wings attached to his stubby body. Both were barefoot and wore rose-colored tunicas that emphasized their smooth shoulders and shapely forms, white teeth gleaming behind seductive smiles.

"Sirs," said the custodian. "These ladies will—"

"We will not be staying," said Stilicho.

Arbo curled his finger to one of the women, and she glided to his side. "What's your hurry?" he asked Stilicho, as the escort wrapped her arms around one of his. "It has been over a month. Why risk it?"

Stilicho clapped his hands together, nearly stamping his feet in excitement. He offered Arbo a toothy smile as the escort ushered the general out of the office. The remaining escort took his hand and led him out of the office, leaving the custodian behind.

Turning to wink at Stilicho, the rosy woman led him down a marble-clad staircase and into a private bathhouse. The moment he entered, Stilicho could feel the heat and smell the sulfur of the thermal waters circulating in the tiled pool. The woman slipped by him, strategically brushing against his groin as she stepped down into the bath, disrobing as she did. Steam enveloped her nakedness and she lowered her glistening body into the water, leaving her breasts exposed. Stilicho hastily unfastened his sandals, pulled off his tunica and waded in after her, moving through the soft layer of rose petals that floated on the water's surface. As he reached her, she slipped below the surface... the sight of her hair spreading out in the water below him, the pull of her lips, forced a groan of pleasure from his throat. Surfacing, she guided him toward the marble seat that ran along the side of the pool, straddling his body and lowering herself onto him. She stroked him slowly, rhythmically, bending over to graze his lips with her nipples.

But it had been too long for Stilicho, and he wanted it faster. He lifted her off and stood quickly, spinning her around and bending her over. With a fervency he hadn't felt in years, he gripped her buttocks and thrust into her from behind, withdrawing and thrusting again, this time harder. He reached climax, and as the orgasm immobilized his body, Stilicho experienced an epiphany. A dawning awareness. A new truth. Or perhaps it had been there all along, asleep in his heart and waiting for these moments of euphoria to awaken and reveal itself. Regardless, as he stood in the fragrant water and clutched the soft flesh of the woman's buttocks, waiting for the waves of ecstasy to end, Stilicho accepted the truth and made a vow to himself then and there. If this was the how the finer half lived, he would do whatever it took—steal, lie, cheat, kill or betray—to join their ranks.

CHAPTER V

Rome

Coelia always imagined the colossal amphitheater to be a living thing, only the massive oval mouth of which was visible on the surface of the earth. It was a mouth that never closed, but rather gaped wide open under the boundless sky, ready to swallow whatever unfortunate souls were fated to never leave its jaws and send them tumbling down into the unseen underworld of its belly. She knew that was a philosophical way to think about it, but perhaps it was exactly the kind of deeper contemplation its architects had hoped to inspire. Or perhaps she was overthinking it. Perhaps it was all about the spectacle on the surface.

Regardless, it was ironic that Vespasian, the most unpretentious emperor to have ruled Rome, had been the force behind the city's showiest structure, one he had built over the previous showy structure—a giant artificial lake that once constituted part of Nero's Golden Palace. The amphitheater's form had taken shape in record time due to the backbreaking work of over fifty thousand captives that Vespasian and his son Titus had brought to Rome after squashing revolts in Judea, and its massive oval mouth still teethed on the spoils of that long ago war. At a height of nearly fifty meters, its towering tiers of gleaming columns and marble arches were decorated with over a hundred and fifty gilded statues of the gods, goddesses and heroes of Greece and Rome—each of them over five meters high—with a dazzling ring of gilded military shields encircling the top level. Such magnificence wasn't just a symbol of supremacy, but a celebration of Rome's journey from modest village by the Tiber to the greatest empire the world had ever known.

At the time of the amphitheater's inauguration over three hundred years earlier, the Vestalis Maxima Cornelia had entered the building to the sound of cheers. She and the other Vestals—favorites of Vespasian thanks to their peace-keeping efforts during the preceding civil war—had walked proudly to the luxury seating box of the Vestal Virgins, one that granted them the same prestigious location on the podium as the emperor and senators. During those inaugural games, Titus had arranged for spectacles—animal hunts, executions, gladiatorial matches, battle recreations, theater productions and more—that lasted for over a hundred consecutive days. Through the centuries and Caesars that followed, the Vestal Virgins had maintained their preeminent front-row position, enjoying the same refreshments and wine as the emperor and spending intermissions talking politics with Rome's elite and visiting dignitaries.

Although the emperor Diocletian had stripped Rome of its status as the capital of the empire almost a century earlier, and the emperor Constantine had subsequently stripped much of its marble and monuments to dress his eponymous capital of Constantinople in the east, none of that political geography mattered in the great stadium. As far as Coelia could tell, the view from the splendid seating box of the Vestal Virgins was largely the same as it always had been. There were only two differences. The first was that the nearby Imperial Box now typically catered to important senators like Symmachus and their circle of friends rather than the emperor and his family. The second difference was the lighting, or rather the lack of it.

Rome was a night-and-day city in every sense. With a population of nearly a million people and no possible way to light every city street after dark, public safety went down with the sun. It had been a Herculean task for Coelia and the other owners of the gladiator schools to convince the outgoing urban prefect to allow this exceptional event—a gladiatorial performance at night. Now, as the vibrant sunlight in the stadium faded to the subdued orange of dusk, leaving the evening's bright full moon and the grid of secured torches placed strategically within the amphitheater to illuminate the arena, she hoped it would pay off.

As she accepted a cup of Falernian wine from an attendant, Coelia spared a good thought for Symmachus, the man responsible for the rarity. His vineyard in Campania was one of the few larger estates that could still produce it in volume, many of the vineyards having been destroyed by the eruption of Vesuvius years earlier. She hadn't taken a sip before she was joined in the Vestals' Box by the priestesses Domitia and Proculeia, cups already in hand. At nearly the same time, a stream of senators in white togas filed into the Imperial Box, each man bowing his head in greeting to the Vestals before taking his seat and being served by attendants. Olympius was among them. He offered Coelia a civil smile before sitting. Things weren't nearly as civil on the upper levels of the amphitheater, however, and the sound of the usual skirmishes floated over the heads of the elite:

"You're in my seat, move it!"

"I need to sit closer to the exit, change seats with me."

"You spilled your drink on me!"

"Don't sit by me if you're cheering for Phobos!"

Domitia and Proculeia regarded the growing crowd inside the massive oval and settled into the seats next to Coelia. As Domitia took the closest, her full lips spread into a wide smile.

"They're still lined up to get inside," she said.

"That's a good sign," replied Coelia. She watched people continue to stream into the stadium, all squinting to read the section, row and seat number carved into their *tessera*, and many wandering around lost until ushered to their seats by one of the circulating torch-carrying attendants. It had been a long time since the amphitheater had been this full. When the bishops weren't trying to close the temples, they were trying to close the stadium. Between the statuary of the gods that decorated the grand structure and the fact that it drew bigger crowds than their churches, they were on a mission to end this chapter of Rome's history. Still, this rare night-time performance had piqued interest. "This has to be at least half capacity," Coelia guessed, surveying the stands.

"More than half," said Proculeia. "Closer to three-quarters. You're going to make some money tonight."

"I'd better," Coelia replied. "We had to bribe the prefect for permission to host the games at night, and with Symmachus replacing him soon, he was determined to squeeze us for everything he could. We had to pay for extra *vigiles* to patrol the streets, too. And that's before what I had to contribute for all the props and the set, which ended up being twice what I was quoted—"

To Proculeia's relief, the sound of a lone horn interrupted Coelia's complaining and a current of energy ran through the stands as the last stragglers hurried to their seats, the sun now fully down. As the torches affixed to the encircling wall of the arena flickered and cast long shadows over the sand, a dusky eeriness descended over the stadium. The crowd grew hushed.

Domitia gripped Coelia's hand. "Spooky," she said, smiling.

Somewhere, a drum began to beat. It started slowly and rhythmically—*thump... thump... thump*—but grew faster and faster by the moment, more frantic and intense, until it morphed into the unmistakable sound and resonance of a panic-stricken heartbeat—*thud! thud! thud!*—culminating in a crescendo of manic pounding that roused the crowd from expectant silence to appreciative cheers.

In the midst of the cheers, a red-robed figure—the master of ceremonies—appeared in the center of the arena floor, rising up from the depths of the amphitheater's underfloor hypogeum.

"*Salvete* Romans!" he called out. "Who among you are quick to fright? You should leave now, before the moon drips madness upon you and spirits steal your breath, for this is no place for the faint of heart! For tonight, the fiery gates of Hades will open below the sand of the arena floor!"

At that, a wide ring of fire roared to life on the arena floor, encircling the master of ceremonies and illuminating the amphitheater so that even those in the farthest, highest seats could see what was happening. The crowd erupted in exuberant applause at the special effect.

Domitia clapped in glee. A fan of the games and of any good time, her round face glowed with happiness. "Oh, wonderful!" she said.

The exuberance settled as the crowd waited for more, and the master of ceremonies continued. "Romans, the *ludi* of gladiators are pleased to bring you the tragic story of a life-loving maiden destined to become queen of the dead! It is the story of sweet-faced Proserpina and foul-breathed Hades!"

As the master of ceremonies descended back into the substructure of the arena, the gladiators took to the sand. Yet instead of charging into the stadium as they usually did, the fighters entered leisurely in groups of six or seven, all dressed in the rough tunicas of simple farmers and carrying the tools of their trade—shovels and rakes, spades and sickles. They did not pay the ring of fire any heed, but remained outside its perimeter as though oblivious to its presence, tilling the sand of the arena as if tilling the soil of their fields.

The crowd quickly recognized two of the men in the arena: Deimos and Phobos, the most famous gladiator duo in Rome. Deimos's trademark scar—a cheetah's bite mark on his left shoulder—had been embellished with orange and black paint to remind the spectators of his prowess, while Phobos's muscular torso glistened with oil to emphasize his physique. Coelia scowled inwardly as the crowd applauded their heroes. Deimos and Phobos—their names meant panic and fear—were Olympius's champions, and it was a rare gladiator match where one or both of them didn't manage to cripple at least one of her better fighters.

Soon, the sound of pipes filled the air above the strange pastoral scene, and a young woman—Proserpina—strolled onto the arena floor. Her hair was long and golden, like stalks of healthy wheat, and the train of her vibrant green dress had what seemed to be thousands of fresh flowers stitched onto it. She meandered around the farmers tending to their fields, cheerfully tossing handfuls of seed from the cornucopia she cradled in one arm over the ground. As she passed, the men—including Deimos and Phobos in their roles as farmers—stopped to greet her with bows of appreciation and gestures of affection, calling out her name and shouting:

"Dearest Proserpina, bless our land!"

"Sweet daughter of Ceres, bring health to our crops!"

But the peace was not to last. A sudden deep blare of trumpets drowned out the happy sound of the pipes while, at the same time, an army of white-and-black cloaked *shades*, agents of the underworld, rose up from below to populate the area within the ring of fire. Some of the ghastly apparitions carried spears and scythes, including Coelia's prize gladiator, Catus, who gripped a blood-red scythe. As the shades scurried about the fiery circle, the crowd erupted again in surprise and delight, stomping their feet for more.

More happened almost immediately as another form rose from the underworld to appear in the center of the fire ring. It was Hades himself, god of the dead, though as none had seen him before. Huge and hulking, he wore black armor that reflected the light of the flames so intensely that it appeared he, too, was on fire. Yet it was the design, not the color, of his armor that truly chilled the spines of the spectators. His helmet was in the shape of a monstrous, snarling dog's head, while his breastplate bore the visage of a red-eyed canine. His spiked scepter was perhaps the most dreadful of all—topped with a growling dog's skull, the animal's long bony ears served as lethal prongs.

Hades screamed into the air. *"Cerberus, ausculta!"*

A breath later, three black dogs rose from the underworld to join their master. A triad version of Cerberus—the three-headed hound of Hades—they ran in circles around their dark overlord, panting wildly and waiting to be commanded as the chains around their necks rattled and swayed back and forth.

Domitia nearly leapt from her seat. She turned to Coelia. "I know those dogs! That is Brogos!"

Coelia tried to remain poised, professional, but it was impossible. "It was my idea!" she boasted, though her words were lost in the cheering of the crowd.

As the stands shook with the force of the spectators' elation, Hades—Brogos—and his trio of hellhounds rushed to the inside perimeter of the fire ring, strategically crossing at the only point where the flames burned low enough to jump over. Charging forward with singular purpose, Brogos ran until he reached the innocent Proserpina, still blithely tossing seeds from her cornucopia. The crowd called out their warnings:

"Look out, girl!"

"Run, sweet lady!"

But it was no use. Hades reached the girl and threw her over his shoulder, carrying her back toward the ring of hellfire as she kicked and screamed, calling out for help.

Immediately, the farmer-gladiators raised their weapons and advanced on Hades to slow his pursuit and rescue their beloved benefactress. But it would not be that easy. In a disturbing display of fidelity to their dark master, the multitude of shades inside the circle of fire crossed the fiery perimeter to attack the farmers. Within moments, the gladiator match exploded into full performance. On one side were the farmers, desperate to save Proserpina from the death god's grip. On the other was Hades, intent on descending into the fiery depths of the underworld with the girl, the abduction aided by the ghastly shades.

The sound of pipes and trumpets was no more. Now, the sounds of shouts and the clanging of weapons, the shrieks of pain and the bellows of coordinated attack and defense strategies rang out as the violent production played out below. All of that rose to join the cries of encouragement or disparagement from the stands as the galvanized spectators immersed themselves in the drama:

"Finish him off, Catus!"

"Phobos, you fool, move your ass!"

Brogos had nearly reached the ring of fire with his abductee—why did she have to shriek right in his ear?—when a lumbering farmer carrying a sickle blocked his path. Brogos lifted his dog-skull spear to strike, but his opponent's weapon was already in mid-swing, and the sharp edge of the blade grazed Brogos's leg just enough to split the flesh. Roaring in outrage, he dropped the girl and lunged forward, impaling the farmer's throat with the iron ears of his scepter. For Proserpina, the clash was an opportunity. She jumped to her feet and scrambled away, just as a ferocious trio of farmer-gladiators strategically closed in on Brogos.

"Catus!" shouted Brogos. "Get the fuck over here!"

Heeding the call, Catus began to hack his way through a group of brawny farmers. Before he could make it to Brogos's side, however, Olympius's man Phobos intercepted him, and the two prize fighters fell into a grueling battle as the onlookers took to their feet. Feeling himself disadvantaged by the cumbersome cloak of his shade costume, Catus hastily shrugged it off—a mistake. For as he stepped forward to block Phobos's incoming sickle with the handle of his scythe, his left foot caught in the discarded fabric. He fell to the sand.

Watching it all unfold from the proximity of the Vestals' viewing box, Coelia had an unobstructed view not just of Phobos's scythe cleanly beheading her fallen prize fighter Catus, but also of the self-satisfied smug that formed on Olympius's face.

Brogos saw it, too. As he desperately fended off the three farmer-gladiators, fully aware that help was not coming but Phobos was, he emitted a series of sharp whistles.

Instantly, the triad Cerberus obeyed. Brogos's three black dogs abandoned pursuit of the farmers and changed trajectory, returning to their master's side to viciously attack his opponents with swift-footed precision and unforgiving fangs. Their sharp turns and high leaps, their barks and growls, the way they didn't just kill but tore apart... it was almost too much for the crowd, and anyone who wasn't already on their feet soon was, punching the air and calling out for more. As the dogs' victims collapsed one by one, the eerie shades swarmed the bodies and dragged them through the sand, rolling them past the fiery perimeter of the circle to plunge into the underworld... or at least into the belly of the amphitheater's substructure.

It was all going pretty well for Brogos, but then he saw a sight that made his stomach sink—Phobos, stepping on the chain that hung from Cosmos's neck. The act pinned the animal's head to the ground, and he twisted wildly but helplessly, biting at the links of the chain and then at the sand, his efforts so frantic that Brogos could hear the snap of his teeth. Phobos raised his scythe to strike.

"No!" Brogos shouted.

But Cosmos's savior came in an expected form—Deimos. He rushed to his partner Phobos's side and grabbed the handle of his scythe just as it moved downward.

"Pay attention, you fucker!" Deimos shouted to Phobos. "He hasn't set the dogs on us! It's all for show. They're only going after the slave fighters!" He gestured to the crowd. "They love the dogs... don't fuck up a good thing!"

Phobos looked around. Deimos was right. The crowd was going mad, and the dogs were a great gimmick. They could work with this. But backing off now would make him look too weak in front of his fans. He raised his scythe again—and felt Deimos's blade open his stomach. He collapsed on top of Cosmos before he had time to process the betrayal.

Domitia applauded, overcome with the drama of it all. "Coelia! Deimos saved Cosmos!"

Coelia didn't deny herself the indulgence of a smile, even as Olympius blinked at her in disbelief from the Imperial Box. Unable to stomach her gloating, he turned back to the arena.

Yet Deimos's good deed was not to go unpunished. Witnessing the treason, a farmer-gladiator swung his iron shovel at

Deimos, hitting him hard on the back of the head. Dazed, Deimos staggered once, twice, just as Cosmos wriggled out from below Phobos's corpse. A shrill whistle of command rang out—Cosmos's ears went up—and the dog leapt up with the grace of a gazelle to clamp its deadly jaws around the throat of Deimos's attacker. Blood spurted from the man's neck and he fell to the side, Cosmos's jaws still in their death grip.

Brogos rushed to Deimos and wrapped an arm around his waist, supporting the stunned gladiator until his senses returned, both men protected by the three black dogs ferociously chasing off any would-be attackers. The stands shook as exhilarated spectators roared their approval of the unlikely new alliance—enemy gladiators uniting to save the life of a loyal dog. What could be more moving? Blood and gore were superb in the arena, but an emotional twist was divine.

Brogos allowed himself a moment of self-satisfaction. The boss lady would be pleased by his performance, but even better, it would have Anthea's heart pounding. No doubt she was seated somewhere out there, watching his every move. *Let's see one of those pretty boys that your parents want you to marry get your blood going like this*, he thought. He slapped Deimos on the back.

"You good, friend?" he asked.

"Never better," replied Deimos. He didn't care what the boss Olympius would say. He would come around eventually. Regardless, it was nice to be rid of that idiot Phobos. Deimos had been covering the fool's ass for too many years.

As the shades and the farmer-gladiators continued their one-on-one battles on the arena floor, and as the black dogs stayed on their master's heels, Brogos and Deimos charged side-by-side through the action. Their destination was a section of the stadium wall where Proserpina was attempting to clamber up and out of the arena.

"Pass something down! Pull me up!" she screamed to the spectators in the front row.

But the spectators only stomped in joy as black-armored Hades approached her from behind. Removing his helmet—Brogos wanted the crowd to get a good look at him—he tossed it aside and again threw the girl over his shoulder. As he marched back to the ring of fire with both his unwilling bride and his new partner, he whistled, and the dogs fell into formation behind him, trotting along with tongues lolling out and tails wagging.

Reaching the fiery circle, Brogos hesitated for only a moment before doing what he had agreed to do—throwing the girl to her fate. He heaved her into the air and she flew over the flames, the last remnants of her torn dress catching fire as she did. Before the crowd could witness more, her burning body plummeted into the underworld. Brogos didn't feel good about it, but business was business, and the performance had gone better than he could have imagined. He gripped Deimos's wrist, and the victors raised their arms in triumph. Together, they crossed into the ring of fire, and the platform descended, lowering Rome's newest celebrity gladiator duo into the underworld to the sound of thunderous applause.

While the lavish rose-scented Vestals' latrine certainly smelled better than the other latrines in the amphitheater, it wasn't any quieter. Even as Coelia stood before the full-length looking glass, waiting impatiently as Ptolema finished fussing over her veil by the light of the large oil lamps affixed to the walls, she could hear the footfalls, arguments, laughter and shouted conversations of thousands of people making their way out of the stadium.

They would stop along the way to purchase food or drink—as if they hadn't indulged in enough during the gladiator matches—or to buy some kind of souvenir, whether a toy gladiator for their child or a cheap necklace for their wife. Some weren't thinking of their children or wives at all, but were negotiating the services of a prostitute. They would agree on the price, do the deed behind the curtain of the worker's rented stall and leave the arena feeling like a new man. As far as the city was concerned, it was a great way to collect prostitution taxes while at the same time draining the games-fueled aggression out of male spectators before they headed into the streets.

The lingering excitement of the games staved off the effects of the late hour, and Domitia and Proculeia chatted as they leaned against a floor-to-ceiling wall mosaic that depicted the arena flooded with blue water. On one panel, soldiers on great ships battled each other to the death. On another, men and animals seemed to walk on water. On yet another, children of all classes raced each other on wooden rafts. As Ptolema finished with Coelia, Domitia pushed herself off the wall and stood straight, permitting the slave to inspect her veil. Ptolema took orders from the Vestalis Maxima only, and Claudia insisted the Vestals never had a hair out of place in public.

"What a show," Domitia said to Coelia. Her face was still flushed from the thrill of it all. "Brogos was amazing."

"Thank *Vesta Felix* for that," Coelia replied. "But Catus… that is going to hurt."

"Coelia," said Proculeia. "Try to relax for once. Brogos is a winner. And that whole spontaneous pair up? It's solid gold. You should think about going into business with—"

"Don't say Olympius."

The Vestals exited the latrine into a relatively peaceful passageway, the torch-lined walls of which were painted with colorful frescos of exotic animals and studded with niches that held the life-sized statues of famous gladiators. Ptolema followed a step behind the priestesses as four red-cloaked soldiers effectively boxed them in, escorting them out of the prestigious section of the amphitheater and out of the building, into the night air.

The area on this side of the stadium was heavily guarded and well lit, and a large congregation of senators and other elites stood socializing around the conical *meta sudans* fountain, talking and drinking, reliving the night's highlights. Coelia's gaze skipped over the familiar faces—Symmachus, Praetextatus, Lampadius—and landed on General Arbogastes. He was dressed in a red soldier's tunica, his face freshly shaven and his fair hair cut short. Although deep in conversation with the senator Pompeianus and a younger soldier—she suspected it was his officer Stilicho—he stepped away the moment he saw her and approached. As he did, those around gave them space. It was no secret that the general was interested in pursuing this particular Vestal once her tenure at the temple was over.

"Priestess Coelia," he greeted. "I was hoping I'd see you. It has been a long time."

"Too long, sir," she replied. "I am happy to see you looking so well. We offered daily in the temple for your safe return."

"Thank you." Searching for the right thing to say next, Arbo laughed suddenly and raised his wine cup in the direction of the stadium. "I did not expect this type of homecoming. Imagine my surprise to see a lowly soldier I discharged in Germania become an overnight sensation in Rome. I thought Brogos would end up destitute and having to eat those dogs, but here he is a celebrity gladiator, getting rich off them."

"He's a long way from rich," said Coelia, "but he is lucky."

"I'd say the dogs are luckier," replied Arbo. "Can't say I blame him for absconding with them. That's how I got my racing pigeons, you know. It all started with a bonded pair of war messenger pigeons that General Bauto told me to kill—the female got injured—but I didn't. I kept them in my gear for the whole march back to Rome."

"That's how you got them?" Coelia laughed. "I didn't know that."

"You're the only person I've told. If Bauto knew, he'd probably convict the whole flock of treason, and me with them." She laughed again, and he pressed on, encouraged. "I've just started expanding the dovecotes on the roof of my house on the Quirinal. You should come see. We can have supper together."

"And dine on your slowest pigeons?" This time he laughed, and she smiled. "I would like that, General." Coelia wanted to stay longer, but she knew that Domitia and Proculeia had already left. Worse, she could sense Senator Symmachus's disapproval as he peripherally watched her interactions with the general. In light of her recent conversation with the high priestess, she decided to exercise discretion. She pulled her *palla* tighter around her shoulders. "*Bonam noctem*, General," she said. "For now."

He bowed. "*Bonam noctem*, Priestess," he replied. "For now."

He watched her move toward the gilded *lectica* that awaited her, the four litter-bearers taking their positions—two in the front and two in the rear—as a grumpy Greek woman pulled back the heavy red curtain to expose the luxurious interior. Coelia stepped inside for the short journey back to the House of the Vestals, offering the general a parting smile as she closed the curtain behind her, and feeling very pleased to see the same smile on his face.

CHAPTER VI

If one could see the passage of time through the eyes of any goddess, thought Symmachus, *the most poignant view would be through those of Victory.*

Her golden frame—a beautiful, winged feminine form descending from the heavens, holding a palm branch and a laurel wreath—had stood atop a marble altar in the Senate House for over four centuries. As the senator waited before the altar and gazed up at the goddess's stately visage, he reflected upon the history that had happened here, in this assembly, under her watchful eyes. His contemplation was quiet but not calm, and soon it was not quiet, either.

The great bronze doors of the Senate House burst open and a gust of noise and energy—the rattle of a wooden wagon, the shouts of senators and soldiers—swept inside the rectangular marble chamber with the force of a sudden invasion. Propelled from thought to action, Symmachus clambered on top of the marble altar, quickly joined by Senator Praetextatus and a centurion soldier whose name he didn't know.

"Bring the wagon closer!" the centurion barked at a subordinate, and the man did as he was told.

Symmachus wrapped his arms around the statue. So did the other two men who stood on the altar with him. "Lift," he grunted.

A scribe in an ink-stained tunica ran into the Senate chamber so quickly that the soles of his sandals sent him skidding across the tile floor. "They're on the Capitoline!" he yelled. "They'll be here any moment!"

The centurion took over. "We can't be dainty about it," he said. "We need to get it in the wagon before they put it in the fucking forge!" Shoving the senators aside, he gripped the statue by the wings and hollered down at the soldiers by the wagon. "Hold it steady! I'm going to push it over."

All at once, the golden statue flew down into the wagon to land face-first with a shocking thud, its fall broken only by the thin covering of straw and manure in the box below. Two of the wooden spokes in the rear left wheel broke, and a hairline crack appeared in the ornate tile floor below it.

Praetextatus put his hands on his head. "Gods above," he said.

The three men jumped down from the altar just as a group of six or seven additional soldiers rushed into the Senate House. The soldiers quickly assessed the situation and arranged themselves around the box of the wagon, propping up the sagging corner as the centurion gripped the wooden yoke to guide the vehicle out of the building. He looked to Symmachus for direction.

"Take it to the House of the Vestals," the senator instructed. "The soldiers will not enter the virgins' home." He wasn't entirely certain of that, but the priestesses' residence was the closest place of possible refuge for the revered statue.

"Move!" the centurion shouted to his men.

Together, the group of soldiers forced the wagon forward, its wooden wheels groaning under the weight of its precious cargo. They navigated it through the senatorial chamber and out the bronze doors, onto the street where a frantic crowd had gathered in front of the *Curia*. A cacophony of sounds—shouts of anger, sobs, gasps—erupted at the sight of Victory face-down in a sanitation wagon, only her golden wings visible above the sides of the decrepit box.

As the soldiers pushed, pulled and supported the wagon along the Via Sacra, surrounded on all sides by the emotional gathering of senators, magistrates and citizens, the scribe in the ink-stained tunica caught up to Symmachus.

"People are trying to hold them back," he said breathlessly. "But they are determined… I saw them stab a quaestor!"

Symmachus looked over his shoulder. At the base of the Capitoline Hill behind him, a mob was trying to delay a large contingent of soldiers en route to the Curia—soldiers sent by Emperor Gratian to remove the pagan idol Victory from the Senate House.

"We're lucky we had the notice we did," said Symmachus. "The fools have never been to Rome before. They went to the Curia of Pompey first."

Two loud pops sounded out—two more spokes breaking— and the wagon shifted, causing the statue to wobble inside the box. The soldiers adjusted their positions and pressed forward, the desperate convoy fueled by determination as much as brute force.

"*They have no right!*" a man's voice cried out.

Another shouted, "*She is ours!*"

Their words were echoed by the irate crowd that was growing larger, more impassioned, by the moment. The statue may have stood in a public space, but its removal felt very personal.

Symmachus felt a lump of emotion form in his throat—rage, grief, disbelief—and did his best to swallow it. It was inconceivable that it had come to this: Victory, bouncing down the street in a trash wagon, trying to escape the melting forge. It was an unceremonious flight for such a dignified statue, one that Rome's first emperor Augustus had placed inside the Senate House after defeating Antony and Cleopatra. At the time, it had been a curious choice of location. Wasn't the symbol of Rome's supremacy better suited to a temple of Mars or Jupiter? Yet Augustus knew that sustaining an empire wasn't just about military conquest. It was about administration. For what good was it to conquer a people if you could not bring the true victories of Rome—law and order, trade, roads, aqueducts, sanitation, prosperity and religious tolerance—to those people? For centuries, that administration had rested with the Roman Senate whose decisions affected the lives of people throughout the Roman Empire.

But in the last few decades, everything had changed. The emperors in Constantinople and Mediolanum had stripped the Senate of its power, at least its power outside of Rome. And now, no doubt at the insistence of their bishops, they sought to strip the Senate of its goddess, too. While Rome's greatest men—Caesars, senators, generals and orators—saw strength in the golden face of the goddess, the bishops saw only their own vulnerability. And none more so than Symmachus's own cousin Ambrosius, the bishop of Mediolanum.

This is his victory, Symmachus thought bitterly as the wagon rattled along.

✻　✻　✻

"Antonia," said Coelia, trying to keep her voice diplomatic. "I sent two shipments of incense directly to the Temple of Isis yesterday."

Antonia sat back in Claudia's chair, tapping a stylus on the chief Vestal's desk. The embodiment of dignity and diligence, Antonia would not outright accuse Coelia of an error... but she had other ways of getting her point across. The slight tilt of her head, the minor tone of questioning in her voice, worked wonders. "Then why did the priest say they didn't arrive?" she asked.

Coelia stepped toward the desk and shuffled through the mounds of scrolls and papyri that covered its ivory surface. Privately relieved to find what she was looking for, she withdrew a piece of paper and, trying to conceal any expression of smugness, held it out.

"Look," she said. "Right here. 'Two boxes of Egyptian cyphi to the *Isis Campensis*.' Signed by me and countersigned by the warehouse clerk. Yesterday." She put the paper back on the desk. "Their slaves probably haven't inventoried it yet."

"All right," said Antonia. "Ask one of the novices to—"

A cry of alarm sliced through the drudgery of the Vestals' work, causing both women to inhale sharply, their hands flying to their chests. Momentarily delayed by the shock of it, they recovered and rushed out of the high priestess's office, into the open air of the courtyard, just as Domitia, Proculeia and three novices emerged from the peristyle, similarly drawn by the cry. Above, the morning sun shone brightly against a calm, cloudless blue sky. Below, a storm was raging.

The Vestalis Maxima Claudia was on her knees beside a pink rosebush, gripping the edges of a papyrus scroll with white-knuckled hands. Everyone rushed to her, Antonia nearly tripping on the bottom of her tunica as she knelt down and put her hand on her superior's back.

"Claudia, what is it?" she asked.

The high priestess stared at the paper, reading, though her hands trembled so hard it struck them all as a small miracle she could even discern the words.

"By order of Imperator Flavius Gratian Augustus," Claudia began, "it is hereby decreed that all state funding of the Order of Vestal Virgins is withdrawn and prohibited, and that all legacies left to the Vestal Order or its members be redirected to the state." Her already hoarse voice broke, and she drew in a breath. "It is additionally decreed that all monies held by the Temple of Vesta be rescinded to the state forthwith. These laws are made in accordance with our desire that" — her fingers tightened on the paper — "that no profit be accrued by the heathen superstitions or those perverting the observance of consecrated virginity."

Antonia sat back on her heels. "Claudia…" She broke off. Whatever she said, it would be insufficient.

"*Heathen superstitions*," Claudia repeated with incredulity. "Christianity spread to our shores from Galilee three hundred years ago. The immortal gods have been here since creation!" She stared at the words on the papyrus, as if they were things she could reason with or rebut. "*We* pervert the observance of consecrated virginity? The Vestal Virgins practiced sacred purity in Rome for a thousand years before the first Christian celibate debased the dignity of it! I myself have served our holy virgin for over thirty years! And now Gratian—an imbecile child emperor—shames *us*?"

"Domina!" shouted Ptolema from the peristyle. She waved Claudia toward the doors. "Come quickly!"

Claudia dropped the papyrus. "*Dei, mihi miseremini,*" she said.

Antonia helped her to her feet, and Claudia hurried toward the doors, trailed by the other priestesses. They all rushed onto the street to see an approaching throng of people led by a centurion pulling a golden statue of Victory in a trash wagon. A band of soldiers framed the wagon's box, supporting a deep slope toward the back and compelling the vehicle along. Senators and magistrates ran alongside, urging the soldiers to move faster and then dashing off toward the rear of the chaotic procession to delay what followed—another group of soldiers, these ones sporting the military trousers customary of soldiers from Mediolanum.

Yet despite the embarrassing delay in executing their task— there was no golden statue at the Curia of Pompey—the trousers-wearing soldiers still had the element of surprise on their side, and therefore the numbers, too. Forcing themselves headlong through the crowd and brandishing their swords without hesitation, they cleaved their way through the resistance until they were only steps behind the men hastening the wagon forward.

As the Vestals watched, a woman in a bright turquoise tunica managed to slip between a trousers-wearing soldier and one of the red-cloaked soldiers pushing the wagon, only to have the soldier from Mediolanum shove her out of the way. She slipped and fell, striking her head against the wooden box of the wagon and slumping onto the street. The soldier pushing the wagon let go and reached down to pull her out of the way, but not before one of the rear wheels of the wagon ran over her leg. The pain roused her and she shrieked, her sharp cry slicing through the clamor.

"They are beating women now!" an outraged voice accused.

Moments later, it began to rain painful shards as the citizens who had scaled the adjacent buildings tore off roof tiles and hurled the sharp pieces down upon the intruding soldiers.

"Get your asses back to Mediolanum!" someone shouted.

"Have you no shame?" challenged another. *"Where is your respect for the gods?"*

Yet the soldiers from Mediolanum had their orders. Only thirty or so meters from the portico of the House of the Vestals, they succeeded in reaching the fleeing convoy and immediately set upon the Romans, forcing them to abandon their cargo and defend themselves. The commanding officer from Mediolanum fought his way to the Roman centurion at the front of the wagon.

"By force of Imperial decree," he shouted, "Tell your men to stand down!"

"Tell *your* men to stand down!" replied the centurion. "This is my city!"

"This is the emperor's city!" said the commander.

As the senior officers argued, the crowd of senators and citizens converged around them. Led by Senator Praetextatus, a number of them jumped into the wagon and struggled to slide the statue out of it, their sights set on the portico of the House of the Vestals.

Claudia spun around. Disregarding the vocal protests of the house guards, she opened the second of the heavy chestnut doors to the residence, widening the threshold to receive the statue. Officially a cloistered house for the priestesses, it would provide sanctuary for the pagan monument, providing the soldiers from Mediolanum would honor the convention. She was privately debating the likelihood of this when a raucous group of men and women appeared from the direction of the Basilica of Constantine, heading toward the tumult. Any hope that they had come to help faded at the sight of their expressions. They were not enraged by the sacrilege, but instead emboldened, and ran directly into the ruckus, clutching rocks and pummelling those men who had managed to maneuver the statue out of the crippled wagon. One of them struck Praetextatus on the back of the head, and he dropped to his knees.

"High Priestess, you must go inside!" insisted one of the sentries, urging the chief Vestal back toward the open doors where a line of his colleagues—weapons drawn and faces furious—guarded the threshold.

Claudia opened her mouth to argue, but grimaced as a thick gob of sputum landed on her chin and slid down her neck. She wiped it away as the youthful face of a red-haired woman appeared only inches from her own.

"Burn in hellfire, you temple whore!" the woman screamed.

Claudia recoiled at the feel of the sputum and the look of scorn on the young woman's face, but it was her words that were the most shocking. The most repugnant. *Temple whore.* Even in the midst of the mayhem and her own revulsion, she knew exactly who had helped paint that portrait of the Vestal Virgins—Ambrosius.

The guard struck the spitting woman in the midsection and she stumbled away, gagging as her stomach contents emptied on the front of her own dress. Now a breath away from using physical force to carry the high priestess inside, he spoke more harshly. "Your safety is my directive," he said, glancing back at the statue and the swarm of conflict around it. "It's too late. They won't get it through now."

Antonia and Coelia rushed to the high priestess's side. Antonia lifted her palla to wipe the rest of the sputum off Claudia's face and neck.

"He's right, Claudia," she said. "We need to lock the doors. The novices are inside."

Claudia cast a glance toward the doors of the house, catching sight of the novices Sergia and the younger Florina inside. It was evident from their repulsed expressions that they had witnessed the red-haired woman spit on their superior... on the Vestalis Maxima of the Vestal Order. Claudia swallowed, as if physically trying to suppress the rising rage she felt. The arrogant audacity of the insult, the sanctimonious entitlement, brought her to a strange crossroads where she hesitated between retreating in humiliation and advancing in fury. A loud crash from the area of the Regia made her momentarily cover her already throbbing ears.

She turned to Antonia. "The archives!"

"The guards will protect them." As the high priestess ignored her and looked toward the temple—it was well-guarded, at least for the moment—Antonia placed her hands on Claudia's face. "Let's go inside."

Slowly, Claudia realized something. She could not feel Antonia's hands on her face. Worse, her body—her lips, her arms, her legs—began to feel impossibly heavy. An intense flare of exhaustion ignited within her, compounded by an overwhelming sense of dread... something extraordinarily wrong was happening to her. She felt the blood drain from her cheeks and her mouth droop with a grotesque weakness that soon spread to her limbs. Her body failed her, and she collapsed into the arms of a house guard. Without waiting for instruction or permission, he carried her into the house, past the sentries who were still blocking the entrance from the mob.

"Blessed Apollo," Antonia said breathlessly. She darted into the house after Claudia.

Not sure which crisis to focus on—the violence, the vandalism of Victory or whatever was happening to Claudia—Coelia's fear narrowed onto the nearby Temple of Vesta. Fifteen or so guards stood around, swords drawn, as Senator Junius marshaled a congregation of men to add an additional layer of protection to the goddess's temple. Coelia could imagine the Vestals inside— Proculeia and Terentia, and probably a novice or two—standing around the sacred fire, praying to the goddess for protection. For peace.

Just then, a sole voice rose above the bluster—above the shouts and obscenities, the cries of anger and pain, and the crash of roof tiles hitting the pavement. It was Symmachus's voice.

"Citizens! Be calm!" The senator clambered into the box of the wagon, standing above the crowd with his arms raised. "You fight your own countrymen!" he called out. "You strike at your own neighbors! This cannot please *any* god!"

The commanding officer from Mediolanum looked up at him, ready to yank him down, but hesitated as a flash of recognition came to him. The senator's cropped but slightly curly hair and authoritative presence, the resonance in his deep voice... he had encountered this man in Mediolanum, watched him consult with Emperor Gratian, and witnessed him receive praise for his work with the peace treaty. Seizing an opportunity, the officer climbed up into the wagon to stand beside the respected statesman. He lifted the whistle that hung from his neck and blew long and hard into it. The piercing signal caught the attention and obedience of his men.

"Stand down!" he ordered.

Gradually, and in fits and starts, the opposing soldiers withdrew from each other. As they did, the centurion who had been pulling the wagon frowned at the spreading savagery of the citizens around him and shouted an order of his own.

"*Ordinem sustinete!*" he instructed.

The opposing soldiers now united in a common purpose, they turned from fighting each other to suppressing the riot and reestablishing order. Many ran off to chase down vandals who were already moving outward from the area sacred to Vesta to ransack other parts of the Forum.

Coelia felt pressure on her arm and turned to find Ptolema gripping her elbow.

"Come inside now," she said. It wasn't a request.

Drained of all emotion save an encroaching sense of wearied helplessness, Coelia complied. She followed the slave toward the grand wooden doors of the house, looking over her shoulder and catching a last glimpse of Victory lying lopsided on the street, her proud face smeared with filth and the tips of her golden wings broken.

CHAPTER VII

Outside of Lugdunum (Roman Gaul)

They had stopped just before nightfall at a small tavern to have supper. Uros had been too nervous to eat anything, but the soldier named Celunno had eaten his weight in pork while the woman, Manta, had drunk hers in beer. Traveling the lonely roads of Gaul with them was like being carted around in one of the tavern's trash bins.

Even if the moon had been free of cloud cover, there wouldn't have been much to see on this obscure dirt road, nothing except for the dense forest of towering yet oddly thin trees that flanked their donkey-drawn cart as it rolled along the barely trodden path. Yet the less the eye saw, the more the ear heard. That included Uros's stomach. It called out for food that he knew he wouldn't be able to keep down. Celunno passed him the reins and leaned back.

"He's just a man," he said, "and a damn scrawny one at that. Manta could strangle him with her own hands if it came to it."

"What do you mean if it came to it?" asked Uros.

"Nothing," Celunno reassured. "It's a just a manner of speaking. Nothing will go wrong."

Manta, who sat behind them in the cart, piped up. "Are you sure Gratian won't have a whole legion with him? We're dead, all of us, if he suspects anything."

"But not dead quickly," said Uros. "He'll have us tortured for days before he'll deliver the mercy of death."

"The emperor trusts me," said Celunno. "He came to me, so he has no reason to suspect anything."

"Including your loyalty?"

"Especially my loyalty." That was true. In addition to serving in Gratian's army for years, Celunno had even stood in as the emperor's *magister equitum* for a while. That had been the good life, but it hadn't lasted. Once a more skilled sycophant managed to clamber over him, it had been back to carrying his own gear. But that was all water under the bridge. As far as Gratian knew, Celunno had done exactly what had been asked of him: He had agreed to secretly transport the emperor's wife to a remote location where they could reunite. Gratian had even shown a rare flash of gratitude when Celunno had wisely advised him to travel lightly and modestly, with only a couple bodyguards and donkeys instead of horses. That would help avoid attracting the attention of Maximus's men who would be combing the countryside for the emperor. *Maximus.* Celunno thumped his hand on the side of the wooden cart. "Magnus Maximus will fill this with gold once we bring him Gratian's head."

Uros groaned and rubbed the back of his neck. It was getting harder to keep his anxiety at bay. "We're going to assassinate an *emperor.*"

Celunno grabbed the reins. His companion's trepidation had a way of inflaming his own. At one time, he had been close to Gratian. Now, no one but Bishop Ambrosius was. After Gratian's vicious persecution of heretic Christians and the insults he had recently delivered to upper-class pagans, he had alienated past allies. His vices didn't help. Between his carousing and, worst of all, his off-putting affinity for foreign mercenaries, he had also managed to lose the respect of the people and the support of the army. Half of his soldiers had already defected to Maximus. The young ruler had made himself vulnerable in a world that had no patience for it.

"He's just a man," repeated Celunno. "He has no magic against the metal of a blade."

He has no magic, thought Uros. But still... it was Gratian's face on the coins in his purse.

The cart hit a bump and Manta grunted. "Are you sure he'll come?" she asked. "If he's hiding from Maximus, he'll be scared to death."

"He'll come," replied Celunno. "He may be Augustus, but he's still flesh and blood. The more afraid he is, the more he'll want the comfort of his soft little wife." He squinted into the shadows ahead, and then turned to look back at Manta, though it was too dark to make out anything other than the outline of her curly hair. "I think I see a torch ahead. We're getting close. Stay low and shut up."

Celunno drove the donkey cart forward. On the road ahead, the light from a single blazing torch gradually carved a sphere of visibility out of the darkness to reveal a similar conveyance as their own—a donkey cart and three figures. Celunno elbowed Uros, and the latter man lifted their single torch from its mount on the side of the cart. He held it out in front of him.

A voice broke through the darkness. "Can you direct us to Parisius?"

"Go north until you see the ghost of Vercingetorix," Celunno replied, completing the passphrase.

Celunno stopped the cart and the form of a shabbily dressed bodyguard, sword in hand but not raised, materialized from the darkness, moving like a phantom toward their transport. "Where is Empress Laeta?"

"She's in the back," said Uros. "Where is the emperor?"

Celunno shot Uros a glare. That was clumsy. The guard thought so, too, and stopped in mid-step. Celunno swore to himself. There was nothing to do now but follow through. He leapt up from his seat and, using his superior position to advantage, jumped down directly on top of the guard, thrusting his blade into the bodyguard's chest. The man collapsed, but pulled Celunno to the ground with him, his thick fingers finding his attacker's throat. Celunno reflexively released his grip on his sword to pry the man's hands off his neck.

Their elaborate and well-rehearsed plan of attack now thwarted by his own stupidity, Uros similarly resorted to instinctual violence and the hope that he would be swift enough to exploit the second guard's confusion. He threw his torch to the ground and jumped down to land on soggy earth. Rushing toward the figure on the road ahead of him, he raised his sword to attack.

The figure lifted his torch and shouted. "Halt!"

At the sight of him, Uros did. He had expected the flame to illuminate the face of a hardened soldier, but instead found himself staring at the same youthful visage that was stamped on the bronze coins in his purse. He hesitated, resisting the ingrained urge to lower himself to his knees in the presence of the Augustus.

"Kill him!" he heard a raspy voice behind him cry out. It was Celunno.

Gratian took a step back and waved the torch in the air, fending off his would-be assassin. "Stand down, you *mentula!*" he shouted, while at the same time his second bodyguard emerged from the darkness and advanced on Uros.

The bodyguard raised his sword, but his foot caught some unseen rock or crevice on the road and he tripped. Swinging his blade even as he fell, he managed to make contact with his opponent's leg. Uros felt his flesh split. Warm blood pulsed out of the gash and ran down his shin to coat his boot in moisture. Too panicked to feel any pain, he raised his sword and brought it down hard... but the guard had rolled away and was already back on his feet.

"*Domine,*" the bodyguard shouted to Gratian. "Run!"

But Gratian was already running—albeit toward the assassins' donkey cart and the curly-haired woman in the back. He dropped his torch and reached into the cart's box with both arms. "Laeta, come on!" Her hands gripped his extended arms, but she felt different, stronger, and he strained to see her in the darkness. Just then, the heavy cloud that had been covering the moon floated past, and a spattering of silvery light revealed her face. "Fuck!" Gratian tried to pull back, but she clung to him.

"I've got him!" screamed Manta. "Celunno, hurry up!"

Still struggling to pry the guard's thick fingers off his throat, Celunno extended a flailing arm in a frantic effort to locate his sword on the ground. Finally finding it, he stabbed wildly, weakly, at the man's body a second, then third, then fourth time, the guard's stranglehold persisting with each puncture of his opponent's blade. "He's fucking Julius Caesar!" Celunno croaked. "He won't die!" But the fifth time was lucky—for Celunno. Either striking something vital or simply exhausting the guard, the man's body went limp. Celunno pushed off the dead weight and clambered to his feet, sucking air into his lungs. He stumbled back toward the cart, the area illuminated by the now clear moon and the two torches that burned on the ground.

Gratian, still struggling to free himself from Manta's grip, glared at his former soldier Celunno in disgust.

"Traitor," he seethed.

Unsure of the second bodyguard's whereabouts, and fearful of a blade in the back, Celunno spared a glance behind him. Uros was there, hobbling toward him.

"The other guard took off into the woods," said Uros, panting.

Celunno turned back to Gratian. "Mercenaries," he said. "You get what you fucking pay for, my lord." He lunged for the emperor.

Utilizing the strength of his youth and the fear of imminent assassination, Gratian mustered all the force within him to deliver a precise and powerful head-butt to the center of Manta's face. Her nose cracked, and she shrieked.

"Don't let—" hollered Celunno.

But it was too late. Gratian had broken free and was already sprinting into the wooded abyss of the black forest. Celunno and

Uros each grabbed a torch and gave chase, lifting their feet high to avoid entanglement in the thick vegetation while snaking through columnar trees with boughs as high as heaven.

"Do you see him?" asked Uros. He could still feel blood trickling into his boot, but the strength in his leg had returned enough for him to keep pace with the larger, though less agile, Celunno.

Celunno pointed. "There!"

"We have to catch him," shouted Uros, stating the obvious. They both knew that if Gratian escaped, if he managed to make his way back to Lugdunum and collect himself, he would have them tracked down and tortured to death. Their families would suffer the same fate. Uros tried not to think of his wife and their two babbling little boys. He especially tried not to think of the last words his wife had spoken to him: *If you take this job, it'll be the death of us all.*

The assassins chased their target deeper into the forest, their torches bouncing before them and their breath visible in the cool night air. Branches snapped under their weight and the forest's floor of thick undergrowth forced them to earn every stride. But their efforts were paying off. They were gaining on Gratian. Uros could see the outline of the emperor's body becoming clearer, closer.

Then, in an instant, he was gone. The forest was gone, too, and Uros had the immediate sense of being encased in black ice. He instinctively held his breath, his mind working it over... yes, he had plunged into a small pond of dark, freezing water. Laboring to free his feet from the muddy bottom, he splashed his way to the surface and dragged himself back onto dry land. His torch had flown out of his hand to land on a clump of wet leaves and, thankfully, was still lit. Uros crawled to it and stood, coughing and surveying the blackness around him. He spotted the point of jouncing light that was Celunno's torch, wiped the frigid water from his eyes, and fell into shivering pursuit.

"He's headed there!" Celunno's voice reverberated within the dense trees.

Uros saw it. A small house in the distance. The faint smell of its hearthfire slipped into Uros's nostrils, again making him think of home. The thought gave him speed, and he caught up to Celunno just as Gratian swung open the rickety wooden door to the home and rushed inside. Voices cried out, something crashed, and a pinpoint of light from an oil lamp danced around in the darkness within the domicile.

Uros and Celunno crossed the door's threshold only moments after the emperor. The home's fading hearthfire and the assassins' torches were sufficient to illuminate the terror-stricken faces of the family within—a couple with two small children—abruptly woken from slumber by what appeared to be mad intruders.

Gratian pointed at the man of the house. "I am your emperor! You will defend me!"

But the man knew where his loyalties lay. Scooping up a child in each arm, he spoke to his wife. "Come." Leading the way, he bulled past Gratian, toward the door. The assassins parted to let the family flee.

Celunno caught his breath and spoke to the emperor. "You have five heartbeats to pray to your god."

"Soldier," said Gratian, "whatever they are paying you—" When Celunno only barked out a spiteful laugh, the emperor stopped. Whatever they were paying him was clearly enough. His indignant posture dissolved, and he lowered himself to his knees, palms pressed together in supplication. "Please don't kill me," he pleaded. "I will abdicate. I will put the purple cloak around Maximus's shoulders myself. I will kiss his feet. I will do anything. I want to live!"

Celunno raised his sword—not high, just to the level of Gratian's neck. Knowing death was a strike away, the emperor took his last stand. He dove for an iron stoker that hung on the brick hearth and swung in the direction of the assassins. In his haste, however, he didn't notice the low flame from the hearth that had caught his hair. It spread as though on a dry field, creeping over his head. It was only when the flames reached the flesh of his forehead that Gratian dropped the stoker and began to swat his scalp. He shrieked in agony.

Celunno laughed again and kept laughing as the flames blackened the panicking emperor's head. Finally, as the humor of it plateaued and the air grew putrid from the stench of burning flesh, he raised his sword and delivered the killing strike. The shrieking stopped, but the crackling of the flames continued.

Not wanting the house to go up with the emperor—why punish these people for Gratian's sins?—Uros began to ransack the humble residence for something to extinguish the fire.

"Try the kitchen," suggested Celunno.

Uros disappeared and returned a moment later with a bucket of water, two live trout within. He dumped the water, fish and all, on the flames. The fire went out with a hiss. He cocked his head and studied what remained: The face he saw in the smoldering mess now looked nothing like the face on the coins in his purse.

Dawn now breaking, the exhausted assassins hauled the emperor's body back through the woods, back to the lonely road and the two donkey carts waiting there. Uros kept an eye out just in case the emperor's second bodyguard was planning to be a hero, but Celunno didn't give it another thought. They emerged from the thick forest and saw Manta's head pop out of the cart. She jumped down and ran toward them, weeping with relief at the look of victory on their faces and the sight of the charred trophy draped over Celunno's shoulder. As Celunno dumped Gratian's body in the cart's box, Uros untethered the emperor's donkeys and slapped their rumps. The animals shook off the dust from their work-swayed backs and brayed before romping off to freedom, their reward for transporting an emperor to his death.

The two assassins and the empress lookalike traveled in happy silence as the sun moved from east to west, overseeing their journey to the designated outpost. There was nothing to eat or drink, but the temporary discomfort was a small price to pay for the riches they would soon receive from the usurper Magnus Maximus. His legions had already proclaimed him emperor in Britannia and Gaul, and his ascension seemed unstoppable. Maximus had promised the defecting Celunno rewards equal to the risk he was taking, and from everything Celunno had heard, the rising emperor was a man of his word.

As the sun took on a deep orange hue and touched the horizon, Maximus's military outpost came into view in the distance. Two armor-clad soldiers rode out to intercept them and, after confirming Celunno's mission and inspecting the corpse in the donkey cart, escorted them the rest of the way. They all moved through the fortified gates and tent-filled military camp to stop before a tent so large and regal it could only have been the headquarters of Maximus. The soldiers retrieved Gratian's body from the cart and lugged it into the Imperial tent, gesturing for the trio of assassins to follow.

The air inside the tent was pleasantly warm and smelled of good food, the scent pulling Uros's eyes to a spread of seasoned meats on a cloth-covered table. He hadn't eaten a morsel of food in two days, and the mouthwatering smell of roasted boar provoked his hunger to the point of nausea. How strange. Here he was, in the presence of a new Augustus, and all he could think about was eating the man's food.

The soldiers who had ushered them inside the tent dropped Gratian's body onto the floor, and the corpse landed soundlessly on the thick carpet. They saluted the purple-cloaked emperor who stood with his back to them, immersed in an intense discussion of strategy with several advisors.

"Caesar," said one of the soldiers. "The assassins, hired by your father." He looked down at the body. "And former Imperator Flavius Gratian."

Even before the purple-cloaked man turned around, Celunno's heartrate had doubled. This was not Magnus Maximus. This was his son, Victor. The assassin struggled to maintain his composure as the stately Victor crossed the floor of the tent, scrutinizing the body sprawled out on the carpet. The usurper's son squatted beside the charred head and frowned.

"Imperator Flavius Gratian," he mused. He stood and silently assessed the three visitors in his tent before moving to a bust of the emperor Caesar Augustus that sat on a nearby pedestal. Victor's fascination with Rome's early emperors—particularly the first emperor—was common knowledge. He even styled himself after the man, his hair fashioned with the same forked locks of hair that identified any statue, fresco, bust or coin of Augustus. Indeed, the fastest way to achieve promotion under Victor's command was to point out his gray eyes and sharp features, and the resemblance they bore to those of the famed emperor. Victor leaned against the pedestal and cocked his head. "How do I know this is Gratian?" he asked. "This could be any drunken fool who passed out in a camp fire."

Celunno bowed. "My lord, your father will be able to confirm the emperor's—apologies, my lord—the *former* emperor's identity."

"My father is on his way to Augusta Treverorum. He will make his capital there. For now."

"Then if you would summon Commander Andragathius, sir. He will also be able to—"

"Andragathius is with him. You wouldn't expect the Augustus to ride out without his master of the cavalry, would you?"

"Of course not, sir." Celunno looked to Uros and Manta, but their blanched faces and horrified expressions only helped his own panic swell. "Domine," he said, a little too desperately, "I swear to you, this is the body of Gratian."

Victor sniffed and rubbed his nose. "You served as Gratian's magister equitum for a spell, did you not?" Celunno nodded and Victor continued. "Then you've already proven yourself untrustworthy to one emperor. Why should I trust you?"

Unable to withstand the tension any longer, Uros dropped to his knees. "My lord, this is Gratian! We met him on the road. Manta here pretended to be his wife... he ran, but we caught him... in this house in the woods... he fell by the fire..."

Victor sighed. "You're probably telling the truth." He signaled an unspoken order to the guards. *Interrogate them.* Or more precisely, torture them to death. "But there's only one way to know for sure."

Ignoring the pleas for mercy from the trio of assassins as the guards dragged them out of the tent, Victor perused the seasoned boar on the table, recalling the Roman historian Suetonius's assertion that Caesar Augustus preferred bread, cheese, fish and figs. He would have to speak to the cooks about it.

CHAPTER VIII

Rome

It was said that when the Vestal Order was first established in the city of Alba Longa—Rome's mother city—it was very poor. It was so poor that the Alban priestesses did not have horses to transport them in fine litters, but rather traveled in donkey-drawn carts. Remarkably, the donkeys tasked with this honor always performed their duty with a dignity not normally attributed to their species, such was their devotion to the virgin goddess Vesta. As time went on and the Vestal Order flourished, the donkey continued to serve the goddess and her priestesses with loyalty. Their strong backs turned the millstones that made the *mola salsa* and hauled endless loads of chopped wood to her temple to nourish the sacred fire.

It was Vesta's appreciation for her hard-working animals that explained the number of plump, rose-garlanded donkeys grazing leisurely on the cartloads of crunchy apples and sweet grapes strewn along the track of the Circus Maximus on this day, the festival of the goddess Ops. As mother to Vesta, Ops was an important goddess to the Vestal Virgins and one whose rites—in addition to those of Vesta, Consus, the Bona Dea, Mars and others—they participated in. For centuries, the Vestals had performed these rites in the temple of Ops on the Capitoline Hill, but since that sanctum had been arbitrarily closed by the emperor Gratian, the city's pagan population had taken the festivities to the Circus Maximus. For it was here, below the first turning point on the racetrack's decorated central *spina*, that Romulus had discovered a subterranean altar to Consus, divine consort of Ops. As bonded deities of the earth, the god and goddess were honored closely together. Such was the natural balance of things.

Yet the Circus Maximus didn't just provide a sacred locale for the festival, it also provided a lively one. Thousands of people were spending the day at the massive oval racetrack, enjoying the chariot races and other performances, as well as the music and food. They ate and drank in abundance—Ops being the goddess of plenty—and chatted with friends as their children sprinted past the grazing donkeys on the track.

Coelia, too, was circulating among the grazing donkeys, though at work and not play. While Antonia had inherited the distinguished task of blessing people during the festival, Coelia and Domitia had been relegated to blessing the donkeys. After saying a prayer for the animals' health, the two Vestals set to work choosing which among them were to be released from the grueling work of turning the millstones and sent out to pasture. Unlike most working animals, their sacred duty spared them from the axe when their backs began to give out.

Domitia sneezed. "These beasts do not agree with me," she complained.

"They are not agreeable beasts," said Coelia. She pointed to a donkey with overgrown hooves and turned to the slave beside her. "That one can go," she said. "Make sure the farrier sees it first."

"Yes, Priestess." The slave made a note on his wax tablet.

"How many more should we release?" asked Domitia.

"We had seven stables of colts and fillies donated during the *Vestalia*. So we can retire as many as we like." She glanced at Domitia. "Or we can save your nose and my sandals—look, they're ruined—and just release the whole lot."

"The whole lot."

"Agreed." Coelia spoke to the slave. "*Omnes.*"

Leaving the slave to the details, the two Vestals made their way along the monumental spina where Antonia was blessing worshippers alongside a priest of Quirinus, the deity that Romulus had become upon his apotheosis.

"I'll wager that Antonia will be made Vestalis Maxima by the *ides*," posited Domitia.

"Maybe sooner," said Coelia. "The priest of Asclepius who visited Claudia yesterday said that she may never fully recover." Coelia thought of the high priestess lying in her bed, barely able to mumble a word and unable to use the latrine without Ptolema's help. It was a denigratory retirement for a woman who had always performed her duties with poise and pride, and who had intended to remain in the office of the Vestalis Maxima until her old age. "Symmachus won't tolerate a void at the top. I'll bet Antonia will be chief Vestal by the *kalends*."

"Do you think she'll turn into a tyrant?" Domitia asked half-jokingly.

"Probably at first," Coelia replied. She glanced back at Antonia who was blessing the worshippers. "But then she'll settle into it, and it'll be fine. She was born to do it."

They continued to the *pulvinar*, a large columned shrine-like building set into the seating of the stadium from which Rome's elite could watch the races in luxury. It was here that some of the Vestal Order's most important benefactors were socializing between mouthfuls of choice meat and swallows of Falernian wine. Since the revocation of the Vestals' funding, these prestigious politicians, powerful generals and wealthy aristocrats—and their well-dressed wives —financed everything from the Vestals' personal stipends and expenses to the wood that burned in the temple and the gourmet foods stocked in the House of the Vestals. Antonia had given strict instructions: *Mix and mingle, smile and flatter, keep them happy.*

Coelia and Domitia entered the pulvinar and headed in different directions to socialize just as a round of congratulations was moving through the gathering. Coelia joined her friend Paulina, the latter leaning against her green-eyed husband, Praetextatus. The rare eye color was a gift from Venus, Paulina said, one that complemented her husband's love of the gardens.

"What's the happy occasion?" Coelia enquired.

Paulina raised her wine cup toward Symmachus and Perses. "An engagement."

Coelia smiled and spoke to the pair of senators. "I had no idea you two were so fond of each other."

The guests laughed obligingly—even Symmachus joined in—and Paulina clarified. "Symmachus's son, Memmius, is to marry Perses's daughter, Anthea." She looked at Symmachus. "When does Memmius return from his studies in Athens?"

"He hopes to be home for the Lupercalia," said the senator. "An auspicious date of return, I would say."

Soon would be better than auspicious, thought Coelia. The young Lady Anthea was spending a great deal of time with Brogos at the ludus these days.

As the best wishes and small talk swirled, Coelia meandered through the gathering, making her way to a lavish spread of delicacies. She was pleased to see General Arbogastes standing nearby, laughing with two other men. His subordinate Stilicho was one and—this amused her—Brogos was the other.

She laughed as she approached them. "Well, I shouldn't be surprised to find the two of you so friendly with each other," she said to Arbo. "Between Brogos's dogs and your pigeons, all you need is one of Hannibal's war elephants and you could open a zoo of wartime animals."

The general smiled widely, warmly, and poured her a cup of wine. "You are a shrewd businesswoman," he said. "What can you contribute?"

"About a hundred swayback donkeys."

"You will have to do better than that, Priestess," he replied.

His tone was perhaps a little too playful, even slightly suggestive, but not unwelcomingly so, and Coelia hoped her cheeks didn't disclose her reaction. She sipped her wine, her gaze flitting down to study him. With his deep blue tunica and the engraved gold cuffs he wore on both wrists, he looked less soldierly than usual. She took another sip of her wine, her demeanor shifting into formality as Symmachus walked by. But it was another un-sought presence that appeared before her and lingered.

Olympius sloshed the wine in his cup as he tipped it toward Brogos. "Have you persuaded your lady boss to join forces with me yet?"

"Not yet, Senator," replied the gladiator. "But I'll wear her down."

Olympius spoke to the Vestal, his words only slightly slurred. "When have you ever seen a better show than what Brogos and my man Deimos put on?" he challenged. "I know that Gratian revoked your funding and so you're here kissing ass, but if you *really* want to make more money, we need to merge our schools. Our boys, fighting together, will bring in the crowds again. Don't forget that—"

Getting caught up in his sales pitch, Olympius's arm moved too quickly, and a small tidal wave of wine escaped over the rim of his cup to land on the sleeve of Arbo's handsome tunica. The senator mumbled something approximating an apology as a cir-culating slave quickly approached the general, passing him a cloth. Arbo stepped back to wipe away the wine, unperturbed. As a veteran of multiple battles, he had suffered far worse stains than a splash of wine. Yet whatever offense slid off him stuck to his subordinate, Stilicho. Not able to stomach any disrespect of his superior officer, Stilicho boldly plucked the cup out of Olym-pius's hands and set it on the table.

"Might be time to pace yourself, Senator," he said.

"Might be time to go fuck yourself," Olympius replied. He jabbed a finger into Stilicho's chest, unconcerned by the soldier's bulkier frame. "I don't know you," he said.

"Commander Stilicho is still new to Rome," interceded Brogos. "He's spent half his life on the battlefields of Germania with General

Arbogastes here." He put a pacifying hand on Olympius's shoulder. "Trust me, *Patrone*, it takes a while for the blood to cool."

Olympius chuckled derisively. "New to Rome, huh?" he asked Stilicho. "They should start teaching manners at the gates. How to act like a civilized human being instead of a backward, illiterate, goat-fucking barbarian."

Arbogastes laughed and handed Olympius a fresh cup of wine. "I'll have tutors posted at every gate," he said, casually attempting to pacify the temperamental senator. "Nobody gets through until they can quote the Twelve Tables and four acts of Virgil."

Although the confrontation had been brief and inconspicuous against the backdrop of the boisterous gathering, Symmachus's omnipresent perception had nonetheless detected it from across the room. He strolled over to investigate. Coelia's present company—a soldier known to be fond of her, a gladiator and a drunken senator—would at least warrant a tacit rebuke. Yet before he could satisfy himself, something more concerning caught his attention: the two unsmiling soldiers who had just entered the pulvinar. Their cloaks were spotted with mud from a hasty journey, and they were making a straight line for General Arbogastes.

Arbo greeted them with a curt nod. The more senior of the two handed him a scroll and Arbo quickly broke the seal as, meanwhile, the guests in the pulvinar formed an inquisitive circle around him. They fell silent as they waited for news, watching the general's brow furrow as he read.

"Don't keep us in suspense," said Olympius, suddenly very sober.

"Gratian is dead," announced Arbo. "Assassinated in Gaul." It looked like he had more to say, but the exclamations of alarm that spread through the gathering stifled him.

Olympius wasn't one to wait. "What else?" he demanded.

"The legions of Magnus Maximus have proclaimed him emperor of Roman Gaul and Britannia."

Like everyone else, Coelia looked to Symmachus. What would this coup mean for Rome? The statesman's arms were crossed and his lips were pursed in thought, his political mind already assessing the assassination, and its myriad of consequences, on a level far above anyone else. With his wavy but prematurely graying hair, masculine features and sonorous voice, he presented as older than his middle age. It was a mixture of attributes that only amplified his reputation for sagacity.

"Gratian is no loss to the empire," he finally said, "and Theodosius doesn't have the manpower or the will for another war. I expect he will come to terms with Maximus and leave the young Valentinian in Mediolanum to govern the west as his vassal. Theodosius himself won't get off his throne in Constantinople unless it is to fornicate."

Arbogastes smirked. "You know him well, Senator."

"I know Maximus just as well," said Symmachus. "He is competent. Even better, he is a zealous adherent of Nicene Christianity and will spend more time persecuting heretics of his own religion than troubling himself with us pagans." The senator's thoughts shifted. "Maximus's son Victor is one to watch," he continued. "He has an obsession with Caesar Augustus. Fashions himself after the man, even down to what he eats, or so I'm told. I would not be surprised to see him touring Rome by the kalends." Symmachus shrugged. "Honestly, my friends, in my estimation, it is more good news than bad for us. I welcome it."

Heads nodded in agreement. After the recent laws that revoked the Vestals' funding, appropriated temple assets and removed the Altar of Victory from the Senate House, not many tears would flow for Gratian in Rome.

Ten or twelve servants entered the pulvinar carrying fresh trays of food and drink, and the circle that had formed around Symmachus and Arbogastes broke apart, those gathered now dispersing to discuss the intriguing developments over the newest delicacies. Symmachus moved off to speak lowly with senators Praetextatus and Junius, while Paulina whisked Brogos off to introduce the celebrity gladiator to a group of bejeweled matrons. At the same time, Arbo retreated to a corner with Stilicho, their voices matter-of-fact. No doubt they would be off to Constantinople by sundown. As former soldiers of Gratian, they would be expected to swear allegiance to Theodosius without delay.

Coelia considered strolling over to the couches to chat with Domitia until the start of the next chariot race, but her sister Vestal was absorbed in conversation with Senator Perses and his wife Helena, so she wandered to the front of the pulvinar and leaned against a fluted column. She stared out at the monuments on the racetrack's spina, her eyes settling on a massive marble statue of a lion—the symbol of Rome's regality and supremacy—attacking a horse. The ferocity in the lion's eyes was countered by the look of terror in the stricken horse's eyes. The doomed beast made her think of Gratian, doomed Gratian, and she smiled.

CHAPTER IX

The extent to which Coelia enjoyed overnight watches in the temple was entirely dependent on her company. Although much of the time she had watch with a novice, she was often paired with one of her sister priestesses. If that was Domitia or Proculeia, the watch would be a lively one as they chatted, played dice or knucklebones, and snacked on whatever sweet surprises the cooks had prepared in advance. Time passed quickly. If she was paired with Terentia or Sergia, the latter of whom had only recently been vested with full rites after training for the standard ten years as a novice, the watch would be quieter and more reverential. Coelia would catch up on reading and lose herself in the duty of caring for the sacred fire after dark. The sound of the snapping flames and the sight of the red embers popping out of the hearth was different at night, and she often found herself standing in awe before the altar, gazing up through the oculus to marvel at the infinity of the silver-starred black sky above. Time passed less quickly than with Domitia or Proculeia, but pleasantly enough.

Tonight, Coelia was on watch with Antonia. As always, Saturn slowed the water clock to a standstill as the chief Vestal's favored priestess—who was to be appointed Vestalis Maxima in mere days—insisted on unwavering adherence to duty. If they weren't diagramming the placement of the wood and how it shifted in the hearth, they were performing an offering or a libation. If they weren't recording the movement of the flames on a grid to divine the goddess's will, they were studying the ash for signs or omens. If they weren't saying a prayer or performing a rite with a consecrated strip of oak, they were sanctifying incense or pine cones for special offerings. If they weren't inspecting every inch of the sanctum for a spot of dust the novices missed, they were reviewing the pontifical books. There was no idle chatting, no snacking, no spirited game of *XII scripta*, and no inessential visits to the latrine. One hour felt like four.

Coelia made a final note on a wax tablet and eyed Antonia. "Domitia asked me if I thought you'd turn into a tyrant when you become high priestess," she said. "My reply was too naïve."

Antonia took the wax tablet from Coelia's hands and read her notes, nodding in satisfaction. She looked up. "Symmachus will be watching every move I make."

"He's always liked you," assured Coelia. "It'll be fine."

"Patting me on the head for keeping the fire going is one thing," said Antonia, her tone crisp and clear. "But he will expect perfection from me, especially now." Her fingers tightened around the wax tablet. "I have always wanted to be Vestalis Maxima. Just think what it must've been like to be high priestess during the reign of a true Caesar, like Antoninus Pius. Imagine dining in the Imperial palace with Empress Faustina and discussing all the goings on in Rome."

"Antonia," said Coelia. "You are the most dignified woman I have ever met. It's like you're from another time. That is what the Order needs, so just be that. The rest is up to the Fates."

Antonia set the wax tablet on a niche in the sanctum's wall and returned to stoke the fire. "Thank you, Coelia," she said warmly. "But you should know that I intend to blame you for any errors I make."

Coelia chuckled. "I know."

The bronze doors of the temple opened unexpectedly—the pair's watch wasn't over for another two hours—and Proculeia stepped inside. Her middle-of-the-night presence was startling enough, but the fact that she was still in her nightdress, an orange shawl haphazardly hugging her shoulders, made it even more so. She rushed to the altar and spoke quietly to Antonia, as if her hushed voice could be heard beyond the thick marble walls of the sanctum.

"There are soldiers here," she said. "From Mediolanum." She turned to Coelia. "They are asking for you."

Coelia's jaw dropped. "Me? Why?"

"I don't know, but they have a scroll that bears the Imperial seal of Emperor Valentinian."

"Have them wait in the tablinum with Domitia," Antonia instructed. "Then get Claudia—I don't care what it takes, find a way to prop her up—and take her there, too." When Proculeia hesitated, Antonia pushed her. "Go!"

As Proculeia hurried out the doors, Sergia and Florina slipped inside the temple, their unveiled heads evidence that they had come straight from their beds to replace Antonia and Coelia on watch.

"What is happening?" asked the novice Florina, her young, freckled cheeks flushed from fright.

"We will soon find out," replied Antonia. She took Coelia's hand and led her out of the temple, down the steps and across the torch-lit street to the portico of the House of the Vestals. One door was already open, and the sentries on guard appeared worried and irate in equal measure. "Are they inside?" Antonia asked.

"Priestess Proculeia took them in," said one of the guards. His dour expression looked even more ominous by the flickering light of the torches that burned beside him. "I don't give a shit about an Imperial seal. Give the order, and we'll throw the bastards out."

"No," replied Antonia. "Whatever it is, they'll just return with twice as many men."

As Coelia followed Antonia into the courtyard, she looked up into the black sky. Silver stars were strewn across the firmament so thickly that they looked as though they might collapse on top of her... or perhaps it was just a crushing sense of dread that made it seem so.

She stopped. "I'm scared, Antonia. What could they possibly want with *me?*"

Antonia moved in front of Coelia and faced her, gripping both of her arms. "I don't know," she said. "But I won't let anything happen to you. Don't panic, please."

They entered the high priestess's ornate office to find it well-lit by a roaring fireplace. Domitia was there, arguing with two of the four soldiers, all of their voices rising by the moment in a mixture of anger and indignation. They fell silent as the composed Antonia swept into the office, Coelia following behind. Antonia sat at Claudia's desk and leaned back in her chair as if the soldiers' intrusion were a mere annoyance and not a gnawing terror that was eating her from the inside out.

"I am the acting Vestalis Maxima Antonia Secunda," she said. She held out her hand. "Give me the letter."

One of the soldiers handed her the scroll and she broke the seal, reading by the light of a candle's thick flame. Coelia knew her well enough to catch the look of shock that flashed in her eyes, but the soldiers only saw an impatient frown.

Just then, Proculeia and Ptolema arrived, both their faces red from the effort of so quickly collecting Claudia from her bed, wrapping her in a shawl and transporting her through the house in the special wheeled chair that the priests of Asclepius had provided. Awake and aware, Claudia was doing her best to sit upright, supported as she was by the high sides of the chair.

"Who is this?" asked the soldier who had given Antonia the scroll.

"Our high priestess Claudia," replied Antonia without looking up. "She has suffered a disability, but she is fully aware." She cleared her throat and casually tossed the papyrus on the desk.

Keeping her voice level, she spoke directly to Claudia. "Priestess Coelia Concordia has been accused of consulting the Oracle at Praeneste," she said, "and of failing to advise Emperor Gratian of the threat against his life. She is to be charged with treason."

"What?" Coelia stepped forward. "I haven't been to Praeneste in ages! And even then, I only went to the Temple of Fortuna. I knew nothing of the threat against Gratian!"

The soldier regarded her coolly. "You were seen consulting the Oracle," he said. "And you" — he looked at all the Vestals — "all of you had the motive to want Gratian dead after he withdrew your monies."

Antonia spoke as cavalierly as she could. "And who precisely says they saw Priestess Coelia consult the Oracle?"

"This is not a tribunal," replied the soldier. "It is an arrest."

"An arrest in the middle of the night?"

"His Highness Valentinian is trying to avoid any public disruption," said the soldier. He set his hand on the hilt of the long sword that hung at his side and looked at Coelia. "The accused will come with us."

"*Mm, muh...*"

Claudia's strident vocalization caught all their attention—but for her part, the incapacitated chief Vestal's attention was focused solely on Antonia. The two women held each other's gaze for a long moment, exchanging silent words.

Finally, Antonia spoke. "The bishops' spies are mistaken," she said to the soldiers. She raised a finger, discreetly signalling for the other Vestals to remain quiet. To not react. "It was not Priestess Coelia who visited the Oracle in Praeneste. It was High Priestess Claudia."

The sun hadn't yet risen as the lives of those who resided in the House of the Vestals changed forever, and it all happened at the point of a sword. Weeping and trembling, Domitia and Proculeia hastily bundled up the infirm Claudia, preparing the high priestess to leave with the soldiers. Refusing any retinue of dignity, they permitted only a single female slave to accompany her—no doubt to spare themselves the unpleasant task of dealing with the woman's personal needs—and would not reveal where they were taking her. While that nightmare was unfolding, Antonia had her own part to play.

The statue of the Vestalis Maxima Claudia had stood in the peristyle of the Vestals' residence for years, life-sized and painted true to life, and accented by a gold gem-studded necklace that caught the light when the sun was just so. But it could stand there no longer, not if the fiction of Claudia's crime were to be believed by the soldiers. As the slaves waited, ropes in hand to pull the statue off its high marble base, it was Antonia's duty to kneel before the statue's pedestal and chisel Claudia's name off its surface. It had to be done. She had to distance Claudia from the Vestal Order, cutting her off like a diseased limb, knowing it was the only way to save the rest of the body.

That sacrilege completed, Antonia stood and stepped back. The effort of marring the hard stone base had torn the flesh from her soft hands. They dripped blood onto her white tunica as she and the other Vestals watched the slaves throw ropes around Claudia's statue. They pulled it forward, and the marble sculpture toppled over to crash into the box of the cart below. The head broke off.

"Stop crying," Antonia whispered to the priestesses. "They are watching. They can't think that—"

She fell silent as a pair of soldiers strode up to the cart. One of them reached into the box to fumble with the marble bulk of the high priestess's smashed statue. When he withdrew his hands, he was holding the gold jeweled necklace that had hung around its neck. He tucked it into his belt. Moving to the wooden handles of the cart, he and his companion grunted with effort as they began to convey the broken statue toward the doors of the house.

A familiar squeaking sound broke through the silent rage of the priestesses, and their hearts sank as one to see Ptolema and a younger female slave wheeling Claudia along the pathway. Her wheeled chair fell into line behind the cart that carried her debased legacy, moving along like spoils of war being paraded in a triumph. The high priestess's shawl was wrapped over her shoulders and her head, obscuring her face from the rest of the Vestals as she was ushered out of her own house like an unwanted guest.

Coelia looked at Antonia. "Can we not say good-bye?"

"No," Antonia replied sternly. "Be quiet."

The bleak procession moved out of sight just as the lights from the torches that lined the peristyle began to fade against the first hues of sunrise. Coelia felt Domitia take her hand and they met eyes, trying to comfort each other as they heard the sound of the house's grand wooden doors close. A moment later, Ptolema rushed back into the courtyard, a cry of agony on her lips and tears streaming down her face. She ran into the arms of Antonia. The two women embraced and moved to sit side by side on the edge of a decorative pool, both of them sobbing.

"*What have I done?*" Antonia shrieked. "Holy Mother Vesta, forgive me!"

Coelia knelt in front of her. "What have *you* done? *I* am the one who saw the Oracle!" She put a hand over her mouth, speaking through her fingers. "I lied to Claudia. I told her the Oracle wasn't there. Maybe if I'd told her what was said... maybe it would've meant something to her. The Oracle said—"

"Do not repeat what the prophetess said," interrupted Ptolema. "The high priestess should have gone herself if she wanted to hear the words." In an unexpected and uncharacteristic gesture of comfort, she smoothed the side of Coelia's veil and looked at the Vestals. "None of you are to blame for this. The high priestess knows that."

Domitia turned to Antonia. "What will happen to her?"

Antonia exhaled shakily. "I will go speak with Symmachus. If anyone can protect her, it will be him." She stood unsteadily and spoke to one of the anxious house slaves who stood watching from the peristyle. "Bring my carriage around," she said. "I'll go now."

* * *

It was strange, but the series of predawn tectonic shocks that had struck Coelia's life—including the accusation of treason briefly leveled against her and Claudia's abhorrent arrest—had largely subsided by midday, surrendering to the forces of routine and nature. The pressing duties she had to perform, the warmth of the sun, the growl of her empty stomach... those had dulled the sharp trauma of it all into a sort of fatigued acceptance. She retreated to the tablinum to lose herself in the distraction of work, waiting for Antonia's return and information about Claudia.

As midday turned to mid-afternoon, news of the high priestess's arrest spread throughout the city. A steady stream of priests, senators, friends and concerned benefactors arrived at the House of the Vestals with endless questions, though Coelia had no answers. Although she had sent a messenger to Symmachus's stately home on the Caelian Hill, he had returned with only the pithiest of responses from Antonia: *Symmachus is assisting. I will come home when I can.*

As afternoon gave way to early evening, Coelia's head began to pound from an aggressive fusion of emotional and physical exhaustion. On top of that, her guilt and her worry were uniting to form a new branch of fear. Antonia had been gone far too long. Claudia's absence was disorienting and frightening enough, but with Antonia gone too, Coelia felt particularly susceptible to whatever outside forces were at work against the Vestal Order. She checked—nervously, repeatedly—on the Vestals and novices on watch in the temple, and then returned to the house to wander the halls before again checking in at the temple. She thought about taking a bath, but knew there was no way she could relax... the idea of disrobing... she felt vulnerable enough.

It was sunset by the time Antonia finally walked through the doors. She shuffled tiredly along the peristyle, wordlessly gesturing for Coelia—and only Coelia—to follow her into Claudia's office. She sat behind the desk, and Coelia sat across from her, trying not to assume the worst. Antonia's red swollen eyes and look of defeat made if difficult not to.

"Symmachus didn't stop," Antonia began. "He probably wrote fifty letters and sent out twice as many messengers. He arranged for her to stay under house arrest at one of Senator Junius's villas in the country. She will be comfortable and cared for."

"What will happen to her?"

"He's written to Theodosius and Valentinian asking for a pardon," replied Antonia. "He is confident they will grant it, though she will be forbidden from returning to Rome. She will be ordered into... how did he put it? Soft exile."

"Exile," echoed Coelia. "After giving her life to Rome."

"They will not stop until they have destroyed us," said Antonia. "They won't rest until they have pulled down every statue in the peristyle and silenced every one of us, one way or another." She pressed her fingers to her temples. "I have made a decision. I spent half the day arguing with Symmachus about it, but I am certain."

"Certain about what?"

"I'm leaving the Order."

Coelia sat back. "You cannot."

Antonia placed her palms flat on the desk, but quickly drew them back. They were still sore and bloodied from the act of chiseling Claudia's name off the marble base of her statue. "You know that I can. My tenure officially ended three years ago."

"So what? You have to replace Claudia as Vestalis Maxima." Coelia shook her head, bewildered. "There is no one else."

"There is you."

"If you force me to wear the veil of the Vestalis Maxima, the bishops' work will be done for them."

"You are more than capable."

"Antonia, I am a plebeian who owns a failing gladiator school and once had a Greek tutor threaten to throw himself off the Tarpeian Rock if he had to listen to me butcher Homer for one more lesson."

"I'm retiring, Coelia."

Coelia's heart was pounding. "I won't do it."

"You have to do it." Antonia leaned forward over the desk. "Your tenure ends in two years. The time will pass quickly, and then you can step down as well. You can marry and move away from Rome. You can do whatever you want. You'll have enough money by then. All you have to do is keep your head down."

"Antonia, we need you. I am begging you—"

"Galeria can be vested with full rites. Domitia will be your second, and you will be Vestalis Maxima." Seeing the horrified disbelief on Coelia's face, Antonia softened. "Symmachus will help you. Praetextatus and Lady Paulina will too, as will the priests in the religious college. You will have support from our allies in the Senate, in the army, in the magisterial offices and—"

"Then why are you leaving?"

"Because I'm afraid, Coelia. It shames me to say so, but it's true. It was one thing when our enemies just fell back on their usual slanders—calling us temple prostitutes and demonesses— but it gets worse every day."

"Rome is still pagan," said Coelia. She pushed the pleading tone from her voice and replaced it with reason. "Think about it. Theodosius listens to Symmachus. Things might get better, and then you'd be stepping down for nothing."

"And what about when Symmachus is gone?" asked Antonia. "What if he is killed? What if he decides that he's had enough of politics and crises and insults, and moves to one of his villas to live in peace? They say countless pagans were tortured and killed under the second Constantius for consulting the Oracles, and many of them on mere accusation. Look what just happened to us. If we didn't have Symmachus to intercede for Claudia, she'd be wasting away in the *Carcer* right now, sitting in her own filth."

"We have other allies besides Symmachus. You said so yourself."

"It isn't about allies," said Antonia. "It isn't about money. It's the indignity of it. The Vestal Order was not meant to beg for protection or coin. We were never meant to be a marginal part of Rome.

We are its very heart. If the emperors don't know that anymore, then it's just a matter of time." Antonia rose and moved to the fireplace. "I have made my decision." She turned to Coelia. "You will be fine if you just wait it out. Do your work and don't make any enemies." She looked into the flames. "Who is on watch in the temple?"

"Go see for yourself."

Coelia stood and marched out of the suffocating anxiety of the tablinum and into the courtyard, although the open sky did nothing to alleviate the sense that the walls were closing in. Not bothering to retrieve a shawl from her quarters, she exited the house and stepped onto the Via Sacra. The Forum was already closed for the night, and the streets were empty except for the sentries lighting torches and the sanitation workers making their regular rounds. She turned toward the Capitoline and walked quickly, hoping to shed some of her stress and resentment, but to no avail. The faster she walked, the harder they clung to her, even as she passed the Temple of Vesta and strode along the arcade of the Basilica Aemelia, gazing up at the great temples on top of the Capitoline Hill, including the greatest of all, the Temple of Jupiter Optimus Maximus.

The gods are fixed in the heavens, she thought. *How could it ever be different?*

Continuing past the Temple of Saturn, she slowed her gait as she reached the wide staircase of the Temple of Concordia and the statues of Mercury and Hercules that stood on either side. Night having fallen, the temple was lit by torchlight and the flickering shadows that moved across the white marble façade seemed to breathe life into the structure's elements: the towering Corinthian columns, the ornate capitals sculpted with pairs of leaping rams, and the roofline topped with statues of the Capitoline Triad—Jupiter, Juno and Minerva. Lifting one tired leg and then the other, she climbed halfway up the colossal staircase before gathering her tunica around her knees and sitting on a marble step. She stared out into the silent, dark Forum.

The silence didn't last long. She heard heavy footfalls mingled with the sound of panting and squinted to make out the approaching silhouette of Brogos, trailed as always by his three black dogs.

"Deimos and I were out hunting in the country," he said as he reached the temple. "I came as soon as I heard the news." He scaled the staircase—the dogs did, too—and stopped a few steps below her, looking up. "Is the high priestess all right?"

"She's under house arrest at a senator's villa. Antonia says she'll probably be exiled."

Brogos sat beside her. "There are worse things."

"I know." She tapped her feet on the marble step below. As she did, one of the dogs nosed her sandals in play. "This step... I once sat right here with Emperor Julian."

"The last pagan emperor."

Coelia nodded. "He came to Rome just before he left for Gaul," she said. "He was the one who initiated me into the Vestal Order when I was a child, not long after he made his own vows to the true gods as Caesar." She touched her head. "He cropped my hair for the veil." Coelia thought back, remembering the day, remembering each word the emperor had spoken to her: *I take thee, beloved one, to be a priestess of Vesta, and to perform the holy rites on behalf of the Roman people. I give thee the name Concordia, daughter and bride of Rome, so that you may always ensure harmony between the gods and the people of our empire.* "Afterward, we walked through the Forum together. It was locked and quiet, but he had one of his scribes find us some sweet ice in the basilica. Then we came here and sat on this step." She looked at Brogos. "And we talked. Just like this, like you and I are doing now." She smiled. "Me and Caesar."

"Eating sweet ice together."

"He seemed so old to me at the time," said Coelia. "But he was younger than I am now." Her smile tightened, and she succumbed to the pressure behind her eyes. Tears formed, and she sniffled. "Imagine if he'd lived longer."

"How did he die?"

"They say he was betrayed by a Christian soldier in his own army. Maybe he was. He despised their religion. He said it was a fiction of men composed by wickedness." She dabbed her eyes with the hem of her veil. "Antonia is leaving the Order."

"What? Why?"

Deciding they'd waited long enough for Coelia's attention, the dogs drew closer. She scratched their ears in turn. "She got scared. I can't blame her." Taking one of the dog's heads in her hands, she looked into its black eyes. "There's no one else, Cosmos. I have to be Vestalis Maxima."

The dog licked her face.

After a pensive pause, Brogos spoke. "Can you still leave the Order in two years?"

"Yes, providing no one wheels me into exile before then. I will have to merge my gladiator school with Olympius's though, may the gods help me. I won't have time to manage it."

"Can't say I hate that. I'd rather fight alongside Deimos than against him."

Coelia leaned closer to Brogos and sniffed. "Hunting with Deimos, you say?" she smirked. "I didn't know wild boar were drawn to perfume." When Brogos avoided her eyes, she shrugged. "Anthea is engaged to Symmachus's son, now. You know that."

He nodded. Coelia knew that she should've forbidden him from seeing the patrician young woman the moment she found out about their relationship. Senator Perses and his wife Helena expected her to, and Ptolema nagged her about it daily: *You have a duty to support the friends of the Order, especially now.* But Coelia had seen how hard Brogos fought in the arena to impress Anthea. It would be bad for business to remove that motivation. And anyway, she had her own problems right now.

Trying to lighten the mood, Brogos snickered as the three dogs contorted over and around each other, each trying to coax another ear scratch out of Coelia. "It will be all right, Patrona," he said. "You'll be the first chief Vestal to be guarded by the hounds of Hades." He twisted around and removed the goatskin pouch that hung from his belt. Pulling out the cork stopper, he passed the pouch to Coelia. "I don't have any sweet ice."

Coelia took a long draw from the wine pouch. Then another. She passed the pouch back to Brogos as they sat together on the temple steps, looking out over the silent Forum.

CHAPTER X

As Coelia stood in the apsidal dressing hall of the House of the Vestals, swallowing another mouthful of Ptolema's stomach-soothing tonic from a mosaic glass *patella* and allowing Domitia to fuss over the folds of her stola, she re-read the letter from Senator Symmachus that had arrived before dawn:

Change is nature's path to eternity. Remember the meditations of the gentle king Marcus Aurelius and know that all things must change. The change in your duties, as prescribed in your vows to the goddess, is therefore necessary for the universal nature. You must commit to the change, to the higher calling, with dignity and diligence.

She tried to wring some comfort from the philosophizing sentiment, tried to remember what Claudia had said about him, but instead only saw shades of condescension and the senator's own panic in the black ink of his words. No doubt he had worn out his knees begging Antonia to stay on as Vestalis Maxima. Ptolema plucked the scroll out of her hands.

"Stop reading this nonsense," she said, and tossed it into the fire that burned in a sacrificial tripod.

"Be careful, Ptolema," said Coelia. "You might end up being helpful after all."

Domitia put her hands on Coelia's shoulders and spun her around to face a full-length mirror. "It is all done correctly," she said.

Coelia looked in the mirror at her imminent self: the *Virgo Vestalis Maxima* of the Roman Empire. In addition to the white ceremonial dress of the high priestess, she now wore a more striking headdress. The customary red and white woolen *infula* headband under her veil, and the *vittae* ribbons that hung down to fall over her shoulders, now boasted a crimson color that was more purple than red. Her white veil was more splendid, too, its border matching the crimson of the infula. The usual fibula she wore to secure the veil at chest level was gone, replaced by a large gold medallion with pearls encircling a central carnelian stone— a gift from Emperor Julian on the day he had initiated her into the Vestal Order. To anyone else, she looked capable and confident, a dignified representative of Holy Vesta. To herself, she looked like an imposter.

She and Domitia departed the dressing chamber to the sound of Ptolema's soft prayers and crossed the central courtyard, exiting the House of the Vestals to find the priests of the religious college, as well as many senators and friends, standing along the Via Sacra. Red and white rose petals lay scattered over the marble stretch of the street that led from the portico of the Vestals' home to the temple. Coelia refrained from making eye contact with anyone and instead focused on gracefully closing the short distance to the temple and ascending its petal-covered steps without slipping or disturbing her ceremonial garments.

The young priestess Galeria and the novice Florina opened the doors for her, and Coelia stepped inside the warmth of the sanctum, noting how the morning sunlight intermingled with the smoke from the fire as it wound its way upward to slip out the oculus in the temple's domed roof. Other than the sharp-toothed self-consciousness gnawing away at her, it was a perfect morning for the dedication of a new Vestalis Maxima. Galeria entered the temple after Coelia and Domitia, joining the rest of the priestesses around the circular hearthfire.

Coelia poured a libation—red wine mixed with white donkey's milk—from a *patera*, into the flames. "*Vesta Mater, tuam altissimam sacerdotem me accipe.*"

Domitia leaned over the fire, reading the movement of the flames from above. "Steady in *postica-sinistra*, but more embers in *antica-sinistra*." She nodded, content. "Very good. Beautiful."

The signs asserting Vesta's acceptance of her new Vestalis Maxima, Domitia passed Coelia a piece of consecrated kindling—a branch taken from the sacred oak tree that grew by the Temple of Jupiter on the Capitoline Hill. The letters VVM COELIA CONCORDIA had been meticulously carved on its smoothed and polished surface. Coelia placed the oak branch into the sacred fire, thus offering her name to the goddess.

"*Gratias, divina Vesta,*" said Coelia.

Domitia placed frankincense onto a specially prepared piece of charcoal within the bronze firebowl. A thick, strongly scented vapor swirled up and out of the flames, its milky whiteness joining the gray smoke from the sacred fire and rising up to escape through the oculus.

Outside the temple, those gathered to witness the appointment of the new chief Vestal saw the smoke signal and broke into a vibrant cheer.

CHAPTER XI

The place was crawling with snakes. Even before Helena and Anthea had crossed the *Pons Fabricius* to reach the trireme-shaped Tiber Island in the middle of the Tiber River, home to the holy temple of the healing god Asclepius, mother and daughter had had to step over several of the sleeping coiled forms. They would not be removed or bothered, for snakes had been protected on the savior's island for over a thousand years.

A vivid sunrise had ushered in a warm early morning, and Helena and Anthea were among the first to arrive for the day's blessings, treatments and advice. Family members of the sick or injured who were being housed on the island were already there, washing the many statues and shrines that graced the pristine island, while the priests and physicians made their rounds, dispensing medicine and prayer to those under their care. The sounds of the Tiber—the rush of water, the song of morning birds, the squawks of squabbling ducks, the shouts of workers and fishermen along the banks—drifted over the complex in a way that only seemed to amplify its serene detachment from the bustle of Rome.

The two women passed under an archway upon which a portion of the physician's oath written by the Greek Hippocrates was inscribed. It reminded healers of their sworn duty to the gods and goddesses of health—Apollo, Asclepius, Hygieia and Panacea—while simultaneously reassuring the weak or vulnerable that those advising them could be trusted. No one read it, of course, but it was nice to know it was there. Emerging from the archway, they proceeded along a footpath until they reached one of the island's curative wells, this one encircled by a low white marble wall. A statue of Hygieia stood in the middle of the clear water. Helena and Anthea drank from the well and received a cleansing blessing from a priestess before continuing to their destination, the larger-than-life statue of Asclepius that fronted the island's largest temple. A whimpering infant lay at the base of the statue while two priests prayed and the child's young mother waited anxiously. It was a visceral reminder that misery and misfortune brought most to this beautiful place.

Anthea said a private prayer for the health of the child. She turned to Helena and spoke softly. "Mother, we do not need to be here. I promise, I won't see him again."

"Enough promises," replied Helena. She pulled her daughter aside. "There is no shame in consulting the priests."

Overhearing their conversation, a priest wearing a white tunica embroidered at the neckline with the snake-entwined staff of Asclepius approached them. "Nothing can heal the healthy, *Mater*," he said, addressing the worried mother while studying Anthea. He pointed in the direction of a white myrtle tree. "Go to the shrine of Venus Verticordia and speak to the priest there."

"*Gratias tibi ago, Sacerdos*," said Helena.

They strolled along the footpath, enjoying the warm morning and the scent of flowers that led straight to a large round shrine to Venus. Fragrant red roses grew from the base of its encircling columns. Shielding the open-air shrine from the sun, a gauzy pink canopy cast a rosy glow over the marble statue of Venus inside. The diademed goddess of love wore a lavender dress and held a set of scales in one hand and a scepter in the other while her mischievous son Cupid, chubby and about to release an arrow, leaned against her leg. The quiet arrival of the mother and daughter startled the old priest who was bent over, busily pruning a rose bush.

"Merciful gods," he muttered to himself. He tried to stand up, but flinched in pain and grabbed his lower back.

Anthea rushed to his side and helped him stand. "You do know you're on the healing island," she quipped. "Are the physicians so ineffectual?"

"Their medicines work well enough," said the old man, "providing you can stomach the taste. I cannot."

Anthea helped the man limp over to a pair of marble benches. He sat on one, while she and Helena sat on the other.

"Would you like some water, Sacerdos?" asked Helena.

"Oh, I never take water before midday," he said. "It goes through the pipes too quickly at my age. What brings you two roses to my roses so early in the morning?"

"It is a delicate matter, Sacerdos," said Helena.

"The goddess does not judge those in love," replied the priest. "And you can see that I am as old as Saturn. I have heard everything."

Helena took Anthea's hand. "My husband and I love our daughter dearly," she said. "We have arranged a betrothal to a respectable young man who is currently out of Rome. He is to return in two months for their wedding, but meanwhile..."

"Meanwhile, she has passion for another," guessed the priest.

"Our family is not as wealthy as it once was, Sacerdos," Helena divulged. "The wedding must happen."

"Ah, the wedding," said the priest. "It is always about the wedding and never about those to be wedded." He turned to Anthea. "Where is your betrothed?"

"He is studying in Athens."

"Do you love him?"

"I do not love either man," replied Anthea. "But Memmius—that's the name of my betrothed—writes good letters. He is wealthy, too, which is all my parents care about."

"I doubt that is all your parents care about," said the priest. "Wealth is good for a young woman. Life will be easier and probably longer." He glanced at the statue of Venus. "Do you know how the first statue of Venus Verticordia, the changer of hearts, came to be in Rome?"

"No, Sacerdos."

"Back in the days of the Republic, two Vestal Virgins were accused of breaking their vows of chastity. They were tried and convicted, and suffered the worst of fates by being interred alive in the underground chamber of the Evil Field. Afterward, the Sibylline Books were consulted, and it was determined that a statue to Venus Verticordia should be dedicated for the benefit of the Vestal priestesses. They could pray to the goddess when their passions grew too strong, and she would invest them with the power to resist."

"So you're telling me to just pray?" asked Anthea.

Helena sighed. "Sacerdos," she said, "I mean no disrespect, but prayer is not enough. We require a remedy."

"The marriage bed is the only healthy remedy," replied the priest. "Not even the Vestals' punishment was enough to deter those consumed with passion. Yet those rigid in judgement, or those who needed a sacrifice for their own crimes, continued to condemn them for it." He turned back to Anthea. "The goddess does not change hearts," he said, "but she can give you the strength to change your own if you truly want to. Pray to her, and she will reveal the many types of love. The love you have for your parents, and that which they have for you. The love you will have for your own child one day. You must respect love." He slapped his hands on his knees. "And then write to this Memmius fool and tell him we have libraries and tutors in Rome as well! Those damn Greeks think they know it all!" Anthea laughed, and the priest stood on shaky feet. He shuffled to the myrtle tree and retrieved one of several cloth sachets that hung from its branches. "This is an ointment made from the chaste tree," he said, passing it to Anthea. "I give it to the Vestals. Wear the sachet around your neck, and apply the ointment to your breasts in the morning. Follow it with camphor oil at night. Along with prayer, the odors will help allay feelings of desire. Only consummation with your husband will satisfy them fully, though." He looked at Helena. "This is the nature of things, *Mater*."

"Thank you, Sacerdos," said Helena.

"Most welcome, my dears," he said, and headed back to his roses.

Helena and Anthea stood, the latter clutching the sachet in her hand while her mother placed two coins on the marble bench. They turned and retraced their steps along the pathway, strolling past the statue of Asclepius, passing under the archway, and alighting onto the footbridge that extended over the Tiber. Knowing her mother was less than satisfied with the priest's advice, Anthea unfastened the sachet and dipped her finger into the thick ointment. She rubbed a little into the skin of her neck and inhaled deeply.

"It is working already, Mother. Take me to Vesta's temple, I shall become—"

"It is not funny," said Helena. She stepped over a coiled snake and huffed, dreading the conversation she would soon have with Perses. He would not be appeased by a partial remedy and prayer, and she didn't know how many more family arguments she could endure. During their last shouting match with Anthea, she had nearly formed the derogative *meretrix* on her lips but—thank the gods—had stopped herself. If she had spoken it, she knew Anthea would have walked out the door forever.

"I am sorry, Mother. I don't want you and Father to be disappointed in me." She hung the sachet around her neck.

"Well, we are disappointed," said Helena. The words were hasher than they should have been, but her frustration was getting the better of her. Why could the girl not show more restraint, more respect?

Nearing the end of the bridge, Helena's frustration swelled at the delay caused by a congestion of people. She tried to shoulder past the man in front of her, but he turned around to reveal a bandaged eye, no doubt his reason for visiting the temple of Asclepius.

"There's nowhere to go, lady. Somebody dumped a load of horseshit on the bridge. They're just clearing it now." He gestured to an ornamental statuette of Hygieia affixed to the bridge. The goddess's breasts had been chiseled off. "And then there's that horseshit."

"*Bona Dea*," whispered Helena.

At last, the path ahead was cleaned and cleared, and they were able to depart the bridge, averting their eyes to avoid the sight of the defiled statuette and the words painted in red along the bridge's stone balustrading: DEI FALSI. *False gods*. Helena spotted a street vendor selling the morning's freshly baked bread and abruptly veered toward the stall, Anthea quickening her step to follow, suddenly aware of just how hungry she was. She waited eagerly as her mother purchased two triangles of still-warm bread. Together, they leaned against the brick wall of an *insula* to eat. The food was soothing.

A voice interrupted their street breakfast.

"Helena, I haven't you see you in ages," said a woman dressed in a plain, faded tunica.

It took Helena a moment to recognize her—she looked different without cosmetics—but then she passed her bread to Anthea and embraced the woman enthusiastically.

"Abigail, it has been too long," said Helena. She looked down at the woman's simple clothing. "How have you been?"

"I have been happy," replied Abigail. "I am doing the Lord's work."

"Oh." Helena stepped back and glanced at the sanitation workers still scrubbing the graffiti off the bridge.

"There are troublemakers everywhere," said Abigail, "but true Christians do not vandalize." She turned to Anthea and smiled. "Last time I saw you, you were trying to ride that big old dog of yours like a horse and ordering your father to buy you a pony. What a beauty you have grown into."

"Thank you, Lady Abigail."

"What are you doing here?" Helena asked her friend. "I thought you and your husband moved to the suburbs ages ago."

"We did," replied Abigail, "but I always come here on the Sabbath to extend the Lord's mercy to the ill before they cross over to the island. We do not seek to convert, only to spread awareness of Christ's healing grace." She glanced at Anthea, then back to Helena. "Helena, how long have we known each other? Twenty years, maybe?"

"At least."

"I have heard the rumors among our mutual acquaintances. I don't care what the gossips say, I know you are a good mother, and I have seen many young women struggle with your daughter's affliction. The idolatry of the games and allure of the gladiators breed sin. There is a healer on the Aventine who can help."

Anthea tensed. She had no affliction and she required no healer, but she said nothing. She had already disappointed her mother enough. She would not argue with one of her oldest friends on the street.

"You have a good heart," said Helena, "but that is not our way."

"This healer," continued Abigail, "he knows the old ways, too." She looked in the direction of Tiber Island. "He used to be a pagan priest at the temple." Her eyes moved to the sachet that hung from Anthea's neck. "He does not dispense useless ointments or potions. His skills are more effective than any medicine a physician can provide."

"That is not our way," Helena repeated, this time more forcefully.

Abigail touched Helena's arm. "I meant no disrespect, my friend. If you change your mind, you know where to find me. May the Lord bless you both."

CHAPTER XII

The section of the Roman Forum that was most sacred to Vesta included more than just the temple and the Vestals' residence. It also included the Regia, the gardens, the sacred spring of Juturna and small but fine shops—most owned by the Vestals themselves—along the Via Sacra that sold religious accoutrements and jewelry. Yet as imbued with holiness as the area was, it was equally infused with a history that stretched back to Rome's founding days and provided the backdrop against which the Eternal City's most momentous scenes had played out, from the intervention of the Sabine women to the spontaneous cremation of Julius Caesar by a frenzied mob.

Coelia moved in the presence of these sacred buildings and this history each time she exited or entered Vesta's sanctum. But there was someone for whom the experience was as novel as it was reverential—Victor, the man who had just been declared co-emperor of Britannia and Gaul by his usurping father, Magnus Maximus. And it was Coelia's nerve-wracking duty to formally greet him on this, the morning of his first visit to Rome. With the priestesses Domitia and Terentia standing respectfully behind her, she waited for him before the Temple of the Deified Julius Caesar. Dressed in the formal white stola and veil of the Vestalis Maxima, she had accented the traditional attire with enough gold jewelry to worry the mint. She wanted Victor's first impression of the Vestal Order to be a memorable one.

Caesar Flavius Victor approached as if from a triumph of the past, boasting Imperial purple and wearing a crown of gilded laurel. Accompanied by a procession of soldiers and senators, he strode over the marble stretches of the Via Sacra with his head held high as attendants played music and a crowd of spectators tossed rose petals at his feet. He waved at them as he passed, his gaze finally landing on the three Vestal Virgins who lowered themselves to their knees before him, their veiled heads bowed in deference, but their gold jewelry suggesting they didn't spend a lot of time in a state of obeisance.

"Rise, Priestess," he said to Coelia.

As Domitia and Terentia remained kneeling, Coelia stood just as Damascus, the bishop of Rome, appeared at Victor's side. Eager to assert his prominence despite recent scandals, he was leading Victor's tour of Rome. He regarded Coelia with a look of contempt. No doubt it had irked him to no end that the new emperor, one already fascinated by the old ways, would deign to speak to a pagan priestess. He opened his mouth to introduce her to the emperor, but Coelia beat him to it. She would not give him the satisfaction of strong-arming this.

"Caesar," she greeted, suddenly realizing it was the first time since her novice years that she had addressed an emperor by that customary title. The other Christian emperors and co-emperors preferred to be called Augustus. "The ancient Roman Order of Vestal Virgins, as ordained by King Numa, is honored by your request for an audience," she said. "I am the Virgo Vestalis Maxima Coelia Concordia."

He smiled and inspected her Vestal dress. "I have seen frescos and coins of our ancient priestesses from the time of the pagan emperors," he said. "Time stands still."

"This is Rome, Caesar," Coelia replied. "Time is a river with a strange current. It moves, but moves nowhere."

The sentiment appealed to his sensibilities and he nodded, his attention turning to the altar atop the tall podium of the prostyle Temple of the Deified Julius Caesar. "To think that the dictator's funeral pyre was on this very spot," he said. "I can almost feel his presence." He looked to Coelia. "The pagan Caesars were always close to the Vestal Order."

Coelia wasn't sure if it was a question or an observation, but she risked taking the statement further. "Close in purpose and in friendship, sir. Julius Caesar took sanctuary in the House of the Vestals during the proscriptions of Sulla. And when he was cremated here, it was by flames taken from Vesta's hearthfire. Emperor Augustus then built this temple for his divine father and interred his ashes here. At the same time, he embellished Vesta's temple and our home. He was one of our Order's greatest benefactors."

Damascus cleared his throat, gently suggesting to the emperor that they move on. Victor flashed him a look of *I'll tell you when it's time to move on*, and the bishop stepped back. Victor again studied Caesar's memorial, admiring the gold-capped columns and the star in the pediment, a reference to the comet that had hung in the sky for days after the dictator's assassination.

"I have heard that some still call this the Temple of the Comet Star," he said.

"They do," Coelia replied. "Traditions die hard."

Intrigued, he faced Coelia, crossing his arms and giving her the immediate impression that he was testing her. "I have often wondered about something," he said. "Before Octavian became Augustus, he took Marc Antony's will out of the Temple of Vesta. It was the contents of that will that justified his war against Egypt and led to his imperium. But removing it from the sanctum was an act of sacrilege, was it not?"

"A sacrilege of the highest order, Caesar," asserted Coelia, "and one that could have cost him the support of the Senate and the priesthoods. He was fortunate that the Vestalis Maxima Occia did not more strongly oppose him."

"And why did she not?"

"We can only speculate, sir. But one must remember that High Priestess Occia and Octavian were both in Rome, both witnessing the famine that Antony was inflicting upon his people from Egypt. Perhaps the high priestess thought that was a greater sacrilege." Wanting to add something more, something that delved deeper into a matter that clearly intrigued him, she lowered her voice. "The writings of High Priestess Occia were lost in the great fire, but it has been passed down to us that she secretly financed Caesar Octavian's armies from the temple's undisclosed coffers and the accounts of Caesar's enemies."

He raised his eyebrows, enjoying the gossipy tidbit. "As you said, close in purpose and in friendship."

Ignoring the way Damascus had slowly inched forward to join the conversation, Coelia bowed her head to Victor. "I hope it will always be so, Caesar."

"I am a Christian emperor," said Victor. "Our friendship will be limited. Even so, I believe the traditionalists have much to teach us about how to manage an empire. It was they who built it."

"I offer our friendship, and our loyalty, in whatever way Caesar requires," she said.

Victor turned to go, but stopped and faced her squarely. "I am told that you own some of the gladiators who will be competing in the arena today."

"Yes, Caesar. I hope I can say the same tomorrow."

It took a moment for Victor to take her meaning, but then he laughed. "I am residing in the domus of Augustus while in Rome," he said, glancing up the Palatine Hill immediately behind the House of the Vestals. "We will travel together to the amphitheater," he said. "We can talk more."

"Thank you, Caesar." Her reply was quick and gracious, an approach that Claudia had taught was best to camouflage sudden insecurity.

Victor gave the Temple of the Deified Julius Caesar another long look of appreciation before speaking to Damascus. "Now the *Curia*."

"Yes, Caesar," replied the bishop, and ushered the emperor away.

Coelia remained standing before the Temple of Caesar until the procession was well on its way along the Via Sacra, reaching the Basilica Aemelia en route to the Senate House. Only then did she exhale a lungful of air, though it did little to lower her stress level. She turned to Domitia and Terentia who were just rising to their feet, and all three of them moved to ascend the nearby steps of the Temple of Vesta. As they entered the warmth of the circular marble sanctum, the Vestals Proculeia, Sergia and Galeria looked up from the sacred fire, eager for news.

"How did it go?" asked Proculeia. "What was he like?"

"Like Roma's long lost lover," said Domitia, "swooning over Caesar's ashes."

"He's certainly more pleasant than Gratian," added Coelia, "may the gods piss fire on his black soul." She pulled off her headdress and leaned against the altar, careful not to dip her long brown hair into the flames. She groaned as the second-guessing set in. "Why did I tell him about Priestess Occia and the money from the coffers? What a stupid thing to do."

"He was hungry for a good Roman rumor," soothed Domitia. "And now he wants to ride with you to the amphitheater? You handled it perfectly. Antonia could not have done better."

"*Gratias, amica*," said Coelia. "I'm just happy he's willing to attend the games. It's a good sign. It'll be good for attendance, too."

Domitia turned pensive. "I wonder if he and Magnus Maximus will truly be content to just rule in the north?"

"Time will tell," said Terentia. She grinned at Domitia. "Did you see Damascus's face when Coelia ignored him?"

The two priestesses laughed in satisfaction, but Coelia refrained. She sprinkled an offering of sweet incense into the fire. "I should go get ready," she said. "He will be returning soon."

"Just keep doing what you did," said Domitia. "He liked you."

Coelia nodded, already thinking ahead to the evening's banquet, the one to be held in honor of her inauguration as Vestalis Maxima. It couldn't arrive fast enough.

I just have to get through this day, she thought, *and tonight I can relax and enjoy myself.*

Her thoughts turned to Ptolema's stomach-soothing tonic. She would need it, and not just for her trip to the arena with Victor. Symmachus would be watching, judging, her every move. Senator Perses would likely be there, too—she had already postponed a meeting with him to avoid his inevitable request that she forbid Brogos from seeing Anthea. On top of that, her mother Lucilla was back in Rome after an extended tour of Egypt—in truth, an exotic shopping trip on Coelia's denarius—and would no doubt be keen to critique everything from her daughter's posture to her complexion.

She strode to the doors of the temple. "I'll see you at the arena," she said to her sister Vestals, while privately praying to the goddess for strength on all fronts.

If the bishops had eyes and ears in every corner of Rome, so too did Symmachus, for Coelia had barely changed out of her formal vestments and into her standard Vestal dress and veil—she kept the gold jewelry, though—before the senator's letter had arrived:

I have just learned that you will be riding to the amphitheater with Caesar. Do not squander this opportunity. Maintain decorum at all times. Secure his friendship at all costs.

She waited just inside the doors of the House of the Vestals, not minding the way Ptolema ceaselessly fussed over her hair and clothing. There was something comforting about it. At the sound of a blaring trumpet and heavy footfalls on the street, she cast the slave a worried look and strode with false confidence through the open doors to meet Victor's approaching litter—an oversized lectica with gilded sides and a purple canopy, carried by eight porters, four in the front and four in the rear. They set the vehicle down and Ptolema pulled back the curtain.

Victor was inside, sitting on a crimson cushioned seat and writing something on a wax tablet. He set the tablet down and gestured for her to enter. Coelia stepped inside, taking the opposite seat and arranging the folds of her stola as the curtains closed. The litter-bearers lifted the vehicle, and she steadied herself against the sudden swaying, interlocking her fingers and smiling amiably at Victor.

"I might be wrong," said Victor, "but I suspect there is someone beneath that vapid smile." He leaned forward. "Shall we speak plainly with each other?"

Coelia tensed, remembering Symmachus's words: *Maintain decorum at all times.* She quickly sifted through her options. She could maintain a façade or counter him with affected innocence. Those were Symmachus's decorous approaches. The safe ones. Yet something in Victor's deportment told her to drop the façade and risk it. *Secure his friendship at all costs.*

"With respect, Caesar," she replied, "the plainer the better."

"Very good. This morning, I told you that our friendship would be limited. Not half a day has passed, and already I find myself needing to test those limits." He drummed his fingers on his legs in thought. "Rome is..."

"Not what you expected."

"The history, the monuments... they are as I expected, if not even greater."

"But the politics," said Coelia, "the people."

"It is impossible to know who to trust."

"You know Rome better than you think."

"I would like to trust you, Priestess."

There was something about the way he said it. Despite the royal attire, despite the penetrating gray eyes and Caesarean haircut, despite the legions of his powerful father Magnus Maximus, Victor was a young man out of his depth in Rome. Coelia sympathized with him, and something told her this was indeed a friendship worth securing.

"I would like us to trust *each other*, Caesar," she said honestly.

Victor sat farther forward. "Senator Symmachus," he put forth.

"Rigid in custom and often critical, but intelligent beyond words. Highly respected. They call him a second Cicero. He despised Gratian and speaks favorably of your father."

"Can I trust him?"

"Implicitly."

Victor took this in. "Senator Lampadius."

"Prideful, but never deceptive. He never spoke against Gratian, but never sang his praises, either. I think he would be open to a friendship with you if it served Rome's interests."

"Senator Praetextatus."

"A traditionalist, as you would say," said Coelia, "and perhaps the only senator with a greater personal fortune than Symmachus. The two are close friends and always of one mind."

Victor raised an eyebrow. That was good to know. "Senator Olympius."

"A viper," Coelia replied, picturing her business partner's fanged eye teeth. "Resourceful, but unpredictable." Victor dwelled on this, no doubt re-evaluating an interaction with the senator. Coelia sat forward, matching Victor's posture. "I will comprise a list of influential senators, and detail their characters and agendas to the best of my knowledge."

"As soon as possible," Victor affirmed. "What do you know of General Bauto?"

Coelia paused. The segue from senators to soldiers was revealing. "Accomplished, obviously, and dedicated to the empire." She thought about this. "Rather, dedicated to Theodosius."

Victor locked eyes with her. This is where the trust would come in. The woman clearly suspected he and his father had no intention of limiting their rule to just the barbarian regions. Italy was the ultimate prize, and although he had come to Rome as no more than an Imperial tourist, he had no plans of leaving. That unspoken truth hung in the air like a seditious breath. But Victor recognized a fledgling ally when he saw one, and this priestess needed him as much as he needed her. Not only had Gratian defunded the Vestal Order, the bishops were now pressuring Theodosius to close even more pagan temples, including the Temple of Vesta. Victor's tolerance of the traditional ways would secure her loyalty.

"General Arbogastes," he posited.

"Powerful and popular with the legions. He formerly served Gratian, but now he's favored by Theodosius. He is second only to General Bauto."

"I have heard a rumor that Bauto is his father."

"I have heard the same rumor. No one knows for certain. Bauto and Arbogastes probably don't even know, though they are very close." She hesitated. "Regardless, I may have some influence over him."

"There may come a time when I ask you to use it."

"Yes, Caesar."

Satisfied with his new alliance and the information it had already bestowed, Victor reclined on his silk couch. He moved the curtain aside and stared outside as the litter passed by the massive vaulted basilica originally named after the pagan emperor Maxentius, but renamed after the Christian Constantine. The young Caesar's heavy thoughts seemed to add weight to the lectica, and Coelia knew better than to interrupt whatever machinations he was constructing. So she sat back on her own couch, and they rode the rest of the way to the amphitheater in silence.

✳   ✳   ✳

"Why are you so flushed?" Lucilla asked her daughter. "Are you feeling faint?"

"I'm fine," replied Coelia.

"You just arrived with Caesar, and I know those cheeks. Did something happen?"

"Everything is fine, Mother. No need to worry."

"You look like a pomegranate."

"I missed you, Mother. Drink your wine."

Lucilla tapped on the side of her cup, her gold bangles softly clinking. "It's good, this."

"It's the Falernian from Symmachus's estate," Coelia replied, her eyes on the newest guests to enter the elite pregame gathering in the stately Imperial Box of the amphitheater: General Arbogastes and Commander Stilicho, escorting a genteel young woman garnished in jewels.

"Well, well," said Lucilla. "Look who has a jealous streak."

"Stop it, Mother."

"Oh, I'm just teasing. The general only has eyes for you. Lucky for both of you that your tenure will be over before you know it. Time flies, and I don't care what those damn Greeks say, cruel Saturn makes it fly faster the older you get. Just look at me. I went to bed last night a soft sapling and awoke as the *Ficus Ruminalis*." She combed her fingers through a long tress, knowing full well that her dark hair, angular face, perfect smile and eyes as bright as Io's had blessed her with lasting looks.

"You are still as beautiful as ever," said Coelia. She had to say it. Her mother wouldn't stop angling for a compliment until she did.

"I do offer to Venus five times a day," said Lucilla. "You should start doing so as well, daughter. It is never too soon." Seguing with flawless precision from glib to graceful, she caught Arbo's eye and waved him over, her bracelets jingling more energetically. "General," she summoned. "Do come and join us."

Arbo approached with his companions. He accepted a cup of wine from a servant and glanced from Lucilla to Coelia, his smile spreading as he neared the Vestal.

"Last time I left Rome, I returned to find Brogos a star gladiator," he said. "This time, I return to find you Vestalis Maxima. Congratulations."

"Thank you, General."

"Tell us," said Lucilla, "who is this lovely young woman with you?"

"This is Lady Serena," said Arbo. "She is the niece of Emperor Theodosius. His Highness had us escort her to Rome." He looked at Serena. "My lady, may I introduce you to High Priestess Coelia Concordia of the Vestal Order and her mother, Lady Lucilla."

"The Vestal Virgins," said Serena. "I have heard of your order, but I did not know you were still so active in Rome."

"Rome is fortunate that we are," said Coelia.

A burst of laughter caught their attention, and they all turned to see Victor immersed in lively conversation with Symmachus and number of other senators—Praetextatus, Lampadius and Perses—all of them plucking delicacies from a draped table.

Lucilla poked Arbo in the arm. "What does Theodosius think of..." she pointed her chin to Victor.

"His Highness is amenable," said Arbo. "He has agreed to expand the domain of Victor and Maximus to Spain and Africa, as well as Britannia and Gaul."

"Ah, good," said Lucilla. "Compromise is better than another wretched war, that's what I say." She nudged Commander Stilicho, tactfully inviting him into the conversation. "Wouldn't you agree?"

"I would, in fact," said Stilicho. "I've taken to the easy life."

"My uncle wishes all his subjects to enjoy an easier life," said Serena. "That is why he prizes peace above all." Her eyes shifted to Victor. "Lady Coelia, can I trouble you to introduce me?"

"It is no trouble," said Coelia. "Come."

The group—the Vestal, her mother, the two soldiers and the emperor's niece—moved as one through the gathering. Victor noticed them approaching and turned from his companions to face Coelia.

"Caesar," said the Vestal. "May I present Lady Serena, niece of Emperor Theodosius. She has just arrived from Constantinople. His Highness entrusted her safe transport to General Arbogastes" — here she put a hand on Arbo's shoulder — "and his commander Stilicho."

Victor had been waiting to meet the general, but etiquette dictated he address the royal woman first. "I am honored to meet a kinswoman of Theodosius," he said to Serena.

"My uncle extends his warmest regards and hopes of friendship," she replied. She smiled, the cheeks of her pretty round face blushing slightly. Her message could not have been more clear had she donned a bridal veil when she delivered it. "Now that you have been in Rome for a while, perhaps you could show me all the best sights?"

"I have only just arrived," Victor replied noncommittally. "There are better guides."

Lucilla nudged her daughter, prompting her for an introduction.

"Caesar," said Coelia. "This is my mother, Lucilla Coelia."

"Ah, Lady Lucilla," said Victor. He smiled as she held out her hand—he was told to expect boldness from certain Roman matrons—and kissed the back of it. "Delighted."

"Nonsense," said Lucilla. "It is we in Rome who are delighted." She took a step back, nodding in approval. "Now *this* is a Caesar."

"Ah, here is the cleverest one yet," Victor replied sportively. "Your daughter and I have—"

"So this is the infamous amphitheater, is it?" interrupted Serena, spinning around to brush against Victor. She surveyed the dizzying expanse and height of the gaping oval, the tiered seating and ornamented arches, the decorated staircases and kaleidoscope of vibrant colors—scarlet, yellow, purple and blue—that dressed the encircling wall. Looking down onto the arena floor, she watched an assemblage of stadium staff working on a section of the elaborate stage. Some hammered away, while others placed huge chunks of red meat in strategic locations. "What are they doing?"

Symmachus spoke. "They are preparing for the beast hunts, my lady. There is to be a rendition of the first labor of Hercules. The slaying of the Nemean lion."

"Is that so?" asked Victor. "How perfectly Roman."

Yet still not enough to fill the seats, Coelia noted dispiritedly. It seemed no hook could reel the crowds back into the stadium.

Victor took a step away from Serena and spoke cordially to Arbo. "General Arbogastes, the high priestess speaks highly of you. I would like to meet with you tomorrow. We will have supper at the palace. I know we will be good friends."

"As you wish, Caesar," said Arbo.

"Well, we're all friends here," said Lucilla, her voice projecting slightly more than was proper. "Oh, excuse me," she said. She poked Symmachus's shoulder. "Your wine is to blame. Bacchus himself planted these vines."

Everyone laughed at Lucilla's exuberance, though unfortunately its volume drew the attention of a chronic critic. Always eager to publicly eviscerate anyone he could for even the smallest breach of social decorum, Olympius traversed the terrace to seize his prey. He took a swallow of his wine and glared at Stilicho over the rim—he had not forgotten their previous encounter in the pulvinar—before turning his predacious eyes to the ebullient older woman standing beside the Vestal. The moment he did, his punitive gaze softened.

"Now, who might this be?" he asked, a flirtatious timbre in his voice. Without waiting for a formal introduction, he bowed. "I am Olympius."

"This is my mother," Coelia said flatly. "Lucilla."

Lucilla swirled the wine in her cup. "Olympius," she noted. "So you are the one who hounded my daughter until she went into business with you."

"Guilty," he said.

Coelia glared at him. *Stop it.*

Amused, Lucilla let out a puff of laughter.

"Mother," said Coelia. "Look" — she gestured to the Vestals' viewing box — "Domitia and Proculeia are here. You haven't seen them in ages. Let's take our seats."

"Oh, they can wait a little longer."

"The master of ceremonies is coming out," urged Coelia. "Let's go."

Olympius slipped in front of the Vestal. "Lucilla, come sit with me. The view from the Imperial Box is superior, and the company...."

he put his hand on his chest and grinned, evoking another puff of amusement from Lucilla.

She hooked her arm through his. "Don't worry, daughter," she said to Coelia. She shook her head at Olympius. "This little one is always worrying about something."

Olympius dipped his head to Victor. "Caesar, I hope you enjoy the show," he said, and led Lucilla away to their seats.

Victor offered his arm to Serena, and together they strolled to the gilded chairs that lined the marble balustrade of the Imperial Box. Their departure prompted the other guests to take their seats as well, though Coelia remained where she was. She couldn't look away from Olympius and her mother.

"Come," said Arbo. "I'll walk you to the Vestals' Box."

"Yes... thank you."

She permitted Arbo to usher her out of the Imperial Box, past the soldiers who guarded the entrance and into a wide passageway alive with frescos and rich ornamentation. They turned in the direction of the entrance to the Vestal Virgins' luxury seating box, though walking slowly to prolong the rare occasion of relative privacy.

"I heard that you rode here in Caesar's litter," said Arbo.

"We met in the Forum this morning," Coelia replied. "I told him some gossip, and the next thing I knew, he was asking me to travel with him."

A wave of sound and shouts from the arena floor rolled into the passageway. For a modest-sized crowd, things were starting off with unusual rowdiness. Arbo looked up and down the corridor. Seeing no one, he stopped.

"What is he like?"

"I think he will be a blessing to Rome," said Coelia. "If it is not impolitic to say so in front of one of Theodosius's top generals."

"I don't care about politics," said Arbo. "Now that I'm back in Rome, all I want to do is fix my dovecotes and train my pigeons for the races." He raised his voice to be heard over the rising waves of raucous arena noise flooding the spacious walkway. "Perhaps now we can have that supper together."

"And dine on your slowest pigeons."

Arbo's smile faded at the sudden appearance of a stern-faced centurion who stepped into the passageway. The centurion frowned and began to march quickly toward them, a hand on the hilt of his sheathed dagger. Coelia instinctively imagined the worst: an accusation of unchasteness and a formal charge of *crimen incesti*, followed by a trial and a condemnation by Symmachus and the old priests of Rome. It would all end with her forced descent into an underground pit where she would either suffocate or starve to death in darkness for breaking her vows. But even as the thoughts persisted—what Vestal hadn't studied the horrid fate of Priestess Cornelia and others?—she knew the soldier wasn't responding to impiety, but rather to something more terrestrial.

"General," said the soldier, an octave of alarm in his voice. "You must take shelter immediately. A number of lions have escaped the arena floor."

"A number of... *lions*?" asked Arbo.

"Yes, sir. Three or four leapt right into the stands. A few more escaped through the gladiators' entrance." Something, somewhere, fell with a crash and the soldier jumped. He drew his blade and spun around just as panicked spectators began to file into the passageway. "The beasts could be anywhere by now!" he exclaimed, and dashed for the nearest exit. A mob of people chased after him as though his single blade could protect them all.

As the stampede quickly grew in size and sound, Arbo sprang into action. "This way," he shouted to Coelia, and led her back the way they had come, toward the emperor's box—but it was too late. The guards had already sealed the entrance from the inside. Short of a battering ram, there would be no way to get through the iron barrier.

"My mother!" Coelia exclaimed.

"She will have followed Caesar into the tunnel below the Imperial Box," said Arbo. "You are the one who is exposed." He backed her against a frescoed wall, protecting her body with his own and debating what to do—find a place to hide or make a run for it?—as a rush of spectators rampaged past. *Keep moving*, he decided. *Safety in numbers.* It had saved his life countless times on the battlefield. "Come on!" he yelled, his voice barely audible over the din of shrieking cries and stampeding footfalls that seemed to shake the very foundation of the stadium.

They entered the herd of fleeing spectators and ran along the marble floor. Ahead of them, the wide passageway curved slightly as a constant stream of people exited the stands to join the exodus. Coelia was suddenly very grateful the stadium was not full. It would have been nearly impossible to make any headway if it were at capacity. Even as it was, it seemed they had a better chance of being trampled to death by humans than torn apart by lions.

The relative safety of that assumption was shattered instantly as in front of them, no more than fifty feet away, a massive lion with shining gold fur and a blinding gilded mane shot like a catapult out of an arched entrance. With its painted gold coat, shockingly wide girth and ferocious eyes, it looked every bit the Nemean lion. It landed on two men, knocking them to the floor and sinking its ivory teeth into the chest of one with a spine-tingling deep growl. The impaled man made no sound, but his companion screeched and twisted, freeing himself from the animal's weight. He slipped on the pool of blood forming on the smooth floor, but found his footing and rejoined the herd without looking back.

Coelia heard herself scream. She couldn't remember ever having screamed in her entire life, and the sound only amplified the surreality of the gargantuan beast—how could an animal's paws be that big?—tearing off the dead man's arm, the spray of blood coating its scarred golden muzzle in red. It was nothing she hadn't seen before from the close proximity of the Vestals' Box, but how different the spectacle looked, felt, sounded, without a barrier. Even in the midst of her horror, she felt a renewed appreciation for Brogos.

Arbo pulled her in the opposite direction.

"There is another tunnel," Coelia shouted. "It goes to the ludus. Brogos told me there are hidden spots to enter..."

"Where?"

She struggled to think of the closest secret entrance, but all her energy was channeled into flight and she couldn't recall what Brogos had said. All she could picture was the shining gold lion leaping out of every archway they passed, springing out from behind every curtained cloister, pouncing on them from behind. She looked over her shoulder, imagining she could feel the beast's breath on the back of her neck, fully expecting to meet its piercing amber eyes and feel its thick ivory teeth sink into her flesh.

"I can't—I can't remember."

Debilitating fear was nothing new to Arbo, so he didn't waste precious time trying to revive her memory. "We just need to get outside," he said, stopping long enough to peer out one of the statue-filled open arches that lined the exterior wall of the stadium.

Coelia remained at his side and looked out with him. From their vantage point, they had a birds-eye view of the chaos below as people fled screaming in all directions, husbands carrying their children over a shoulder while dragging their wives along behind them. Here and there, someone fell or was knocked over. No one dared stop to help, but instead left them to be trampled underfoot or, more usefully, to serve as unwilling bait for the lions. Coelia counted three of the shining beasts running wild.

"*Iuppiter*," she said, and pointed to the base of the colossal statue of Sol. There, an elderly vendor named Gnaeus—Coelia had been buying sweets from him since her novice years—was struggling to push his portable little food cart through the crowd. "Leave it, Gnaeus!" she called down, knowing there was no way the man could hear. "Run!"

Someone knocked the old vendor's cart, sending small terracotta jars of honey smashing to the street. Gnaeus bent down to salvage the ones he could. Coelia gripped the sleeve of Arbo's tunica, watching helplessly as one of the lions stepped out from behind the far side of the statue's base. Spotting the easy prey, it stopped and shook its massive mane, sending a spray of gold paint into the air. A splatter landed on Gnaeus and he looked up, locking eyes with the beast. The animal advanced slowly, almost lazily, seemingly indifferent to its location in the center of Rome and not the plains of Africa, until it was only a leap away from the petrified vendor. Only then then did it lunge forward and clutch the old man in its mammoth paws, no different it seemed to Coelia, than a cat catching a mouse. The man's feeble limbs only gave fight for a moment.

"*Sancta Diana, ei miserere*," said Arbo. He led the Vestal out of the archway, noting that the stadium had now cleared out significantly. That was good and bad. They could run faster, but there were also fewer bodies between them and the lion with the scarred muzzle. Praying to Diana that it was still licking the bones of the man it had killed farther back in the passageway, he guided Coelia down a wide staircase, along another wide ornate passageway, and finally out through one of the numerous exits.

By now, the stadium's animal handlers, gladiators and a contingent of soldiers had organized a spontaneous animal hunt, and were fanning out around the amphitheater grounds with nets and weapons to catch and slay the escaped lions. Arbo stopped a centurion he recognized.

"Report," he ordered.

"Sir," said the man. "Two animals have been caught and killed, but four are still unaccounted for."

"There's probably one still in the stadium," said Arbo. "Last spotted north of the emperor's entrance, licking its lips. I saw another one by the colossus."

"Yes, sir."

The soldier headed off to convey the message to whoever was in charge of the hunt, though never taking more than six or seven steps without spinning around to anxiously scan for threats.

Coelia felt it, too. The unnerving sensation of being completely exposed, the skin-prickling awareness that one of the escaped beasts might be crouched behind any statue, hiding in any niche or doorway, ready to pounce.

Arbo drew his blade and they walked swiftly to the fortified iron gates of the Forum. The guards recognized them and opened a gate for the pair to enter, closing it again so quickly it almost caught the Vestal's dress.

"What do you know?" Coelia asked the guards.

"About twenty lions escaped from the stadium," replied one. "Thank the gods we had the gates locked. You are safe, High Priestess."

"Twenty," grumbled Arbo. "There were only *six* lions that escaped, and two are already dead. Don't make it worse."

"Yes, General," said the guard.

Coelia fell into step beside Arbo as they began to make their way—their hearts still pounding and their breaths still heavy—along the Via Sacra, toward the House of the Vestals. Feeling her veil tug at her scalp, and assuming it looked as lopsided as it felt, Coelia pulled it off. She fished for the pins in her hair and withdrew them one by one.

"Do you think my mother is all right?" she asked.

"I know she is all right," replied Arbo. "She will be in the Imperial palace by now, worrying about you."

They strode a little farther in silence, trying to calm themselves, though Coelia could not blink away the mental image of Gnaeus's lifeless body in the golden lion's blood-stained paws.

"Victor wanted to see Rome," she said, bundling her veil in her hands. "I wonder if he'll decide that he's seen enough."

CHAPTER XIII

The Imperial Fora were closed for business and the gates were locked. Trajan's grand market was also closed, as was the cattle market in the Forum Boarium. Shops and vendors elsewhere in the city were open, but were prohibited from hanging meat in their stalls. Those shopkeepers willing to risk disembowelment to stay afloat went door to door selling their wares, their customers still not hungry enough to venture into the street. The area around the amphitheater was heavily patrolled by armed soldiers, and an army of professional hunters had been hired to capture—dead or alive—the four gilded lions that were still on the loose and reportedly inside the city limits. The hunters roamed the unusually quiet streets nonstop on foot and on horseback. So did a brave or foolish few who were less skilled but equally eager to collect the large reward offered by the Senate.

Brogos and his fellow gladiators found the whole thing hilarious and fairly morale-boosting. Uncultured as they were, they at least had the balls to walk the streets like men, carrying nothing more than a gladius, while the smooth-skinned aristocrats of

Rome refused to travel even when surrounded by a bodyguard of well-armed soldiers. Even better, the ladies knew it, too. That explained the recent uptick in love letters the fighters had been receiving from the only other demographic willing to brave the streets—pretty, doe-eyed gladiator fanatics. They could wait to see their dressmakers and jewelers, but not their lovers.

As Anthea struggled to slip back into her tunica within the small space of the curtained archway, Brogos almost wished her soon-to-be husband was already back in Rome. That way she could see him for the effeminate type Brogos fully expected him to be. A man didn't study ethics and logic in Athens for four years without developing a certain limpness. Brogos opened the heavy red curtain and glanced down the wide passageway. Here, on the top level of the amphitheater, like on the other levels, things were quiet. The only activity—other than what he and Anthea had been doing—was the methodical movement of the cleaning crews that swept and shone the marble floors, removing all traces of blood and gristle left behind by the man-eating lions.

"We have to find someplace else to meet," said Anthea. She retrieved the cloth sachet the priest of Asclepius had given her and hung it around her neck. "Somewhere nice."

Naked, Brogos pushed himself off the thin straw-filled mattress in the archway—one of the many used as pop-up brothels in the amphitheater—and put his arms around her waist. "How about your bedchamber?" he teased. "That soft bed, those stuffed little dolls everywhere. Your chamberpot is probably lined with gold."

Anthea rolled her eyes. "Our home has a proper latrine," she said. "Though if I had a gold chamberpot, my parents would sell it for my dowry. They've sold everything else. My mother even sold her jewelry."

"What does Memmius need with your dowry? The *Symmachi* are made of money."

"My parents are proud. I cannot fault them for that." She pushed him away. "Take me home. Pray Fortuna my mother isn't yet awake, or I won't have to worry about some measly lions."

"As you command," said Brogos.

He dressed, and they walked slowly through the still stadium, enjoying being alone in so vast a space, their only companions Brogos's three black dogs. The animals trailed behind obediently, occasionally quickening their step to press a wet nose against Anthea's hand, prompting her for an ear scratch.

"Oh, my spoiled little kittens," she said, obliging them.

It was only when they stepped outside into the early morning air that Anthea grew more apprehensive, her eyes darting here and there.

"The beasts will be long gone from here," Brogos assured her as they walked along. "The *venator* Clemens says they will take to the trees to hide, if you can believe it. Just imagine walking along with your sweetheart and saying" — he pointed to a nearby stone pine — "'*look at the size of that sparrow, darling!*'"

"You have no natural humor, Brogos."

"Who needs humor when you have these?" he asked, flexing a bicep. "Don't worry. We are safe. It's those fools on the Caelian who are in trouble. Let's see how they boast about their orchards after a lion snacks on their fattened little brats."

They continued on to the Esquiline Hill, the morning air dewy and filled with birdsong, and reached Anthea's walled home in good time. Nonetheless, Anthea's heart sank when she saw the large oil lamps outside the entrance had already been extinguished, something her father did himself every morning. That meant her parents were already awake.

"Go," she said to Brogos. She rushed into the house without looking back at him.

Her mother, Helena, was waiting in the atrium, still her in her nightclothes. "Silver buys more dresses than sand does," she said sharply. "But if you feel being a gladiator's wife will bring honor upon this family, then by all means."

"Where is Father?"

"He is in the tablinum. It is better he stays there for now." Helena moved to the *lararium* where statuettes of Vesta and the household gods graced the temple-shaped shrine. She sprinkled a pinch of salted flour into the thick flame of a beeswax candle and knelt, quietly thanking the gods for her daughter's safe return. Pushing herself to her feet, she moved to a chair by the *impluvium* and sat, staring into the clear water. "You are not a child, Anthea," she said, "and you are not a whore. Your father is a Roman senator with nothing left but a respectable name, and you bring shame upon it."

Anthea sat at her mother's feet and wrapped her arms around Helena's legs, looking up at her in earnest. "I will not see him again, Mother."

Unconvinced but softened by her daughter's affection, Helena stroked Anthea's hair. "I was young once," she said. "I know how difficult it can be."

They heard a shuffling and looked up to see Perses enter the atrium. His face tightened at the sight of his daughter's messy hair and flushed cheeks. He opened his mouth to speak, but seemed to think better of it and simply walked away.

"I do not wish to hurt Father," she said. "Truly, I do not."

Helena kissed the top of her daughter's head, her eyes falling on the sachet that hung from Anthea's neck. *I hope it works better for the Vestal Virgins*, she thought.

CHAPTER XIV

Coelia crossed the courtyard to greet Brogos, who was helping the house slaves carry heavy sacks of grain from the street to the mill and kitchen. The Vestal Order's grain providers were refusing to deliver their goods, partly due to the rumors of a looming famine that had drastically increased roadside theft, but mostly due to the reports that one of the escaped lions had attacked a donkey-pulled cart of grain. It had left the barley, but devoured the donkey and driver. Coelia was lucky her gladiator was willing to step in.

"*Salve*, Brogos," she said.

"Good day, Patrona." He slapped his palms together, shaking off the grain dust. "That was the last load. You'll have full stomachs to the Neptunalia."

"Did you take some to my mother's house?"

"Yes, just as you asked."

"And?"

Brogos looked down at his sandals and scuffed a sole on the marble pathway. "I didn't see him, but his lectica was there."

"*O dei, cur?*" Coelia cogitated. "Of all the men in Rome, why does it have to be Olympius?"

"I have become more familiar with the senator," said Brogos. "He's an arrogant prick, but he's not all bad."

"Not all bad," mused Coelia. "A high standard, indeed. Never mind. I can't worry about my mother's battle with insanity right now. I have to go make an offering to Roma. The last thing we need is a famine stalking us along with the lions."

"I'll go with you."

"There is no need. The Forum is secure."

"From wildcats, maybe, but not from hooligans. They've been scaling the walls to raid the grain stores and generally stir up shit. Anyway, I'm under orders from Arbo. I'm supposed to keep an eye on you."

Coelia tried to appear unaffected by that disclosure... but it was nice to hear. "Fine. Let's go." She led Brogos out of the House of the Vestals and turned right to walk along the Via Sacra, passing the temple of the emperor Antoninus and the empress Faustina—how generous they had been to the Vestal Order in their day—followed by a circular temple dedicated to Romulus. "Victor wrote to me yesterday," she said. "He asked me which Romulus this temple was originally dedicated to, the founder or the young prince of the emperor Maxentius. Since the historians cannot agree, I gave him the answer I thought he would like better."

"Which was?"

"The founder." She stopped and stood in front of the great bronze doors and porphyry columns of the round temple. "This sanctum should be dedicated to the founder, shouldn't it? Right here, when there was nothing in the Forum but Vesta's fire and Romulus's vision, his army fought the Sabines and made peace with them."

"It is a good story."

"It's the kind of story that Victor loves," Coelia said smilingly. "I invoke the spirit of Virgil whenever I speak with him."

They continued along, reaching the stretch of street that ran between the Basilica of Constantine on the left and a row of arched porticos and warehouse spaces on the right. Farther ahead, in the space dominated by the thick columns and colorful pediment of the Temple of Venus and Roma, they heard a commotion—shrill shouts suppressed by the heavier bellows of soldiers. Hooligans, no doubt, being rounded up after trying to empty the warehouses of their precious grain reserves.

"What else did Victor write to you about?" asked Brogos.

"Nothing. He just asked about the history of a few temples."

"I thought it might've been you who gave him the idea about Agrippa's villa."

Coelia turned to him abruptly. "What do you mean?"

"Oh." Brogos grimaced. "Forget I said it."

"Impossible. Tell me."

"Victor purchased the old villa of Agrippa on the Tiber and gave it to Arbo in recognition of his service to the empire. The foundation has been sinking for decades, and the house needs a lot of work—eels dine in the triclinium—but the history of the place is what matters."

"Arbo worships the memory of Agrippa," said Coelia. "The villa will be in good hands." *An ingratiating gift*, thought Coelia. It was clever of Victor.

"Don't tell Arbo I told you about it," said Brogos. "He made me swear to Harpocrates I wouldn't say anything. He wanted to surprise you." He turned to Coelia. "He asked me how many more years you had to remain with the Order now that you are Vestalis Maxima."

"Oh?"

"I told him ten."

"*Ten?*" exclaimed Coelia. "Why ten? It is only—" Brogos burst into laughter, and she swatted him on the shoulder. "Any more news about the lions?"

"They almost caught one overnight. Somewhere on the *Via Latina*. But it mauled two of the hunters and got away. They're trying to catch them alive. They want to haul them back into the stadium and kill them there."

"Did you ever find out how they escaped in the first place?"

"Some barrier screens failed, that's all I've heard."

"The whole thing is so awful," said Coelia.

Brogos clucked his tongue. "Depends."

"Depends on what?"

"You've been tucked away in your fancy house for days, but I've still been out and about, and I'll tell you one thing. The lions are all that anyone is talking about. People can't wait to get back into the amphitheater. If the hunters can catch at least one of those bastards alive and give me a second chance to slay the Nemean lion, I'd make both of us rich as Pluto."

Coelia pondered that potential as they continued walking toward the Temple of Venus and Roma, a vast gleaming structure that was actually comprised of two temples placed back-to-back. The one dedicated to Venus faced the amphitheater, while the one dedicated to Roma faced the Forum. As they neared the temple to Eternal Roma, the entirety of the wide marble staircase that led up to its *cella* came into full view. So too did the source of the shouts and bellows.

Along the southern side of the monumental staircase, a cluster of perhaps thirty men, women and children were kneeling on the stairs, resisting the efforts of Forum guards to remove them. As soon as the guards dragged one away and went back for another, the one they had removed was already sprinting back to rejoin the others.

"*The hour has come!*" they chanted.

"Go get a prison cart, for fuck's sake!" shouted out of the guards, and two men raced off to fulfill the order.

"What in the name of the gods?" wondered Coelia. She looked to Brogos for insight, but he wore the same look of bafflement.

Spotting a familiar guard—he was usually assigned to Vesta's temple, but had obviously been called to help manage the ruckus—Coelia waved him over.

"High Priestess," he said, winded from wrestling with the trespassers. "It is some kind of Christian occurrence. They say their god is about to return."

"Well, it is not a good time for me," Coelia said, frustrated. "I need to make an offering to Roma." She needed to make it quickly, too. It was already late afternoon, and she still had to get dressed for the night's banquet in honor of her inauguration as chief Vestal. The banquet had initially been scheduled for the night of the Nemean lion performance, but the chaos of the beasts' escape had delayed it.

"I apologize," said the guard, "but it will take some time to clear the entrance."

He gestured to the temple's staircase, and it was only then that Coelia noticed the damage. Large chunks of the marble columns and stairs had been chipped away, leaving debris scattered everywhere. On the landing atop the staircase, directly in front of the gleaming doors to Roma's sanctum, the marble altar had also been vandalized. Its bronze firebowl lay upturned on the ground, spilled gray ash and burnt wood all around. *The great whore.* That's what some Christians called Rome. Perhaps that is what had drawn them here, to Roma's temple—the idea that it would happen before the eyes of the goddess that personified the city. Ignoring the guard's protests, Coelia moved closer to the group and stood watching, transfixed by the sight of one humble family—husband, wife, and two small children—huddled together. They had their arms wrapped around each other as the husband and wife looked up into the blue sky in terror, expecting the heavens to fracture and their god to appear. The two children pressed their faces into their parents' bodies, weeping. Coelia could see the tiny fingers of a young girl clutching the cloth of her father's tunica. "Papa, I want to go home!" she cried. But her father's eyes were riveted to the sky.

This religion from Galilee... in that moment, Coelia could not fathom how it had taken root in Rome, how it had intruded upon the ancient and natural gods and goddesses that had harmoniously inhabited the soil, the water, the air, the flowers and the fire of the city for so very long. Gods that had inspired the founder, and the ancestors, to build Rome and all it stood for. She heard scraping and clunking, and looked to Roma's staircase where a sanitation crew was sweeping up the ash and tossing chunks of marble into a trash cart. She thought of Claudia's smashed statue and turned away, heading back to the House of the Vestals.

Serena's uncle Theodosius had warned her that Victor would not be an easy man to seduce, but she had not listened. She had assumed it would be a foregone diplomatic conclusion, one that would require nothing more than striking an inviting smile and setting a date. She had expected Victor would be eager to secure a marital alliance between himself and her Imperial uncle. Instead, she had received courteous rejection after courteous rejection from the young Caesar.

From her guest residence in a villa on the Aventine Hill, she had sent letters to his palace on the Palatine Hill expressing her eagerness to see the great sights of Rome with him as guide. Even though he could have sprinted the distance on foot without breaking a sweat, it had taken him days to send a reply via messenger, stating that the escaped lions made such recreation too dangerous. His concern for her was too great, he had said, and his respect for Theodosius too sincere, for him to be so reckless with her safety.

Failing to reel him in to her, she had no choice but to swim out to him. She had therefore invited herself to the inauguration banquet of Rome's chief Vestal priestess. Her uncle would obviously disapprove of her attending such a nefarious event, but necessity trumped principle. The Vestal was the only bridge to Victor that Serena could cross at the moment, and crossing it she was—quite literally—thanks to the banquet's venue on a luxury floating barge in the middle of the Tiber River.

The chill she had felt when she first stepped out of her lectica and onto the banks of the Tiber was gone, kept at bay by the rows of firebowls that illuminated the footbridge leading to the barge.

Stepping into the splendor of the barge's immense cabin was like returning to a world she knew, one full of music and conversation, shining ornamentation, well-dressed elites and exotic foods. As she had expected, Victor was there, dressed in a royal purple tunica with gold embroidery, wide silver cuffs on both wrists and a large Aquila pendant hanging from a chain around his neck. She made eye contact, forcing herself to appear impervious to the brief look of annoyance that crossed his face. As protocol required, he stepped away from the senatorial company he was in and greeted her.

"Lady Serena," he said. "You look lovely."

"Thank you, Victor," she replied, disregarding his irked expression. It was a risk to use his personal name, but she needed things to get personal. She touched the thick tapestry-woven neck trim of her blue gown. *Touch your neck,* her uncle's concubine had told her. *It draws their eyes there.* "I thought I would bring some eastern fashion to the west."

"Hmm," he sounded. "I would not have expected to see you at a function like this."

"It was Lady Coelia who introduced us," said Serena, as if that held great meaning. "And anyway, I haven't been to a good party since I came to Rome."

"It is *High Priestess* Coelia," corrected Victor. "A prestigious position in traditional Roman society."

"So you use her heathen honorific?"

"I respect the ways of the traditionalists in their own city," said Victor. "I consider it a form of cultural eclecticism."

A servant came by with a tray of olives stuffed with goat cheese, and Serena inspected the selection, using the distraction to conceal her dissent. A woman had no business holding a high religious position in society. Not only was it forbidden in the scriptures—no woman was permitted to teach or assume authority over a man— but they would simply come to think too highly of themselves.

"These look very nice," she said, and popped one of the olives in her mouth. It was larger and firmer than she had anticipated, forcing her to chew gauchely and turn away from Victor as if drawn by the pipe players who had just started another lively tune. He took a sip from his wine cup and pivoted slightly away. Serena could tell he was summoning General Arbogastes with his eyes. She was losing him. She felt a bead of perspiration on her forehead. She couldn't lose him. Her uncle had made that painfully clear. "Victor," she said. "Would you like to step outside? I would love to see the famed Tiber under the stars."

"I would like that," said Victor, "but I have a matter to discuss with the general first."

"Nothing bellicose, I hope," she said.

"Of course not. I have no enemies that I am aware of."

He stepped away to converse with the general, not bothering to connect her to another guest and thus leaving her to stand awkwardly on her own, without even a wine cup in hand. Thankfully, the solitude didn't last long as Commander Stilicho joined her, tactfully filling the social void left by the emperor. Whether because of his handsome tunica or his sympathetic look—she didn't get many of those in her life—Serena was happy to see him.

"I am a rough substitute for a Caesar," he said, "but I would also like to see the Tiber under the stars. Would you do me the honor?"

It was precisely the salve that Serena's wounded ego needed, so she accepted his arm. Why not? Stilicho traveled in Victor's inner circle. He was an acceptable companion, and one that might serve a greater purpose. *Let him see you with another man... it will rouse his jealousy and he will desire you more.* And besides, walking with the charismatic Stilicho—that tall frame, light brown hair and sensuous smile, those warm eyes—was no chore. Strange she hadn't noticed his finer attributes earlier.

They arrived on the deck of the barge to find the party was more outdoors than in. Servants circulated with wine and refreshments as guests gossiped among themselves, the space lit by thick flames that spewed from the nostrils of the bronze bull statues lining the perimeter of the deck.

"They are the *Khalkotauroi*," said Stilicho. "Wild fire-breathing bulls created by the god Vulcan."

"Tell me you do not believe in such things, Commander."

"No, my lady. I am a Christian, like you."

"But your general is pagan."

"He is."

"So you learn his stories to impress him?"

"Stories do not impress the general," replied Stilicho. "Only performance does." He gazed out at the moving black waters of the Tiber as flashes of light from the bulls' bronze nostrils danced on its surface. "If you spend any amount of time in Rome, you will find the old legends sculpted on every building, painted on every wall, and despite yourself, you will learn them."

"The heathens should be learning our stories, not the other way around."

"I once tried to tell the story of Jonah and the whale to the granddaughter of General Bauto," said Stilicho. "He broke my nose with a kitchen pot and told me not to fill the child's head with Jewish fables."

"You should have reported him," said Serena. "He would have been executed."

"Yes," said Stilicho, "and the army would have lost one of its best generals. My nose" — he tapped its slightly crooked bridge — "pretty as it is, is not worth the life of a good soldier. It is hard enough to find men to enlist."

"I admire your humility, Commander, but some might say you are too permissive."

"I only oppose that which threatens the empire," said Stilicho. "Invasion. Civil war. The unpredictability of the Goths within and beyond our borders." He took two cups of wine from an attendant and passed one to her. "The superstitions of the past are no threat to the empire or to our Lord." Catching sight of Arbo strolling onto the deck, he was suddenly reminded of his friend's fallen expression by the desecrated shrine to Diana on the road to Baiae. "Religion should not come between friends." His voice adopted a more intimate tone. "If I may be so bold, my lady, I would advise against engaging in religious debate with Romans. It is an open wound for many." He clinked his cup against hers. "Restraint gets one invited to more parties."

"That is good advice," replied Serena. "I shall try to restrain myself." She permitted herself to stand a little closer to the commander as Arbo approached.

"Lady Serena," he said. "It is good to see you again."

"And you, General. Are you friends with the" — there was no way around it, she would have to say it — "high priestess?"

"I am," replied Arbo, and then dipped his head toward Coelia as she strode onto the deck of the barge. "*Lupa in fabula*," he said, loudly enough for her to hear.

Coelia smiled and approached, noting the spark of surprise in Arbo's eyes at her appearance. As Vestalis Maxima, one of her greatest joys was having the freedom to infuriate Ptolema with impunity by choosing her own wardrobe. She had therefore left her formal stolas hanging in her closets, and instead chosen a more fitted ivory gown and a veil embroidered with delicate green laurel stitching. Her eyes and complexion were enhanced with light cosmetics, dangling gold earrings brushed against her veil, and the large circular gold medallion that Emperor Julian had given her now hung from a pearl station necklace.

"What a striking piece," said Serena, noting the medallion. "Interesting design. Is that not the cross?"

Coelia touched the medallion. "The round carnelian in the center represents Vesta's fire," she said, "while the pearls symbolize her priestesses gathered around it. The four points—a cross, as you say—represent the cardinal directions of the earth and how the goddess's light reaches the entire world."

"I see."

"You will find similar cross symbols in other religions. The Egyptians and the ankh, and the barbarians and their sun crosses. Last I knew, some of these were some on display in the Temple of Concordia and the Palatine Library. I don't know if they are still there or not. I haven't been to the library since the bishops started removing so many of the books."

Either not catching the subtle jab or not caring, Serena lifted her chin and perused the guests. She had lost sight of Victor.

Arbo tossed Stilicho a look that indicated he wanted to speak to the high priestess in private, and the commander quickly obliged. He pointed toward a couple on the other side of the platform. "I don't think you've met Senator Perses and his wife Helena," he said to Serena. "I'll introduce you."

As they departed, Arbo directed Coelia to a quiet spot along the balustrade of the deck and laughed. "You will find similar cross symbols in other religions. The Egyptians and the barbarians..."

"Maybe it was a bit much."

"I thought you were going to recite the entire *Naturalis Historia* to her."

"I'd love to," said Coelia. "I'm sure she'd find the volume on agriculture to be riveting." She raised her eyebrows. "Did you know, Lady Serena, that bracken dies in two years if you can prevent it from leafing?"

He smiled, but then grew more serious. "How is Priestess Claudia?"

"Theodosius granted her a full pardon," Coelia said quietly. "As a favor to Symmachus."

"Where is she?"

"We've moved her to a villa in Tivoli. A former chief Vestal bequeathed it to the Order. It's close to where Claudia's niece has an estate, so she is happy there."

"Did Gratian not have the property confiscated?"

"We took it off the books years ago. He didn't know about it."

"Good."

She felt a tap on her shoulder and turned to find her mother wagging a finger at her, gold bangles jingling as always. "It is bad form to stand by the gift table," she chided. She turned to Olympius, who was at her side. "Do you see, Olympius? The younger generation has no respect for etiquette, not even this one, trained to the teeth like she is."

"It's a shame," he agreed.

"Mother," said Coelia. "I was just speaking with—"

"Oh, I'm just joking," said Lucilla. "Let's see what these patricians have brought you." She shouldered Coelia aside and stepped closer to the large table, the gold-inlaid surface of which was covered with extravagant gifts. She poked through the fineries. "Look at this pearl bracelet, oh and these silver cups... the rims are diamonds, that's a nice touch. And this shawl... the silk and beads are so exotic, this can only be the work of the Seres." She tapped a large ivory carving of the amphitheater, complete with an intricate battle scene raging within. "It is Brogos and Deimos, and the dogs, too! What a clever gift from those two boys." She gasped. "Oh, but here is my favorite! These gold lion earrings are divine... just look at that majestic little snarl."

"Those are from me," Arbo said proudly. "So your daughter never forgets my heroics that day in the stadium."

Lucilla slapped him playfully on the shoulder. "You men are all alike." She turned to Coelia and brushed her daughter's veil aside, plucking the earrings she wore from her earlobes. She replaced them with the lion earrings. "She will wear them now."

"They are lovely," Coelia said to Arbo. "Thank you, General. Very thoughtful."

"*Libet*," he replied.

Coelia glanced around the deck of the barge. A legion of staff meandered among the high-class guests to serve a variety of expensive foods and even more expensive wine. Several pedestals stood around one of the fire-breathing bronze bulls, each holding a selection of fine oil lamps that Lucilla had had designed for the occasion—costly take-home trinkets for the guests. And on the far end of the barge's platform, a troupe of professional dancers were preparing for their performance. They had been surreptitiously brought in from Athens, even though theatrical dancing had been banned by the bishops. The Vestal turned back to Lucilla.

"Don't get too attached to the silver cups, Mother. I'll have to sell them to pay for all of this."

Lucilla drew back and gave her daughter a surprised look. "Oh, don't you know? I didn't pay for any of this. Olympius wouldn't have it. It is his gift to you."

Coelia turned to the senator, and he bared his teeth in a smile, the flames from the bronze bulls illuminating the white tips of his pointed eye teeth. He raised his wine cup to her.

"Congratulations on your appointment, High Priestess."

"*Gratias ago*, Senator," she said. "This was very generous."

"I've been hearing that Victor—Caesar—favors you," said Olympius. His eyes moved from Coelia to Arbo. "Favors both of you."

Ah, there it is, thought Coelia. *Not a gift. An investment.*

Knowing it was safest to face Olympius head on—he was less likely to think of her as prey—she nodded. "He does. And as long as he does, I will do what I can for my friends."

She wasn't sure if Olympius was convinced—she certainly didn't mean a word of it with respect to him—but he nodded contently and sipped his wine. His face soured, though, as he spotted Stilicho chatting with Serena closer to where the dancers were set to perform.

"Not that prick again," he murmured.

Coelia glanced at Arbo, expecting him to defend his commander, but the general was indifferent. Stilicho was more than capable of defending himself, though if his flirtations with Lady Serena were any indication, he was going on the offensive. A personal connection to Theodosius would be good for his career. Arbo had told him as much for years.

"Lady Serena best be careful," said Lucilla. "I don't think our Caesar is the type to fall into the jealousy trap."

"I doubt Victor would court her regardless," Arbo opined. "He will want to build his own dynasty, not be a brick in the house of Theodosius."

"Do you think Maximus will invade Italy?" Olympius asked him pointedly.

"Victor has assured me that his father has no such plans."

Coelia looked into her wine cup and risked it. "Would it be so awful if he did?"

"War is awful," said Arbo.

Olympius rocked on his heels. "For some," he countered. "For others, it brings opportunity."

Lucilla patted Olympius on the chest. "This treads too close to politics," she mediated. "The performance will begin soon." She pointed to the far end of the deck. "Let's go."

The four of them moved together across the length of the deck, passing by all the usual faces. Victor was immersed in conversation with Symmachus, Praetextatus and Junius. Paulina was sharing a spirited bit of gossip with a clique of noblewomen. Everyone was enjoying the clear night sky and the ambiance of the ancient Tiber River, the surface of its flowing waters gleaming with firelight. There were only two people Coelia hoped to avoid—Senator Perses and Lady Helena. She knew they would be looking for an opportunity to discuss their daughter's infatuation with her gladiator. Brogos knew the same, and so had chosen to avoid the banquet... and any awkward confrontation with Anthea's disapproving parents.

After stopping multiple times to accept congratulations and offer blessings—no Vestal, not even the high priestess, could refuse to perform a blessing when asked—Coelia and her companions reached the viewing area for the performance. Domitia, Proculeia and Terentia were already there, elbows resting on the marble railing, drinking wine and giggling in a way that suggested none of them were on their first cup. They took turns kissing Coelia on the cheek as she joined them. As a horn sounded and the rest of the guests crowded around, Victor ascended to a small throne set on raised dais. A subtle reminder, perhaps, that despite his relative informality at this gathering for a pagan priestess, he was still very much the man at the top.

The head of the dancing troupe, a well-coiffed man dressed in flowing red robes, cleared his throat. "The great Pliny put it best," he boomed, his arms out. "*Ex Africa semper aliquid novi!*"

On cue, a great roar sounded from the river, causing several women and a few embarrassed men to gasp in surprise, spilling their wine and sheepishly laughing at the blunder. All eyes turned to a large rectangular platform that floated almost invisibly on the surface of the Tiber.

Illuminated by torchlight, a menacing being took center stage—a huge man, draped in a golden lion skin. His face and head were covered by a maned lion mask, and his hands were gloved in enormous lion paws. The beast's head turned this way and that, flaunting its smooth ivory fangs and black-beaded eyes. All around, shaking in mock fear, lithe dancers leapt and twirled, coming within inches of the lion's deadly claws before somersaulting away. The lion-man roared again and dashed with elegant aggression to one side of the stage and then the other, taking ferocious swipes at the dancers and showering the air with gold glitter. Desperate to escape the beast's claws, the dancers began to dive off the stage into the black water, each departure more graceful and acrobatic than the one before.

The gathering applauded gleefully. Talk of the four escaped lions—the Gilded Lions of Rome, as they were now called—was everywhere. Lion graffiti was painted on walls throughout the city, with the beasts' impromptu but now household names sprawled over their giant heads: *Umbra, Rapax, Lucens* and *Nox*. Each morning brought bloodier and more terrifying accounts of their overnight victims: a mutilated soldier near the *Ager Vaticanus*, a missing family dog on the Quirinal Hill, a whole herd of pigs silently devoured in the market, flecks of golden paint left on the victims' bones. The whole thing had taken on a mythic quality, and the performance's theme was perfect for a city on the edge.

As the show continued and the excitement escalated, Coelia sensed a new presence standing beside her. It was Lady Helena.

"High Priestess," said Helena. "I wonder if I might have a private word with you after the show?"

"Yes, by all means," Coelia replied. "I shall find you before I leave and we will speak."

Helena smiled and politely stepped back to her husband's side. She said something to him, and he nodded with resignation. Their minds were on matters larger than the show. The rumors about Anthea and her gladiator lover were getting louder, and no doubt the young woman's parents were fearful they would reach the ears of Symmachus and his son Memmius, if they hadn't already.

For a moment, Coelia considered doing the right thing and forbidding Brogos from seeing the girl. But then another roar from the lion-man filled the night air, and the crowd cheered and clapped louder, eager for more. She remembered Brogos's words:

People can't wait to get back into the amphitheater. If the hunters can catch at least one of those bastards alive and give me a second chance to slay the Nemean lion, I'd make both of us rich as Pluto.

She didn't need to be rich as Pluto. But from what Olympius had told her, if they could indeed snare one live lion and bring it back to the arena, they stood to make more in one show than they had in the last five years. This was not the time to sap her star gladiator of his motivation. Not when so much money was—

Her thoughts took an abrupt turn.

So did her head, toward Olympius. With all eyes on the performance, she stepped around her mother and clutched the sleeve of his tunica, pulling his ear close to her mouth, her voice full of sudden revelation. "The lions... it wasn't an accident, was it?"

Olympius looked at her, grinning. "It's about time," he replied.

CHAPTER XV

The house of the healer on the Aventine Hill looked a lot like Abigail's tunica. Plain and faded. A small fire set into the corner took the chill out of the room, but still left it cooler than was comfortable. The frescos that had once enlivened the walls had been scrubbed away to the point of unrecognizable fragments, and a large wooden cross had been nailed directly into the stucco. One man in a long brown tunica and four women in thin blue ones knelt in prayer before it, all of them rising as Abigail escorted Helena and Anthea into the humble room. The man—middle-aged, with a lanky stature and longish black beard—greeted them with open arms.

"Sister Abigail," he said. "You just missed breakfast. A baker from the Forum Pistorium brought by the most delicious *panis candidus.* It was most brave of him to venture out with the lions still at large."

"The Lord protects the charitable, brother," replied Abigail. She put her hand on Anthea's back. "Brother Aulus, this is Anthea and her mother Lady Helena. They are dear friends of mine." She took the sachet from Anthea's hand and passed it to the man.

He opened the sachet and smelled the ointment, his eyes flick-ing up to Anthea. He took four large strides to the fire and tossed the sachet into the low flames, ignoring Anthea's gasp of protest. "I am familiar with such concoctions," he said. "I used to dis-pense them myself until I bore witness to the Lord's healing. He is the divine physician."

Bidding the women to follow him, he led them all into an ad-jacent room, a smaller space that was even cooler. A narrow mattress set on a high wooden frame was in the center of the room. On the table beside it lay a single scroll, a wooden cross, and a small bottle of water.

"Sir," said Helena. "What is your practice?"

"I perform a ritual that can free your daughter of her wanton-ness," he replied. "It has never once failed."

"Mother..." said Anthea.

Helena met her daughter's eyes. After enduring yet another family argument that morning, and having accepted that the high priestess would never call off her gladiator, she had been willing to try anything. Now that she was here, though, she wasn't so sure.

"Perses would not approve of this," she said to Abigail. "I am sorry to have bothered you."

"Perses is a man of dignity," said Abigail. "Brother Aulus can help him remain so. Anyway, there is nothing in the heathen be-liefs that forbids you from consulting healers of a different faith."

Aulus smiled and put his hand on Anthea's back, gently guiding her toward the mattress. "It is a common affliction with your sex," he said. "You have been seduced by trickery and evil spirits. Yet you can be freed with nothing more than words and a little water."

It sounded like nonsense—if the ointment didn't work, words and water probably wouldn't either—but Anthea could see the con-flict and worry on her mother's face. Perhaps if she did this, she could pretend it worked. That might give her mother some peace.

Anthea followed the healer. "Words and a little water," she said to Helena, and gave her a private look. *It's all right, Mother. It cannot hurt to try.*

She climbed onto the little mattress and stared up at the ceiling, only then noticing the scene sketched above her: a nearly skeletal depiction of Jesus Christ affixed to a cross, his mouth hanging open in agony, eyes looking upward, as black blood dripped from his hands and feet. Three women knelt at the base of the cross, weeping as a man wearing the red cloak of a Roman soldier pierced Christ's body with a lance. The morbid imagery filled Anthea with a sudden sense of desolation, and yet she found it hard to look away.

The four women in blue—Aulus had not introduced them to Helena or Anthea—moved as one. Two took their places at the bedside, while the other two stood on either side of Helena and pressed their palms together, whispering soft prayers into their fingers.

Aulus picked the wooden cross off the little table and held it over Anthea. "Behold the cross of the Lord." He looked down at Anthea. "What is your name?"

Anthea met his eyes. He already knew her name. "My name is Anthea."

Holding the cross in the air with one hand, he placed his other hand on her stomach. "In the name of Jesus Christ, I compel you to speak your name, demon!"

The sudden fury and strangeness of his words, combined with the unwelcome intimacy of his cold hand on her stomach, made Anthea's heartbeat quicken. She pushed his hand away and tried to sit up, but more hands gripped her shoulders, pressing her down against the bed. She tilted her head back to see one of the women staring down at her... and a moment later felt pressure around her wrists. They were tying her down.

"No!" she screamed. "Stop it!"

The man's face reappeared above her.

"I beg thee, Almighty Christ, deliver this woman from the foul sorcery of her lover! I beg thee, Almighty Christ, deliver this woman from the demon of lust she has allowed to enter her!"

Witnessing it all from across the small room, Helena's face reddened with anger. "Take those ropes off her! My daughter has no demon inside her." She stepped forward, but felt hands restrain her. The women in blue.

"The demon cannot be called forth without being vanquished," one of the women said to her. "Brother Aulus must complete the exorcism."

Helena twisted to release herself from the women's grasp, but could not. "Let go of me! Are you mad?"

The sound of her mother's panic-laced voice made Anthea's heart pound even faster and harder. Her own panic mounting, she pulled at the ropes around her wrists, but there was no give, so she kicked her legs, frantically trying to liberate herself from the hands on her body. Immediately, a tight pressure around her ankles added to that around her wrists, and she shrieked in protest at the terrible realization that they were tying her down completely. She was at their mercy.

She glared at the man above her. "Let go of me, you *fucking prick!*"

He looked down at her in awe. "The demon is with us!" he declared. He inhaled, his nostrils flaring as his eyes slowly closed. Bending over, he brought his face close to Anthea's, so close that the oily bristles of his patchy beard brushed softly over her lips. The feeling of intrusion repulsed her and she closed her lips tightly, cranking her head to the side as his nose grazed her cheek and neck. He stood and opened his eyes. "Yes, it is as the masters say," he declared. "I am able to smell the thing. The *odor* of the thing."

"Stop it! Let go of my daughter!" cried Helena. She tried to extricate herself from hands of the women in blue, but could not. Her head pounding as hard as her heart, she turned to her friend. "Abigail, make them stop!"

Abigail folded her hands in prayer, but said nothing.

Aulus retrieved the vial from the table and snapped his wrist forward, splattering Anthea's body with cold water. Her flesh twitched from the unexpected sensation and she wriggled furiously, trying to break free of the restraints. Her tunica tore in the struggle, exposing her left breast. Even as she fought, she could see the man's eyes linger on it. Rage consumed her.

"Get your hands off me! He will *kill you* for this!" She thought of Brogos, the way he looked at her, touched her... what he would do to this man once she told him what had happened. She stayed there in her mind, retreating there, the only place of dignity and power she could find.

"I beg thee, Almighty Christ, cast out the demon whores Venus and Pertunda, false gods and agents of Satan!"

Anthea sputtered out a half profanity, half sob. It caught in her throat and she coughed.

"The Almighty is casting out the demon!" Aulus exclaimed. He put his hands around Anthea's throat. "In the name of Christ, I expel thee from this woman!"

The terror she felt as the man's hands tightened around her throat, the glazed look in his eyes, the unbearable sense of helplessness and violation... it curdled in Anthea's stomach and came up in a sour broth of vomit. It spewed from her mouth, but restrained as she was on her back, it quickly slid back into her mouth and drained into her nostrils. She inhaled, desperate for air, but the thick acridness filled her throat and nose. She heard a disturbing gurgle emerge from her own body. Mute and helpless, Anthea opened her eyes as wide as she could and stared up at the man. *I cannot breathe! I cannot breathe! I cannot breathe!*

"You're killing her!" screeched Helena. She dropped to the floor, kicking and flailing, but the arms and hands of the women in blue seemed to be everywhere, clutching at her and holding her down. "Abigail! They're killing her! They're killing my baby! I will do anything, I will give you anything, make them stop!"

Anthea could hear her mother's voice. She could hear the panic, the pain, and it broke her heart to know that her mother would never forgive herself for this. She wanted to tell her that it was all right. That it was not her fault. But the taste of the sour vomit and the suffocation seemed to converge in a coming darkness, and as it drew closer, she was filled with the desolate awareness that she would never speak those words, any words, to her mother again.

CHAPTER XVI

When the caretaker responsible for the grain stored in the *Horrea Galbae* opened the first warehouse to find the rot, he swore under his breath. When he opened the second, he beat his subordinates. When he opened the third, the fourth and the fifth, he thought about committing suicide, but instead decided it was the perfect time to retire. He and his family had packed up their belongings and headed south before the true extent of the devastating loss had been calculated and reported to the Senate. And as the caretaker had accurately predicted, the Senate was so distressed by the scope and inevitability of the coming famine, his abscondence quickly faded into irrelevance. Rome was about to starve. If anything, he was just one less mouth to feed. Immediately, officials were sent to Egypt and Hispania to oversee an increase in production and shipments, and a motion was passed to consult the Sibylline Books for further instruction.

Since her inauguration as Vestalis Maxima, Coelia had been studying the most secret rites and prayers of the ancient Vestal Order. These were the words and rituals known only to the high priestess and which were only to be used during times of crisis, whether it was war, invasion, plague or famine. Now, as she stood over the holy fire in Vesta's temple and offered the best of the bad grain Rome had to spare into the flames—following the rituals to the letter—she took note of the goddess's indifferent response to her pleas. It was a bad sign. She might have blamed it all on her own incompetence had the other priests and priestesses not told her it was the same everywhere.

The *sacerdotes* of Ceres had appealed to the goddess of grain to protect the remaining crops, both in the field and in the warehouses. They had also prayed to Robigus, the god of blight, begging for mercy. But the gods were apathetic, and the reason why was no mystery. With the recent revocation of the Vestals' stipend, Rome had offended her guardian goddess. That offense was compounded by the criminalization of sacrifices customarily performed to alleviate famine. As if those reasons weren't enough, the emperor Valentinian's recent call for public order—one that specifically forbade the despoiling of pagan temples, shrines and statues—had been ignored. The vandalism and desecration continued with impunity, and Rome's gods were losing patience with the city's impiety.

The doors to the temple opened, and Proculeia and Terentia stepped inside. "Senator Olympius is requesting an audience with you," said Proculeia. Seeing Coelia's unhappy reaction, she crinkled her nose. "Sorry."

"Tell him—"

"Ptolema already put him in your office."

"Bloody Ptolema," mumbled Coelia.

She left the temple and entered the House of the Vestals, heading straight to her office and entering the high-ceilinged space to find Olympius stoking the fire. He leaned the iron stoker against the wall and looked at her seriously.

"Have you seen Brogos today?"

"No."

"Do you know where he is?"

"I have no idea. With Deimos at the ludus, probably." When Olympius shook his head, she added, "General Arbogastes has a house on the Quirinal. They're friends. He might be staying there."

"I had a man check there, too. The general hasn't seen him since yesterday."

"A day's absence is hardly cause for alarm," said Coelia.

Olympius looked at her quizzically. "You haven't heard."

"About what?"

"Perses's daughter. She died during an exorcism on the Aventine yesterday. Her mother took her to a charlatan, hoping the girl would stop fucking our Brogos—you knew about that at least, right?—and now Brogos is nowhere to be found."

Coelia's breath caught in her throat. She moved slowly behind her desk and sat. "Where is the charlatan?"

"On the run. When he found out the girl's lover was none other than Hades himself, he took all the gold he could carry from his congregation and took off. He'll be halfway to Caledonia by now."

"And Brogos after him."

"And Brogos after him," echoed Olympius. He slumped into a chair. "*Futuo.* I had it all planned out. Who better to slay the Gilded Lions of Rome than Brogos and Deimos? What have we been training the bastards for if not to face the beasts in the arena?"

"He'll come back," said Coelia. "Why wouldn't he?"

"I can think of a thousand reasons," replied Olympius. "All of them shaped like the gold coins in the exorcist's luggage."

"Brogos will come back," Coelia insisted. "He won't abandon Deimos. And if he doesn't come back, we'll find someone else."

"A missing gladiator isn't our only problem." Olympius looked at Coelia, a rare shade of concern on his face. "The barriers in the arena, the ones that failed... I didn't do that alone. I owe people money. *We* owe them money. A lot of it. It was supposed to come out of the proceeds of the big lion-slaying finale, but once they learn that Brogos has left Rome, they'll want to be paid. Especially Clemens. He's a weasel."

"Who is Clemens?"

"The head animal handler in the amphitheater."

Coelia put her elbows on her desk and leaned forward. "Olympius, I am the chief Vestal of Rome. I cannot have people accusing me of being complicit in your little stunt. How many civilians and soldiers have the lions killed now?"

"I know. We'll be broke if this gets out."

"We'll be *executed* if this gets out." She put her head in her hands. "What if we hired mercenaries to find the exorcist? Brogos is probably on the same trail. They could find him too, and tell him—"

"Spending more money isn't the solution," said Olympius. He sat up straight. "The Senate is meeting this afternoon so that Symmachus can make a formal statement of condolence to Perses. I'll ask that funds be allocated for a manhunt."

"Will they do it?"

"Probably not. These charlatans and fraudsters are on every street corner. If the Senate pays to catch one, they'll be inundated with requests to catch others." He gripped the arms of the chair and pushed himself to his feet. "I'll let you know how it goes."

He departed without saying goodbye, leaving Coelia reeling from the news. Her throat felt dry and restrictive, so she poured herself a glass of water from the jug on her desk and drank. When she lowered her glass, Ptolema was standing before her.

"If you're going to say 'I told you so,' I'll have you thrown to the lions," said Coelia.

Ptolema set the iron stoker back on its stand and left the chief Vestal alone.

As Senator Symmachus, prefect of Rome and leader of the senatorial assembly, stood in the center of the Senate House's ornate multicolored marble floor and listened to the storm of discussions and debates reverberating within the high walls of the rectangular chamber, he found himself reflecting upon the ground under his feet. For it was here, over a millennium earlier, that Romulus had inaugurated the *Comitium*, that world-changing meeting space where Rome's allies and enemies alike had gathered to make peace and expand the Roman virtues—dignity, piety, fairness, tenacity, industriousness and human civility—beyond its own walls. It was here that people brought the skills, customs and gods of their lands to live as free Romans with a common purpose. It was from this spot that Rome's light first shone into the void to show the dark world a better way to live. A way to build things up, not constantly tear them down, and for a long time, it had worked. There had been mistakes and missteps along the way, but Rome had always reembraced her true self and Romulus's vision. These days, how-ever, the flame was flickering and the darkness was creeping back. Symmachus could feel it happening, see it happening all around him. And despite being invested with some of the most significant powers in Rome, he felt powerless to stop it. That didn't mean he would stop trying.

The presiding magistrate gestured for calm and quiet before calling the Senate into session and nodding at Symmachus to begin.

"How fortunate each of us is at this moment," declared Symma-chus, "to be sitting here in this great house and not curled in our beds, weeping into the sheets as Senator Perses must be doing right now." He paused as the thoughtful murmurs rose and fell. "On be-half of this Senate, I offer to the divine our prayers for the soul of our friend's beloved daughter." After a few moments of respectful silence, he continued. "I have read the motions put forth by several members of this assembly. To those of you calling for a state-funded manhunt to capture the charlatan responsible for the young woman's death, I understand your anger. I share it. But a senatorial order to that effect would only attract accusations of favoritism and set a precedent for a flood of similar requests. I instead propose that we increase patrols within the city walls, focusing on the districts where these fraudsters are known to operate."

A swell of affirmation and agreement went up. Only one man stood in opposition—Senator Lampadius. As a member of the Christian minority that comprised the Senate, his was often the loudest dissenting voice. He stood and lifted his chin.

"No one can deny the abuses committed by religious charlatans," he said. "They sell dog-piss love potions from rickety stalls behind every pagan temple in Rome, don't forget. So I must ask, which districts do you speak of?"

"Those with the most public disruption," replied Symmachus.

"You mean those with the most anti-pagan sentiment," Lampadius challenged. "Your proposal is not meant to prevent fraudsters at all, but rather to suppress the rights of our Christian citizens."

"Suppress *your* rights?" asked Senator Nicomachus. "Your religion is the law of the land, and still you claim oppression?"

The white-haired senator Junius put his hand on a fold of his toga—it was a gesture that called for civility—and addressed Lampadius. "The purpose of the increased patrols is to suppress public disruption, and that is all," he insisted. "The vandalism in certain quarters makes Rome look like a ruin."

"The suppression of public disruption," mused Lampadius. "The timeless assertion of the Diocletians and those whose persecution of the Christian faith taught the vandals their art."

"You have a selective memory of history, Senator," replied Junius. "This assembly has often suppressed pagan disruptions as well. It is a matter of public order."

Senator Pompeianus, another member of the Christian demographic in the assembly, stood. "I support Senator Symmachus's motion," he said, his high cheekbones and lofty tone infusing his words with patrician authority. He turned to Lampadius. "The prefect is correct. The charlatans wreak havoc, and then disappear with their money and leave us with the mess. Worse, they corrupt the Lord's work and spread misery in his name. Senator Perses and I have often been at odds in this chamber, but I grieve for his loss. I know you do as well. Order must be restored."

Lampadius nodded, albeit reluctantly. "Order must be restored," he agreed.

Pompeianus and Lampadius sat. Content that his first proposal was accepted, Symmachus moved on to the second matter on the agenda.

"On the ides of this month," he began, "a motion was passed in this assembly to consult the Sibylline Books with respect to the worsening famine. With the oversight of the Greek scholars and our own priests, I have done so." He turned to address both sides of the floor. "The Oracle instructs the Senate to write a special *relatio* to the emperor, one which begs for the return of the Altar of Victory to this house and for the restoration of the Vestal Virgins' funding. The Oracle's message was clear: The words of this *relatio* will outlast he who writes it and all who read it."

The senator Nicomachus stood and addressed the assembly with outstretched arms. "This oracular pronouncement should be no surprise to anyone in this chamber," he said. "Too many have turned away from the customs of our ancestors. The grain wilts without the blessings of the goddesses, and he who stripped us of those protections—the tyrant Gratian—quickly answered for his sacrilege at the tip of an assassin's blade. We cannot ignore these signs."

Senator Junius stood and dipped his head to Symmachus. "Many in Rome and in this house have called you a second Cicero," he said. "You will write to the emperor on behalf of the Senate. We must bring the winged goddess back to this chamber and restore the dignity of our Vestal Virgins. We must restore the freedom of the people of Romulus, and the right of every Roman to worship the divinity he feels in his own heart, whether it is Christ or Juno. We cannot feed Rome's stomach without first feeding her soul."

CHAPTER XVII

The time of day made no difference in the catacombs. It certainly made no difference to the dead, but even to the living who worked as diggers, painters, tilers, perfumists, cleaners and priests within the endless winding tunnels of the subterranean cemetery, it made no difference. It was always black as night, the darkness broken only by whatever oil lamp a person brought with them into the depths. The sole indication of the passage of time, as far as Gabinus could tell, was the state of his stomach. If it was growling, it was either midday or late day. Since he had already taken lunch, and since his stomach was grumbling so loud as to echo in the narrow stone passageway, he surmised that it had to be early evening. His wife would be fully irritated by now, clanging pots together and staring at the door, willing him to enter before supper was ruined completely. With the famine tightening everyone's belts, there was no food to waste.

Gabinus held his paintbrush between clenched teeth and gripped the sides of the scaffolding, pulling back just enough to assess his work by the light of several oil lamps: a depiction of Christ carrying the cross, painted across the back wall of a stone niche within which the sheet-wrapped body of a man named Audax now rested eternal. The painting was quite good, if Gabinus said so himself, though bleak. Personally, he preferred more colorful scenes. The painting he had finished the day before—a vibrant pastoral scene of Christ as a shepherd—was more to his tastes. Still, it was the family's coin. He just painted what he was told to paint. That included the deceased's epitaph.

He held onto the scaffolding with one hand and took his paintbrush in the other, printing the words HIC IACET VIR FORTIS AUDAX—*Here Lies the Hero Audax*—above the funerary cavity, careful to leave enough room for the tilers to seal the space without covering the words. They were words that Gabinus doubted were fully deserved, for he had heard of Audax. The man had broken into a granary along the Appian Way, one of the last facilities to have healthy inventory. Charitable sort that he was, he had distributed much of it among his hungry neighbors and the poor before being charged with stealing state property. Many had petitioned for his pardon, despite the inconvenient revelation that he had secretly sold much of the grain at an exorbitant price. Ultimately, he had been put to death. But one man's hypocrite was another man's hero, and Gabinus supposed Audax's family preferred the latter as the man's lasting legacy.

His work complete, the tomb painter descended the scaffolding from the third level of the catacomb to the second, stopping to say a prayer over the linen-wrapped child's body that lay curled up in another stone niche, forever asleep in a green pasture with Christ. The savior cradled a lamb in his arms, and Gabinus suddenly very much wanted to be home with his wife and daughter, even if he had to kiss his wife a hundred times before her scowl cracked into a smile. He began his descent to the ground level of the claustrophobically narrow tunnel when a deep, strange sound coming from somewhere beyond the bend in the passageway made him stop.

"Hello?" he called into the darkness. "Who is there?" He waited several moments. *I am imagining things,* he thought. *Too much time in the dark with the dead.* He stepped down onto the next rung in the scaffolding, again stopping—this time with a gasp—as the sound intensified in the unseen distance, expanding outward to roll toward him through the tunnel like a confined rumble of thunder. "What is that?" he exclaimed. "Is anyone there?"

White-knuckled from clutching the sides of the scaffolding, Gabinus forced his fingers to open so that he could step down another rung. That brought another sound, a strange rhythmic crunching. He would have thought it was footsteps, but it sounded nothing like the footsteps he was accustomed to hearing in the labyrinthine underground world. He tried to convince himself that it was only the sound of the scaffolding shifting under his weight, but then he heard it again, louder and closer this time. He clung to the scaffolding and stared down into the dark abyss. Below him, a figure of shimmering gold materialized by the light of the oil lamps... and took the shape of a lion.

"Father in Heaven," he said weakly.

Slowly, the animal lifted its massive head and looked up, leveling a mesmerizing gaze on Gabinus. Its eyes—amber irises encircling widely dilated black pupils—narrowed slightly as the lion curled its top lip and opened its mouth, exposing pointed white fangs that looked as long as daggers, its muzzle crinkling as it studied the scent of the strange creature clinging to the rickety scaffolding. Either unsure that the creature was prey, or just deciding there was an easier meal to be had, the lion lowered its head and sniffed at a shrouded body tucked into one of the countless niches pock-marking the top-to-bottom surface of the stone walls. It raised a thick leg and pawed at the corpse, pulling it off the stone shelf to land on the ground with a grotesque thump. With a motion that looked as lazy as it did effortless, the beast bit the heavy linen and tore it off the deceased to reveal the body of a large man. He was dressed in a brown tunica, his bare legs and arms a macabre shade of purplish red.

Gabinus could not bear to watch what happened next. He turned away and pushed his face into the wooden frame of the scaffolding, praying softly. "What should I fear when Christ is with me?"

A short, throaty growl burst out of the animal, striking Gabinus as a shockwave of sound and terror that knocked an involuntary sob out of his own throat. The growl ricocheted off the narrow walls and then faded, only to be replaced by a louder, longer, deeper growl. The sound touched something primal inside Gabinus, and he understood the beast's mind. It was perturbed by the rotting flesh, irritated, and just hungry and angry enough to explore its other option: the fresher-smelling creature suspended overhead, the one that looked not so different than a baboon hiding in a tree.

With a swift agility that seemed discordant to its bulk and the constrictiveness of the stone passageway, the lion reared up on its back legs and swatted Gabinus, its huge scalpel-like claws slicing open the side of his right leg from the ankle to the hip. Gabinus screamed in pain and tried to clamber higher up the scaffolding, but lost his footing on the slipperiness of his own blood and fell downward in an awkward series of descents that ended when he landed on the ground, on his back. Without sparing a moment to orientate himself or see where the lion was, he leapt to his feet and charged into the black void of the catacomb's maze-like tunnel system.

"*Adiuva me!*" he shouted. "*Leo est!*"

Gabinus had roamed these tunnels for ten years, and he knew workers and clerics who had roamed them for much longer. Yet neither he nor any of them claimed to have traveled down every passageway in the underground cemetery. Its endless stretches of trench-like walls were patterned with a network of multilayered rectangular funerary niches carved into the tufa, with miles of tunnels that snaked into curvatures, broke into intersecting corridors, led to abrupt dead-ends and opened into elaborate arched private tombs before shooting off again into the tangled void. Moving through these passageways was challenging and unnerving enough during the workday, when men of various guilds moved to and fro, each carrying light and supplies, each following a rough map to their destination, everyone calling out to each other for the reassurance of companionship as much as anything else. But moving through the tunnels alone, without even a single candle to pierce the oppressive blackness, with a man-eating lion in pursuit, was something else entirely.

And so Gabinus did the only thing he could do. He fell back on the most basic instinct imbued in his living bones, the instinct infused in his blood since those long ago ages when men were prey and not predator—he ran. He ran as fast as he could, lifting his legs high to avoid tripping over the changing slopes of the ground or the forgotten tools of some workman. He ran with his arms out, frantically feeling his way along the walls with his hands, his fingers passing over a variety of textures: the bumpy tufa of the wall, the smoother face of brick, the polished surface and engraved letters of marble plaques, the soft linen of a shrouded body, the ridges and hollows of human bones.

Similarly unaccustomed to navigating the subterranean tunnels of a village-sized cemetery in the dark, the lion fell back on instinct, too. Its long, rigid whiskers guided it through the foreign stone channels, and its nostrils flared as it assessed the smells on either side: stone, dust, paint, fabric, quicklime, bone, decaying flesh and the pungent oils and balms left by the perfumists to mask it all. The only appealing smell was that of the fresh blood spilling out of the fleeing creature ahead. So the hungry animal followed that smell, gained on it, ready to strike it down when its senses said it was close enough.

As Gabinus continued to run deeper into the crushing blackness, his sandal caught something on the ground—it felt like a pile of rags left behind by a laborer—and he stumbled, falling forward and hitting his nose on something... another scaffolding. Workers were supposed to remove their scaffolding at the end of the workday to prevent exactly this kind of thing—well, not *exactly* this kind of thing—but there was always one too lazy or too entitled to follow the rules. The explosion of pain in Gabinus's face and the tears that streamed from his eyes slowed his progress... but he also found himself presented with an opportunity. After squeezing his body through the legs of the scaffolding, he turned around in the dark and pushed the structure with all his might. It crumbled noisily into a disjointed heap of pipes and planks.

Panting, he scrambled forward. Behind him, he heard a sound that filled his pounding heart with a glimmer of hope—a loud crash as the lion ran headlong into the twisted debris of the scaffolding. The beast let out an ear-splitting roar of angry surprise, of frustration, and struggled to extricate itself from the pretzeled pile of broken wood. No match for the weight and strength of the lion, the scaffolding's shattered frame gave way, and the animal pushed through to resume its pursuit.

Gabinus gasped for breath, knowing that he was coming to the end of his fight. It was harder to fill his lungs now, his chest was frighteningly tight, and the muscles in his legs felt weak and unresponsive, like they weren't even part of his body anymore. Although fear and shock had initially shielded him from the pain of his leg injury, he felt it now. He kept running, but began to cry, his arms still outstretched as he felt his way around yet another curve in the tunnel.

And then he saw it. The tiny flame of an oil lamp in the distance. The small point of light turned into two, then three, and Gabinus heard the most beautiful sound he had ever heard in his life—the sound of human voices. A wave of relief washed over him. Even if he died, he wouldn't die alone.

"*Adiuva me, obsecro!*" he screamed.

"What is wrong?" a voice called out.

"*Leo adest!*" he called back. "It is chasing me!"

As if providing evidence to substantiate the wild claim, the lion roared again, loud enough, Gabinus thought, to wake the dead that lined the walls on either side of him.

The points of light quickly retreated.

"No! Come back, you cowards!" Gabinus screamed, again finding himself plunged into total darkness.

Another voice, this one deeper. "This way! Follow my voice!"

So Gabinus did. The fingers of his right hand lost contact with the wall, indicating the mouth of another tunnel, and he turned sharply to run down it in the direction of the bodiless voice. The lion followed, gaining now with every step.

"This way! Follow my voice!"

This time, the fingers of his left hand lost contact, and he pivoted in that direction. As he did, the sudden blinding light of a torch appeared before him, and he reflexively raised an arm to shield his eyes.

"It is just behind me!" he shrieked. "It will be—"

An indescribable pain shot through his body as the lion's fangs sank into his backside, the ivory blades of its teeth scraping against the bone of the tomb painter's pelvis. A moment later, Gabinus felt the meat of his right buttock separate from his lower body. He screeched in agony and horror even as he felt human hands on his arms pulling him away from the beast, even as he heard the clanging of metal weapons and voices shouting orders at each other, coordinating their attack on the animal.

Now liberated from the animal's jaws, Gabinus struggled to get his bearings, to clear his mind. He was propped up against a marble sarcophagus in a large arched niche, sitting in a pool of his own blood as three men fought the lion, stabbing at it with long swords—efforts that only seemed to enrage the beast more—by the light of a single torch perched in a wall sconce. As Gabinus watched, the lion lunged forward and grabbed one of the men by the shoulder, forcing him to the ground and tearing the man's arm out of its socket even as the other two men continued to assault it. Gold paint flecks from the gilded lion's thick mane flew into the air and floated there like glimmering subterranean stars.

The sight was a surreal one, and it rendered Gabinus motionless. But then the man in the lion's jaws screamed and the tomb painter's fear transformed into resolve. Gripping the top of the sarcophagus, he struggled to his feet. Nearby, he spotted a large glass bottle of perfume sitting at the feet of a marble angel statue. Gritting his teeth against the pain, he shuffled toward it. Without giving himself time to rethink the wisdom of getting closer to the animal instead of farther away, without listening to his wife's voice in his head—*Run, you fool, run!*—he broke the lid off the bottle and advanced on the beast, spraying its eyes and nose with the powerful perfume.

Instantly, the lion released its prey. It lowered itself to the ground and slunk backward, its muzzle crinkled and its eyes closed. Raising its massive head, it opened its mouth and began to sneeze involuntarily. This was exactly the distraction—the opportunity—the lion hunters needed. They set upon the beast as Gabinus stumbled backward, the trauma of his injuries and blood loss now sapping what remained of his strength. He felt the sarcophagus against his back and slid down it into unconsciousness, though still sensible enough to wonder what scene would await him if he ever woke up again.

CHAPTER XVIII

Choosing to arrive in style—Victor could not resist pomp—Coelia rode to the church of Laurentius in the Vestal Order's finest *carpentum*. Gleaming with gilded highlights and topped with a deep purple canopy, the brilliant two-wheeled transport was pulled by two white horses dressed as finely as its occupant. As the driver pulled up to the church's entrance and parked behind Symmachus's carriage, one of Coelia's two guards opened the door at the rear of the vehicle. Even the door was embellished, displaying a bronze medallion that depicted the sacrificial implements of the Vestal Virgins. He lowered the steps, and the high priestess alighted onto a red stone pathway to the sound of mourning chants. Just that morning, Bishop Damascus had died.

But Coelia wasn't here to pray for Damascus's soul. She was here at the request of Victor. After having attended numerous pagan festivities, including her own inauguration banquet, it was now time for him to reassure Rome's Christian population that he had the power and the will to command high-ranking pagans like herself and Symmachus to tread on Christian ground whenever it suited him. Coelia didn't mind. It was a small price to pay for his friendship.

The Vestal waited, hands clasped before her, as a brown-robed cleric approached. His eyes moved up and down her body, silently chastising her attire. With her silver and garnet tiara, delicate white veil, form-fitting tunica with elegant shawl, and dazzling silver-banded wrists, she was not the species of religious woman he and his brethren approved of. That is precisely why she had chosen to drape herself in jewels, brazenly emphasizing the difference between herself and the widows and virgins who frequented the church. Years earlier, Claudia had visited the same church to meet with the head of the Christian women's monastery, hoping to foster civil relations between the orders. The woman had not shown up, and within days a rumor had begun to circulate that the high priestess was renouncing the Vestal Order and converting. Claudia had spent the better part of a month raging at her own gullibility. Coelia was determined that if any rumors were to arise from her visit, they would orbit around her extravagance and nothing else.

"I am to take you to Caesar," said the cleric. "This way."

The curt tone was undeserving of a reply, so Coelia did not offer one. She spoke only to the closest of her guards, a young man barely out of his teens, named Teo. "Wait here." The command was unusually abrupt, but she was proving a point. She would make it up to him later.

The cleric led her to the open double doors of the church, though he remained outside as she entered the rectangular space. Symmachus was already there with Victor, the two men dressed in formal togas and leaning against wooden benches at the front of the church. A life-sized model of Christ, nailed by the hands and feet to a wooden cross, hung on the marble-faced wall behind them. As with most renditions of the man's execution that she had seen, the Christian god was thin, long-haired and bearded. He looked upward with an expression of pleading agony, streams of blood coating his cheeks from his crown of thorns.

As she reached the front of the church and the two men conversing there—the words *famine* and *crisis* hung in the air—she bowed her head in greeting.

"*Salve*, Caesar." She turned to Symmachus. "Prefect."

"Good morning, High Priestess," said Victor. He smiled at her presentation. "A pearl among the barley."

"We've been discussing the theft along the grain routes," said Symmachus.

"I have news of even greater drama," Coelia replied. She adopted the stance of the two men and rested against a wooden bench, facing them with a sportive affectation and a private desperate prayer that Victor hadn't yet heard the news. "They caught a lion last night."

"Ah ha!" exclaimed Victor. "Where?"

She leaned forward slightly, playing into the dramatics of it. "In the catacombs, if you can believe it. The hunters tracked it to the area, but it escaped down a shaft and they had to chase it through the tunnels for hours. Can you imagine?"

"I can," Victor replied enthusiastically. This was exactly the kind of Roman excitement he had come to the *Caput Mundi* to experience. "What else?"

"One of the hunters was killed. The beast ripped his arm right out of its socket, and he bled to death. There was a tomb painter in the catacombs at the time. He was injured, but still managed to throw a bottle of perfume at the thing. That distracted it long enough for the other hunters to take it down. They say the man's a hero."

"What theater!" said Victor. "Brilliant. So the painter lived?"

"He did," said Coelia. "He left half his backside in the tunnels, but emerged with a third of the reward. A net gain, I would say." Both Victor and Symmachus laughed out loud.

His thoughts turning to more serious matters, Victor signalled to the cleric still standing by the church's entrance. The man closed the doors from the outside.

"I value my friendship with you both," said Victor. "That is why I am at least grateful that you will hear this from me. Bad news is worse when delivered by the unfriendly." He glanced at Symmachus, giving the strategist the opportunity to guess.

"Emperor Valentinian has rejected my petition to return the Altar of Victory to the Senate House," he said.

"Unfortunately, yes," replied Victor. "Although I did persuade him to order the return of some statuary and other riches looted from temples. It was the best I could do under the circumstances. Strictly speaking, I am not Caesar of Italy. I must respect the bounds of my imperium." He looked at Coelia. "He likewise refused to restore your funding."

"I expected no other outcome, Caesar," said Coelia. *Especially not now*, she thought.

Since the famine had struck, and as circumstances grew more direful by the day, an increasing number of voices had been calling for the return of public pagan rites and the reopening of shuttered temples. But Coelia suspected the emperors and their bishops would let Romans turn to eating each other before they let them turn back to their gods.

"I read your relatio," Victor said to Symmachus. "It was an eloquent plea for the freedom of thought and belief that Rome was built on." He extended his arms, reciting Symmachus's words, words he had clearly read more than once. "'We see the same stars, we share the same sky, the same world is ours. What should it matter by what knowledge each one comes to the truth? By only one path, we cannot arrive at so vast a secret.'" He rested his hands on his thighs. "Your defence of the Vestal Virgins and your pleas to respect Rome's ancient customs were equally compelling." He shook his head. "Valentinian's father was a reasonable man and no harsh persecutor of pagans. I had hoped he would follow his father's example."

"As had I, Caesar."

"The word from Mediolanum is that Ambrosius panicked when he heard of your relatio," said Victor. "He got his hands on a copy before Valentinian had even finished reading it. He then wrote a rebuttal to the emperor and sealed it, or so I'm told, with the threat of excommunication. I've read the rebuttal myself. It is full of the usual mockery and sanctimony, which is unsurprising. His envy of your Ciceronian reputation is well known. Regardless, I've had my scribe make copies for both of you. I wouldn't read it sober." Victor frowned. "You should also know that Ambrosius didn't act alone. Damascus told Valentinian that the Christian senators vehemently opposed the presence of the altar. He even presented a list of dissenting names."

Symmachus looked surprised. A rare reaction. "There is no such list, Caesar," he said. "These falsifications grow by the day."

Victor released a heavy, exaggerated sigh of discontent. "It would be different if Rome were ruled by another breed of Caesar—a Christian Caesar, to be sure—but one strong enough to curb the self-serving antics of the bishops and restore legislative powers to the Senate. We need an emperor capable of restocking the army with loyal soldiers who can protect our borders, and who respect the customs and virtues that, as you said in your relatio, brought the whole world under Rome's sway." He paused and looked at Symmachus for a long, expectant moment.

"We are agreed," Symmachus said forcefully. "Rome needs another breed of Caesar."

"My father plans to invade Italy," Victor revealed, the bold admission suffused with a gravitas that Coelia had never before heard in a man's voice. "He wishes to be Caesar of the entire Roman Empire, and I with him. With your support, with your influence in the Senate and among the military, we can achieve it."

Immediately, without so much as a moment's reflection, Symmachus extended his arm. "You have my support, Caesar. To the end."

Victor clasped his arm. "*Gratias tibi ago, mi amice.*"

Coelia's mind was working so fast she felt perspiration under her dress. She had long known that Victor had treasonous intentions. Driven by her vitriol for the bishops and persecutory emperors—they had nearly killed Claudia—she had even courted involvement by helping him align himself with the right people in Rome. It had almost seemed like a private game, a way to pretend that she had the power to exact some kind of revenge upon the enemies of the Order, from the shadows, just as the influential Vestals of years gone by had done. But now she was being dragged into the light.

Victor looked at her, waiting.

"You have my support as well, Caesar," she said. "To the end."

"*Gratias ago, Sacerdos.*" His demeanor relaxed now that their common purpose was in the open. "The time has come for you to use your influence with General Arbogastes," he said to the Vestal. "He and I have become friends, but he will not approve of my father's actions. I don't wish to make an enemy of him."

"We have been dining together quite often these past weeks," said Coelia, keeping her eyes on Victor but wondering what Symmachus would make of that revelation. "I will make whatever inroads I can, Caesar."

"Very good," said Victor.

"Nourish a deeper friendship with him," added Symmachus. "It may be crucial."

The comment was heavy with an implication that Coelia would never have expected the Pontifex Maximus to make, certainly not one as rigidly devout as Symmachus. The suggestion only amplified the magnitude of their cause. She felt her perspiration worsen.

Symmachus crossed his arms. "Your father's legions," he said to Victor, quickly turning to the business of usurpation. "Which are the strongest?"

Before Victor could reply, Coelia interjected. "Caesar, I bring nothing to this discussion. With your permission, I will return to my duties until called upon."

He nodded. "Go with confidence."

As the two men fell into a hushed discussion of logistics, Coelia made her way back down the church aisle and stepped into the airy freedom of the outside world. The cleric who had met her upon her arrival was standing a few steps away.

"Caesar has business with the prefect and does not wish to be disturbed," she said to him. "Keep the doors closed."

Without waiting for him to escort her back to her carpentum, she retread her steps along the red stone pathway and caught the attention of her chatting guards. The boy-faced Teo quickly disengaged and opened the vehicle's rear door.

"A messenger left a scroll for you, High Priestess," he said. "I put it inside."

"Thank you, Teo."

She stepped inside the carriage and exhaled a trembling breath as the door closed behind her, cocooning her within the safety of solitude. She pulled off her tiara and veil, ignoring the painful snags and leftover hairpins, and collapsed onto the silk cushion of the sumptuous interior. She pushed her face into the smooth fabric and groaned as the carriage began to roll along.

Immortal gods of heaven and earth, she thought, as the cold sweat on her limbs sent a shiver through her body. *I hope I have not made the worst mistake of my life.*

Victor would expect more from her than just wielding any influence she could muster over General Arbogastes. He would also expect money. Specifically, the money kept in the secret coffers of Vesta's temple. It was money that had been hidden from the state since the time of the Vestalis Maxima Occia, an emergency fund to be used only in times of civil war to covertly finance whatever faction supported the Vestal Order. And it was Coelia who had so clumsily alluded to its existence during her first meeting with him. Even then he had been strategizing how he would pay his legions and bribe his way to the curule chair. Whether he had played her from the beginning or whether his friendship was sincere, she couldn't know.

Drained and now looking as disheveled as she felt, she pushed herself upright. In the silk pocket of the vehicle's interior, she spotted the scroll and retrieved it with a sigh. At the sight of the wax seal, however, the tension that had been slowly leaving her body returned with sudden force. The scroll wasn't from Caesar.

Rather, it was from the Office of the Basilica of Mediolanum and addressed to her by name. She broke the seal and read:

Lady Coelia,

On the occasion of the faithful Emperor Valentinian's refusal to restore the funding of your heathen temple, you are urged to avoid the disgrace of your predecessor and instead find redemption in the Lord. Like Rome, like the whole world, you should not be ashamed to convert. Rather, adopt the sweet chastity of the bashful virgins who serve Christ out of virtue, who delight in poverty, while the Vestals sell their virginity for a price. Accept that your rewards, the rich banquets, the pomp and extravagances, the purple-trimmed veils and set term of your virginity cannot save your order. Look to the good works of Lady Marcella on the Aventine, whose reputation far exceeds yours. Follow her example. Open the house of the Vestals to the poor as she has opened her home to them.

Why persist in stubbornness? Like the illustrious prefect of Rome and your fellow pagans, you support that which cannot be true. It is right that Rome moves from godless superstition to the truth of Christ. It is right that your customs die, for they do not agree with ours, and we Christians know what you do not know. There are not many paths. There is only the path of the savior. Accept the truth that he who named you Concordia—I speak of Julian the Apostate— came to accept. His dying words were, "Christ, you have won!" You too can—

Coelia pulled one of the hairpins from her tangled hair and stabbed the papyrus as if with a blade, shredding the paper into little bits that landed all around her like miserable confetti. She scooped the pieces up in her hands and shoved them past the curtain, throwing them outside onto the street and again collapsing onto the cushion in a heap of anger. The emperor Julian had never spoken those words.

She closed her eyes, but could not block out the sight of the words on the papyrus. Claudia had received similar letters over the years, always written by an anonymous hand from the basilica, though peppered with the bishop Ambrosius's words and teachings, often on female virginity. The work, perhaps, of an overzealous scribe or clergyman. Ambrosius himself would never write to a Vestal. He preferred to insult the Vestal Virgins in his texts while pressuring the emperors to strip the Vestal Order of its status and power.

As Coelia breathed through her rage, reminding herself what it had done to the last Vestalis Maxima, she decided that she didn't care if Victor's friendship was strategic or sincere. They had a shared purpose—to destroy the enemies of Rome. Not the ones outside the gates, but the ones inside. The ones who, as Cicero had said, undermine the pillars of the city from within. If it would take war to restore the concord of Romulus's vision to the Eternal City, then so be it.

CHAPTER XIX

The feathers fell like rain on top of Arbo's stable located on his large Quirinal Hill estate. Below, the structure comfortably housed thirty horses. Above, it supported a city of pigeons housed in fifteen separate columbaria that, along with supplementary structures like feeders and baths, covered just about every foot of the rooftop. The birds flew and fluttered overhead, forming winged clouds and cyclones of energy, landing in groups to splash in a water basin before flapping off to peck at the bread crumbs that Coelia and Arbo tossed all around. Rome might be starving, but the general's pigeons were plump and happy, feeding on premium grain.

"I would hate to know what the top of my veil looks like," the Vestal said to Arbo.

He checked, and grimaced. "It is still white," he said. "Though it is good you brought another. With all the down stuck to your head, the Forum guards might mistake you for one of Juno's great white geese and cart you off to the Capitoline."

He laughed at his own joke. For someone who had slain countless men on the battlefield, and under the most horrific of circumstances, his jokes—his whole temperament, really—seemed to Coelia usually tame, even wholesome. He just didn't seem to have that edge of ruthlessness, of violent ambition, she had seen in other soldiers like Bauto or even Stilicho. She sometimes wondered how Arbo had risen so high in the military. Perhaps he wore his armor like she wore her veil: dutifully and competently, but with the nagging sensation that it didn't quite fit. Or perhaps he just kept the fiercer side of himself from her so they could find peace in their time together. After the recent goading letter she had received from the basilica in Mediolanum, she needed all the peace she could get.

That is why she had stepped away from a desk full of work and had her guard Teo escort her to Arbo's estate. While Teo was helping the general's stablemen shoe some horses—the boy was a natural equestrian—she was spending the day on Arbo's rooftop, helping him repair dovecotes while awaiting the return of some racing pigeons whose speed he was testing.

Fifty of his most promising birds had been released from Sicilia at sunrise, and the fastest of the flock were expected to arrive back home in Rome before sundown. For Arbo, it was a big day, and he could barely contain his anticipation. For Coelia, watching him was as enjoyable as watching for his birds, and sharing in his excitement was the perfect distraction. Indeed, over the last month or so, Arbo had become her favorite distraction. The feeling was mutual.

The first hue of sunset had just painted the sky when Coelia spotted a white speck in the distance. "Is that one of them?" she asked, pointing to the south.

Arbo followed her gaze. "It is," he said happily. "You are a good little augur."

"I could spend all day out in the open on the *auguraculum*, looking for signs from the gods in the flight of birds. A good job. Until it rains, at least."

But Arbo wasn't really listening. He was too absorbed in the bird's approach. "This confirms my suspicion," he said with satisfaction.

"The birds will not fly over the sea, but will choose to follow the land."

"How do you know that?"

"Because we would've seen them return by midday if they'd crossed the sea." He turned to her, a smug grin on his face. "Helvius owes me two stallions. He said they'd take the water."

"Poor Helvius," said Coelia.

Arbo kept grinning, kept looking up, as the pigeon drew closer. It landed on the ledge of its home dovecote and tilted its head, eyelids blinking rapidly over large eyes. Arbo scooped it up and cradled it in the crook of his arm, holding it steady as he removed the small piece of papyrus tied to its right leg. He released the bird and unfurled the paper, reading the print upon it. His voice was slightly breathless with the thrill of it all.

"This is Velox," he said. "Record him as number one."

"Yes, Patrone," Coelia replied lightly. She picked a wax tablet off a stool. Finding the bird's name in the ledger, she documented the information. "Velox is the first." She looked at Arbo. "Maybe we should put the last in the dinner pot."

"As you wish," said Arbo.

Coelia scoffed. "You coo at them more than they coo at you. I would like to see the day you have the heart to close the lid on one of them. Look at old Saxum over there, lazing in the bath all day. He's missing a leg and he's so fat you have to carry him to his pigeonhole at night. Good meat on those bones, yet he lives."

Arbo laughed, but despite his joviality and the amusement Coelia found in their task, the aggravating memory of the anonymous letter she had received from the basilica in Mediolanum days earlier suddenly returned, as it had repeatedly done all day long. She could not stop rereading the words in her mind.

Look to the good works of Lady Marcella on the Aventine, whose reputation far exceeds yours. Follow her example. Open the house of the Vestals to the poor as she has opened her home to them.

"The Aventine..." muttered Coelia. "You heard about the ascetics who were staying there. The ones who left Rome before they could even be investigated for—"

"I set aside some fresh peas for the first birds to arrive," interrupted Arbo, gesturing to a terracotta pot by one of the dovecotes. "Go get some for Velox." He looked at her. "Why ruin a nice day talking about such people?"

Coelia retrieved the peas and fed Velox, frustrated with herself for continually going back to the same well and drinking the same poison. It wasn't any more fun for Arbo than it was for her.

Accept the truth that he who named you Concordia—I speak of Julian the Apostate—came to accept. His dying words were, "Christ, you have won!"

But it wasn't just aggravation that Coelia felt. Ever since Victor had revealed his intent to become Caesar of Rome, Coelia had felt something else growing inside her... a seed of defiance against those who had for too long slandered her and her sisters with impunity... a seed of resistance against those who conspired to relegate the Vestal Virgins to the ashes of history so the Christian virgins—they wore a copy of the Vestal veil, though they wore it in poverty and subordination—had no competition. Her mind's eye returned to the sight of Claudia's statue being toppled in the courtyard, its head breaking off and the soldier tucking its gold jeweled necklace into his belt. She could still see Antonia's bloody hands trembling as she chiseled Claudia's name off the marble base. If Magnus Maximus and Victor succeeded in taking Rome, Coelia vowed to herself that she wouldn't just replace Claudia's statue, she would gild it in bronze. And she wouldn't stop there. She would give all of Rome a good chastising for letting it happen in the first place.

"Did I tell you that I gave Caesar a tour of the Tabularium yesterday?" she asked Arbo, who was now refilling a basin with clean water for his birds.

"No. How did it go?"

"The same as always. Whether he's reading an ancient record or climbing Trajan's Column, he's equally impressed." She pointed at a white spot in the sky. "Look, Arbo. I think that's another one."

"So it is."

The bird drew closer, circled, and landed on its home columbarium with a little stamping of its pink feet. It fluffed its feathers as Arbo scooped it up and removed the papyrus around its leg. "Silva is number two," he said, dropping the papyrus to the ground. "Make a note."

Coelia did. As Arbo let go of the bird and tossed it some bread crumbs, she bent down to retrieve the small rectangle of papyrus that had been fastened to its leg. She stared at the words printed upon it: SILVA • VIA SACRA T CONCORDIAE

"Arbo," she said. "Where did you say the birds were released from?"

"From the temple city of Agrigento in Sicilia."

"The papyrus says the Temple of Concordia."

"Yes," he said, looking upward as more incoming birds appeared in the sky. "It's a good landmark."

Coelia looked back at the paper. She hadn't been searching for signs from the gods in the flight of Arbo's birds, and yet she had found one just the same.

It was midday in the Roman Forum. Government offices, civic trials, public tribunals and merchant shops temporarily suspended their functions or services, the booms and hammers of construction ceased, and everyone turned their attention toward the day's most pressing matter so far—what to have for lunch. Senators and shoppers, lawyers and taxpayers, they all made their way to the Basilica Julia to purchase sustenance from the vendor stalls that lined its peristyle. Yet as they perused the food stalls, they grumbled along with their stomachs to discover that the famine had simultaneously increased the cost of food and decreased the pleasure of it. A fresh, thick wedge of bread made with the tastiest ingredients used to cost less than a *sestertius*. Now, a stale slice of gum-shredding crust cost triple. A decent cup of wine used to cost five *asses*. Now, half a cup of slave's *posca* cost double.

To make matters worse, more than half of the food stalls in the city were unmanned. Some vendors were tired of having their stores cleared out by thieves, while others were hoarding what they could for their own families. The food shortage was causing as much panic as the three still-at-large Gilded Lions of Rome, one of which had been spotted the day earlier picking dry the bones of a hungry mother and daughter who had been plucking berries on the side of the *Via Labicana*. It had bolted away before an effort to capture it could be mounted. But as the graffiti scribbled on the city's buildings and bridges noted with optimism, SED LEONES SATURI SUNT. *At least the lions are full.*

It was against this backdrop that the midday crowd in the Forum saw—or rather heard, and then saw—a most unusual display.

"All make way for the Holy Virgins of Vesta!"

Approaching from the east, six *lictors*—prestigious attendants of magistrates, emperors and Vestal Virgins—strode regally along the Via Sacra, leading a procession of three bronze-embossed chariots. Each chariot was drawn by a pair of meticulously groomed white horses, their manes and tails interwoven with red silk ribbons. Inside each chariot stood two Vestal Virgins dressed in their formal attire. One priestess drove the horses ahead with effortless skill, while the other stood and regarded the crowd with a look of commanding dignity that sent many to their knees. As the red wheels of the chariots turned, like circles of flame spinning around and around, the gold spokes caught the sunlight and threw fiery reflections against the white marble of the structures they passed.

"All make way for the Holy Virgins of Vesta!"

The Vestalis Maxima Coelia Concordia rode in the first chariot with Priestess Domitia, who drove the horses. In the middle chariot rode the priestesses Proculeia and Terentia, followed in the third chariot by the priestesses Sergia and Galeria. At the back of the procession marched six more lictors carrying the *fasces*, the ancient symbol of Roman authority—an axe within a bundle of smooth sticks.

The procession moved along the Via Sacra, parting the crowds and eliciting gasps of surprise and wonder, everyone forgetting lunch and walking alongside the chariots to see where this pageantry was headed to. They followed it all the way to the foot of the Capitoline Hill and the wide staircase of the Temple of Concordia. As befitting its dedication to the goddess of concord, the temple was often used for senatorial meetings during times of civic crisis. But perhaps most uniquely, it also served as Rome's finest museum, one that housed the empire's most splendid works of art. It was a shrine not just to Concordia, but to the Eternal City itself.

The procession stopped at the bottom of the staircase, and the Vestals stepped out of their chariots to follow Coelia up the steps toward the wide platform at the top, upon which burned an altar fire. The spectacle of the six resplendent priestesses ascending the staircase together, the way they moved with ostentatious confidence, was a rare sight, and by the time they reached the decorated marble landing, a large and mesmerized crowd had gathered to watch.

Coelia ordered the doors to the temple opened wide, revealing the bright marble statue of the goddess Concordia inside, seated on a throne. Adjacent to the goddess of harmony stood a life-sized bronze statue of Vesta. Against this majestic backdrop, the chief Vestal moved closer to the altar fire, letting those congregated below absorb the powerful imagery of her white ritual stola, the deep red and white ribbons of her infula, and her crimson-bordered suffibulum, the veil pinned at the breastbone by a large gold medallion. Domitia stood close but slightly behind her, while the other priestesses stood on either side in pairs. Lifting her arms, Coelia addressed the crowd.

"I am Coelia Concordia, High Priestess of the Roman Order of Vestal Virgins. Behold the goddess from whom I take my name, holy Concordia. Behold also the goddess that I serve, Mother Vesta." Here, she glanced at the statue of Vesta before turning back to the crowd. "This statue of Vesta, holy virgin of the Roman Empire, was brought to this temple from the islands of Roman Hestia by Tiberius Caesar. That Caesar, like so many others, knew that Rome's survival depended on reverence for the goddess, on the perpetuity of her sacred flame, and that the concord between Rome and the gods could be entrusted to us, Vesta's consecrated virgins." She paused, letting a murmur move through the gathering, and then continued. "Rome starves because its people have broken the pax deorum with the gods. It is my duty, as the guardian of the flame and your Vestalis Maxima, to make this public offering to the ancestral gods and goddesses of Rome so that harmony may be restored to our souls and to our nation."

At that, Domitia retrieved a round sacred wafer from a terracotta vessel on the altar. Made with the Vestals' mola salsa, the virgins had for centuries been tasked with creating the holy wafers and using them to purify sacrificial offerings to the gods. Domitia passed the sacred cake to Coelia, and the chief Vestal held it high enough for those gathered to see the pagan cross stamped upon it. There would be no more cowering. These were the Vestal Virgins and their traditions. Their duty.

Coelia held the wafer over the fire that burned on the altar. "*Vesta Sancta*," she said, crumbling the wafer into the flames. "We six, your virgin priestesses, make this offering in honor of the ancient and peaceful accord between Rome and the gods. We do so on behalf of the Emperor, the Senate, and the people of Rome."

The murmurs grew louder, but were hushed by the devout. It had been a long time since pagan Romans had seen such a bold display of their customs.

Coelia looked upon those who had gathered below. "This famine is a plague of impiety," she said. "Go home. Offer to the goddess that burns in your hearthfire. Feel the warmth of her breath on your face. Hear her voice in the crackles of the fire. The goddess loves you. Rekindle your love for her. Restore concord with the immortal gods, and Ceres will again touch our harvests with her shining hands. Reclaim the dignity to honor the gods in your heart, just as those who built this temple—this temple to Concordia, to our past, to our future—had the liberty to do. I say this in the name of Father Quirinus and our holy virgin, Vesta."

CHAPTER XX

"Aeneas, Son of Heaven, art thou on watch? Keep watch."

Ignited in the founding year of the city, the eternal fire of Vesta had burned in the same spot in the Roman Forum for over ten centuries, watched over and kept alight by the Vestal Virgins. But the goddess's flames were much older than that. They had sprung from the sacred hearthfire of Troy that had existed for thousands of years before Rome's birth. As the Trojan city fell to the invading Greeks, the Trojan hero Aeneas had escaped to the shores of Italy with embers from Vesta's fire, embers that he and his descendants had nourished back to vibrant life in cities like Lavinium, Alba Longa and finally Romulus's Rome, each city appointing Vestal priestesses as guardians of the goddess's perpetual fire.

So as the Vestalis Maxima Coelia Concordia stood with her sister priestesses in the circular sanctity of the Temple of Vesta and invoked the name of holy Aeneas on this day, the annual renewal of the sacred fire on the kalends of March—the first day of the new year according to the old Roman calendar—she did so with the poignant and humbling awareness that she was but one of countless women who had spoken the same words, said the same prayers, performed the same rites. It was that pious constancy that had maintained the peaceful accord between Rome and her gods. It was that certainty of purpose that had secured the protection of the gods and brought comfort and unity to the city from its earliest days to this day.

Coelia looked down into the wide bronze firebowl set into the round marble altar. The fire had been carefully supervised to the point where only a few red embers still glowed in the gray ash. Domitia passed her a terracotta *culullus* and the chief Vestal carefully poured wine over the embers to extinguish the old fire. It was a frightening act, but death was necessary for the fire to be reborn with renewed strength. Or perhaps it wasn't death followed by rebirth. Perhaps it was, as Claudia had always said, a brief slumber followed by a reawakening.

In complete silence, the priestess Proculeia lifted the bronze firebowl off the altar while Terentia set a new firebowl in its place. Inside were dried grasses from Vesta's grove arranged in a birds-nest formation, plus two smoothened branches of oak taken from Jupiter's sacred *arbor felix* and made suitable to start a friction fire. Yet the sunlight flooding into the temple from above convinced Coelia to try an even purer method of ignition, so she removed the branches and accepted a polished bronze *vasculum* from Sergia. Positioning the tool to catch the sunbeam streaming into the sanctum through the oculus, Coelia directed the beam's focus onto the tinder. The other priestesses stood around the altar, palms up in silent prayer to Vesta and Sol.

"*Vesta Aeterna*," said Coelia. "First and last, your inviolate priestess begs you to enter the sun's flame so that we may renew your eternal fire."

After several moments, a black spot appeared in the tinder, followed by a small red ember ignited by the force of the sun. More embers soon appeared, spreading into infant flames that began to consume the tinder and send delicate wisps of smoke upward. Coelia passed the bronze implement to Domitia and leaned over the newborn fire, covering her mouth with the fabric of her veil so as not to overwhelm the fledgling flames. Softly, so softly that not even the other priestesses could catch the words, she whispered the words of the Precatio Vestae, the secret sacred prayer that called upon the goddess to enter the rekindled fire.

"*Laus Vestae*," said Coelia, as the fire grew in size and strength, "*ignis inexstinctus*."

Following the pattern prescribed by the Vestalis Maxima, the priestess Galeria gently placed six strips of sanctified oak into the fire. The moving orange flames spread out to explore the nourishment while the thin wisps of smoke thickened and swirled up and out the oculus. Soon after, the first snaps and crackles of Vesta's fiery voice popped out of the fire to resonate within the round marble walls of the temple.

As Coelia crumbled a sacred wafer into the holy flames and the other Vestals offered gentle libations, the sound of an exuberant collective cheer embraced the temple. The priestesses exchanged happy smiles. Many people had gathered around the temple, along the Via Sacra and out farther into the Forum to observe the annual renewal of Vesta's fire. They had been watching from the street, from the high steps of the neighboring temple of the *Dioscuri*, and from the large square in the center of the Forum as the smoke from Vesta's domed roof first disappeared then reappeared. Coelia had not heard the joy of such a large pagan gathering since she was a child under Emperor Julian.

"That is a good sign," said Domitia.

"It's a sign of piety," added Terentia, "and of full stomachs."

They all knew why the hunger pangs had ceased. Coelia's bold public offering on the steps of the Temple of Concordia had ended the famine. It had brought the people back to the gods, the gods back to the city and the grain back to the warehouses.

The chief Vestal brushed the crumbs from the sacred cake off her formal stola and touched her head, making sure her veil was still properly positioned.

"Continue with the prayers," she instructed the other Vestals. "I need to greet Sacerdos Symmachus. The day can't be perfect."

Coelia crossed the floor of the temple and opened one of the bronze doors, the bright sunlight striking her eyes. The size of the gathered crowd, now socializing under scarlet banners emblazoned with the letters *SPQR*, again took her by pleasant surprise. The *flamines maiores*—the high priests of Jupiter, Mars and Quirinus—were present, as were various other priests and their wives, many of whom also held positions in temples around the city. She spotted Paulina by the Regia, overseeing the distribution of fine cakes donated from her personal stores in memory of her husband Praetextatus, who had recently passed away. Even in death, the man celebrated Vesta and cared for Rome. Behind her, Victor—looking every inch the Caesar—conversed with Lucilla and Olympius, plus a number of other high-ranking senators and soldiers, including Arbo. Deimos was there, too, looking a little lost without Brogos by his side, though the fawning young women mustered around him competed to fill the void.

Just down the Via Sacra, before the doors of the nearby House of the Vestals, an assortment of jewelry, perfume, small paintings and ivory ornaments had been left as gifts for the Vestal Virgins. For a moment, Coelia felt as if she had been transported back in time, back to the ages where the whole city, the entire empire, celebrated the renewal of the sacred flame.

She caught sight of Symmachus. Dressed in the robes of the Pontifex Maximus and holding a golden vessel with garnet and pearl inlay, he wore a look of pride. She descended the steps to speak with him.

"High Priestess," he greeted. He passed her the rich vessel. "*Oleum ex albis ulivis est.* Offer this libation to the goddess on behalf of the Senate."

"Of course, Sacerdos." She viewed the crowd. "Times have changed."

"There is not a temple in Rome with empty steps," said Symmachus, watching as temple attendants ascended ladders and began to wrap fresh garlands of laurel around the sanctum's columns. "Some

Christians are converting, but the greatest numbers come from those who have been merely living as Christians. They are putting the gods back on their larariums." He checked over his shoulder. Seeing no one within earshot, he continued. "I have just spoken with Caesar. His father's invasion of Italy is imminent. Once it happens, the Senate will proclaim the two of them co-emperors of Rome. You cannot delay any longer. You must push the matter with General Arbogastes. Today."

"I will," Coelia replied.

"There is one more thing. I have learned that you are commissioning a statue of Praetextatus."

"Yes, I am. What of it?" The reply was more defensive than Coelia had planned, but it was too late now.

"I do not need to dictate religious custom to you," said Symmachus, "but it is highly unusual for the Vestal Order to commission statues of men."

"Unusual, but certainly not unheard of," replied Coelia.

"You must be careful not to overstep the traditional bounds of your posting. We are at a pivotal place, religiously speaking. Custom must prevail."

"Pontiff," said Coelia. "You encourage me to exploit the general's interest in me to advance our cause, but you chide me for commissioning a statue? Praetextatus was a close friend of the Order, and Lady Paulina still is. We will show our respect for his legacy in the way that we see fit."

"Of course. Yet—"

"I can assure you, Pontiff," continued Coelia, her irritation growing. "The statue will be fully clothed."

Symmachus's expression tightened. "That is not the concern."

"We can agree on that much," said Coelia. "I hope we can also agree that we have much larger concerns."

A young girl in the simple white tunica and veil of a novice Vestal approached Coelia. She bounced on her feet, waiting for permission to speak. When Coelia nodded, the girl asked, "High Priestess, can we do it now?"

The girl's appearance interrupted the escalating discussion, and Coelia smiled at her as much in gratitude as affection. "Yes, Rufinia. Go ahead."

The novice let out a squeak of excitement and waved to three other novices. Together, they began to hand out baskets of figs to the children waiting around the temple. Soon, figs were flying through the air to the sound of laughter as the children gleefully competed to throw them onto the roof of the temple, aiming for the oculus. It was the one day of the year where the sacred fire accepted the sweet offerings from Rome's children, and in the way that only children could think to offer it. An old and forgotten custom, Coelia had stumbled upon it in the Regia's archives and had decided to revive it.

Yet as she had expected, it didn't take long for the fig-throwing to take a mischievous trajectory. Within moments, the temple attendants on the ladders found themselves pelted with the fruit, reacting with exaggerated cries of pain, dropping the garlands of laurel they carried and clinging to their ladders for dear life. Their overplayed cries — "*Stop! Stop! You're killing me!*" and "*Your aim is terrible!*" — sent the children into wild-eyed fits of laughter as their parents applauded the attendants' self-sacrificing performance.

Symmachus chuckled at the show. That was a relief, and a surprise, to Coelia. Not only was the custom an irreverent one, but she had not discussed it with him beforehand and had fully expected a rebuke. After all, he had sent a total of five letters chastising her for not consulting him before making her speech on the steps of Concordia's temple, even while admitting it had catalyzed important change. Perhaps he was finally making his peace with the fact that she, and not Antonia, had inherited the office of the Vestalis Maxima. Perhaps he felt hope on the eve of Magnus Maximus's invasion. Or perhaps he just didn't want to argue with her again on this special day. Regardless, it was good to see him smile.

"Praise our loving goddess," he said, as the figs flew overhead.

"*Nunc et semper,*" Coelia replied.

✳   ✳   ✳

As if illustrating the old statesman Seneca's sentiment that one who suffers before it is necessary suffers more than is necessary, it so happened that Coelia's worst fears surrounding the Vestal Order's loss of state funding hadn't materialized. Indeed, the amount of the traditional stipend had been surpassed by the personal donations of pagan benefactors. The biggest worry had been the state's hijacking of legacies left to the Order, though thankfully, the last few chief Vestals had hidden bequests with the same zeal they had hidden the relics.

But the matter went beyond money. As esteemed priestesses and legally independent women, the Vestals had long enjoyed additional privileges and rights not possessed by other women or even men. The right to move about the city in a lectica or a carpentum, these transports having the right of way in all circumstances. The right to speak in the Senate House and to testify in court, to buy and sell property, to run a profitable business and to emancipate slaves and pardon prisoners. The right to be accompanied at all times by guards and to enjoy prestigious seating in the amphitheater and Circus Maximus. Neither Coelia nor any of the other Vestals had stopped benefitting from any of these customary entitlements, and no one had tried to change that.

That's why, as she usually did when travelling outside the Forum, Coelia rode to the Campus Martius—the Field of Mars—in the same horse-drawn carriage she had taken to the church of Laurentius on the day Victor had revealed his father's plans to invade Italy. The only difference, it seemed, was the growing number of people on the street who, instead of just moving aside so the lavish carriage could pass, actually stopped to bow or kneel out of respect for the passing Vestal Virgin.

As her carriage arrived at its destination, Coelia pulled back the silk curtain to admire the massive multilayered rotunda of the Mausoleum of Augustus. Built in the style of the earliest Etruscan tombs, though reimagined with the grandeur necessary to house the ashes of Rome's first emperor, the towering structure had been built in tiers and faced with white Luna marble. The topmost temple-like portion of the tomb was ringed by a small forest of cypress trees and crowned with a colossal bronze statue of Augustus, his arm raised to command not just his legions, but the whole world. The sprawling memorial complex also boasted manicured flower gardens and fragrant orchards full of birdsong. Peacocks leisurely strolled along the marble pathways, perturbed only by the occasional chattering squirrel darting past.

Teo opened the door at the rear of the carriage and Coelia stepped out. Now dressed in a belted tunica and informal veil instead of her full Vestal regalia, she felt more relaxed than she had all day. She reached back to retrieve the lit oil lamp she had brought with her from the temple, the one that burned with Vesta's renewed flame, and carried it toward the obelisks and bronze tablets that decorated the mausoleum's entrance. The tablets were inscribed with the *Res Gestae*, Augustus's own account of his greatest accomplishments and deeds, which included his generosity toward the Vestals.

Crossing the columned threshold and entering the cylindrical inner chamber, she moved deeper into the enormous structure, smiling despite the solemnity of the space to find Arbo already there. He was standing in front of a marble niche and admiring the life-sized gilded statue of General Agrippa that stood by the funerary urn of the man's ashes. As Augustus's powerful general and dearest friend, the emperor had ordered that Agrippa's ashes would rest with his own for all eternity.

"Rome's generals are a handsome sort, aren't they?" Arbo asked grinningly as he looked at Agrippa's statue.

"The gilding process covers any flaws," Coelia wisecracked.

He feigned a wounded scoff, and she moved to the large niche that contained the golden funerary urn of Augustus's ashes. The urn sat on a marble pedestal, behind which a larger-than-life gold statue of the emperor gazed down at the tomb's visitors, his subjects, even in death. She set the oil lamp on the pedestal and lowered her head, speaking to the emperor across the ages and bringing the renewed flame of his empire before him.

"*Divine Augustus,*" she said, "*fida sacerdos tua Imperii tui renovatam flammam tibi fert.*"

Arbo allowed her a few moments of silence as he studied the other statues and urns in the chamber. The empress Livia Drusilla was there, as was Augustus's beloved sister Octavia and his favored nephew Marcellus. Arbo could imagine them all together in life, dining or strategizing or arguing, celebrating or grieving, talking about the matters of empire and their plans for the future. How quickly death, which did not distinguish between great and small, could silence such discourse.

"Bauto and I came here together years ago to honor Agrippa," he said. "Seems like yesterday."

"I was sorry to hear of his passing," said Coelia, suddenly hating herself for not mentioning it sooner. She had learned of Bauto's death the day before and had intended to send a messenger to Arbo with her condolences, but with the business of the flame's renewal, it had slipped her mind. "I know he was like a father to you." She realized the scope of her words before she had finished speaking them. "*Was* he your father?"

Arbo shrugged. "I don't know. I do know that he slept his way through Germania for forty years, and my mother was en route, so it's possible."

"Did you ever talk to him about it?"

"No. He had a wife and family."

"I see."

Arbo shook off his melancholy. He had a happier purpose for meeting her here and had been waiting for this special day to tell her. "I have news," he said. "Victor gifted me the old villa of Agrippa along the Tiber."

"That is wonderful," Coelia said with exuberance.

"That bloody Brogos! He told you, didn't he? I made him swear to Harpocrates he would keep his big mouth—"

"You can't open the gate and blame the goat for escaping."

"I do miss the bastard," reflected Arbo. He clapped his hands together, the sound echoing in the chamber. "Come see it. The frescos are the finest in Rome."

"Come see your villa? Now?"

"Why not?"

"Because I cannot swim."

"It is not underwater," assured Arbo. "Well, not *all* of it. I will carry you over the puddles."

"Who could say no?" Coelia followed him out of the mausoleum and back toward her carriage. Her young guard Teo's caution had grown commensurate with the increased attention on the Vestal Order, and he looked relieved to see it was Arbo at her side. "I am going to see the general's new villa," she said to him. "He will ride with us."

"Yes, High Priestess," replied the guard, as he helped her into the back of the carriage.

As Arbo and Teo fell into conversation over the horses, Coelia noted the friendly way the general interacted with her guard. It was typical of how he treated everyone, whether senator, soldier or servant. It was remarkable that a pagan of such humble origin and disposition had risen so high in the service of the elitist Theodosius, but considering the constant threat of the barbarians and the declining number of quality recruits, merit still counted for something in the military. Yet it wasn't just the high powers in Constantinople that trusted him. From what Coelia had been told by men under his command, men like Stilicho, the self-effacing General Arbogastes made it a practice to eat the same tasteless gruel and sleep in the same damp tents as his subordinates. If a wagon got stuck in the mud, he helped pull it out. That comradeship, as much as skill, had earned him the loyalty of his men. It wouldn't be easy, Coelia knew, to persuade him to do what she needed him to do.

She sat back in the enclosed comfort of her carriage and opened the curtain as Teo drove the horses forward, chatting with Arbo. As they moved along the streets of the Campus Martius, to and over the Bridge of Agrippa that stretched from one bank of the Tiber River to the other, the Vestal tossed handfuls of coin outside. Those who had stopped to let the Vestal's carriage pass dove to the cobblestone to retrieve them.

Soon, the noisy crowds outside the carriage thinned, replaced by a thicket of stone pine trees and solitude, while the smooth ride of the paved streets morphed into a jarring journey on the more neglected road that led to the villa of Agrippa. Built on the banks of the famous river, and offering an unmatched view of the structures, temples and monuments in the Campus Martius—that area of Rome that owed so much to the celebrated general's patronage—the multiterraced villa was fronted by a semicircular columned portico. It was there that Teo brought the carriage to a halt. Coelia opened the door from within and stepped out, already surveying the residence in pleasant surprise.

Arbo noted her expression and smiled with satisfaction. "Let's go inside. Watch yourself though, the stone is slippery... oh, look out for that big slug, you wouldn't want to step on that one."

Leaving Teo with the carriage, she followed Arbo along an overgrown footpath to reach the portico, the general struggling only slightly to open one of the doors. He gestured for her to enter first and she did, quickly lifting the bottom of her tunica as a layer of cold liquid sludge sloshed against her feet.

"Gods, Arbo."

He slipped by her and patted the fresco on the wall. "Look at this."

Coelia nodded, impressed despite the seepage clinging to her feet. Unlike the floors, the walls were nearly pristine: Pompeiian reds and yellows, blues and greens, all animating depictions of the gods and heroes of Rome.

"This place is beautiful," she said, "even if it has been forgotten."

"It's beautiful *because* it's been forgotten. No bored matron has had a chance to paint over Agrippa's walls. Come on, it gets better." He led her farther into the home, rounding a corner into a wide corridor and then proceeding to a large room with a vaulted stuccoed ceiling. More intricate murals vitalized the space, extending from the ceiling to the flooded floor. "I've already had the restorers look at the frescos," he said. "It's just the lower part of the walls that need to be repainted. And guess what? They said it's the same paint that's on the *Ara Pacis.*" He looked around proudly. "It just needs love."

"It needs drainage," said Coelia. She covered her mouth, speaking through her fingers and her laughter. "I have leeches on one sandal and fish eggs on the other."

Arbo swished a sandal in the water and laughed with her. "Let's find higher ground." He led her back the way they had come, and then veered off to follow another corridor before climbing a staircase—the marble was dirty, but flawless—and emerging onto a splendid terrace that overlooked the flowing waters of the Tiber. Fetching two tipped-over wooden stools, the only furnishings in the place, he placed them before the balustrade. "Sit." Coelia did, and he sat next to her. Together, they looked out over the river. "The best view in all of Rome," he said.

"It just might be, Arbo."

"There used to be a stable on the property, but just the foundation remains. I'm going to rebuild it and put my columbaria on top."

"Will you move all the birds?"

"It'll take a while, but yes. I'm going to build a giant water basin for them in the shape of a trireme."

"Very clever."

"It was Caesar's idea."

"The place will come to life again," said Coelia. "There is no one better to make it so. You and Victor are both pupils of history. It was a thoughtful gift from him."

"Indeed."

"He tells me that you and he have become friends. I know he wishes for that friendship to continue."

Arbo's eyes shifted away from the Tiber and onto her. "Why wouldn't it?"

Coelia wondered how to broach it. She had no idea how Arbo would respond to Magnus Maximus's usurping ambitions. She had no idea how *she* would respond if he rose up in anger and loyalty to Theodosius, who he had sworn allegiance to. There was every chance he would storm off to mount the nearest horse and gallop nonstop to Constantinople to fight alongside Stilicho, his friend and comrade who had recently left Rome to wed Serena. Coelia decided to broach it in the fashion that suited Arbo's temperament. Head on.

"Magnus Maximus is going to invade Italy," she said.

The general's voice was steady, but uninterpretable. "When?"

"Imminently."

Arbo stood and took a short step to the front of the terrace, gripping the balustrade and leaning on his arms. "*Mars Pater, miserere,*" he muttered, staring out at the Tiber. "Who else knows about this?"

"Symmachus. He's already been talking to the other senators."

"Has he told them of your involvement?"

"I'm not involved," said Coelia. "Not like the others are."

"I don't give a fuck about the others, and you are involved. You're conspiring with senators, and you just admitted to treason. I'm Theodosius's general, for the love of the gods!"

Coelia rose from her stool and stood beside him. "Would you prefer that I kept it from you?"

He scoffed in response, though his acrimony quickly dissipated. There was too much at stake to be angry. "Why take this risk, Coelia?" he asked. "You can retire now. We have been waiting so long. I thought this place..." He turned to face her. "I thought we might live here together."

"We can... but after."

"After what? After Victor's troops seize Rome?"

"After I fulfill my promise."

"Gods," he said gravely. "What have they talked you into?"

"They didn't talk me into anything." She laced her fingers together in a nervous gesture. "It was my own doing. I told Victor about the Order's secret coffers... about how previous Vestals had helped finance the legions they supported."

Arbo sighed, deflated. "I should've seen this coming."

"I am going to give him the money," said Coelia, forcing resolve into her voice. "I support him. I want him to be Caesar of Rome."

"So does half the bloody empire, but that doesn't mean you have to march yourself to the fucking frontlines of his war." Again, he calmed himself. "You told me what Antonia advised you when she left the Order. She told you to wait it out, do your work, don't make enemies." He took her hand. "Retire now. We can live here and mind our own business, or we can leave Rome altogether until it all blows over."

"I can't retire now. I need to see this through. Domitia is too much like Antonia. She won't give him the money, I know it."

Arbo turned back to the balustrade and leaned on his outstretched arms, ruminating. "Symmachus... who is with him?"

"Seventy-nine out of hundred senators are with him, and the rest are ambivalent. There is no serious opposition. The Roman Senate will recognize Magnus Maximus and Victor as co-emperors of Italy. There's no stopping it now. Victor has made them a lot of promises."

"Like what?"

"Like reinstating their legislative authority, for one. And restoring the religious liberties of Constantine's edict. You know how many times the senators have petitioned Theodosius for those things. The emperor won't even hear their petitions anymore, never mind grant them."

"I'll wager that Victor has also made some promises to you," said Arbo. "Like restoring the state funding of the Vestal Order."

"The funding be damned," said Coelia. "It is against the laws of Rome to worship our own gods. It is only the safety of our numbers, and the leverage of pagan senators and generals, that prevent Theodosius from enforcing the laws more harshly. But they exist. They hang over our heads like a sword suspended by a thread, and they embolden the hateful. How many statues of

Jupiter have had crosses carved into their foreheads? How many bronze roof tiles have been peeled off the temple of Venus and Roma to decorate churches?" She spun around and sat back down on the wooden stool, balancing herself as it wobbled below her anger. "The tide is turning. We may never have a better chance than now to regain what we have lost. I am the Vestalis Maxima of Rome, and I know that the bishops will not stop until the Vestal Virgins are as forgotten as Agrippa's frescos. Shall I just ignore it all, pick flowers with you along the Tiber, and let them erase us from our own history? Is that how Rome's great generals deal with their enemies?"

For a long while, he stood with his back to her, his thought-heavy stare fixed on the moving waters of the Tiber. He had sworn fealty to the house of Theodosius, and the emperor had entrusted him with great power—power that had the potential to expand even more now that Bauto was dead. His long-time friend Stilicho had just married Theodosius's niece. Those were alliances he could not easily cast aside. Yet like all pagans, he abhorred the boarded-up temples, urine-stained shrines, and pilgrimage routes that trampled over Rome's ancient sacred sites. And despite having endured years of trauma on the battlefield, fighting for all Romans, he had seen the contemptuous glares of Christian Romans when he knelt in his soldier's cloak to pray before the Altar of Mars.

Coelia was right. They might never have a better chance than now. The famine had led many to turn to the true gods, to observe and honor them, and the gods had responded with abundant, healthy harvests. Things were changing. The boards were coming off the temples and more and more Romans were boldly practicing the ways of their ancestors. Those customs and virtues were in their blood, passed down through generations, and they were reclaiming their true nature. Something along the water's edge below caught his eye, something stuck in the muddy river bank—an old *amphora*, painted but cracked. At one time it would've held the finest wine for Rome's greatest general.

He turned around to face Coelia. "I want us to be together," he finally said. He returned to sit on the stool next to hers. "What do you want me to do?"

"Stay in Rome," said Coelia. "Talk to Victor. Let him tell you his vision for Rome, and then decide if it is your vision, too." He nodded, and she touched his hand. "You were meant to do more than mop Agrippa's floors. You were meant to follow in his footsteps."

CHAPTER XXI

It was Rome's birthday—April 21st, the day Romulus founded his city—and Victor was the guest of honor. At *precisely* noon, the giant bronze doors of the Pantheon temple opened and he crossed the threshold, dazzling himself and those gathered inside the massive circular sanctum with the building's famed special effect: a thick sunbeam that streamed down through the oculus in the high coffered ceiling, slanting just so, to bathe the entering emperor in the divine light of Sol. It happened like this only once a year, only at midday, and only for moments. And yet once witnessed, it remained in the mind forever.

A vision begun by General Agrippa but completed by Emperor Hadrian, the monumental rotunda of the Pantheon—a temple dedicated to the Roman gods and the deified emperors—was arguably the finest structure in the Campus Martius. Its breathtaking dome, towering columns, multicolored marble floor with geometric designs and its encircling niches filled with statues of the gods all provided a grandiose sanctum in which to honor the *Dii Consentes*—the twelve major gods and goddesses of Rome. Yet as Victor strode into the temple, wrapped in Imperial purple and wearing a crown of golden laurel, he brought another god with him. For just steps behind him followed the new bishop of Rome, Siricius, carrying a cross atop a high staff. Victor may have seen the day as a tribute to tradition, but to the bishop, it was yet another opportunity to march the cross before the pagans of Rome.

Coelia joined the other priests, senators and elite of Rome in applauding the emperor and the special sunbeam effect, though her thoughts were with Proculeia and Terentia inside the Temple of Vesta. At this moment, they would be offering into the sacred fire as sunlight similarly entered through the oculus in Vesta's domed ceiling to illuminate the hearthfire below. For it was on this day that the goddess's eternal fire had first burned in the Eternal City.

Domitia spoke quietly to her. "General Arbogastes will miss the show if he doesn't stop looking at you."

"You'll miss the show if you don't stop looking at everyone else to see what they're looking at," replied Coelia.

As the sunbeam moved on—even the emperor couldn't command it to stay—those tightly gathered to watch the spectacle broke apart to socialize. Coelia smiled at Arbo and he winked, though his duty took him to Victor before her. Indeed, since the Senate had declared Victor emperor of Italy, the new Caesar's trusted general was always close by. Victor and Arbogastes, Rome's reimagined Augustus and Agrippa.

Coelia and Domitia exchanged the usual obligatory pleasantries and small talk with Symmachus and a number of visiting dignitaries before exiting the temple to enjoy the warm midday sun. Stationed at regular posts around the Pantheon, armed soldiers kept watch. There hadn't been a sighting of the Gilded Lions for some time, but knowing that guards were on the lookout nonetheless settled the stomach enough for celebrants to enjoy the good wine. Happy to be outdoors, the Vestals gravitated toward a group of well-dressed women already overindulging.

"The *Vinalia* isn't for a couple days," Coelia said smilingly, as she greeted her friend Paulina.

"We are no slaves to the calendar," Paulina replied, and waved to an attendant who passed the priestesses their own wine cups.

Coelia had no sooner taken a sip—it was very good—than Victor and Arbo approached, Caesar receiving bows of deference from women not particularly known for showing docility.

"Ladies," said Victor, holding out his hand for a wine cup. "I was told to hurry if I wanted to sample the year's best."

The women grinned as Victor tasted the wine. He raised his cup, impressed. "No wonder the traditionalists see a god in wine," he said, eliciting wider smiles from Rome's rich matrons. He looked back at the Pantheon, its soaring dome seeming to cut a section out of the blue sky. "It is hard to believe that men can build such things," he said.

"They say it is here where Romulus ascended to the heavens and became holy Quirinus," said Coelia.

Domitia chimed in. "When I was a novice, the *flamen* of Mars— you remember old Orus, don't you Coelia?—he brought me here and told me that Quirinus holds up the dome from the heavens. He said only the divine could suspend such a great roof. His timing was tragic, though, since a group of visiting Greek engineers overheard him. They argued for so long that I fell asleep just over there by the fountain."

Victor's attention was riveted to the anecdote, and it took a physical tap on the shoulder from Arbo to break it away. The general gestured to the Imperial messenger who was kneeling on the ground an arm's length away, holding out a scroll.

"Caesar," said the messenger. "A letter from General Andragathius."

They all knew the name. Andragathius was Magnus Maximus's top general, the one in charge of the military campaign against Theodosius. A competent and clever soldier, he was also rumored to be Maximus's illegitimate son and Victor's half-brother, though Maximus had never formally acknowledged him. The wine-sipping matrons and priestesses politely stepped aside to give the emperor and his general privacy as they received word from the frontlines of battle.

Victor broke the seal and read. He looked up at Arbo. "Commander Stilicho remains in Constantinople with his new wife," he said. "It is General Richomeres who leads Theodosius's army in the field."

Arbo nodded. It gave him some emotional relief to know that Stilicho, like him, was remaining on the sidelines. At least for now. But it did nothing to quell the larger problem.

"Richomeres is nearly undefeated," he said. "I will write to Andragathius and detail his strategies. He can be a tricky bastard, especially when his back is against the wall."

"I only hope Andragathius will listen to you," Victor said seriously. "He is a decent soldier, but he covets my father's attention. He will not want to share his victory with you."

"Victory is always shared," said Arbo, glancing at the great dome of Agrippa's vision. "Not even Agrippa went to war alone."

CHAPTER XXII

The young Caesar Flavius Victor stood on the marble floor of the Senate House, gripping a fold of his purple and gold-embroidered toga with one hand and raising the other before the turbulent assembly of senators, magistrates and high-ranking soldiers. This included his top man, General Arbogastes, dressed in the red tunica and leather cuirass of the Roman soldier. Arbo didn't need the cuirass, but Victor preferred him to wear it as a reassuring symbol of strength to the Senate.

"Senators and friends," said Victor, and the vocal commotion settled to an expectant silence. "It is my duty to officially declare what you have already learned. My father was captured in battle by the forces of Theodosius. He was executed in Aquileia." He waited for the dutiful rise of grief to abate. "His general Andragathius, unable to endure the burden of failing my father, fell on his own blade in Siscia."

Senator Junius stood among the cries of anger and frustration. "Caesar," he said. "This assembly mourns with you. Emperor Magnus Maximus brought the promise of peace and stability to Rome. As we supported the father, we will support the son."

"I thank you, friends," said Victor, pivoting to address the assembly as a whole. "But this bad news is tempered with good. Our legions are in a more advantageous position than ever. Theodosius is desperate to return his vassal co-emperor Valentinian to the throne in Mediolanum, but by fighting the juvenile's battles for him, he has stretched his own forces too thin."

Senator Lampadius addressed the chamber. "An emperor who cannot raise his own army—who cannot even raise a sword!—has no right to rule Rome. Are we Romans to kneel before a prince who yet has no need for a razor?" He grew more indignant. "Valentinian cowers behind the throne of the tyrant Theodosius. He is tethered to it, like a dog is tethered to a post. The only way to free ourselves is to kill both master and mongrel!"

A spirited chorus of *Hear, Hear!* resounded within the chamber. Victor gave it time to ebb before speaking again. "It will be done," he announced. "The loss of my father, may God rest his soul, changes nothing. Our army is strong and loyal. At dawn, General Arbogastes will leave for the frontlines at Poetovio to assume command of the legions."

The senators roused another boisterous clamor of approval, this one louder and longer. Though few would say it aloud, many had been eager for the day that Victor, not his father, would be in charge, and thus could put Arbogastes in command of the war. Between Arbo's military ability and his intimate knowledge of Theodosius's battle tactics, he could succeed in all the ways that Maximus's general had failed. All in all, this was a good day and a promising development.

The proceedings came to a close, and those present dispersed to attend to their various duties. When the chamber was empty save for Victor, Arbo and Symmachus, the senator spoke.

"Theodosius's army is stocked with Huns and Goths," he said to Arbo. "There is no one more capable than you of defeating such patchwork. What will be your strategy, General?"

"Secrecy," replied Arbo. "No disrespect, Senator."

Symmachus slapped the general on the back. "May Father Mars protect you, sir," he said, and left the emperor and his most senior officer alone in the chamber.

Victor sat in his curule chair. "My father and his general were too proud to heed your advice," he said to Arbo. "It is written that pride comes before destruction."

"Richomeres is a true warrior," said Arbo, his mind turning to the formidable opponent. "But even Achilles had a weakness."

A clerk carrying a box of scrolls cleared his throat to be noticed, and Victor waved him closer. He began to shuffle through the scrolls of correspondence. There was much work to be done before morning. "We will speak at dawn, General," he said. "Take a woman and sleep well."

"Yes, Caesar." He rose to leave, but Victor's words had summoned images of Coelia and he hesitated. "Sir, I would like to raise another matter with you. Before morning."

"What is it?"

Arbo eyed the clerk. He trusted no one. "In private."

"Then you will stay on the Palatine tonight," replied Victor. "We could use the time."

"Yes, Caesar."

Arbo bowed to the emperor and headed out of the Senate House. Behind him, he heard Victor and the clerk fall into a discussion about money—specifically, the recent pay hike for legionary soldiers. It was coin that no one could quite account for, but Arbo knew exactly where it had come from. He again pictured Coelia. She would be wondering, worrying, about his deployment to Poetovio, and there was no point making her speculate any longer. He strode to the stables behind the Curia to find his horse already saddled and restless—precisely how he felt—and mounted the animal for the trip home to Agrippa's villa. If he couldn't ride his own horse through the streets of Rome without an upbraiding from a *vigile*, what was the point of being Caesar's top man?

His thoughts made the trip pass quickly, his horse seeming to find its own way from the Forum to the Bridge of Agrippa. It clip-clopped over the Tiber and snorted in excitement at the scent of the stone pine trees that marked their destination. The animal knew what awaited it at the newly built stable: sweet hay, crunchy apples and a bath from doting stable hands. One of the stable hands, along with Coelia's guard Teo, greeted Arbo at the gate. They led the horse away to its indulgence, while the general proceeded to the semicircular portico of his impeccably restored home. He glanced up at the rogue pigeon nest tucked into the entablature, scuffed some droppings off the bottom of his sandals and crossed the threshold. Passing by the vibrant frescoed walls, he continued over the polished marble floors that gave way to fine carpets, and finally emerged onto the terrace.

Coelia was leaning against the balustrade. "I saw you cross the bridge," she said. "Have you eaten?"

He shook his head. "Caesar has ordered me to depart Rome at dawn and take command of the legions. I am to stay on the Palatine tonight."

She laced her fingers together, fidgeting, her thoughts as heavy as his. Perhaps heavier. She was the one who had allied him with Victor. She was the one responsible for the fact that, once again, he would be thrust into the peril and trauma of war. It was too late for second thoughts, but she had to wonder... if she could go back, would she do it all again?

"I see," she said. "I don't know why I feel surprised. You said to expect it."

"Let's have supper together," he replied. "Some wine. Then we will say our goodbyes."

Coelia turned and looked out over the Tiber. "I will try to say goodbye without sounding like Penelope weeping for Odysseus."

"I would not mind a few tears." He wrapped his arms around her waist from behind and spoke, his mouth close to her ear. "How many times in these last few months have we stood right here and watched the fishermen pull their nets from the water, or the merchant ships go by, or a drover chase down an escaped cow wading through the tall grasses on the banks?"

"How many times have we raced down to pull one of your overfed pigeons out of the current?"

His arms tightened around her. "I fight only for the life we could have. I have prayed to Juno and Venus that you want the same." A trace of hope lifted his weighty voice. "Have you made a decision about retiring from the Order?"

"There was a time I could not wait to do it," she said. "So why is it so difficult now?"

"Change is frightening."

She leaned back against him, feeling the slight irregularity in his breaths as he struggled to suppress his own apprehension on this eve of battle. He had spent months restoring Agrippa's villa, and she knew he wanted nothing more than to stay where he was, look out over the Tiber with her, and spoil his pigeons. "I am ready for a change."

He brushed her light veil and long hair aside and kissed the side of her neck. "I will always do what is best for us." He kissed her again, this time moving his fingers under her veil to touch the back of her neck.

Coelia pulled away. "I am still bound by my vows."

"Your tenure is complete," he said. "The goddess knows your decision. If we are not destined to be together after this day..." he nestled his face into her veil, whatever words he was going to say lost in the soft fabric. Gently, he turned her around and pressed his lips against hers.

... the Vestals sell their virginity for a price.

It was a strange time for those words to fly back into her mind... or perhaps it was not so strange. Coelia didn't care what the bishops thought of her—they were no paragons of virtue— but ever since Symmachus had tacitly suggested she compromise her vows to secure Arbo's allegiance, she had become even more certain that she would never do so.

"I cannot sully my vows." She took a step back. "Especially not with a war starting. We cannot risk offending the goddess. When you are back, I will leave the temple and we can be together."

He advanced and placed his hands on either side of her head, kissing her more forcefully. Coelia's heart pounded, though now from anger and a beat of instinctual fear more than arousal, and she twisted her head out of his grip. Arbo clutched her arm as she tried to withdraw.

"Would you have me see a whore on the day before I ride into battle?" he asked.

Coelia's gaped, having no idea how to respond to such crassness, nor to the sudden hurtful image of another woman in Arbo's arms. The emotions ran through her—shock, indignation, jealousy—and she teetered on the edge of two choices: succumb and follow him into Agrippa's bedchamber, or slap him in the face and leave. She had not yet decided which path to follow when Arbo's demeanor eased.

"Forgive me," he said.

"You can see a whore if you want," she said coldly.

"I will not take another woman before we marry," he replied. "Nor after."

The words melted Coelia's anger. The anxiety of war, the pain of their parting, those were to blame.

"We cannot part like this," she said.

"No, we cannot." He took her hand affectionately. "Let's take supper out here and watch for any pigeons that might float by. It might be some time until we can do it again."

The House of Augustus on the Palatine Hill, former residence of the illustrious emperor, was Victor's favorite place in all of Rome. Sitting among Augustus's statuary and trophies, walking his floors, passing by his shrines, and enjoying his gardens and baths brought the young Caesar peace and made him feel connected in purpose to Rome's first *imperator.* That in turn helped him clear his mind and focus on strategy. With his father dead and gone, it all fell to him now. He sat on the marble edge of a pool in one of the many courtyards on the palatial grounds and hung his sandaled feet into the clear water, just as he heard the voice he had been waiting for.

"*Salve*, Caesar."

"Arbo," said Victor, pointing at a statue. "Look what I found."

The general studied the statue: a life-sized bronze of Augustus. Unlike many of the other statues of Rome's first emperor, this one depicted the man in later life. His trademark hairstyle, refined features and princely deportment was the same as always, but there were also the unmistakable signs of age.

"He looks tired," observed Arbo.

"He looks like he's headed an empire for forty years," said Victor. "Sit, General."

Arbo sat next to the emperor, dangling his feet in the water beside his. The two men sat like this often. Theirs was an easy companionship forged not only by their political alliance, but a common interest in Rome's past.

"Where did you find it?" asked Arbo, looking back at the statue.

"In one of the underground storehouses on the Oppian Hill. My men also found a stash of very nice gladiator armor, an ivory bust of Alexander, and Julia Domna's lectica." Victor leaned over to remove his sandals, letting them drop to the bottom of the shallow pool. "How is your stable coming along?"

"It has been finished for some time." He smiled at the emperor. "I put the two horse statues you sent—the ones from the racetrack in the Campus Martius—on the roof. My stable looks like the Temple of Castor and Pollux."

"Ha," said Victor. "Excellent." He twisted around and gestured to a linen-draped table. "Get us wine."

"Yes, Caesar."

Arbo stood and stepped away from Victor, shaking the water off his sandals. He took a deep breath... and then unfastened his leather belt, wrapping the ends tightly around his hands. Turning back to Victor, he closed in on him from behind.

But the sudden motion had triggered Victor's imperial instincts. He glanced at the water, and at the last moment saw the assassin's stealth attack reflected on its surface. It was all the time he needed. A younger and faster man than Arbo, he lurched himself forward into the pool only a breath before the general's belt constricted his neck. Arbo plunged in after him.

"Guards!" Victor cried out.

Scrambling to get his feet under him—the bottom of the pool was slippery—but sensing Arbo would reach him before he did, Victor turned and kicked with all his strength. His foot met Arbo's right knee and the general cursed aloud, but did not falter. Still gripping the belt, he descended on the emperor, but again, Victor's agility outmaneuvered Arbo's brute force, and he found traction on the pool's floor. He leveraged it, and his adrenaline, and scrambled out of the pool. For a moment, Victor felt like he had the advantage, but then he felt Arbo's vice-like grip on one of his ankles. He fell forward, fast, striking his head too hard against the marble edge of the pool as Arbo dragged him back into the water. A flare of pain and panic shot through his skull.

The world turned red. Victor wiped the blood from his eyes, and saw at eye-level the boots of soldiers.

"Help me!" he shouted.

The boots rushed toward him. But then Arbo's commanding voice rang out.

"Stand down, soldiers!"

The soldiers stepped back.

Victor slumped back into the water, waves splashing against his chest. He tried to shake off the sickening dizziness, but it only grew worse. He lost vision in one eye and glared up at the general with the other.

"Arbo," he spat. "I had you wrong. You're no Agrippa. You're a fucking Brutus."

"It can't be helped, Caesar," said Arbo. "Not this time."

Again, Victor wiped the blood from his eyes. "Whatever Theodosius has promised you, he will never do it."

Arbo coiled his leather belt around his hands again, shortening its length. His hands throbbed from the pressure and his knee ached, but nothing pained him as much as the look of betrayal in Victor's eyes and the knowledge that he would face far worse with Coelia. He tried to suppress the rising, gnawing fear that Victor was correct: that Theodosius would renege on his promises, and that he had made a horrible mistake by backing the wrong man. But it was too late now. Even if he relented, even if swore renewed allegiance to Victor before every shrine in Rome, the young emperor would have him executed the first chance he had. He'd be a fool not to.

The general waded through the water and moved behind Victor's back, wrapping the garrotte twice around his neck and pulling it tightly. A croak sounded from Victor's throat. His hands flew up to claw at the leather strangler, but realizing it was no use, curled into fists that struck out but hit nothing. Wanting it to be over, Arbo submerged Victor's head under the water. He didn't know if it would make the man die any faster, but at least it would mute the pathetic croaks still emanating from his throat. Even so, the young Caesar thrashed and kicked longer than Arbo would have thought anyone could.

When the thrashing finally ended and the water calmed, Arbo uncoiled the leather belt from his swollen hands. Without looking down at the body—he couldn't bring himself to see Victor's lifeless, accusatory eyes looking up at him from below the surface—he trudged through the water and stepped out of the pool.

The four guards who had answered Victor's call stared at General Arbogastes with expressions of bewilderment and uncertainty.

"Cut off his head and take it to Constantinople," Arbo said to one of the soldiers. "Deliver it to Commander Stilicho directly. Leave after dark. Quietly."

The soldier nodded. He could deal with a clear order from the general. The rest was above his pay grade. "Yes, sir."

Arbo turned his back as the soldiers entered the pool to remove Victor's body. His breaths still labored from the exertion and his mind racing, he walked out of the courtyard as quickly as he could, feeling the tired bronze eyes of Augustus watching him go.

CHAPTER XXIII

Lucilla and Olympius greeted Coelia in the same manner they always did. Lucilla was exuberant despite the clouds that hung in the morning sky over the ludus, happy for any opportunity to see her busy daughter, while Olympius was indifferent to both the weather and the Vestal. His relationship with Lucilla had emboldened him with even greater informality toward the high priestess, and he spoke plainly to her.

"I assume you've heard the news," he said, standing beside Coelia in the peristyle that framed the gladiator school's training field.

"General Arbogastes and his men rode out at dawn," Coelia replied. The wind picked up, and she fastened her cloak at the breastbone. She was already unhappy knowing that Arbo was galloping his way toward the frontlines, and the chilly visit to the ludus had done nothing to distract her from her dourness.

"Everyone knows about that," said Olympius. "I'm talking about the other news."

"I've been here for hours, working while you've been sleeping in with my mother, so no, I haven't heard." She pointed to one of

the swordsmen training with Deimos in the rectangular courtyard. "That's the bald retiarius I was telling you about. Not as big
as Brogos, but maybe if Kaunos can muscle him up and Deimos
can—"

"They caught another lion last night."

Coelia perked up, hopeful. "Alive?"

Olympius crossed his arms and watched the fighters while,
meanwhile, Lucilla perused the fresh selection of breakfast foods
the servants were rolling into the peristyle.

"You're going to love this," he said. "A group of twenty hunters
tracked it for miles along the *Aqua Marcia*. They surrounded it
and forced it up an incline, consummate professionals they are,
then netted it. And then while the idiots were busy congratulating themselves, it fell down and impaled itself on an iron rod."

Coelia looked skyward. "*Dei, date mihi vires.*" She accepted a
fig from Lucilla and spoke while chewing, casting Olympius a
sidelong look. "Maybe we should buy one ourselves from Africa.
We can stage its capture and put it in the arena."

"Olympius," Lucilla scolded softly. "See what a bad influence
you are on my daughter? She never used to be the scheming sort."

"Desperate times call for desperate measures, Mother," said
Coelia.

Olympius shook his head, refuting Coelia's suggestion. "What
happens when they catch the last two? They'll know it was a fake.
Either that, or we'll end up having to pay off more people to keep
them quiet."

Coelia ate another fig, ruminating. Calculating. She had given
nine-tenths of the secret Vestal monies to Victor to pay his
troops, and the last tenth to Olympius to help silence those he
had bribed to release the lions from the stadium, lest she be implicated alongside him. She wasn't sure how he had achieved
their silence—whether he had simply paid them off or hired an
assassin to permanently muzzle them—but either way, it had
taken a lot of money to solve that problem. The perfidious senator was right. They couldn't afford another bout of extortion.

"Oh, don't look so despondent," said Lucilla. "There are still two lions left. One of them is surely to be caught alive." She wrapped her fingers around a cup of hot honey water and looked into the courtyard where the gladiators were still strenuously training. "You are right. That bald one is very good. Stuff him into Brogos's spooky armor and call him Zagreus, son of Hades. There's nothing Rome loves more than a legacy drama."

A voice called down from the ludus's top story. "Is the high priestess still down there?"

Coelia stepped out of the colonnade and craned her neck, looking up to see Kaunos peering down. "Yes, I am here."

"Very good, Domina. There's a messenger coming down."

He had barely finished speaking when the breathless messenger sprinted into the peristyle. "High Priestess," he bowed. "Priestess Domitia requires you to return to the House of the Vestals immediately. She said it is a matter of extreme urgency."

"All right. Go back and tell her I will—"

The messenger bowed more deeply, speaking to the ground. "Forgive me, High Priestess, but I am to insist that you return without delay."

Lucilla passed her cup to the servant. "Let's all go," she said to Coelia. "Your cooks can make us a proper breakfast. We cannot survive on figs. We are not woodpeckers."

They left the ludus together and walked quickly, hastened by the cool morning, to Coelia's carriage. Teo opened the door and Coelia stepped in first, taking one seat while Olympius sat on the seat opposite, Lucilla wedged in beside him. She poked him flirtatiously.

"Stop it or walk, Mother," said Coelia.

Lucilla laughed and folded her hands in her lap. As the carriage rounded the stadium and headed back into the Forum, she peeked out the curtain and frowned. "Something has happened."

Coelia pulled back the silk curtain. As the carpentum rolled down the Via Sacra and neared the flower-lined stretch of the street where the House of the Vestals was located, she spotted small groups of people huddled together to talk, their expressions wavering between confused and concerned. The undercurrent of anxiety and the near certainty of impending bad news compelled Coelia to open the door of her carriage even before it had come to a complete stop in front of the Vestals' residence. The guards opened the heavy wooden doors of the house, and she passed over the threshold quickly, sensing her mother and Olympius on her heels.

Of all the scenes she had imagined walking into upon her return, this one was even more astonishing: Symmachus, battered and bruised, bleeding profusely from the nose while Ptolema dabbed his wounds with a kitchen cloth. Domitia was there too, an apprehensive frown on her face.

"He is requesting sanctuary," Domitia said to the chief Vestal.

"Why?" asked Coelia. "What is going on?"

Symmachus took the cloth out of Ptolema's hand and held it against his nostrils, trying to tamp the bleeding. "Men came to arrest me," he said. "Theodosius's men. If my staff hadn't helped me fight them off and escape, I'd be in the Carcer. Maybe worse." The cloth grew saturated with blood, and Ptolema passed him a clean one. He pressed it against his nose. "I need sanctuary."

"Of course," said Coelia, "but what is the charge against you?"

"Treason." He coughed and looked at Coelia. "Victor is dead." An aura of defeat settled around him, and his shoulders fell. "Assassinated on the Palatine last night."

Coelia's felt the strength leave her body. The chill she had felt all morning tightened into a frightful cold that gripped her limbs, and a shiver ran through her. After the death of Magnus Maximus, Victor was their last hope. She clung to it.

"Are you sure? Maybe he—"

"There is no doubt of it. He is dead."

Instinctively, Coelia's thoughts turned to survival. Theodosius would act quickly to prevent Victor's allies from regrouping. As demonstrated by the attempted arrest of Symmachus, his Imperial tentacles were already reaching out to seize Victor's strongest supporters. He would also be searching out those who had financed Victor's legions. People like her. His most pressing matter, though, would be to cut off the head of the treasonous army as quickly and decisively as possible.

"We must get word to General Arbogastes," she said. "They will be looking for him." She could already picture Arbo riding straight into an ambush, being set upon by a throng of Theodosius's men, fighting for his life.

"Coelia," Symmachus said firmly. "It is Arbogastes who killed Victor."

The Vestal balked. "No," she rejected. "I saw him last night."

Domitia placed a sympathetic hand on her shoulder. "Maybe he had a reason," she said warily. "Maybe... I don't know."

"Domitia," said Coelia. "It's just not possible. Trust me."

"Someone is feeding us a falsehood," asserted Lucilla. "The general would not betray my daughter."

"Victor's scribe at the *Domus Augusti* saw it happen," Symmachus said wearily. "Arbogastes strangled him in the courtyard. In a pool. He ordered soldiers to take the head to Commander Stilicho in Constantinople." He dropped the blood-soaked cloth onto the ground and looked glumly at Coelia. "The general betrayed Victor, and he betrayed us. It could only have been him that ordered my arrest."

Coelia returned in her mind to the night before, when she and Arbo had stood together on the terrace, when he had put his arms around her... the things he had said and done. Slowly, inescapably, it all took on a new meaning.

Olympius broke the incredulous silence.

"There is no sanctuary to be had here," he said to Symmachus. "Arbogastes might not do it, but Theodosius's Christian soldiers will take a battering ram to these doors if they have to. They don't give a shit. You need to get out of Rome right now. You can hide in one of my country villas."

Lucilla gripped the sleeve of Olympius's tunica. "We are trusting you," she said.

"I know, Lucilla," he replied. He kissed her on the cheek. "Go to my house on the Caelian. I'll return as soon as I can." Putting a supportive arm around the weakened senator, he made to leave.

"Follow me," said Domitia. "It's better if you leave through the slave's door. Ptolema, have a carriage brought around."

The slave rushed off to arrange for the men's transport, while Olympius helped Symmachus limp across the courtyard, Domitia urging them to move faster. They exited the House of the Vestals through the back. As their voices retreated, Lucilla guided her daughter to a decorative pool framed with pink roses. They sat on its edge, engulfed by the traumatic silence. In the water, a fish snatched an insect from the surface with the faintest of splashes.

"Whatever the general was to you, he is nothing now," said Lucilla. "You must only think of yourself, Coelia. How deeply involved are you?"

"To the neck."

"Then let's gather what coin you have and leave Rome right now, together. We will go to Cumae. You can announce your retirement from the Order from there."

"I cannot just leave Rome."

"Of course you can."

"That will look more suspicious than anything."

"Out of sight is out of mind," insisted Lucilla. "If you aren't here for them to target, if you withdraw from public life, they will focus on other conspirators."

"Arbo won't let anything happen to me."

"Are you certain of that?"

The Vestal's temples throbbed. "No, I'm not," she conceded. A tightening band of anxiety around her chest gave her the sudden urge to head to her bedchamber and claw her way out of her clothes. She stood to do just that, when one of the new novices—a petite girl, the bottom of whose tunica was wet—approached.

"High Priestess," the girl said timidly. "I was at the spring collecting the holy water when a man came up to me. He wants to see you. He said not to be angry because he can explain."

Lucilla stood. "Not to be angry," she seethed. "You stay here, Coelia. I will handle him." The Vestal's mother marched across the courtyard, through the peristyle and to the front doors of the house. "Open the door!" she commanded one of the guards.

"Yes, my lady."

Lucilla burst onto the street, teeth and hands clenched, ready for battle with her daughter's betrayer. Yet at the sight of his long hair, untrimmed beard and rough tunica, she stood down and scoffed.

"So the messiah returns," she said to Brogos. "And on judgment day, no less."

CHAPTER XXIV

Rome's emperor, the youth Valentinian, sat in the curule chair in the Roman Senate House like a puppet dressed in purple and gold. His master, General Arbogastes, sat facing him, wearing the white toga of the Roman Senator. Yet Arbo's powers went far beyond any senator's, beyond any prefect's, and in reality, beyond Valentinian's. His loyalty to Theodosius had earned him twofold authority: regency over the teenaged Valentinian plus the coveted title of *magister militum*—master of soldiers. The combined political and military command made him the second most powerful man in the empire, answerable only to Theodosius himself.

Yet Arbo's loyalty to Theodosius had meant disloyalty to those he had called allies and friends in the Senate. Some had even been arrested on his orders for conspiring against Theodosius, and though most had been quickly released without charge, his presence in the assembly was nonetheless met with an anxious, angry silence. He looked at Valentinian, pulling the puppet's strings with his eyes, and the juvenile emperor stood. It was his first time speaking before the Senate, and he extended an arm in the fashion he had been advised to. The imperious gesture elicited a few mocking chuckles.

"Senators," he said, "by the force of my imperium, I order this assembly to pass a decree of *damnatio memoriae* against the usurpers Magnus Maximus and Flavius Victor."

A low grumble sounded from the senators, but settled. They all knew that decree was coming, and they all knew it was futile to resist. At this point, they would have to choose their battles carefully.

Senator Junius stood. "Highness," he said levelly. "The Senate requests a pardon for Prefect Symmachus. There can be no bridge to peace while Rome's most dignified statesman is in exile."

"And yet there is peace," said Valentinian. "I hear no shouts of sedition on the streets. Those have departed Rome with Symmachus. The senator will remain in exile. Moreover, the investigations into his collaborators and the usurpers' financiers will continue."

At that, General Arbogastes stood. All eyes, including Valentinian's, turned to him.

"Symmachus will remain in exile for now," he stated. "But there will be no further inquisitions."

Valentinian's smooth angular cheeks reddened. "I am new to Rome, so will defer to my regent's judgment," he said. "It is true that inquisition can too easily turn to persecution. There will be no further investigations. For now."

The session drew to a close, and the senators exited the chamber amid hushed conversations of relief and even words of hope. Things could have gone a lot worse. Arbo had betrayed them, but perhaps not completely.

When the hall was empty, Valentinian rounded on Arbo. "Why did you contradict me in front of everyone? I could have had you gutted on the spot!"

"And who would wield the blade, Highness? You?"

"I could tell Theodosius that you—"

"Theodosius has given me command over you," snapped Arbo. "And if you had any wits about you at all, you would realize that he is more *your* enemy than mine. He will prop you up on the throne until one of his sons is old enough to replace you, and if you give him any grief, he'll do it a lot sooner. Best to keep your head down and your mouth shut." Arbo signalled to four guards—the same four who had transported Victor's head to Constantinople—and they stepped into the chamber. "His Highness will reside in the *Domus Tiberiana* on the Palatine Hill," he said. "Escort him. Get him a whore or two to keep him busy."

"Yes, General," said the most senior of the guards.

The emperor departed under guard, and Arbo sat alone in the Curia, again telling himself that he had made the right decision: that remaining loyal to Theodosius and Stilicho was a safer bet than tossing the dice of war. It was safer for him and safer for Coelia. He sat for some time immersed in his thoughts and plans, ignoring the doubts that always crept in, before exiting the cool marble walls of the chamber and stepping into the warmth of the outdoors.

As expected, Brogos was there, waiting with lunch. Two bowls of spiced sausage with sweet apricots. He passed a bowl to the general.

"How'd the boy do?" he asked.

"What he lacks in competence he makes up for in arrogance," replied Arbo. "A natural politician." He stared into his bowl of food. "Did you give the high priestess my letter?"

"Yes," said Brogos. "She threw it in the fire with the others."

"Tell her the investigations are over. She is safe."

"Why would she have been in danger?"

Arbo stuffed a clump of meat into his mouth. There had only been two men he had fully trusted in his entire life. The first was Bauto, who was dead and therefore still fully trustworthy. The second was Stilicho, who had proven his continued trustworthiness by negotiating Arbo's regency over Valentinian and his appointment as magister militum. But Stilicho was in Constantinople with his wife Serena and their newborn son. There were things Arbo needed done in Rome. He would need to add a third man to his shortlist of confidants.

"She gave some money to Victor," Arbo divulged. "Actually, she gave him a lot of money. I know how to get it back to her. Quietly."

"I doubt she'll take anything from you," replied Brogos. He set his empty bowl on the ground. "She is planning to leave the Order at the end of this month."

Arbo swallowed and looked at Brogos, concerned. "Will she stay in Rome?"

"No. She's going to Campania. To Cumae. Her mother's already left to buy a villa."

Arbo took another mouthful, but bit into a bone shard. He spat it out angrily, tossing his bowl aside. But he was only angry at himself. He should never have lied to Coelia about Victor, though at the time it had seemed the only choice. She would have opposed him, and viciously so, such was her loyalty to that Caesar and her belief that he could restore Rome's founding values. *I made the right decision*, he told himself again. *Remaining loyal to Stilicho and Theodosius was the right thing to do... look how the emperor has already rewarded me. I am master of Rome.* Little good it did with Coelia, though. Even if he could make her understand his reasons for the deception, she would never forgive him for his inept attempt at seduction. He had lied to himself about that, telling himself that intimacy would secure her unquestioning allegiance. Or maybe he had simply wanted the pleasure of coupling with her while he could, before she hated him, and to hell with her vows. That was the certainly the conclusion Coelia had drawn.

"This money," he said to Brogos, "I know she'll take it."

"Don't be so sure," replied the gladiator.

"It's for the Vestal Order, not for her. She'll take it."

Arbo stared absently at the sanitation workers making their rounds in the Forum, collecting discarded lunch bowls and scrubbing wine stains off the stone benches. A beam of hope shone through his gloominess. Every mess could be cleaned up. He would get Coelia to listen to him, to understand that he had acted in their best interests—and in the best interests of Rome— even if he had to buy her time.

Coelia stepped out of the bath and called for a servant to help her slip into a tunica. The garment had been warmed by the fire and felt good against her skin, though as she strode out of the baths and back to her office, the warmth morphed into an unpleasant chill. She lifted a red wool blanket off a chair and wrapped it around her body, hair dripping wet and skin goose-bumped below it all. Moving behind her desk, she leafed through the memos and scrolls that covered its surface.

The novice Rufinia appeared in her doorway and smiled. "High Priestess, the hounds of Hades are here."

"Show them in."

Trailed by his three dogs, Brogos entered—giving the teen-aged Rufinia's veil a playful tug as he passed—and stoked the fire before sitting in the chair closest to Coelia's desk and commanding the dogs to sit. He watched her shuffle through the mounds of documents and correspondence, stylus in hand.

"If you're here playing Cupid for the general" — Coelia pointed to the fire — "you know where I file his letters."

Brogos leaned over the Vestal's desk, speaking quietly in case anyone was lingering outside the office. "He's put an end to the inquiries, Patrona. You don't have to worry about anything."

"I wasn't worried," she lied.

"He also wants to restore your Order's coffers."

Coelia looked up. She twirled her stylus in her fingers. "How?"

"He's grown friendly with the magistrate who administers Valentinian's office. The man handles everything from his letters to his finances."

"Eugenius," said Coelia. "I know of him. He's Christian. I think the general" — she couldn't bring herself to speak Arbo's name — "must have converted, for all the faith he's placing in the Galileans these days."

"Eugenius is pagan," said Brogos, "at least behind closed doors. And from what Arbo says, he's a magician with money. He can make it disappear and reappear at will, untraceably." A log shifted and tumbled out of the fire, and Brogos stood up to push it back into the flames. He sat back down. "Should I tell him to do it?"

"Yes."

The gladiator scratched his freshly shaven chin. "There is one condition."

"Then no."

"He wants you to remain in Rome as chief Vestal. Just for a little while longer."

Coelia tossed her stylus onto her desk and stared at Brogos for a long moment. "How do you do it?" she asked pensively. "How do you live with the knowledge that Anthea's murderer is still out there, still eating and coupling and making money, while she's in ashes?"

It was a harsh question, though presented gently, and Brogos recognized the Vestal's particular species of anger—the kind veined with bitter powerlessness and injustice. He had spent countless hours, days, weeks, searching for the answer himself.

"I suppose I tell myself that I did the best I could to find him," he replied," but the Fates had other plans, and those plans are not my business."

Coelia leaned back in her chair. "The Christian faith offers something more certain," she said. "They are taught that those who wrong them or reject their god will burn in hellfire, and let me tell you, there are some people who rejoice in the idea of their enemies liquefying in flames... that's how I've heard it said. When Praetextatus died, the ascetics mocked Paulina's grief and said that her husband was suffering in the foulest darkness for being pagan. I used to think such pettiness arose from a person's character. That is what Symmachus would say. But now I see it has a greater purpose. It lets a person feel good because they believe a horrible punishment awaits their enemy. I doubt their god would approve of such gloating, but it's a pragmatic invention for use among men." She chewed her lip. "If I could believe that the general would burn in hell for murdering Victor and for lying to—"

"I also tell myself that I have other responsibilities," interrupted Brogos, "and that running off to hunt an enemy I might never find, or feeling sorry for myself in the bath, or philosophizing about useless shit, only makes a bad situation worse. It means I'm not there for the other people in my life—like Deimos, who has become my brother, and you, who I also think of as family—and it means the bastard who killed Anthea gets to keep hurting people I care about." He stood and headed for the door, speaking over his shoulder as he led his dogs out of the office. "Eugenius will contact you about the money, Patrona. It's up to you whether you accept the general's terms."

CHAPTER XXV

It had been a long time since the emperor Valentinian had sat in the curule chair in the Roman Senate and ordered a decree of *damnatio memoriae* be passed against Magnus Maximus and his son, Victor. Since then, he had not sat again in the Senate House, had not been seen in the Forum or on the streets of Rome, had not hosted a banquet nor been invited to one, and had not visited the palace of the Roman bishop. Instead, he preferred to sequester himself on the Palatine Hill—his private oasis of indulgence—while his regent Arbogastes managed Rome and his administrator Eugenius briefed him on civic matters. It was easier that way. It spared him both the boredom and the stress of attending the notoriously cutthroat Roman Senate. It also spared him the public humiliation of Arbo's defiance. It was clear to everyone who was really in charge, and Valentinian had no choice but to sign whatever documents were put in front of him and find contentment in the good food and very good prostitutes that his handlers provided.

Rome also found contentment with the arrangement that saw their emperor living inside the city and outside of it at the same time. Every once in a while, Valentinian could be seen on top of the Palatine, looking down into the Forum like an apparition or a ghost, but some even felt that was too much of a presence. The truth was, no one liked him. Where Victor had exuded imperious confidence and magnanimousness, a lion of Rome, Valentinian was more a lapdog—spoiled and elevated, yet keenly aware of his own vulnerability, yapping and nipping at anyone who came close. A pawn of greater players, he had rarely made an independent decision as emperor. His ruling to deny both the restoration of the Altar of Victory and the reinstatement of the Vestals' stipends was not truly his, but the bishops'. That didn't garner any sympathy from those in the Eternal City, though. If there was one thing Rome despised more than a tyrant, it was a coward.

Although many in Rome had lamented Victor's death, all in all, life went on as usual. General Arbogastes and the Senate continued to follow Victor's policies of increasing religious tolerance and returning legislative powers to the Senate. The granaries remained well-stocked. People still complained about their taxes and their wives' spending, still shared sightings of the two remaining Gilded Lions of Rome—Lucens and Nox—who had become legends in their own right, yet the city was at relative ease. It helped that General Arbogastes also controlled Valentinian's correspondence, effectively cutting him off from Theodosius and Ambrosius. The young emperor's outgoing letters traveled directly from his desk to Arbo's hands to the fire, while any incoming letters were intercepted by Eugenius.

Yet Valentinian—never one to be accused of being a fast learner—had begun to suspect as much. As he lay in his silk-sheeted bed, his favorite prostitute curled up against him, he heard the faint voices of Arbogastes and Eugenius slip into his bedchamber through the open window. He kicked off the sheets, got up, and peeked out the window to see the two men standing in the garden below, leaning against a fountain and talking.

The woman raised her head. "What is going on?" she asked sleepily.

"Shut up, Delilah," Valentinian hissed. "I'm trying to listen." He stood quietly by the window for a long while, straining to hear what his two keepers were discussing. The northern borders: Nothing interesting there, just the usual criticisms of Theodosius's policies. Prominent citizens returning from exile: That was slightly more interesting, since Senator Symmachus was among them. Valentinian's legions: This was most interesting of all, and for all the wrong reasons. "*Futuo*," swore the emperor. He returned to the bed and sat dejectedly on the edge. "They're restructuring command of my legions without even consulting me. It is going too far!"

Delilah sat up and rubbed his shoulder. "Maybe it isn't as bad as you think. Maybe they're just talking about it and they will consult you later."

"That fucking Arbogastes... who does he think he is?"

"It is the Frankish breeding, Highness."

He swatted her hand away. "It gets worse every day. I don't care about their humdrum senatorial business and petty politics. Who *could* care what districts need new water pipes, or what days the markets must close, or how many public latrines are in disrepair, or what trade agreements must be amended, or what senators are guilty of corruption—they *all* are, by the way—but he cannot make military decisions behind my back!" The sound of trumpets in the distance caught his attention. "Don't tell me," he said. "Another pagan festival."

"The Vestalia, Highness."

"The Vestalia," he echoed, diving deep into regretful thoughts.

When he had first received Senator Symmachus's petition to restore the Vestals' stipend, he had initially planned to do it. His father had always advised him to avoid antagonizing Rome. But then Ambrosius had issued his not-so-thinly veiled threat to use the pulpit against him. He had done the same to Theodosius, and last Valentinian had heard, Theodosius was refusing to see the bishop. Looking back, perhaps Valentinian should've resisted the clergyman's meddling and just let Rome be Rome. But he never could have foreseen this: living in the belly of the beast, held a virtual captive by those he was supposed to rule. And if he reversed his decision now and conceded to the Senate, he wouldn't just be their captive, he would be their slave.

Delilah combed her fingers through his hair. "It is not fair that they treat you so," she said earnestly.

"I'm not even supposed to be here. My court is supposed to be in Viennensis. It is the general who wants to remain in Rome, not me."

She rested her head on his shoulder. "I would love to see Viennensis. I would love to see anyplace other than Rome. I hate this city." Her hand caressed his bare chest. She did hate Rome. She had served in the brothels since she was thirteen, although her blond hair and pretty face had at least helped her find employment in the better ones. "Would you take me with you?"

"What?"

"Would you take me with you to Viennensis?"

"I suppose so."

Delilah bounced excitedly on the bed. "You would not regret it, Highness. I know how to behave in fine company. I could be your courtesan. I would be very discreet and respectful to your wife, when you take one. Not all courtesans are."

"All right, Delilah."

"When can we go?"

"I'd go this moment if I could."

"What is stopping you? Why can't you just order the general to take you there?"

"Because every time I give him an order, *any* kind of order, he responds with the same words. 'At once, Highness.' His perception of time is skewed, though, since 'at once' means 'never.'" He pointed to the carved chestnut desk that stood on the other side of the bedchamber. Writing supplies littered its surface, and several scrolls with broken seals lay scattered on the floor all around. "And that? That is just there for show."

Delilah flopped back onto the bed. "Come lie down."

"I'm tired of lying down."

Valentinian stomped to his desk and leaned over, ignoring the cold chestnut against his bare genitals. He grabbed a stylus and a sheet of papyrus, writing furiously and rolling the paper up into a scroll before the ink had even dried. He didn't bother to seal it. Another blare of trumpets from the Forum below, this time accompanied by a distant swell of laughter, floated gallingly through the open window.

"What are you doing?" Delilah asked.

Valentinian turned to face the open door to his bedchamber. "*Servi, venite!*"

Three female attendants rushed into the bedchamber. "Yes, Highness?" asked one.

"Dress me," he said. "Very finely."

"At once, Highness."

Valentinian blew an angry torrent of air out of his nose and stood naked in the center of the room while the three slaves buzzed around him like bees around the hive, washing his body, perfuming his skin, grooming his sparse beard and setting his hair. That done, they dressed him not in the traditional toga of a Roman emperor, but rather in a *loros* of the style worn by the eastern emperors, draping the fabric—blue and red satin, heavily patterned with embroidery—around his body and leaving a length of it to hang down over his left arm. His non-Roman choice of attire would in itself send a message to the general. *I am not yours to command. You are mine.*

Delilah hopped naked out of bed and brought a full-length mirror before him. "The rightful king of Rome."

Valentinian strode out of his bedchamber, chin held high, and marched through the corridors and courtyards of the house of Tiberius, the emperor who ruled Rome during the time of Christ's crucifixion. *He houses me here of all places*, thought Valentinian. *It cannot go on.*

Emerging from the grand portico and stepping into the warmth of the early afternoon sun, his four personal guards—the same quartet that Arbo always had watching him—greeted him with surprised looks.

"Your Highness," said one. "We were not aware you were venturing out today."

"You're aware now," said Valentinian. "Fetch my lectica. I am going to the Forum."

The guards traded looks of uncertainty. General Arbogastes had already departed the Palatine, and they were certainly not invested with the authority to refuse an order from the emperor.

The senior soldier called for the emperor's lectica, and as the litter-bearers helped Valentinian step inside, he whispered to one of his subordinate men.

"Go find the general and tell him the emperor is coming."

"Yes, sir." The soldier ran off.

Valentinian reclined in the lectica, thinking that it was only his second time riding in one in Rome. Typically, he preferred to walk. Litter-bearers moved too slowly, and he loathed the sound of their laborious grunts and, worse, the tipping and bouncing as they navigated the streets. Back in Mediolanum, he had once been traveling in a lectica with his mother when one of the porters had tripped on a loose stone. The rear of the vehicle had crashed to the street, sending him tumbling backward out of it. His mother had laughed uproariously, but he hadn't seen the humor in it. He hadn't ridden in a lectica since without constantly fearing a repeat.

Nonetheless, he endured the slant of the lectica as it moved down the slope of the Palatine Ramp and proceeded into the Forum. With every step, the noise of Rome closed in around him— the blare of trumpets and the lilting music of pipes, the chatter of people, the high-pitched laughter of children, and the sound of footsteps on the cobblestone. As he neared his destination—the square in the center of the Forum—the soldier at the front of his procession called out.

"Hear this! All make way for His Highness, Imperator Valentin—"

The comical bray of a donkey drowned out the full pronouncement of his name, and a roar of laughter enveloped his litter. *I will never ride in another lectica*, Valentinian swore to himself as the porters set the vehicle down. The soldier who had announced his arrival pulled back the curtain.

The emperor stepped out, framed by his guards, and revealed himself to the Roman public-at-large for the first time. Yet this particular demographic—pagan, celebrating the Vestalia—was perhaps not the ideal crowd for Valentinian's debut, and his unexpected appearance was met with shouts of derision and looks of scorn.

General Arbogastes emerged from the crowd. He nodded curtly to the soldiers stationed in the Forum, and they spread out to restore order. It was done easily enough, people turning their backs to the emperor and returning to the festivities. Romans knew how many emperors had graced the Forum—how many triumphant Caesars had worn the laurel before the Curia, how many had delivered great speeches from the decorated *Rostra*, how many had left their ashes under that temple or their heads by that monument. This emperor, with his ruddy adolescent complexion and provoking costume, was nothing special.

"Have you come to honor the goddess, Highness?" asked Arbo.

Valentinian scoffed at the strange festivities around him. The liveliest seemed to be taking place in the Forum's square near the Rostra and the Temple of Concordia just behind him. Fresh flowers, coins and gifts —statuettes, jewelry, pots of incense and expensive fabrics—covered the marble steps of the temple, while on the platform atop the high staircase, the Vestalis Maxima and three other priestesses made offerings into an altar fire. At the nearby triumphal arch of Septimius Severus, some kind of game seemed to be underway as women competed to push, pull and coax garlanded donkeys through the arches while their husbands and children cheered them on. Musicians and food vendors meandered through the crowd, while the scent of frankincense hung in the air from the various altar fires that burned in the public square.

The emperor scowled at Arbo. "You know I do not approve of this," he replied, and cast a look of disgust up at the Vestals. "The question is instigation."

Arbo glanced up at the high priestess and turned back to Valentinian, a shade of warning in his expression. *Behave yourself, Highness.*

The impertinence of the general's posture, combined with the amused impudence on the faces of those who stood around watching, catapulted Valentinian into sudden action. He withdrew the scroll he had tucked under the fabric of his robe and thrust it high into the air.

"I am your emperor!" he shouted, directing the declaration toward a cluster of senators. "By the power of this Imperial decree, I relieve General Arbogastes of his command! My court will immediately be moved to—"

Arbo stepped forward and snatched the scroll out of Valentinian's hand. In front of the senators, in front of the magistrates, priests and public of Rome, he tore it in half and let the pieces fall to the ground.

"You didn't give me my command, boy," he said, "and you can't take it away." He turned to the emperor's senior guard. "Take him back to the palace. Keep him there this time."

The four soldiers boxed Valentinian in, urging him to turn and walk back to his lectica. Knowing there was no other option—at least none other than continued humiliation and further disempowerment—he retreated, shrinking back to his litter and disappearing inside the vehicle.

As the porters carted it away, Eugenius bent down to retrieve the torn papyrus. He held the two pieces together and reviewed the script, appalled by what he saw. "When did our emperors abandon penmanship?"

Arbo smiled at the erudite gibe. With Eugenius's groomed black hair, short beard and sapient eyes, he looked every bit the academic snob he was. Yet the typical uselessness of his kind was tempered by the gruff sensibility of military service, experience that Eugenius had the scars to prove—a particularly deep one ran in a near horizontal line under his right eye. Born of a respected Roman lineage and pragmatic enough to keep his pagan beliefs private in the Christian court of Valentinian, he had risen naturally through the Imperial ranks. Arbo had added him to his shortlist of confidants some time ago.

"Perhaps you should tutor His Highness," Arbo suggested. "Teach him to properly hold a stylus."

"A monkey can be trained to properly hold a stylus," replied Eugenius. "But nothing worthwhile will ever appear on the papyrus." He crumpled the torn paper into a tight ball and tossed it into the fire of a sacrificial tripod. "Excuse me, General," he said, and left to attend to other matters.

Arbo remained where he was, thinking it over. The drama could serve as a bridge to speak with Coelia. They had only spoken a few times in the last year, and always with brevity. Deciding to risk it, he strode up the steps of the Temple of Concordia, approaching the Vestal with a slight bow.

"Apologies for the display, High Priestess," he said. "I wasn't aware the emperor would be present."

She smiled civilly. "It is no trouble, General," she replied. She turned to Domitia. "I should return to the sanctum. Remain here."

Leaving Arbo and Domitia in an awkward silence, Coelia descended the steps of the temple. As she reached the base, soldiers parted the crowd so she could continue along the Via Sacra back to the temple, escorted by lictors and stopping here and there to bless those who knelt along the street or tossed flower petals in her path. Although her flowing attire concealed it, she could feel her body trembling from the brief encounter with Arbo. The ire she held for him had not abated, not even a little, and he had done nothing to change that. Instead of filling the Order's coffers all at once, as he implied he would do, he had extended the process as long as possible through regular disbursements intended to keep her from retiring to Cumae.

He is like a controlling husband, thought Coelia, *only placing one coin at a time in his wife's hand.*

Her spirits improved as she arrived at the temple, noting that the trend of recent festivals had continued. A long line of Roman matrons had formed along the street, all waiting patiently for their turn to enter the normally cloistered sanctum, behold the sacred fire with their own eyes, and place an offering to Vesta—figs, dates, bread, cakes—on the floor beside the altar. At the bottom of the temple's steps, a novice greeted each worshipper with a blessing. Coelia walked past her en route to the House of the Vestals, passing by piles of terracotta votives on the street. Molded to resemble deceased men, women and children, the dedications had been left by mourning family members who wished for the Vestal Virgins to offer them into the eternal fire.

Coelia entered the house and headed for her tablinum, spotting Rufinia and Florina standing by the statue of the Vestal Occia in the peristyle. The young priestesses were taking a scolding from Ptolema for some real or imagined transgression, but Coelia was suddenly too fatigued to rescue them. Disregarding Rufinia's pleading eyes, she slipped into her office.

As expected, Brogos was there, standing on a ladder and spreading fresh plaster over a cracked section of the vivid swan fresco that decorated the high ceiling. He looked down at her.

"After I fix it, I can repaint it, if you'd like." He grinned. "A fresco of me in the arena with my sword in the air, bodies lying all around and the whole stadium on their feet cheering. What do you think?"

"Very appropriate," said Coelia. "A gladiator painted on a Vestal's ceiling."

"Better here than in your bedchamber."

"I'll stick with Venus and her swans," replied Coelia, sloughing off the ribald comment. Of course, Brogos meant no offense—it was just his irreverent nature, and he routinely said much worse—but it made her wonder. Had Arbo told him of their kiss? That was unlikely. He would not risk making things any worse between them, if worse were even possible.

She moved behind her desk and sat down, glancing up at Brogos to make sure she wasn't in the path of any falling plaster. Feeling reasonably safe, she looked down to find the entire surface of her desk covered in white splatters of the stuff. The sight instantly transported her back to the rooftop of Arbo's stable, to the dovecotes covered in pigeon droppings, to the days they spent recording the return of his homing pigeons and sitting on Agrippa's terrace, looking out over the flowing waters of the Tiber and talking about their future.

"On second thought," she said to Brogos, wiping the mess off her desk. "Plaster over the whole damn thing. The artists can paint whatever they please."

CHAPTER XXVI

"And then what, Highness?"

"And then what? I already told you! A couple brats followed my lectica all the way back through the Forum, braying like donkeys the whole time. The guards didn't even chase them away. I actually think they *slowed* their pace to amuse themselves!" Valentinian threw his empty wine cup onto the floor, and it tumbled under the couch opposite him. "I can live with being ignored or told what to do, that is the narrative of my life, but I cannot live with being publicly humiliated and laughed at."

Delilah rose from her couch in the triclinium of the Domus Tiberiana and fetched Valentinian another cup of wine. She handed it to him and he reclined, putting the cup to his lips and drinking.

"You should not let the general ruffle your feathers, Highness," she said. "You are an eagle of Rome."

"A flightless eagle," grumbled Valentinian. "A caged eagle." He sat up and tossed the empty wine cup aside. It rolled over the floor to join the first one under the couch. "I must escape."

Delilah thought about it. "What if we say we're going riding and just run away?"

"My guards won't let me do anything without the general's permission. I can't even walk freely on the Palatine anymore, never mind getting on a horse. Just this morning I wanted to have a peaceful breakfast by the fountains in the house of Domitian, but two guards followed me the whole time, prattling all the way about their pathetic little lives. Why should I have to listen to them complain about their salaries or their back pain or the fact they can't find a good woman? I just want to enjoy my morning cheese in solitude!"

"Let's go to bed," said Delilah. "It's late. You'll be able to think more clearly after a good night's sleep. That is how the mind works."

"Maybe you're right."

Delilah rose from her couch, and Valentinian followed her into the expansive lamplit bedchamber and toward the four-post bed, careful to not trip on the various tunicas, cloaks and pairs of sandals she left lying around. The woman was a perfectionist in bed, but a slob out of it. He let her undress him, and then sat on the edge of the mattress while she disrobed, though in his distracted state he took little pleasure in it. She pushed his body back onto the bed and knelt on the carpet, spreading his legs and raking her fingertips gently against his bare thighs, teasing him.

"Relax," she soothed.

But it was no use. He pulled his legs up and tucked them under the covers. "I cannot," he said. "I just want to sleep."

Delilah climbed into the bed and cozied up to him. "You will feel better in the morning, Highness." She kissed his cheek. "Good night."

Valentinian lay awake, staring at the stuccoed ceiling as the candlelight cast dancing shadows upon it. He sensed Delilah's breathing change as she fell into sleep, but her easy slumber only amplified his insomnia and he sat up, raking his fingers against his scalp in frustration. He had never felt so alone. After his father's death, his mother had been his protector and strategist, always seeming to find a way to advance his interests. Since her death, he had been left to fend for himself... and to fend off those who used him only to increase their own power.

For my part, I don't care about power anymore, he thought. *I just want to go to Viennensis and live in peace.*

The thick flame of a candle flared, and something shiny caught Valentinian's eye. He squinted and recognized it—the large deer-shaped bronze brooch on Delilah's favorite cloak, the only one she took the time to hang over the top of the dressing screen.

An idea came to him. Without giving himself a moment to reconsider, he slipped soundlessly out of bed and moved about the bedchamber in the low light, picking Delilah's tunica and sandals off the floor and squeezing his body and feet into them. He plucked her blue cloak off the dressing screen and wrapped it over his shoulders, pulling the hood over his head. And then he began to walk, as calmly and womanly as he could, through the corridors of Tiberius's grand palace.

It can work, he told himself. *Delilah often leaves after I'm done with her.*

He neared the front portico of the home—all other entrances and exits were sealed—to find the doors open and the guards standing just outside, gossiping over a crackling spit. The smell of roasted pig filled his nostrils, and he caught fragments of their conversation. More banal talk of women, though louder and bawdier now that night had fallen and they had wine in their bellies.

Forcing himself to maintain a steady pace, to adopt the posture of a prostitute who had departed her patron's house a hundred times before at this time of night, Valentinian pulled the cloak's hood down over his face and clutched it closed at the breastbone the way women always did when chilled.

If I can get by these guards, I can make it. The ones at the checkpoints won't look twice.

He walked briskly over the threshold and past the guards, feeling the heat of the fire briefly pulse against his body as he passed.

"Have a good time tonight, honey?" one of the guards called after him, and they all laughed.

The emperor nodded his head and kept walking. Behind him, the guards turned their focus back to their food.

"The damn pig's near burned," one of them complained. "Cut me a slice."

Valentinian let himself exhale and continued to put distance between himself and the men... until a voice, close and unexpected, made him stop.

"Whoa, slow down, my peach. I almost walked right into you."

Valentinian held his breath. Directly ahead of him, a torchlit figure emerged from the darkness—another one of the guards. He swore to himself. Yes, there had only been three of them around the fire. No doubt this one had stepped away to relieve himself, at least if the piss stain on his soldier's tunica and the smell of wine on his breath were any indication. Head down, Valentinian veered off to the left and kept walking.

The guard sniggered and began to make his way back toward the fire, drawn by the enticing smell of the roast pig. But then something inside him, some sober instinct or flare of caution, made him think twice. His colleagues were even deeper into the wine than he. If they hadn't followed proper protocol, if they hadn't searched the girl... he turned and sprinted to catch up to her, grabbing the back of her blue cloak.

Valentinian gripped the cloak tighter at the breastbone and twisted his body, trying to escape the guard's grasp, but that only solidified the guard's suspicion. He yanked harder, and the cloak flew off Valentinian's body.

"Leave me alone!" cried the emperor.

The guard jerked his head back—he didn't quite know what he had expected to see, but he certainly had *not* expected to see the emperor dressed in a long tunica and women's sandals. Valentinian darted into the black night.

"*Attat!*" exclaimed the guard. "It's him! He's out!"

The three guards around the spit dropped their midnight suppers and raced into the darkness, all four soldiers now tracking the emperor more by sound than by sight. There was scant light in this section of the grounds. They called out to each other, searching.

"Where is he?"

"I can't see a bloody thing!"

"He's this way... follow my voice!"

As Valentinian propelled himself forward into the darkness, he could feel them closing the distance from behind, the sound of their footfalls and the clinking of the metal daggers at their sides getting louder, more threatening, more inevitable. He took a sharp right turn and felt the stone pathway below him disappear, replaced by the feel of vegetation—he was in a garden. He ran more forcefully, trying to make some headway, but the thick branches and leafy plants grew nearly waist-high, miring his progress. His left sandal—Delilah's sandal—caught on something, a root or a low bundle of tight branches, and things suddenly became much worse. He fell forward, yelping as the rigid branches lacerated his face on the way down.

"I've got him!" shouted one of the guards.

Valentinian felt strong hands clamp onto his arms, yanking his body out of its branchy trap. He let his legs go limp as the guards towed him out of the garden and back down the footpath, the ill-fitting sandals dragging along the ground. As they reached the firelit portico, he scrambled to get his feet under him and wrenched out of their grips, standing to face them in indignation. All four guards stared at him, eyes blazing with anger... but then one snickered and began to laugh, his joviality a hybrid of relief and amusement. The others joined in, and soon all four were bent over at the waist, wheezing with the hilarity of it, slapping each other on the back. The emperor turned around and shuffled back into the house. The doors closed heavily behind him and locked from the outside. He paused long enough to remove the restrictive sandals from his bleeding feet and continued back to the bedchamber. Delilah was still fast asleep. Valentinian struggled to pull her long tunica off over his head, dropped it to the floor, and sat naked on the edge of the bed.

"Now they know," he whimpered. "Now they'll be watching me closer than ever."

"What?" Delilah sat up in bed. The emperor's ragged appearance and anguished expression jolted her to full wakefulness. "Highness, what has happened?"

"I tried to escape," he said quietly. "They caught me."

"You tried to escape without me?"

"I wore your clothes and tried to get out," he said. "I would have sent for you once I was safe." He probably meant it. He rested his head on her shoulder.

"But you know they search me when I come and go."

"I couldn't stop myself," said Valentinian. "I just did it on impulse."

Delilah took the edge of the bedsheet and dabbed the blood off the emperor's face. "Highness," she said. "Why can I not just relay a message to Theodosius for you?"

"You would never be granted an audience. Not even a clerk would meet with you."

"With Ambrosius, then."

"Even less chance. His staff wouldn't let you get close. He is paranoid of scandal."

Delilah fell silent for some time. "What if I could get a letter to one of their offices? Something in your handwriting, with your signature on it. I could use the *cursus publicus* to courier it. One of my clients—before you, of course—oversees part of the route. He will help, I'm sure of it."

"Maybe," pondered Valentinian. "But the guards search you—"

"There are places they do not search, Highness," said Delilah. "If can hide a letter..." she shifted her eyes downward, between her legs.

Valentinian followed her eyes and her meaning. His deepening despair held fast and then began to rise again as renewed hope. "How?"

She shook her head, thinking, and glanced at his desk. "If you roll the paper small, and cover it in wax. I can put it inside. I can try, at least."

Valentinian leapt up and dashed to the desk. He sat naked in the chair and used the flame of one candle to light two more. Picking up a stylus, he stared at the blank pieces of papyrus before him. Then he got to work. He wrote to Theodosius first, conveying what he suspected the emperor already knew, but chose to ignore: *General Arbogastes, my regent and your magister militum, mistreats me, holds me captive, and does not consult me on Imperial matters.*

He wrote to Ambrosius next, disclosing what he knew would cause the bishop to act: *Senator Symmachus is returning from exile, and despite his treason, has been promoted to consul; General Arbogastes seeks to keep your religious counsel from me, while heathen festivals are openly celebrated on every street in Rome.*

He folded both sheets of papyrus lengthwise and rolled them up tightly. After dumping the miscellaneous contents of a desk tray onto the floor, he poured the melted wax from all three candles into the tray and carefully dipped the spool of papyrus into it, slowly molding a layer of wax around it. He set it aside. He and Delilah waited for it to cool, which it did, into a small, smooth cylinder.

"Are you sure that I should do it tonight?" asked Delilah. "Won't they be extra vigilant now?"

"They will be drunk now," said Valentinian. "And they won't expect me to try something twice in one night. Now is as good as ever."

Delilah took the wax cylinder in her hand and brought it between her legs. She looked at Valentinian. "I love you," she said.

"When we are free and living in Viennensis," he replied, "I will make you the wealthiest courtesan in the history of the Imperial court."

Delilah inserted the wax cylinder. That done, she dressed carefully, feeling it inside her body as she moved. It felt strange, but secure enough, and not so different than some of the cheap wool inserts she used when she menstruated. She could do this. As she brushed her hair and quickly pinned it back, Valentinian plucked one of her discarded cloaks off the floor and draped it over her shoulders. He put his hands on either side of her head, pulling her close to place a long kiss on her lips. She placed her hands on top of his and looked into his eyes.

"I will not fail you, Highness," she promised.

She waited for him to say something else, but he didn't. That left no reason to delay, so she turned and strode out of the bedchamber, through the dimly lit palace to the main portico. The doors were closed and secured from the outside. She rapped on the thick wood with her knuckles.

One of the doors opened, and a guard with glazed eyes and a lopsided grin permitted her to exit. As she stepped outdoors, she noticed the three others standing nearby. One of them stumbled over and lifted her cloak to peer underneath.

"You're not hiding anyone under there, are you?" he teased.

"No, sir," she replied.

Another guard clutched the fabric of her long dress and hiked it up. "Nothing under there either, honey?"

She smiled, playing along. "Only what the emperor has paid for." She put a hand on her hip. "I don't know what happened, but His Highness is inconsolable. Burst into tears and ordered me to leave."

The guards erupted in laughter.

"*Burst into tears,*" chortled one. He slapped Delilah on the bottom. "Off you go, love," he said.

"Thank you, sir," she said.

She strolled away from the guards, her breaths coming easier the more their voices receded. She followed the familiar street, clearing one checkpoint and then another, until she reached the foot of the Palatine Hill and the liberty of the larger city, all the while carrying the emperor's official correspondence in a manner that she suspected was a first in the history of Rome.

CHAPTER XXVII

Ostia (one day by horse west of Rome)

Most Roman men whose wives indulged in the women-only bath complexes in and around the port city of Ostia correctly assumed that said baths were decorated in a manner similar to the men's baths. They would expect to see the same kinds of splendid statuary—great Neptunes, muscly horses, naked Venuses and cute Cupids, beautiful dolphins—and stroll across the same kinds of exquisite tile mosaics on the heated floors. They would expect the turquoise waters to be just as clear and hot, the columns and walls to be just as marbled, the bath attendants and aestheticians to be just as hospitable, the air to be just as humid and fragrant, and the food and drink to be just as delectable.

They also assumed, often less correctly, that it was only their neighbor's wife who might let her eyes linger on the rumored erotic frescos of naked gladiators in the women's baths or receive a massage from those gossiped-about masseurs whose skilled hands delivered more pleasure than was decent or, worst of all, take advantage of the reputed male prostitutes who offered one-on-one services in the private bath chambers. Of course, the men's baths swarmed with erotic masseuses and prostitutes of both sexes... but that was different.

Abigail knew that her husband would make the same assumptions. Despite their extended time apart, he would never think that she might feel a twinge of sexual need or corrupt their marital vows with impure thoughts or deeds. But it had been so long, and Senator Perses's search for her—he held her responsible for the exorcism death of his wanton daughter Anthea—showed no signs of abating. The man had hired mercenaries to, in his words, "bring her to justice" for her involvement, but Abigail knew—everyone knew—that if his mercenaries found her, no one would ever know. There would be no public investigation or trial. They would murder her on the spot and desecrate her body in every way the grieving father could think of.

That is why Abigail had still not returned home to her villa in the suburbs of Rome, but had instead traveled to one sumptuous retreat after another under an assumed name. She had even changed her appearance. Her natural dark hair was now as fair as any Gaul's, and the white lead pigment that she regularly applied to her skin had lightened her face at least two shades. Not that she minded. It was kind of fun seeing a different reflection in the mirror. And although there were times when she missed the familiarity of home and the comforts of her marriage, there was a part of her that had come to love the freedom of life as a single woman. A single wealthy woman.

So when her husband's last covert message had arrived with the news that he had secretly purchased property in northern Hispania, thus enabling them to again live as man and wife, Abigail had mixed feelings. Soon, it would all be about him again. What *he* wanted for supper. When *he* wanted to couple and how—which meant her on her back and him finishing before she had started. It would be back to prayers and scripture studies, and pretending not to notice that while she was doing the Lord's work, he was in the pantry with one of the young housekeepers.

She pushed thoughts of the impending lifestyle reversal out of her mind, choosing to just enjoy the day. The sun was high and hot, her poolside couch was soft and the water was glistening. Although the baths were full of women and attendants, it was tranquil and quiet, and she was glad she had chosen to stay at a retreat in the countryside just outside of Ostia. The whole area was surrounded by stone pines and expansive gardens, which she preferred to the noisy markets, apartments, temples, churches and other buildings that filled the city itself. Even that morning, she had awoken slowly in her guest room to the gentle sound of a deer munching on a tree just below her window. It was so much better than being jarred awake by pounding hammers, ringing bells, bellowing vendors and rattling carts.

An attendant came by with a tray of delicacies, but Abigail declined. The heat from the afternoon sun had become too much for her to stay outside, but more than that, her thoughts had again started to wander to the male prostitute she had already hired twice during her stay. He called himself Antinous—he probably didn't use his real name either—and she didn't have to search long to find him. He was sitting on the edge of a Triton fountain, waiting to see if she was ready for a third encounter. She rose from her couch and preceded him into the same private bath chamber they had used the day before, and the day before that.

He did his work without speaking, undressing her and leading her into the warm water, his mouth and hands not hesitating to do all the things her husband had neither the care nor the skill to do. At first, she had been reserved, but now she held her legs open for him as she lay on her back on the heated tile, giving herself entirely to the feel of his tongue as it glided over her most sensitive spots, and writhing under his fingers as they moved up to touch her breasts. He brought her to another slow but strong climax, stroking her thighs as her breathing returned to normal. And though he asked for nothing in return, nothing other than his well-earned payment, she now knew his body well enough to stroke him to a quick release. That done, he kissed her in parting and left her to soak in the warm water, enjoying the afterglow.

As the last of the feeling left her, Abigail stepped out of the private pool and wrapped herself in one of the fresh linen shawls that hung on the wall. Suddenly thirsting for some sweet lemon water, she sauntered outdoors where pools of varying sizes, shapes and depths dotted the colorful tile floors. Encircling it all, a colonnade of red marble columns created a striking boundary against the forest of green trees that lay just beyond.

She was gazing contentedly into this verdant forest when she saw a form so out of place, so wildly unlikely, that for a fleeting moment she wondered if she had fallen asleep after Antinous's services and was actually curled up on a couch, dreaming. But then someone screamed.

"Lion!"

As if responding to its name, the beast leapt out of the woods and bounded directly toward two women tossing a ball back and forth by an oval pool, idly exercising while chatting. The lion seemed to prefer the woman who currently held the ball, but then she threw the sphere with all her might at its head, and although uninjured, it changed its mind and headed for the other one. She shrieked, dodged it, and dove into the oval pool.

The lion didn't chase its prey into the water, but pinned its ears back and lowered its head, appraising its other mealtime options. It walked slowly, teeth bared, as pool guests frantically sought the correct course of action. Should they run, try to hide, dive into a pool, or stay put and pray to whatever god they thought was most likely to intervene? It seemed like everyone made their respective decision at the same moment, and in a burst of terrified activity, women variously ran into the woods or deeper into the bath complex, tipped over couches to hide under the frames and cushions, jumped into the water of the nearest pool, or dropped to their knees and began to pray.

In keeping with her character, Abigail decided to hide. She darted for the closest couch, but it was already shielding its capacity of women under its heavy cushions. One of them clawed at her.

"Get away! Find your own spot!"

She ran to the next couch and tried to crawl under it, but again she was refused, this time with a foot to the face as one of the women already there kicked her away.

"There's no room for you under here!"

Abigail clambered away and started to run. She didn't look back as an impossibly loud roar rattled her skull and seemed to impact her physically, jolting her heart to beat harder and her legs to move faster. Screaming, she realized that she was fleeing the predator within a larger group of panicked women all running along the tile floor, perhaps too much like a herd of startled gazelles bolting across the plains of Africa. She hoped she was not the weakest or the slowest... that was always the herd's sacrifice.

She had made it about halfway across the outdoor pool complex when she saw a problem approaching, as if in slow motion. Just ahead, the surface of the floor changed to a smoother tile—she had almost slipped on it twice already today—compelling her to slow down before falling down. But the tile was even slipperier than she remembered, and her legs went out from under her at the same time that she felt a shocking, fur-covered force strike her from behind.

Like a mythical monster formed from the body parts of different animals, three women—including Abigail—plus two male attendants and the lion itself, merged into a single amalgamation that slipped on the floor together, their limbs mingling and entangling. The mass of their intertwined bodies slid over the smooth tile to land with a heavy splash in a small but deep pool. Flecks of gold paint from the beast's fur swirled in the water.

The sights and sounds of the world disappeared as Abigail plunged below the surface, held there by the awful weight of the lion. Flailing arms and legs struck at her head and chest, creating a whirlpool of current around her. Holding her breath, she opened her eyes and looked up. The lion was thrashing madly above her, its protracted claws tearing the flesh of the bodies closest to it. As the water grew red and opaque, one of its curved claws sliced her left breast open. Her cry of agony was lost as the beast's roar sounded in the water, gurgled and muted, but horrifically sonorous all the same. Ignoring her pain, Abigail extended her arms upward in the red water, one moment trying to push the lion up and out of the way, and the next moment trying to drag it down and use it as leverage to reach the surface... she needed to breathe!

For those still hiding behind couches or praying on their knees, and for the remainder of the herd, the watery havoc created an opportunity. The male prostitute Antinous was the first to see it.

"Don't let it get back out!" he hollered. Spotting a neat row of thick linens hanging against a wall, he scooped them in his arms and then rushed back to the pool to toss them, one by one, on top of the monster. "Help me!"

The others joined in. They emptied shelves of their linens, grabbed them off the floor, fished them out of other pools and even tore them off their own bodies, throwing each piece of absorbent fabric on top of the monster, weighing the beast down, trapping it within twisted lengths of cloth, and not sparing a self-endangering thought for the parts of the monster that were human.

It took a lion's weight in linen, but the strategy started to work. The big cat became more tightly constricted in the tangle of water-logged fabric. Confined by that, and anchored down by the human animals clambering onto it from below, it sank below the surface and stayed there.

Gradually, the thrashing and muted roars and shrieks stopped, and the surface of the water grew still. The pile of soaked fabrics draped over the floating mound of the drowned monster masked a sight—a menagerie of entwined dead bodies—that no one looking into the pool wanted to imagine, so instead they stepped away, giving thanks to their respective gods and proudly congratulating each other on working together to slay one of the famous Gilded Lions of Rome.

CHAPTER XXVIII

SENATUS POPULUSQUE ROMANUS INCENDIO
CONSUMPTUM RESTITUIT

S uch was the inscription on the pediment on the Temple of Saturn in the Roman Forum: *The Senate and people of Rome restored this temple which had been consumed by flames.*

But the temple hadn't merely been restored. Since its destruction some thirty years earlier, it had been rebuilt and reimagined as an even grander testament to Saturn and the true gods of Rome. It was both the timing and the attitude in Rome that had made it so.

For decades, the people of the Roman Empire—most of whom were still faithful pagans—had lived under laws that criminalized the worship of their gods. Depending on the place, time and people involved, some of these laws were observed and enforced, others totally ignored. Regardless, the constant assault on their freedoms, and the clergy's relentless campaign to stir up fear and hatred toward them, had become a way of life for pagan Romans. So when it came time to rebuild the Temple of Saturn, they decided that they'd had enough. Every gleaming column, every gilded capital, every shining statue in, on and around the enormous temple was a symbol not just of religious veneration, but of political resistance. They would build the temple they wanted, one that hearkened back to Rome's golden age.

It was therefore no coincidence that Symmachus—only recently returned from exile—had chosen this temple to meet with Rome's pagan elite. In attendance were many of the influential senators, magistrates, officers, priests and aristocrats who had petitioned Theodosius to forgive his charge of treason and rescind the order of exile. Not only had Theodosius done so, but he had gone a step further by appointing Symmachus as a consul of Rome. It was a position even higher than his previous one. The promotion had a dual purpose: to preserve Symmachus's dignity and to satisfy General Arbogastes, who had only reluctantly agreed to arrest the respected senator in the first place.

Coelia had been among the first to welcome Symmachus back to Rome, noting that he looked no worse for the experience. Indeed, his healthy countenance confirmed the general suspicion that his forced absence from Rome had been more vacation than exile. Just like the almost fully recovered Claudia, whose letters practically burst with carefree joy, he was proof that life outside of Rome wasn't just less stressful, it was more pleasant. Coelia imagined her villa in Cumae—she had to imagine it, since she had yet to actually visit—and looked at Arbo. Only two more disbursements from him, and the Vestal coffers would be as full as they were before she had secretly funded Victor's legions. He felt her eyes on him and met her gaze. Yet instead of smiling hopefully at her as he usually did, his expression remained level, even dour. Something big was on his mind.

A mirthful voice drew her attention away from him.

"Have you heard the latest, High Priestess?" asked Senator Junius, speaking in the tone reserved for only one topic.

"Tell me they caught one alive," she replied. "Please."

"Not alive," said Junius. "It struck at a bathhouse outside of Ostia. A bunch of women drowned the thing in a pool, if you can believe it."

"Let that be a warning, Senator."

He smirked, but his levity faded when he saw Arbo. "I don't like the look on the general's face," he said.

"I was just thinking the same thing."

Senator Nicomachus called the meeting to order. Those gathered, including Coelia and Junius, took to the comfortable chairs arranged around the perimeter of the temple's magnificent rectangular sanctum, a space that often served as a meeting hall for religious or civic matters.

Symmachus stood in the center. "Friends," he said. "Tomorrow in the Senate, it will be my duty as consul to read the newest Imperial edict. It concerns our religion." He held out his hands, pushing back the uproar of anger. "Outrage will get us nowhere," he said. When the chamber settled, he continued. "It is decreed that the observance of the immortal gods is a *religio illicita*." He raised his voice, shouting to be heard over the clamor. "All forms of pagan worship—even private worship—are a criminal offense. The temples are to be closed, and anyone honoring the ancestral gods is to have his property confiscated and his assets seized. At the discretion of the state, anyone performing or observing a pagan ritual may be executed. My friends, if any spirit of religious equality remained from Constantine's edict, it is gone now."

Nicomachus stood. "Then we must do what we have always done," he said. "Ignore it."

"Perhaps," said Symmachus, "but this edict is a harsh one, and it comes at a pivotal time. Theodosius knows of our religion's widespread resurgence. He knows about the public festivals and rituals, and he knows that our temples prosper. He is likely to enforce this edict more than previous ones."

"And who will he find to enforce it?" asked Perses. Since the death of his daughter, Perses rarely spoke publicly, and all eyes flew to him. "No magistrate or officer in Rome will dare."

"It has been that way until now," agreed Symmachus, his tone softening slightly, "but with religious power hanging in the balance, Theodosius will not take any risks."

"There are more of us than them," said Nicomachus, his already rough complexion reddening with indignation.

"True," someone else shouted. "They can't prosecute all of us."

"They don't need to," said Symmachus. "If they confiscate one man's home—his sense of security, his life's work, his son's inheritance or his daughter's dowry—a thousand other men will fall into line. And make no mistake. Those ordered to enforce these laws will do so. If they refuse, they risk losing their own meager assets, or their heads, for insubordination." A doleful tone settled into his voice. "Laws such as these are not enacted to maintain public order, or punish a crime, or protect a citizen's rights. They are enacted only to instill fear and capitulation, so that an iniquitous few can control the many." He looked at Nicomachus. "That is why it doesn't matter that there are more of us than them. Our oldest laws, the Twelve Tables, restrained the abuses of the powerful few. These new laws unleash them."

"So what do you advise?" asked Junius. "Sending another senatorial delegation to Theodosius to protest?"

"There is no point," Symmachus replied. "The last two have been turned away." He gestured in the direction of the Palatine Hill. "Valentinian is co-signatory of the edict. Perhaps if he could be persuaded to revoke his support for it... " He dropped his arms to his sides. "Otherwise, we can only wait and see. An opportunity may present itself."

The structure of the meeting broke apart into clusters of discussion and debate, though to Coelia there wasn't much point in either. Symmachus was right. Only time would tell to what extent the laws would be enforced. As for other options, there wouldn't be any until something changed at the Imperial level, something big enough to create opportunities below.

Feeling deflated at the thought of yet another persecutory Imperial edict, Coelia made a round of small talk with the other pontiffs and sacerdotes, said a few farewells to those senators closest to her, and headed for the grand doors of the temple. Domitia and the others would be waiting to hear Symmachus's news. She stepped outside into the fading light of the day, looking for her guard Teo.

"I sent him back to the temple."

Coelia turned around to see Arbo exiting the temple behind her.

"It was not your place to do so, General," she said. "But no matter. The Forum is secure. I can walk back alone."

"I will accompany you," said Arbo.

She would have resisted, but those gathered within the temple were now streaming out, taking their discussions into the otherwise quiet street. She could hardly be seen arguing with the general in public.

"Thank you, sir," she replied.

He fell into step beside her, and they walked along the cobblestone street. It wasn't until they reached the Temple of Castor and Pollux that Arbo broke the silence.

"This edict," he began. "I will do my best to—"

"To what?" Coelia interrupted. "To have it revoked? To prevent it from being enforced?" She scoffed. "If Victor were Caesar, it would never have been written in the first place. Now, the best you can do is plead with Theodosius to have mercy, to show restraint, to not destroy the things you honor or impoverish your friends, half of whom you once arrested just to please him!"

"Symmachus and the others have forgiven me," asserted Arbo. "They understand that I did what I thought was best. And I have protected them, Coelia, just as I've protected you. Who hasn't been promoted or made richer since Theodosius made me regent?"

"And yet the noose of the law tightens around our necks a little more every day," said Coelia. "General Bauto risked his life for Gratian, for Theodosius, for Valentinian. He kept them in power and was loyal, yet just like you, they ignored his pleas for religious equality. You *must* be Bauto's son, since you are just as gullible. You are not Theodosius's top general. You are his most useful fool."

"I was trying to avoid a war."

"So you surrendered without a fight? How heroic."

The derision in her voice, the ferocity of her words, slowed Arbo's step and he fell behind as Coelia stomped toward the doors of the Vestals' residence. She disappeared into the house, leaving him standing alone in the street and reeling from the kind of fatigue—the fatigue of assault—that he hadn't felt since the last time he had stood, wearied and traumatized, on a battlefield. He knew she resented him deeply, but hearing it spout from her with such bitterness... he could not stop his thoughts from returning to that time and place they so often did. That moment in Caesar Augustus's courtyard, when he had strangled Victor to death.

Needing to put distance between himself and the lingering echoes of her words, he marched toward the Palatine and began to make his way up the ramp, toward the palace of Tiberius. But the echoes followed, and by the time he reached the principal tablinum of the palace—the one Eugenius could almost always be found working within—Coelia's words were pounding in his ears.

Eugenius looked up from a large desk and set down his stylus as the general entered the office. "How did they take the news about the edict?" he asked.

"As men with no other choice always do," Arbo replied. "Resigned, but hopeful."

"*Dum spiro, spero*," said Eugenius. "A valiant thought, but in my experience, hope is what men fall back on when they know they are fucked."

Arbo slumped into the chair opposite him. "Valentinian has been getting letters out via the cursus publicus," he revealed. "One of my men discovered it at a random checkpoint. I found out just before the meeting."

"That explains a lot," said Eugenius. He spoke to himself as much as to Arbo. "So he's found an ally here in the palace... someone to move letters in and out." He sat back in his chair. "One of the guards?"

"I don't know. Could be a guard, a cook, a servant, a gardener, or any one of the whores. Regardless, I have two choices. I can torture and kill everyone who has had contact with him and look like a paranoid despot to the Senate, or I can just cut the problem off at the source."

It was several long moments before Eugenius spoke. "It would be better if it looked like an accident."

"No one would believe that."

"Suicide, then. Everyone knows Valentinian is as spineless as they come."

"Cowards fear death more than anyone. People would know the truth of it."

"A claim of suicide leaves room for speculation," said Eugenius. "If you want him dead, but you want to deny involvement, at least officially, I see no other way." He leaned forward and spoke encouragingly. "Give the people of Rome what they want, General."

"And what is that, Eugenius?"

"You, sir. As their emperor."

The cooks were getting lazier with each passing day. When Delilah had first started providing her services to Valentinian, the kitchen had always been well-stocked with the freshest ingredients, the finest exotic delicacies and the best wines. Before the cooks left for the day—General Arbogastes prohibited overnight servants—they would prepare elegant platters of meats, cheeses and sweets, and leave them in the kitchen for her. That way, when she and Valentinian had finished coupling, she could bring him a snack. But no more. Now when she did her late-night dashes to the kitchen, the cupboards were as deserted as the rest of the palace. She was lucky if she could scrape together some bread and salted fish. The wine was second-rate now, too. No doubt the cooks were pouring the good stuff into their cups at home.

Naked except for the costly silk *subligar* that served as an erotic loincloth, Delilah stood on a low stool in the kitchen and reached up to the top shelf of the cupboard, feeling around in the hopes that her fingers would land on some forgotten treat. She touched something, but it rolled away, so she stood on her tiptoes until she could grab it. An old egg. How disappointing. She stepped off the stool and slunk into the pantry, but it was too dark to see anything. She sighed. If she waited long enough before heading back to his bedchamber, Valentinian would just fall asleep. That way, she wouldn't have to listen to him complain about her returning empty-handed. At this rate, she would have to start bringing food from her own shelves to stock the emperor's kitchen. Wasn't it enough to be his favorite courtesan and secret courier, or did she need to be his cook as well? She stubbed her toe on something in the dark pantry and cursed under her breath, reaching out to feel her way out of the stockroom, back toward the flicker of the lamp's flame in the kitchen.

But chaos got there before she did. It started as a single shout somewhere else in the palace, but within a breath it was an endless howl from Valentinian, one that grew louder as he burst into the kitchen completely naked, running directly into the edge of the butcher's table and knocking the wind out of himself. Instinctively, Delilah shrunk back into the darkness of the pantry as the sound of fast, hard footfalls on the tile floor outside the kitchen kicked her heartbeat into a similar rhythm. She peered around the corner to see General Arbogastes invade the kitchen. He reached out with a strong hand and grabbed Valentinian by the scruff of the neck. The emperor dropped to the floor, slipping out of the general's fingers.

"Stop!" shrieked Valentinian. "I order you to stop!"

Arbo wasted no energy and no time responding. He knelt down and wrapped both of his hands around the emperor's thin neck, squeezing. Valentinian kicked and thrashed, the soles of his bare feet and the palms of his hands slapping at the mosaic floor as he desperately tried to squirm out from under the larger man. From her place of hiding, Delilah put a hand over her mouth and stared down at Valentinian's face. His eyes were bulging and his lips were turning blue, but he was still conscious enough to catch sight of her gawking down at him. His lips sputtered something breathless and inarticulate, but she knew what he was saying: *Help me Delilah! For Christ's sake, he's killing me! Do something!*

From her hiding spot, Delilah glanced around at the shelves in the dim kitchen, assessing the cooking pans and utensils that hung from the walls. There were heavy pots and thick knives, and all sizes of butcher's hooks that could serve as weapons. If she were quick, quick as a mouse and just as quiet, she could skirt around the edge of the room unseen. More than likely, she could get her hands on a knife and have the blade in Arbogastes's back before he knew what or who had struck him. She licked her lips and inhaled deeply, targeting the closest and largest knife with her eyes, and leaned forward to run toward it. But then she hesitated. If she wasn't quick or quiet enough, if the general saw her first, if the guards came in, if she slipped on the floor... there were so many if's. She looked down at Valentinian and saw the recognition in his eyes, the panic that came from realizing that she wasn't going to help him. She felt a rise of guilt, but then remembered: *You did try to escape without me.*

Her state of indecision outlasted Valentinian's struggle for life, and death gradually soothed the look of panic in his eyes. General Arbogastes released his hold on the emperor's thin neck and stood. From what Delilah could tell, he hadn't even broken a sweat by the effort. He grabbed Valentinian by the ankles and began to drag the emperor's corpse out of the kitchen. Before he disappeared, he spoke.

"You made the right decision by staying put," he said. "Keep your mouth shut."

Delilah nodded in the dark and did as she was told, watching in silence and second thoughts as her one-and-only chance to become the wealthiest courtesan in the history of the Imperial court slid across the kitchen floor and out of sight.

CHAPTER XXIX

It was the second time that Coelia had stood before the eternal fire in the temple to pray for the soul of an emperor she wholly detested. The first time had been for Gratian. Following the instructions of the infirm Vestalis Maxima Claudia, the Vestals' prayers had been brief and formulaic, and their offerings scant. Now, as high priestess herself, Coelia led the same short prayers and spare offerings for the soul of Valentinian. After all, she knew that Vesta did not care to receive them any more than her chief Vestal cared to deliver them. But duty was duty.

I will go through the motions, she told herself, *and then have a very good lunch.*

"The flames are active for such a small offering," Domitia observed. "I wonder what that means?"

"Make a note in the records," said Coelia. "We will interpret on the ides."

Domitia nodded and leaned against the circular wall of the temple. "Valentinian, found hanging in his bedchamber," she reflected. "Do you think he really killed himself?"

Coelia stoked the fire and joined her, leaning her shoulder against the cool marble wall so they could speak face to face. "I don't know. I don't think so."

"You think the general killed him." It was a statement more than a question.

"He's done it before," said Coelia.

"My uncle fought for the general in Gaul," said Domitia. "He's retired now, but says there's already talk that the legions will declare Arbogastes emperor."

"Where did he hear that?"

"Those men gossip like spinsters. I honestly don't know how they manage to keep any war strategy a secret. Anyway, my uncle says that's why Eugenius left Rome so suddenly. He thinks he's going to Gaul to marshal the general's forces."

"Hm."

Domitia raised her eyebrows. "You know what that would mean, right?"

"What?"

"If the general became emperor and you married him..."

"That will never happen."

"... you would be empress." She grew more serious. "It's hardly a secret that the two of you were close. You won't convince me that you didn't care for him. Perhaps if you could forgive him for what happened to Victor, you could start again."

"It's been too long," said Coelia. "Feelings fade. And we were never a good match to begin with."

"A good match," considered Domitia. "Who's to say? Look at your mother and Olympius."

"Gods, I can't believe they're still together. My mother's letters are full of the most revolting flattery for him." Coelia put her hand to her chest, speaking with exaggerated adoration. "'Oh, daughter, you should see how Olympius has repaired the garden walls at our villa! Oh, daughter, you would not believe the quality of the new hypocaust system Olympius has installed in our bath! Oh, daughter, you would be amazed at what a good fisherman

Olympius has become! He caught the most amazing flounder right off our dock!'"

"Your villa," said Domitia, "aren't you dying to see it?"

"Of course I am. It will happen soon enough."

"What is stopping you?" The question was a reasonable one, but delivered with an unintended edge of frustration.

"I know you want to head the Order," said Coelia, glancing at the fire as it crackled loudly. "You will have your turn, I promise. But I made a mistake, and I have to fix it before I can step down."

"What kind of mistake?" When Coelia hesitated, Domitia pressed on. "We have been friends and sisters since we were girls. Not once in thirty years have I betrayed your trust or spoken against you. I deserve to know what is going on."

Coelia rolled her body so her back was against the curved wall. "Do you remember the first time Victor came to Rome?"

"Yes. We met him by the Temple of Julius Caesar."

"Do you remember what I said to him?"

"I remember you were nervous."

"I was trying to impress him," said Coelia. "So I told him the rumor of how High Priestess Occia had financed Caesar Octavian's armies from the temple's secret coffers. He never forgot the story. And then when his father invaded Italy..."

"Jupiter's stones..." said Domitia. "How much did you give him?"

"Almost all of it."

"Coelia!"

"But I have almost all of it back," assured Coelia. "I have to wait for three more disbursements from the general, and then it's back to where it was."

Suddenly feeling compelled to offer into the flames—the revelation was a shocking one—Domitia plucked a fragrant pinecone from a terracotta bowl and set it into the fire. She watched the flames slip under and between the scales to blacken the cone. "Who else knows about this?"

"Other than the general and now you, only Eugenius and Symmachus." Coelia joined her at the hearthfire. "When the coffers are full again, I will retire. The office will be yours if you want it." She shrugged. "Unless you think you'd be happier in a villa outside of Rome as well."

"And do what?" asked Domitia. "Learn to spin wool? Get married and listen to a husband snore all night in bed? Maybe at one time I would have thought about it, but not now. I'm needed here. Even with the latest Imperial edict, there are ample applications from families who want their daughters to enter the novitiate."

"That may change if Theodosius decides to enforce his laws," said Coelia.

"He won't be able to enforce anything if General Arbogastes is made emperor in Rome."

"Maybe," said Coelia.

She wasn't convinced. Everyone saw the general as being so powerful, so noble and courageous. She used to see him like that, too. Now all she saw was a liar, a man who had murdered Victor and deceived her, both acts of betrayal carried out by someone too afraid to bite the hand of his abusive master, Theodosius. Perhaps Arbo had changed and was no longer Theodosius's loyal pet. Perhaps he had killed Valentinian or at least driven the weakling to kill himself. Perhaps he was positioning himself to be named Augustus. But regardless of any of that, and regardless of what he had planned for the future, it wouldn't change the past.

"Now I know where all your pigeons went," said Brogos, only slightly winded. "You ate them all."

Releasing a long, exhausted breath, Arbo struggled to extricate himself from his armor. "It is tighter than it used to be," he conceded.

Spent from their sparring match, the two men sat heavily on the ground in the training field of the Campus Martius, their weapons and armor scattered around them. The air reverberated with the shouts of soldiers, the clashing of metal blades, the rattle of chariots and the loud whinnying of war horses being trained alongside drivers and riders.

"Fuck," said Arbo. "I can barely catch my breath."

"You vomited yesterday," Brogos jested. "So today's already an improvement."

"Kind words, Brogos."

"You just need to get your edge back. I was getting fat as a dinner hen before things picked up in the arena, but look at me now." He sat up and patted his tight belly. "Could bounce a denarius right off it."

"You and Deimos are doing well," said Arbo. "The hounds of Hades, and all that. I was at Senator Nicomachus's house for supper the other night, and the wine glasses had the pair of you engraved on them. You were running along the banks of the River Styx."

"Silver cups?"

"Gold."

Brogos nodded approvingly. "Good. Wouldn't want my face on the cheap shit."

Arbo struggled to his feet. "Let's go get something to eat."

"Last thing you need," said Brogos, standing. "But all right."

Leaving their armor for Arbo's subordinates to clear away—the general insisted on extreme order during military exercises—the pair headed directly to a kitchen tent to down two steaming bowls of gruel. That done, they ambled through the Field of Mars, Arbo inspecting the men and drills all around, never hesitating to stop and converse with even the most junior soldier. Whether the men who saluted the general were war-hardened veterans or new recruits who had never before wielded a sword, they all regarded him with the same fervent loyalty. Shouts of *"Ave, Caesar!"* and *"Augustus Arbogastes!"* followed him wherever he went. They wanted their general to be the emperor of Rome. What was good for him was good for them.

"I received word from Eugenius this morning," said Arbo. "The numbers are impressive. There is even more discontent among the legions than I thought."

"It isn't merely discontent," replied Brogos. "It's sheer hatred of Theodosius."

"I will have forces equal to his by the end of summer."

"And then you'll have your army. What will you do with it?"

"Move it to Mediolanum."

Brogos turned to the general. "It will mean war."

"Not necessarily. Opposing armies of equal strength can be good peacekeepers."

"Well, you would know better than me. I don't have a mind for politics."

"Theodosius refuses to receive delegations from the Senate," said Arbo. "He ignores petitions from the Senate. Rome's voice has grown too soft. I want it to be heard in Constantinople and Mediolanum, and in every corner of the empire. The army will speak for it." He paused, his voice losing its assertiveness. "I fucked up, Brogos. I should never have killed Victor. You know what his last words were? He said to me, 'Whatever Theodosius has promised you, he will never do it.' At that moment, I knew he was right, but I carried out my orders anyway."

"That moment is dead and buried, brother," said Brogos. "No point digging it up."

Their wanderings through the Campus Martius led them to the Pantheon, the place Arbo always gravitated to when he needed to feel the grandeur of the gods. As they approached the colossal columns of the portico, a memory returned—standing here with Victor and Coelia on the *Dies Romana*, drinking good wine under the bright midday sun. *If I could go back...* he thought, but pushed the caustic thought away. *Dead and buried.*

Entering the rotunda, Arbo's eyes moved upward to stare thoughtfully at the giant oculus in the ceiling just as a flock of birds flew by, black specks against the blue sky. He wondered: Did it look so different inside the Temple of Vesta? That sanctum was much smaller, of course—you could probably fit three of Vesta's temples inside the Pantheon—but as the sound of the altar fire in the Pantheon crackled within the circular walls, he could almost picture Coelia standing inside the goddess's temple, offering into the sacred flames. Leading Brogos to a larger-than-life statue of the goddess Diana, he poured a libation of wine into the fire that burned before it.

"I will never again beg for the honor of worshipping the gods," he said.

The two men moved on to a statue of Mars, both offering wine into the flames, before Arbo felt a presence behind him. He turned around to find a young soldier, helmet tucked under an arm, waiting to speak. His face was red and his breaths heavy, evidence he had been scrambling to find his superior.

"General," said the soldier. "A military convoy from Emperor Theodosius is requesting permission to enter the gates of the city."

Arbo nodded slowly, soberly. "Who leads it?"

"General Stilicho, sir."

CHAPTER XXX

"I cannot remember the last time we got drunk together," said Stilicho. "It has been too long."

"The last time we got drunk together, you were young and I was old, "Arbo replied. "Now you are old and I am ancient."

"Then you are in the right house." Stilicho stood and refilled his wine cup, surveying the traditional frescos that adorned the walls of Agrippa's triclinium. "From another time," he observed. He returned to recline on the couch opposite Arbo. "I keep expecting to see Bauto come stumbling in, a wine jug tucked under one arm and a woman under the other."

"He was a reaper, that man. Cut through swaths of women in every land." Arbo tilted the rim of his wine cup toward Stilicho. "Can't say you didn't do the same."

"I emulated my heroes," said Stilicho. "That includes you, Arbo. You took me in when I had nothing. Not a sestertius to my name. I didn't even have armor. You gave me your hand-me-downs." He smiled at the memory. "The cuirass was all dented and smelled like a swamp, but I felt like Achilles."

"It wasn't dented until you wore it," joked Arbo.

"It was you who introduced me to Bauto and brought me up through the ranks," Stilicho continued. "I never would've risen to general without your tutelage." He canted his head. "I certainly wouldn't have had the connections to marry into the house of Theodosius."

"Well, you always did have an elitist disposition. I remember how you used to pick through your barley, nose in the air."

Stilicho laughed. "I do enjoy life's indulgences."

"You've earned them. I hope Theodosius feeds you well."

"Well enough."

Arbo drained the last of the wine in his cup. He thought about getting up to get another, but the slight spin of the room changed his mind. He would pace himself. "How is your son?"

"The boy is smarter than I was at his age," said Stilicho. "He is already learning to read."

"I am sure you have high hopes for him."

"Doesn't every father?" A pair of servants entered the dining room with more wine and trays of freshly baked food, setting it all on the low table between the two men. They left as quickly as they had entered. Stilicho retrieved an oyster shell, tipping its contents into his mouth. "You're still in working order," he said to Arbo. "Ever think about having a son to run through this big house and get fingerprints on these old walls?"

"Not really."

"I always thought you'd marry that priestess you had your eye on."

The wine had already rendered Arbo a bit vulnerable, and the sudden thought of Coelia made his heart sink. "She is still at the temple." He peeled a slice of chicken off one of two roasted birds on the table and stuffed it in his mouth. "Your son," he said, quickly changing course. "He's only a few years younger than Theodosius's youngest, Honorius, is he not?"

"Yes. They play together."

"Hopefully well."

Stilicho wiped the oil from his lips with the back of his hand. "What do you mean by that?"

"You know what I mean," said Arbo. "You're no fool."

"My son is perfectly safe."

"Your son is too close to the throne to be perfectly safe," countered Arbo. "Too close in age and too close in blood to the heir apparent."

"I haven't had cause to worry."

"Perhaps, but who knows what worries cross the emperor's mind."

Stilicho sat up. "Right now, he has only one worry, my friend. The legions that your man Eugenius is mustering in Gaul."

"Drills and restructuring," said Arbo. "There are entire cohorts wandering the woods up there, wondering what to do with themselves."

Stilicho stood abruptly, knocking the table with his knees and spilling the wine. "You must stop, Arbo. Call Eugenius back to Rome."

"I'll call him back when it suits me," Arbo asserted. "I am still magister militum, and your superior. Or has Theodosius demoted me?"

"The emperor wants to trust you, but he cannot ignore the rumors that you're carving your own army out of his." Stilicho held out his arms entreatingly. "I too want to trust you, but I cannot ignore what I've seen with my own eyes. I have been back in Rome for less than a day, and already I've seen the graffiti painted on the walls—you, wearing the laurel crown. I've seen the open defiance of the laws against pagan worship." He let his arms drop to his sides, at once noticing a statuette of Diana that stood in a wall niche. It was the same one that Arbo had taken from a desecrated shrine years early on the road to the resort town of Baiae, though the cross that had been carved into its forehead was gone. "We have been like brothers, Arbo," he said. "I have always loved you as one. Truly, I have. I still do."

Arbo stood and approached him. The two friends faced each other silently for several long moments, each in his own thoughts, before Arbo put his hand on Stilicho's shoulder. "Then let's eat and drink as brothers, just like we used to," he said. "This night will not come again."

CHAPTER XXXI

The cloistered life of a Vestal Virgin wasn't very cloistered. Indeed, the Vestals were Rome's most visible priestesses. Not only had the first kings of Rome built Vesta's earliest temples in the heart of the Roman Forum, erecting the Eternal City around it in all directions, they had invested the priestesses with so many duties and privileges that it was impossible for them to stay put. When they were not on watch in the temple, they could often be seen overseeing the administration of other temples, presiding over public rituals, managing their private enterprises, attending games in the stadium or races at the Circus Maximus, lending their support to a friend or family member's endeavors, or socializing at some aristocratic banquet.

In the last several years, all of that had increased in frequency and demand. In life, Gratian had stripped the priestesses of their stipends; however, his death had ultimately led to a renewed push for open and official recognition of the customary gods. It was a trend most recently promoted by Julian, the last emperor of the house of Constantine, who had rejected Christianity to embrace the profundity of the immortal gods and the higher philosophies of mankind.

Yet there were times when Coelia wished her life was more peaceful. A day didn't go by without her having to meet with a priest or magistrate, or point out repairs to an engineer, or chase down a missing order of grain from the bakers. Since becoming Vestalis Maxima, she had inherited those kinds of administrative duties and stepped further away from the two she used to enjoy the most—regular watches tending the fire in the temple and days spent teaching the novices their sacred duties. The priestesses Terentia, Sergia and Galeria now conducted most watches with a register of subordinates, while Domitia and Proculeia oversaw both the curriculum of the existing novices and the applications of new ones.

I am not a priestess, thought Coelia, as she hunched over her desk to sign yet another document set before her by Ptolema. *I am a bureaucrat.*

"Daughter, put down the stylus. Come see the new fish."

Coelia's eyes shifted upward. Her mother was leaning against the doorway to her office, blithely twirling the end of her green silk shawl in the air. "Work is a poor distraction."

"What would you know of work, Mother?"

"Now, don't be so sour. I have come all this way to see you."

"Any word yet?"

"Not yet, but I told Olympius to come back here the *moment* the Senate is out and tell us the news. 'No standing around afterward gossiping,' I told him. 'Come straight back here.'" She dropped the end of her shawl. "Come on."

Coelia rose from her desk and followed her mother out of her office and into the courtyard. Domitia and the younger priestess Florina were standing beside one of the decorative pools as three novices leaned over, tickling the surface of the water with their fingers. The chief Vestal patted the novice Tertia on her head and looked into the pool to see six large, showy orange fish swimming languidly amongst the aquatic plants and ornamental shells, living flames moving underwater.

"Very pretty," she remarked.

"High Priestess," said Tertia, "we have already named them. That is Cetus, and that is Charybdis" — the fish darted this way and that, and she sighed, trying to keep them straight — "no, *that* is Cetus over by that conch shell... no, I think that is actually Scylla."

The other novices laughed, and Coelia felt a swell of affection for their innocence, though mingled as it always was with the gravity of knowing it was she as Vestalis Maxima who was ultimately responsible for them. Their competency and conviction, their happiness and temperaments, and their future independence—it all depended on how she managed the Order. It was a daunting responsibility at any time, but even more so during these times when the bishops and Christian women's monasteries were doing everything possible to undermine the Vestal Order.

Catching movement in the corner of her eye, Coelia turned to see Ptolema leading Olympius into the courtyard. Terentia and Sergia—no doubt alerted to the senator's arrival by the guards—were close behind, their eyes greedy for information.

Olympius spoke directly to Coelia, his blunt manner for once a blessing. "Senator Nicomachus made a motion to declare General Arbogastes emperor of Rome," he began. "The general refused."

"What?" exclaimed Domitia. "Why would he refuse?"

"Because he's gotten smarter, thank blessed Minerva. Since he fucked up and killed Victor, Theodosius has been stocking the Senate with his sycophants. There's no way they'd elect a pagan emperor."

"So what happened?" prodded Coelia.

"All hell broke loose, that's what happened. Arbogastes chose that moment to inform the assembly that the legions in Gaul have declared their commander Eugenius as emperor."

"And the general will let that stand?" asked Coelia.

"Of course he will. Think about it."

Coelia did. "Eugenius is Christian," she said. "At least..."

"At least that's what Theodosius thinks," said Olympius. "And that's all that matters. Anyway, it was all just theater after that. The general threw his full support behind the legions and

     Debra May Macleod

Eugenius, Senator Junius made the motion to proclaim him emperor of Rome, and after the usual round of bickering and *bravoes*, the motion passed. Arbogastes has his second figurehead, though this one will be more useful. Eugenius is a thinker, and the two are of one mind. They both want to restore the glory of the gods."

"*Gratiae deis*," said Coelia.

Lucilla put her arm around Olympius's waist. "My darling Mercury," she said, speaking to all the Vestals. "See what good news he brings to your house?"

"Oh, I'm just getting started," said Olympius. He bared his teeth in a smug smile and tongued one of his pointed canines, pausing for effect. "Eugenius wasn't emperor for more than a heartbeat before General Arbogastes delivered our new Caesar's first edict to the Senate. Before the seal was even broken, the doors to the Curia opened up and in rolled the Altar of Victory. Half the assembly rushed the floor and started fawning over the statue like it was their new bride on their wedding night."

"What else?" asked Coelia.

"Just this." He held a scroll out to her. "From the general."

Coelia accepted the document. She broke the seal—the seal of Emperor Eugenius—and unfurled the papyrus. "To Coelia Concordia, Vestalis Maxima," she read aloud. "By the force of Imperial decree, it is proclaimed that all privileges, stipends and dignities of the Roman Order of Vestal Virgins be restored without delay." She reread the words silently several times before rolling the paper back up, slowly absorbing the full meaning of the edict, and allowing herself to bask in the expressions of joyful surprise that formed on the faces of her sister Vestals.

"Oh, daughter," said Lucilla. She kissed Coelia's cheek. "Praise the goddess."

Coelia turned and embraced Lucilla, burying her face in her long and perfumed hair, and not caring in the slightest that the astonished novices were watching their high priestess weep in her mother's arms.

CHAPTER XXXII

The advent of Rome's new emperor, Eugenius, was staged with all the fanfare of a triumphant Caesar from days gone by. Wearing the laurel crown and waving to the lively masses, he stood in his horse-drawn chariot as it traveled along the Via Sacra en route to the stadium, his procession attendants flinging coin—Eugenius's diademed head on the front and the goddess Victory on the back—in all directions as red *SPQR* banners hung from every temple and monument. The jubilant, music-fueled mood was bolstered by the fact that, in keeping with the tradition of Rome's great Caesars, Eugenius was personally sponsoring three months of spectacles in the amphitheater and Circus Maximus. It was the kind of bread-and-circuses celebration that the Eternal City had not seen in generations. If Victor had stirred echoes of Rome's customs, Eugenius was blaring them from all seven hills.

The stadium was already packed and ebullient when Coelia strolled into the Vestals' luxury seating box accompanied by Domitia, Proculeia and Florina, and trailed by two novices. A cheer went up, and she looked down at the arena floor before realizing the acclaim was for her and the other priestesses—Rome's guardian Vestal Virgins, dressed in the regalia of their white stolas and veils, taking their rightful place of privilege. Regaining her composure, she raised an arm to the crowd before nodding at the priestesses to all settle in.

Domitia took the chair beside her, marveling at the gold letters—IMPERATOR CAESAR EUGENIUS AUGUSTUS—affixed to the gleaming marble of the adjacent Imperial balcony. "The walls of Rome work miracles," she noted. "Eugenius departs as an administrator, but reenters as an emperor."

"It worked that way for Symmachus, too," replied Coelia. "He left as a traitor and returned as a consul. Not that he's going to remain so. He told me that he's stepping back from some of his duties. Virius Nicomachus will be urban prefect."

"Symmachus is afraid to be seen backing Eugenius. At least openly."

"Can you blame him?" asked Coelia. "He was fortunate that Theodosius didn't strip him to the loincloth on the Capitoline and pauperize him for supporting Magnus Maximus."

Another spirited cheer, this one louder and longer, rose up to disperse in the boundless blue sky. Emperor Eugenius had arrived in the Imperial Box. His entourage of senators, magistrates and aristocratic allies, including Olympius and Lucilla, filed in behind him. General Arbogastes was last. He smiled in satisfaction at the crowd's reaction to the emperor's appearance.

The Vestals stood, and Eugenius paused long enough to put his hand on his chest and acknowledge them with a respectful bow. He proceeded to the balustrade at the front of the terrace and lifted his arms in greeting as the jocund spectators called out his name—*Ave, Caesar Eugenius!*—and stomped their feet. Not everyone in Rome supported him, but everyone in the arena knew who was paying for their good time. Or at least they thought they knew. In truth, Arbo had been bleeding Mediolanum dry of gold for longer than anyone knew, so much so that Eugenius's coinage was being minted there. It was long past time, in both men's opinion, that Rome started reclaiming the gold that other emperors had stolen from it.

The final rush and push for seats now mostly finished, the audience—emperor, elites, sacerdotes and the remaining fifty-thousand spectators—sat and waited for the performance to begin. Food vendors made their rounds selling the usual treats, while other sellers made a small fortune on popular trinkets. Gold-painted figurines of the Gilded Lions of Rome and wooden gladiator playsets of Brogos and Deimos always sold out quickly. Yet the anticipation in the stands was laced with some trepidation. The Roman public had been hoping for big things, but the bare arena floor and lack of staging or props—it was all level sand, nothing more—had many wondering, loudly and accusatorily, if despite the initial promise he had shown, Eugenius would prove to be disappointingly thrifty.

A lone trumpet sounded. Yet instead of the gate opening and a pre-show parade of musicians, chariots, performers and palm-bearers flooding into the arena to make a few rounds and enliven the crowd, a platform in the centre of the stadium floor rose upward to reveal an unusual master of ceremonies—a strikingly large man dressed as the god Mars. Wearing a plumed helmet and draped in a blood-red cloak, he held the shield and spear of the war-bringer, his booming voice amplified by the stadium's acoustics.

"Romans," he called out, turning in all directions as he spoke. "I, your divine father, Mars, today bring to life those mighty battles that spilled the blood from which *you*" — he jabbed the tip of his sword toward the crowd — "the people of Quirinus were born, just as the Furies were born from the blood of Uranus! For we gods know that only the blood of great sacrifice brings forth great reward! This story of sacrifice and greatness begins now, Romans, and it begins..." he thrust his sword into the air, paused for effect, and finished with a resounding "...on the bloody battlefields of *Troy!*"

On flawless cue, a world—a world at war—rose from the bowels of the amphitheater, hoisted up from below by an unseen army of robust arena workers laboring in the hypogeum, the stadium's substructure of tunnels, rooms, ropes and pulleys that brought its special effects to life. In the center of this world at war were the high city walls of Troy.

Dazzling wooden constructions of the temples and palaces of Troy arose on one side of the walls, as citizens frantically fortified their city gates from within. Outside the walls, Trojan soldiers engaged in hand-to-hand combat with bloodthirsty Greek soldiers trying to break through. Elsewhere, more Greek soldiers assailed Troy's walls with weapons or tried unsuccessfully to scale them, their shouts intermingling with the crashes and thuds of weapons. Yet the wartime clamor was instantly drowned out by the impassioned uproar of the audience. This was precisely the kind of spectacular excess and unapologetic violence they had been hoping for. They shouted and whistled, stomped and cheered, in appreciation.

The Vestals cheered as well, especially Coelia. Empty stadium seats and the struggles to scrounge up enough coin to put on a good show seemed like the trials of another lifetime. She interlaced her fingers in excitement and watched the Trojan War unfold below, proud that at last she could be part of the brilliant overindulgence the amphitheater was made to showcase. And it wasn't just the extravagant props, either. The fighters—professional gladiators, free men, slaves and criminals—were just as diverse, and just as assailable. Billed as a fight-to-the-death performance, the battles and the blood were real. That's what made it exciting. Nothing could match the drama of a man truly fighting for his life.

First, the fearsome Greek soldier Achilles faced the Trojan Prince Hector. They battled and fought, fought for their lives and for glory, until Hector fell—Coelia wasn't sure if the gladiator in Hector's armor was really dead or just faking it—and the enraged Achilles dragged the valiant prince's body around the walls from his horse-drawn chariot. King Priam and Queen Hecuba sobbed at the sight of their son's plight as Paris, Hector's brother, exacted quick revenge. He shot an arrow into the heel of Achilles when the warrior's back was turned, downing the famous warrior-gladiator and setting upon him fast and hard, bludgeoning him to death. Blood poured from his skull to soak into the sand and spawn a wild roar of approval from the stands.

But the death of Achilles only riled the Greeks to a new level of brutality. The Greek warrior Ajax—enthusiastically played by Deimos—took on five Trojans himself. Meanwhile, a powerful new player charged onto the sandy battlefield with a blood-curdling war cry—Brogos, in the role of the Greek archer, Philoctetes. Coelia couldn't stop herself. She rushed to the balustrade of the Vestals' balcony in excitement, Domitia at her side, leaning over the balcony to cheer on her gladiators.

"You are cheering for the enemy," laughed Domitia, but joined her nonetheless.

Brogos—Philoctetes—let loose an arrow that flew, guided by the gods, directly into the chest of Paris. The young Trojan prince's body fell onto the sand. Dead.

And then, just as choreographed, the tone shifted. Brogos, Deimos and the other gladiator-soldiers lowered their heads in grief... in sadness and bewilderment... in regret and shame at the human toll the war had taken. Pipes played and women wailed as the men wandered among the corpses littering the ground, collecting their dead. Moved to humility by the scope of the loss, and accepting that they would never break through the impenetrable gates of Troy, the Greek soldiers laid down their weapons. They would fight no more.

At that, something new rolled onto the floor of the arena—a tremendous wooden horse, its skyscraping body painted as blue as Neptune's sea and its long main blowing in the wind. It creaked and groaned on gargantuan wheels as no fewer than thirty Greeks dragged it over the sand, toward the gates of Troy. There they left it, as a peace offering to the gods and the people of Troy. And then the Greek army retreated.

Inside the walls of Troy, the people celebrated. They embraced one another and sang and danced, reveling in the end of ten long years of war. They pointed to the magnificent horse—only its head was visible over the top of the city gates—and marvelled at its impossible size.

"*Bring it into the city!*" voices demanded. "*It will please the gods!*"

The voice of a woman protested: "*Leave it, leave it!*" she screamed, though her countrymen ignored her warning.

The spectators in the stadium added their voices to hers, as shouts emanated from every tier of the amphitheater. The crowd was deeply, personally, involved in this war.

"*Don't open the gates!*"

"*You fools, think twice!*"

"*Listen to the prophetess! It is a trick!*"

But the Trojans didn't listen. As they opened the gates of their beloved city and pulled the massive gift horse inside, the stadium's audience went mad with the knowledge of what was to come. For no sooner had the gates closed behind the horse than the wooden planks of its belly burst open. A wave of Greek gladiator-soldiers poured out and began to massacre the Trojans, striking them down and flinging infants—these at least were dolls, thankfully—from the battlements. The invaders seized as captives the royal women of the city to serve as trophies of war, their future slaves and concubines, unmoved by the women's tears and laments.

The bloodshed and brutality was too much for the softer hearts in the stadium's crowd, and a few cheers turned to pleas for mercy. It had been years since such a large-scale *sine missione* spectacle had been seen in the stadium. But Rome soon remembered itself, and the tide of the spectators' emotions turned from sorrow back to feverish exhilaration as a startlingly loud *whoosh* went up—and the temples, palaces and houses of Troy became engulfed in orange flames. Within moments, the entire sprawling wooden stage of the battle was on fire, sparks snapping out of the conflagration and heat rising into the stands.

The novice Tertia tugged on Coelia's stola. "I am scared, High Priestess."

Coelia wrapped an arm around the young girl. "You, a novice Vestal, are afraid of fire?" she asked lightly, and Tertia smiled. "Do not worry," assured Coelia. "It is all part of the story." She pointed into the flames. "Look! There is Aeneas! See what he carries?"

"The Palladium!" cried Tertia, clapping at the sight of the sacred statuette of Athena tucked under the Trojan hero's arm. She pointed to the little boy who ran behind Aeneas, her fear now fully yielding to excitement. "Ascanius has the embers from Vesta's temple!"

As the gladiator playing the role of Aeneas hacked through Greek soldiers and navigated his way through the fiery streets of the doomed city, the spectators in the amphitheater grew even louder and more raucous. That included the emperor. Eugenius leapt to his feet and rushed to the balustrade of the Imperial Box, gripping the marble railing and shouting along with his subjects.

"Take care, Aeneas!"

"Look out, don't go that way!"

"Run faster, man!"

As the city fell around them, Aeneas and Ascanius fled through the crumbling ramparts and kept fleeing toward a Trojan soldier who called out for them, pointing to the ground. When the father and son reached the soldier, all three of them descended underground—or more accurately, into the arena's substructure—to escape burning Troy through the tunnels below the city. It was several long moments before the trio reappeared, this time on the opposite side of the oval arena, pulling themselves out of the tunnel and assessing their surroundings. They were in a lonely forest setting now, quiet and safe.

Exhausted, they stopped to rest and comfort each other. Meanwhile, the smoldering ruins of the city and the great wooden horse began to disappear before the audience's eyes, descending into the hypogeum. At the same time, the platform supporting Mars again rose up.

"This heartsick father and son," narrated Mars, "do you recognize them, Romans? You should, for they are your ancestors!

Watch, my children, as they rise from the ashes and journey from fallen Troy, over the waters of the *Mare Nostrum*, to the warm shores of verdant Italy!"

At that, platforms rose up like waves from the arena floor, each ejecting—like fountains of water—women dressed as sea nymphs. They sprinted off in all directions, leaving swirling trails of Egyptian blue pigment in their wake, their movements painting a beautiful landscape on the blood-stained sand of the arena floor. The audience gasped in awe, while those irreverent enough to shout leers at the scantily dressed sea nymphs received quick, silencing justice from those who sat near them. Why did someone always have to try and ruin things?

Aeneas and Ascanius stood and began to wander over the arena floor, downcast refugees searching for a home, still clutching the sacred items of Troy. Before them, a towering temple with a soaring pediment rose dramatically from the stadium floor. The father and son approached it with reverence and knelt to pray. As they did, the doors of the temple opened and a procession of kingly men wearing crowns of gilded oak and carrying golden scepters streamed out.

Mars raised his arms. "The progeny of Aeneas and Ascanius were great men," he said, "but most glorious of all were the Silvian kings that sprang from their virtuous bloodline." The descendant kings circled their ancestors once, twice, and then led them into the temple as Mars continued his narration. "From this Silvian line came the princess Rhea Silvia, holy priestess of Vesta, the mortal light in this immortal god's dark heart!"

On cue, a lone woman wearing a white dress and carrying a bronze firebowl stepped out of the temple. At the same time, the platform that held the war god lowered, and Mars strode toward the young woman. He knocked Vesta's fire out of her hands and took her in his arms, carrying her back to the platform. Together, they descended into the unseen depths.

For several moments, nothing happened. All was quiet. It was so quiet, in fact, that murmurs began to move through the stands—was something wrong with the set? But then a lone, spine-chilling sound rose up and resonated throughout the stadium. It was the howl of a wild wolf. The *Lupa*. The platform rose again, and the spectators fell into a frenzy unmatched by any Coelia had ever witnessed in the amphitheater. For upon the platform stood two men—the famed twin sons of Mars, nursed as infants by the war god's she-wolf—and every Roman knew their names. Romulus and Remus.

Or rather, Deimos and Brogos.

This masterful conclusion, this splendid conflation of Rome's founding story—abbreviated as it was—and its two favorite gladiators was almost too much for the stadium to bear. The stands shook with such joyful mayhem that the floor beneath Coelia's feet rattled, though she felt no joy. The breath left her body, and she leaned against the balustrade for support. This performance was fight-to-the-death, but that didn't mean the owners of the gladiator schools hadn't taken precautions to protect their assets. Most of those doomed to die were ill-trained slaves and criminals, while the more valuable gladiators were assigned the roles of victors. Accordingly, Olympius had assured Coelia that Brogos and Deimos would only fight on the same side. *They will both be Greeks and fight together,* he had told her. He had left out the rest. He had left out the part where they would also headline the finale by playing brothers who themselves would fight to the death for the honor of founding Rome. And by the stark look of shock on the faces of Brogos and Deimos, they had just been informed of that fact as well. Dressed in identical rough tunicas, without armor, and each holding only a simple gladius, the winner of this lethal match would be Rome's first king. The loser would be its first sacrifice.

Coelia craned her neck to look at Olympius in the Imperial Box, but his attention was on the crowd's reaction. It didn't matter that Brogos and Deimos were like brothers—that was probably what gave him the idea in the first place—he would always put profit over sentimentality. She should never have left business in his hands. Her horrified stare shifted to Arbo just as he rose from his chair and walked rigidly to the front of the terrace. Even after all this time, Coelia could read him well enough to know that he was feeling the same panic, the same helpless dread, as she was.

She thought about returning to her chair, but her head was spinning, so she remained where she was, with one hand clinging to the balustrade for balance and the other reaching out to Domitia for support. Her friend took her hand and squeezed it.

"How can I stop it?" Coelia asked her.

Domitia shook her head. "They have to fight," she said. Her lips went dry, and she licked them. "Brogos is the better fighter. He cannot lose."

On the sand, Brogos and Deimos took several steps away from each other. They turned to face each other, their arms hanging at their sides and their knuckles blanched from gripping the hilts of their gladii. Their despondent yet resigned expressions, the fatalistic imprints their sandals left in the sand, the somber way they held their weapons... it drained the murderous, pitiless energy in the stands until the shouts for blood grew fainter and less frequent. Only now was the audience grasping the true scope, the brutal inevitability, of the day's performance.

"Brother," said Deimos, "I did not know."

Brogos looked toward the Imperial Box. His stare targeted Olympius. "Do you think we could get to him before the guards do?"

"No." Deimos glanced down at his gladius. "But we could kill ourselves and not give him the satisfaction of watching us hack each other to death."

"We could," Brogos replied. "But brother, I do not want to die."

Exploiting Deimos's unpreparedness—he was still looking at his gladius, deliberating—Brogos lunged forward, the movement propelling fifty-thousand spectators to jump to their feet as if they themselves were escaping the blade. But Deimos was not one of Rome's best gladiators by chance. He sensed the movement early enough to protect himself. Brogos's blade missed its lethal mark, but opened the flesh on the side of Deimos's body. Blood soaked through his tunica and ran down his right leg, dripping into the sand.

The first blood now spilled, the brothers turned against each other in full force. Weapon raised, Deimos rushed at Brogos and their blades met with a clash so forceful those watching wondered how they managed to keep hold of the hilts. Brogos moved next— leaning to the side, he kicked with one leg, his heel impacting Deimos's kneecap. Deimos clenched his teeth and limped several steps away, inhaling deeply to stifle the pain. He tried to turn around again, but fell to his good knee and then onto his back. Brogos was on him instantly. He raised his gladius and brought it down, but not before Deimos rolled away from the bloody tip's trajectory. He scrambled to his feet, clutching a handful of sand as he did, and throwing it into Brogos's face. The shards flew into Brogos's eyes and mouth, and he stumbled backwards to regain his vision. He spat out sand.

Brogos moved to advance on Deimos again, but his momentary blindness had cost him ground. He felt something he had never felt before—the blade of an opponent's sword sink deep into his belly, the agony amplified by the disorienting uproar from the audience. Yet instead of subduing him, it had the opposite effect. Suddenly overcome with an extraordinary panic that pumped strength into every muscle in his body, he raised his own weapon hard. Its metal hilt struck Deimos's chin from below and knocked his head backward. Blood sprayed from Deimos's mouth, and he shuffled away to regroup.

Brogos wouldn't give him the chance. With one arm pressed against the open wound in his midsection—it did nothing to hold back the pain or the blood—he set upon Deimos again. He raised his gladius, but the movement tore his gash open wider, and a warm gush of blood streamed freely down his left leg to coat his sandal. Striking at the only level he could manage, he stabbed at the back of Deimos's already injured knee. The blade went straight through, dislodging the man's kneecap. Deimos screamed in pain and collapsed onto the sand, the blade still stuck in his knee. Brogos tried to hold onto the hilt, but felt his grip slip and fail. He was weaponless.

But Deimos wasn't. Roaring in agony, his left kneecap gone and Brogos's blade protruding grotesquely from his knee joint, he used his gladius for leverage and pushed himself back onto his feet. He swung wildly at Brogos, but only sliced at air. Worse, the movement threw him off balance and he found himself falling again. Brogos hit him like a battering ram, and the two of them fell to the ground. Brogos tried to rip the weapon out of Deimos's grip but, failing that, reached for his own gladius and yanked hard, pulling it out of Deimos's knee. He positioned it to strike—but Deimos maneuvered under him and he lost the opportunity. For a heart-beat, Brogos wasn't sure where Deimos was, but then he felt a sickening constriction around his neck as his opponent's thick arm tightened around it. He instinctively dropped his weapon, frantically trying to pry Deimos's arm off him. But Deimos had the advantage. Unable to breathe, Brogos felt an impossible pressure build up inside his skull. His vision grew blurry.

"Brogos! Don't give up!"

It was the priestess's voice. How he could discern it among the tens of thousands of other voices, and in the midst of his own desperate struggle for life, he had no idea... but he heard it all the same. He gave up trying to pry Deimos's arm off his neck, and instead used his last moments of consciousness to bring a hammering fist down directly on Deimos's ruptured knee joint. Deimos swore through gritted teeth but held on, though his grip loosened just enough for Brogos to twist free. He hastened to his feet—but stepped on the bloody blade of his gladius, slipped, and fell back onto the sand.

By now, the two men had fought, fell, stabbed and scrambled nearly to the stone wall of the arena floor, and had ended up immediately below the Imperial Box, only a short distance from where Arbo stood beside Eugenius. The general looked down at his friend fighting for his life in the sand. He glanced at Eugenius.

He could ask the emperor to show mercy, to grant a reprieve... but then he surveyed the euphoric multitude in the amphitheater. Like those in the Imperial Box, they were on their feet, waving their arms, shouting support for the gladiator they wanted to win. This crowd did not want a draw. They did not want leniency. They wanted to see this through to its end. They wanted to see Romulus become the king of Rome. Anything less, and they would take it out on their new emperor.

"Arbo! Do something!"

The general's head swung toward the Vestals' Box. Coelia's hands were clasped in front of her, pleading with him to intervene. He looked away... away from her and away from his friend in the sand. Instead, he stared into the crowd to watch the match proceed on their faces. Their expressions—horror, revulsion, fear, exhilaration, savage exuberance—told him the struggle continued. But then there rose a collective gasp of surprise and a riotous cry of victory that told him it was over. He forced himself to look down. Brogos was leaning against the stone wall of the arena floor, heaving for breath and dripping in blood. Deimos lay dead at his feet.

Coelia fixed her eyes on Brogos. His eyes found hers in the crowd, and as they held each other's gaze, he began to weep. Unable to withstand the force of his guilt or his grief, Coelia looked away... and met eyes with Olympius. He was smiling widely, overjoyed with the crowd's reaction. Coelia had known it all along. Those who did business with Olympius always ended up regretting it. It had taken years, but the inevitable had finally happened, and it was her own fault. She had become too complacent with him, had let their business partnership and his romance with her mother lull her into some idiotic sense of safety. A look of confusion crossed Olympius's face—was she not as delighted as him with the results? Coelia looked away from his elated smile. For her and Brogos, it was personal. For Olympius, it was just business.

On the arena floor below, Mars returned. Carrying a gilded crown of oak leaves, he strode to the gladiators—the living and the dead—and put his hand on Brogos's shoulder.

"My two sons," he shouted. "Both born of the virgin, both born divine, but only one destined for greatness!" He placed the crown on Brogos's head. "Romulus, king of Rome!" he exclaimed. He clutched the victor's hand and raised it into the air.

The crowd hailed their new king.

"*Ave, Romulus! Ave, Romulus!*"

Brogos looked down at the body of Deimos. But instead of celebrating his hard-won coronation, he continued to weep—not theatrical tears, not tears of relief, but rather tears of sorrow and shame for the brother that he had killed with his own hands.

Slowly, he fell to his knees, lowering his head until it touched Deimos's bloody skull. The act touched something in the hearts of the spectators, and the cheering ebbed until the stadium grew quiet enough for Brogos's sobs to be heard in the stands. And it was only in that moment, when they realized that their star gladiator was forever changed, forever a little bit broken, that fifty-thousand Romans felt in their hearts, however fleetingly, what it had taken to found the Eternal City.

CHAPTER XXXIII

In the year since Eugenius had been proclaimed emperor, Theodosius's scribes had rubbed raw the flesh on their fingers, such was the volume of persecutory laws against paganism that their emperor had them writing, each law harsher than the last, each law determined to suppress the worship—even private worship within the walls of one's own home—of the gods. But Eugenius didn't care, and neither did his subjects.

Indeed, since Eugenius had become Augustus, he had redecorated Rome with the single-minded zeal of a new wife moving into her husband's outdated house. It had started with the return of the Altar of Victory to the Senate House and the appointment of senators loyal to him, thus returning the Senate to its strong pagan majority. The Vestals' funding had been restored, as had the funding of various other priesthoods and temples, while the city's extensive roster of magistrates and officials had been restocked with men loyal to Eugenius, not Theodosius. Coin and pride were once again being injected into traditional pagan festivals and rites on a large scale. And something remarkable was happening... or rather, nothing remarkable was happening. Romans were living together in peace and order, and despite the occasional burst of belligerence from those extremists unhappy with coexistence—would anything make them happy, though?—life was carrying on as usual.

Yet while Eugenius was restoring Rome's customs, Coelia was proposing change and had therefore called for an informal midday meeting of the College of Pontiffs in the courtyard of the Regia. As the priests entered, she acknowledged them in order of rank: Symmachus as Pontifex Maximus first, followed by the flamines maiores of Jupiter, Mars, and Quirinus, and then the lower priests who served the other gods. As they all reclined on couches, servants presented them with trays of lunchtime delicacies.

"Pontiffs," Coelia began. "It is easy to forget that not so long ago, the Vestal Order was on the brink of serving you locusts for lunch. Worse, High Priestess Claudia nearly drank herself to death on posca out of fear that our Order wouldn't have the numbers to staff the temple. The thuggery of the times were to blame, but the long-standing constraints of the Vestal Order didn't help. Our roster of novices, active duty priestesses and senior Vestals has had to adapt over these past years, but we are moving past stability, toward abundance. This time of strength presents an opportunity. I have spoken with the senior priestesses of Bovillae and Tivoli, and they stand with me as I propose three changes to the Vestal Order. First, reducing the years of service from thirty to twenty, the same time traditionally prescribed to our soldiers. Second, accommodating requests for early retirement. And third, removing crimen incesti—and its punishment—from the pontifical laws. These changes will attract even more candidates to the priesthood, while ensuring the Order never again has to deal with the scandal of an absconding priestess like Primigenia."

"I know how we should have dealt with her," said Symmachus. "In the customary way."

"Yes, I remember your opinion," replied Coelia. "You said the full severity of the ancient law should be brought against her for breaking her vows. Let's imagine that for a moment. All of Rome watching you noble men lash the naked back of a high-born woman, gag her, drag her to the *Campus Scleratus* in a wooden box, and then force her into an underground pit to slowly suffocate or starve to death."

The high priest of Jupiter, a chiseled man named Statius who was rumored to have had more illicit love affairs than his patron god, bit into a dormouse, scoffed, and glanced at Symmachus. "I can't see it," he said, chewing.

"Yet if a transgressing woman thought that it could happen, her instinct would be to run," said Coelia. "Just like Primigenia did. Perhaps we're lucky she ran off into the country somewhere, and not into the nearest church to beg for sanctuary." A few of the priests nodded in agreement, and she pressed on. "I don't need to tell you how the bishops would've exploited that. Every man, woman, child and family dog in the empire would know the story of the pagan priestess who turned to Christ in her hour of need." She paused for effect. "Not a single Vestal Virgin has converted, and these proposals ensure that none ever will."

"There is little risk of that regardless," said Symmachus. "It is well-known that many Christian virgins grow embittered with the severity of monastic life, but age and poverty make it hard to leave. No Vestal would put herself in that position."

"And yet every Vestal must still bear the insult of knowing this antiquated punishment remains on the books, even if it is unlikely to be used," said Coelia.

"This 'antiquated punishment' has distinguished the Vestal Order since its inception," argued Symmachus. "It has distinguished the Vestal Virgins from all other priestesses. How much reverence would a Vestal's vow command if breaking it did not come at so great a cost?"

"We are more than our vows, Pontifex," said Coelia. "It is time for change."

"Change is the *opposite* of what we need now," countered Symmachus.

Coelia sighed. "Sir, our Order has always promised women a life of dignity, even independence. Such are the rewards that Vesta wishes for her priestesses and that Rome has provided. That is why I believe that serving her should be a matter of esteem and privilege only, not fear. *Especially* now."

The pontiffs digested the debate with their lunch, though it was only Symmachus's face that continued to betray resistance. Before he could say anything further, however, a bell rang in the Forum and the pontiffs rose from the couches.

"The customary punishment for crimen incesti does seem antiquated," said the high priest of Quirinus. "And the old constraints have been loosened before." He looked at Symmachus. "Vespasian and Titus let the Vestals govern themselves, and yet the pax deorum endured. I see no harm in reforming the pontifical laws." Several other priests voiced their concurrence, and he nodded at Coelia. "Draft your proposals in detail, and submit them to the college. We will consider them." He offered her a bow. "*Bene vale*, High Priestess."

"Thank you, sir," said Coelia. "*Valete, Sacerdotes.*"

As the chief Vestal followed the pontiffs out of the Regia and onto the Via Sacra, a loud intoxicated voice struck her ears.

"High Priestess, I've been waiting... how come you don't... wait, wait a minute! I just want to talk."

The pontiffs rolled their eyes at the drunkard and headed back to their business in the Forum. Reluctantly, Coelia stopped. She held her nose.

"Olympius," she said, "the bathhouses are free."

"I know that Lucilla is in Rome," he said. He pointed to the portico of the House of the Vestals. "I know she's in there."

"She is not."

"Then where is she?"

"That's none of your bloody business."

He stumbled closer to her. "I need you to tell her that I—"

Teo and another guard intercepted, each grabbing one of Olympius's arms. The manhandling and his drunken state were unmistakable signs of the man's decline in the wake of Lucilla's rejection, though Coelia felt no sympathy for him. Olympius had certainly spared none for Brogos or Deimos. Not only had the heartless stunt that pitted brother against brother turned both Coelia and her mother against Olympius, it had changed Brogos. He hadn't been the same since.

"Leave my mother alone," Coelia snapped. "She despises you as much as I do." She spoke to the guards. "Throw this inebriate out of the Forum. Arrest him if he gives you any grief."

"Yes, High Priestess," said Teo.

"Wait!" shouted Olympius, trying to break free of the guards. He faced the portico of the Vestals' home. "Lucilla! I know you're in there! Come out and—" he made a pained expression, and promptly retched onto the street.

The guards tightened their grips and dragged him away, his sandals sliding through his vomit, as Coelia held her breath from the stench and entered the house. Her mother was in the triclinium, dressed in a pretty tangerine tunica and azure shawl, blithely relating some anecdote that had Domitia and Sergia nearly doubled over in laughter.

"Oh," said Domitia, and grew serious. "What did the priests say?"

"A roundabout yes," said Coelia. "They want to see a proposal."

"Then why do you look so grim?" asked Sergia.

"Because Olympius just accosted me on the street, drunk as Bacchus, and because I could've died happy never having seen his stomach contents spewed out in front of me."

Lucilla shook her head. "He never could hold his wine."

"He knows you're in Rome."

Sergia turned to Lucilla. "He is persistent. He must really love you."

"His ego makes him persistent," said Lucilla. "Not his love for me. Men cannot stand rejection. First, they will beg for your forgiveness, then rage when you deny it, then turn to drink, and then finally go mad. You will see. Madness is next."

"A quiet madness, I hope," said Coelia. "I cannot have men shouting outside the doors of this house."

"I am sorry, Coelia."

"It's not your fault, Mother. It's strange, though. I never would have expected Olympius to fall apart like he has."

"I did," said Lucilla, plucking a cube of cheese off a lunch platter and pushing it between her lips. "I put a curse on him. Well, *I* didn't. A priestess of Proserpina did it for me. She has a good business just outside of Cumae. There's money to be made in curses, that much is certain. It took me three days to see her." She waved the half-eaten cube of cheese in the air, the three other women her captive audience. "It was all very dramatic. Lots of calling upon the Furies and condemning his mind and penis to wither, things like that. I quite enjoyed it. Found the whole thing quite cathartic. Anyway, when she was done, she gave me a scroll with the spell to break the curse if I wanted to—you have to speak words in a certain order and use some salt, I can't really remember—but I burned it just in case I ever had a weak moment. But it wasn't all bleak. I made an offering for the soul of poor Deimos, and she said the man was drinking with Priscus and Verus in Elysium. I was very happy to hear it. I really should tell Brogos. It'll make him feel better." Lucilla finished the rest of her cheese, brushed off her dress, and looked at Coelia. "Shall we go to the market?"

Olympius had been banned from most of the respectable taverns in Rome. That left him with two choices. He could go home and drink alone, or he could venture into the Subura district where tavern owners couldn't afford to be quite as picky about their customer base. If you had coin, you were welcome. And while Olympius didn't have as much coin as he used to, he still had more than most who lived on the wrong side of the massive firewall that separated the gleaming marble and colorful excesses of the Forum of Augustus from the wooden structures and worn cobblestone of the notoriously rowdy Roman precinct.

Yet to Olympius, there was something comforting about the plebeian character and low expectations of the Subura. He didn't have to worry about offending some fragile senator's sensibilities or insulting some magistrate's favorite chariot driver or getting slapped in the face for giving a rich matron a lascivious eye wink. He didn't have to listen *ad nauseam* to some aristocrat brag about how much he had donated to the temple of Orbona for the maintenance of Rome's orphanages. No one was showing off in the Subura. It was liberating. The anonymity was a bonus, too. No one knew him. Rather, no one knew him *before* his life had become Rome's longest-running shitshow. That meant he could spare himself the whispered gossip and the looks of pity—or more often, the looks of amused satisfaction—from those patricians who had witnessed his fall.

The music in the gruff tavern grew louder—a necessity as the night wore on if it were to rise above the shouts and brawls—and Olympius ordered another drink. The servant brought him two cups of wine, plus a tray of dry bread and olives that looked like they'd been sitting in the sun for three days. He pushed the olives aside and took a cup.

He was sinking further into his wine and his despair when a young man joined him at the wobbly table.

"*Salve*," said the stranger. "I've seen you before, friend."

Olympius looked up from his drink. "So what?"

The man smiled and draped his long fingers over Olympius's arm. "My name is Adonis," he said. "I thought you might like some company."

"I don't fuck men," said Olympius. "These days, I barely fuck women."

Adonis sighed and sat back in the chair, folding his arms across his chest and regarding Olympius with a shrewd though supportive look. "I also give advice," he said. "Lady advice."

Olympius laughed. "What in the name of the gods would you know about the ladies?"

"Just about everything there is to know," replied Adonis. "Women talk to men like me." He took one of Olympius's cups of wine and drank. "Why is she mad at you?"

"Because I killed someone that she didn't care about."

"Then why is she mad?"

"Because someone she does care about cares about someone who cared about him," Olympius met his eyes. "Which I didn't think would carry over to her caring."

"You really don't understand women at all," said Adonis, "or you would have seen that coming. Some women care more about the things other women care about than they do about the things they care about."

"I know that *now*," replied Olympius.

"Buy her something pretty," Adonis volunteered. "Not jewelry, that's too predictable. An exotic dress is better, something from Egypt. Or perfume."

"She has her own money."

"Tell her the devil made you do it."

"She's pagan."

He clucked his tongue. "Damn."

"Maybe you should just stick to sticking it," said Olympius, gesturing toward the young man's genitals. "Leave the love advice to Ovid."

"Who is Ovid?"

Olympius scoffed derisively. "Fucking barbarians, everywhere I go."

"I'm not a barbarian," said Adonis. "And I'll tell you what, sir. I might be a prostitute, but it is still a more noble profession than others. Like my uncle's job, for example."

"What's your uncle's job?"

Adonis emptied his wine cup and set it down on the table with a certain premeditated firmness, a certain beat of deliberate delay that made Olympius suddenly wary.

"He worked in the amphitheater. He was a venator. His name was Clemens."

It had been a long time since Olympius had heard that name, and he was drunk, so it took him an extra moment to place it. But then he remembered. Clemens was the name of the lead animal trainer in the stadium, and the man Olympius had bribed to arrange the escape of the gilded lions.

"Venator," said Olympius. "A shit job."

"That's what my uncle always said," agreed Adonis. "Put his neck on the line every day for years, training lions and bears to put on a good show of devouring people, yet barely made enough money to buy a third-floor apartment in the Subura. But then one day, the strangest thing happened." He leaned forward. "He struck gold. Suddenly, he was villa shopping on the Esquiline." He waved a finger thoughtfully in the air. "As a matter of fact, it happened right after those lions escaped from the amphitheater..." He sighed with feigned sadness and put his elbows on the table, holding Olympius's stare. "And then he just disappeared. No one has seen him since."

I know where to find him, thought Olympius. *At the bottom of the Tiber with a concrete slab tied around his waist. Had he not extorted me for more money, he'd be living the high life on the Esquiline with his dandy of a nephew.*

"Why the fuck are you telling me this, boy?"

The young man grew smug. It was time to reveal all. "My uncle told me what he did for you, *Senator Olympius*," he said, placing prolonged emphasis on Olympius's name. "I wonder what people would think if they knew you were responsible for the lions escaping?"

Olympius sniggered. "Look at me, boy. Do you think I give a shit about protecting my reputation at this point?"

"It isn't just your reputation on the line," said Adonis. "I know you didn't act alone."

"Yes, you fucking idiot, I did."

"No, you didn't. You have a business partner, and she's a fancy one, too." The young man let that hang in the air for a moment before standing up. "I will be back here tomorrow night," he said.

"Right here, at this table. If you don't come with money, and a lot of it, I will tell the authorities what you did. Your lady friend's reputation will be as rank as yours, although that will be the least of your worries. You'll be lucky to escape the hangman. Goodbye, Senator."

Sobering up by the moment, Olympius watched the young man leave the tavern. If the little weasel implicated the high priestess in the lions' escape and the carnage that had ensued since, any chance he had of reconciling with Lucilla would be lost forever. He quickly ran through his options. He could deny everything, but once the rumor started, it would spread like wildfire. He could pay off the little prick, but like his uncle, he would only come back for more. He landed on his third and only option and stood, stumbling out of the tavern and hoping it wasn't too late.

It was a warm night, and despite the late hour, the area was fairly well-lit thanks to the full moon and the torches that lined the streets. Olympius looked to his left, then to his right—and spotted Adonis promenading along the street, offering his services to those he passed. Olympius followed behind at a safe distance, ducking into porches and hiding behind fountains to avoid being seen. At last, Adonis seemed to accept that no one was buying tonight. He picked up his pace and turned onto a quieter street, one more residential than commercial, with long rows of multistory *insulae* on either side and gangs of lanky dogs, fearless but not aggressive, scrounging for food.

Olympius discreetly trailed the young man to the end of the street, careful not to trip on the uneven pavement. As Adonis stopped before the humble porch of a large apartment block, Olympius slipped behind a small cart that had been left along the street—one wheel was missing, no doubt to deter theft—and stayed there until Adonis had disappeared inside the building. Again, Olympius weighed his options. He could follow the man inside, into his apartment... but the effete extortionist could too easily call out for help. There was really only one thing to do.

Olympius peeked into the cart's box. It was half full of scraps of wood and broken slabs of stone. Leaning over the side, he fished through the debris until he found a large, angled stone. Checking over his shoulder to ensure the street was empty, he carried it to the entrance of Adonis's insula and shoved it, hard, into the space under the door. Certain it was as snug as possible, he hurried to the closest street torch and pried off the metal protective cage, ignoring the flames that licked his fingers. Ushering the exposed flame back to the insula, he held it against the dry wooden wall. It caught fire easily. Olympius shuffled along the wall and did the same to another section, then another. Soon, the insula was on fire.

Mesmerized by the sight—the fire was consuming the entire building now—Olympius looked up to see the thick smoke rise into the night sky, a grey cloud obscuring the full moon from view. Despite the intensity and heat of the fire, it raged in near silence, the only sounds being the occasional crack of wood or whoosh of flames. But then a strident sound pierced the strange peace. A man's voice, ear-splitting and urgent:

"Ignis! Ignis!"

The residents of the Subura might have been poor, but they weren't stupid and they weren't ill-prepared for the dangers of fire. Between their community fire brigade and the state-funded *vigiles* that patrolled the neighborhood, a plan was ready. Soon, an army of amateur and skilled firefighters swarmed the street in front of the burning insula, forming an assembly line that moved buckets of splashing water back and forth to fight the fire.

From inside the building, screams and cries for help rang out. Although the doors of insulae opened outward to permit quick escape in the event of fire, this one refused to budge no matter how hard the choking tenants inside pushed it—the angled stone, now hidden in smoke and flame, held firm. As the flames resisted the efforts of the firefighters, and as the conflagration raged on, the vigiles abandoned the engulfed infula and took axes to the adjoining ones, desperate to stop the fire from spreading.

Fully sober now, Olympius lowered his head clandestinely, turned around, and began to walk back the way he had come. He hadn't passed the length of the insula, however, before he felt a hand on his tunica. He spun around to see a young woman in a ratty nightdress glaring at him accusatorily.

"It was him!" she screamed. "I saw him start the fire!"

"Get off me, you fucking lunatic," said Olympius. He broke free and kept walking.

The woman's voice rose above the roar of the flames. "Stop him! He started it!"

And then there were more hands on his tunica—men's hands, hands he couldn't break free from. Olympius fought and swore, threatened and denied, and finally pleaded... but his pleas were cut short by the butt of an axe that struck the back of his head, extinguishing the flames, at least from his vision.

CHAPTER XXXIV

Constantinople

General Stilicho faked a lot of things in his life. Most of them, like a coin or the pagan god Janus, had two faces. His admiration of Emperor Theodosius, for example, was false, though his loyalty to the man was true. His fidelity for his wife Serena was false, though his love for her was true... mostly. There was one person, however, for whom his feelings were absolute and unqualified—Honorius, the emperor's son. Stilicho hated the boy with every fiber of his being. He hated the dead eyes that were a little too far apart, the elongated face, the droopy mouth, and he especially hated the high-pitched whistle that accompanied his speech and that made every vapid word he spoke sound even hollower. But his hatred of the young prince wasn't just an unadulterated one, it was a dangerous one, too, and he had never revealed it to anyone. Nothing in the world, no treason or infidelity or mistake, would lead him to the gallows as quickly as Theodosius discovering that his trusted general and kinsman prayed nightly for the death of his son and heir.

There was only one person in the empire who suspected Stilicho's feelings for Honorius weren't as pure as he let on—General

Arbogastes. Arbo had correctly surmised that Stilicho did indeed worry about his young son's proximity to the heir apparent, especially since anyone who saw the two together could not help but note how superior Eucherius was to Honorius in every way. That truth was on full display in the Hippodrome, the great racetrack in Constantinople—a copy of the Circus Maximus in Rome—where the two boys were taking lessons from their riding instructor. Honorius sat precariously on horseback, his jumpy uncertainty making the animal as skittish as he. Eucherius sat with confidence on a horse nearly two sizes too big, holding the reins loosely in relaxed hands.

If anything gets the boy killed, thought Stilicho, *it will be his competency.*

Serena appeared at his side and smiled at their son's horsemanship. "An expert rider already," she said, boasting in that way she always did—the praise was for Eucherius, but somehow it sounded like it was for herself.

"He is a natural," agreed Stilicho.

"My uncle wishes to see you."

"All right." He kissed her on the cheek. "I will see you tonight."

"Don't say it unless you mean it," she said, her playful tone poor camouflage for her frustration. He hadn't slept in their bed for three nights, and she knew what—who—was keeping him from it. Her own train of female attendants. They were supposed to be focused on amplifying her beauty, not indulging her husband's lasciviousness.

"I mean it," he replied with a grin.

Stilicho waved goodbye to Eucherius and strode out of the Hippodrome, walking quickly enough to work up a good sweat by the time he reached the *Palatium Magnum*. The great palace had been built by the emperor Constantine when he had decided to transform the Greek city of Byzantium into his new Rome, Constantinople. Now, the palace complex housed Theodosius's residence and sprawling administration. Finally reaching the basilica where the emperor held court, Stilicho stepped into a washing room and let two slaves wipe away his sweat and dress him in a fresher, more presentable tunica before his audience with Theodosius. The emperor was Stilicho's family now—his uncle by marriage—but Theodosius was informal to no one. It was rumored that he hadn't even visited his own son until the boy had passed his third birthday, thus reassuring the emperor that he would survive childhood and be of Imperial use.

As Stilicho emerged from the washing room, his second-in-command, Constantius, fell into step beside him. To Stilicho, the man was the perfect subordinate soldier—dependable and capable, yet not more capable than Stilicho himself.

"Sir," said Constantius. "The emperor has been reading letters from the bishops all day long." He turned to Stilicho with a heedful look. "Just so you know."

"Thanks for the warning," said Stilicho.

Constantius veered off to other duties while Stilicho proceeded into the basilica, past the colossal columns and desks of hunched scribes, across the tile floor and toward the large golden throne positioned within a raised apse at the far end of the space. Theodosius sat formally upon it, watching his general enter but not reacting to his presence. Stilicho continued until he reached a respectful distance from the emperor, then lowered himself onto one knee and bowed his head, waiting for the emperor's permission to rise. Such was royal etiquette in Constantinople. While the Caesars in Rome had always demanded loyalty, ostentatious displays of subordination were typically frowned upon, and most Caesars had addressed senators and generals with at least a façade of respect. Not so in Constantinople. Stilicho waited for Theodosius's permission to stand, trying to ignore the sharp flare of pain in his kneecap from the hard marble floor.

"Rise," said the emperor.

Stilicho did, proceeding deferentially to the emperor's throne and kissing the large gold ring on his hand. He stepped back, at liberty now to make eye contact with the emperor. As always, he was struck by how much Theodosius resembled his son Honorius:

the same elongated face, though the trait was exaggerated on the emperor by the tall golden crown that topped his head.

"The situation in Rome is becoming more problematic," said Theodosius.

"I am aware, my lord," replied Stilicho.

"Eugenius is openly funding pagan temples and causes. I am told that the Senate approved a massive expenditure for the embellishment of the Temple of Venus and Roma, and that libraries throughout the city have reopened. The Tiber Island of medicine is ready to sink, it is so full of physicians and their patients." He tapped an index finger on the arm of his throne. "I am also told that the statue of a heathen priestess now stands openly in the Roman Forum." The finger tapping grew more insistent. Irritated. "Were you aware of that?"

"I have sent messengers to General Arbogastes, my lord," said Stilicho. "I still believe I can bring him back into the fold. I did it before, when he was allying himself with Victor."

"I am losing faith in that," replied Theodosius, with an edge of *and also in you.* "This is a Christian nation, General."

"My lord," said Stilicho. "Eugenius is a Christian emperor."

"Ambrosius is not so sure. He fears Eugenius is a heathen sympathizer, if not a secret pagan himself."

"Ambrosius fears his own loss of influence," replied Stilicho. "He instigates conflict only to inflate his own importance."

"Ambrosius is a soldier of peace," said Theodosius. "His hands are cleaner than yours, or mine."

Stilicho tensed. Criticizing the bishop had been a misstep. Whatever strife had arisen between he and the emperor had clearly dissipated. "Of course, Highness."

"Any news from Gaul?" asked Theodosius.

Stilicho's tension tightened. He hadn't wanted to share this information with the emperor. Not yet. But if he waited any longer and Theodosius learned of it elsewhere, it could be interpreted as collusion. "Nothing certain, my lord, but there are some initial signs that Eugenius may be planning to move his army to Mediolanum."

Theodosius drummed his fingers harder on the arm of his throne. "I have been counseled to declare Eugenius's rule illegal."

"Highness, I do not believe—"

"And to name my son Honorius as emperor in the west."

Stilicho's mouth went dry. There was no way around it. If Theodosius did it, it would mean war. War with Arbo. "I see," he said simply.

"Do we have the troops?"

Stilicho's mind turned to the practicalities of battle. "Not Roman ones," he said. "But our alliance with Alaric of the Visigoths would supply the needed manpower."

"For a price."

"Yes, my lord." *Of course for a price*, thought Stilicho. *The Visigoths will not fight your war for free.*

"I will think on it," said Theodosius. "Dismissed."

"Yes, my lord."

Stilicho bowed deeply at the waist and walked backward, not turning his back on the emperor until he had crossed most of the basilica. Theodosius stood from his throne, the act prompting his yellow-uniformed attendants to orbit around him like wasps around a disturbed nest. Stilicho pivoted on his heel and exited the court, his mouth still dry and his chest tight.

If there were a million duties he had to perform in the service of Theodosius, going to war with his friend and mentor Arbo was the last one he was ready to do. Or rather, it was the last one he wanted to do. If the general couldn't be reasoned with, there might be no way around it. As Stilicho put distance between himself and the basilica, he spotted his private scribe and waved the man over.

"Come with me," he said to the man. "I want to write a letter."

Another letter to Arbo. Another letter pleading with him to keep Eugenius's troops in Gaul. To keep the clergy in Rome happy. To keep the peace. To keep communicating, for as long as their styluses were moving, their swords would stay sheathed.

CHAPTER XXXV

Rome

For years, a fine marble statue of Coelia Concordia as Vestalis Maxima had stood in the lavish public gardens donated to Rome by Senator Praetextatus. For almost as long, various senators had called for the statue to be moved to the Roman Forum and placed near the Temple of Concordia in honor of the high priestess's public oration during the despair of the famine. They remembered the sight of her standing on the high steps of the temple, boldly offering to Vesta and the gods of Rome, and they remembered her words to the city's despondent people:

This famine is a plague of impiety. Go home. Offer to the goddess that burns in your hearthfire. Feel the warmth of her breath on your face. Hear her voice in the crackles of the fire. The goddess loves you. Rekindle your love for her. Restore concord with the immortal gods, and Ceres will again touch our harvests with her shining hands. Reclaim the dignity to honor the gods in your heart as those who built this temple— this temple to Concordia, to our past, to our future—had the liberty to do. I say this in the name of Father Quirinus and our holy virgin, Vesta.

Coelia's public offering had ended the famine by restoring the pax deorum. It had also emboldened Romans to once again openly honor the gods of their ancestors. Nonetheless, the statue had remained where it was until recently. In honor of Coelia's piety and leadership, the high pontiffs of the religious college had voted to relocate the statue. Coelia had requested it be placed inside the House of the Vestals to join the other Vestal statues in the peristyle, including the repaired and now gilded statue of the former Vestalis Maxima Claudia. Yet the pontiffs had instead chosen to place Coelia's statue outside of the Regia, emphasizing the Vestalis Maxima's proximity to both the religious headquarters of Rome and the Temple of Vesta.

At first, Coelia had felt self-conscious whenever she saw it. After a few days, however, she had begun to take a measure of pride in it, even appreciating the workmanship: the similitude of her face, stance and attire, the pious way she held a patera and the brilliant reproduction of the medallion Emperor Julian had have given her as a novice. After a few more days, she had simply stopped noticing it. The streets of Rome had as many statues as the night sky had stars. There were statues of emperors and empresses, statues of gods and goddesses, statues of heroes and celebrity gladiators, statues of generals and benefactors, statues of animals and birds, statues of legendary creatures... hers was just one more.

Yet for those Romans significant enough to see their faces in marble, there was one unavoidable fact. Many statues, particularly those that stood in the fora, were of dead people. And as Coelia's lectica passed by her statue, she found herself reflecting upon that. *My stone body will outlast my flesh-and-blood one,* she thought. *I cannot decide if that pleases me or terrifies me.*

She knew one thing for certain, though. Her musings on mortality were amplified by the day's event—the public execution of

Senator Olympius, charged with the capital crime of arson. It was an event that she couldn't wait to watch unfold. She had barely slept, such was her excitement.

Olympius's execution site in the Roman Forum—specifically, on the platform atop the staircase of the Temple of Saturn—was a rare venue for the death penalty. Most criminals sentenced to death met their end outside of the city walls, with the Forum's prestigious location reserved for the most noteworthy of state enemies or traitors. Olympius wasn't either of those things, but he was guilty of two unforgiveable crimes. The first was murderous arson, and the second was general unpalatability. The truth was, he didn't have a lot of friends. He had backstabbed, swindled and exploited almost all of his peers and associates at one time or another, and recently some formidable ones.

Deimos hadn't just been a fan favorite, he had also been a close personal friend of many men who moved in Rome's most aristocratic circles. He had been an even closer personal friend of some of their wives. The gladiator's body had barely hit the sand—it was a cheap death, many thought—before people began to lay bets about when, where and how Olympius's enemies would exact their revenge for the stunt. Yet not a single one of those wagerers, or Coelia herself, could have predicted that Olympius would make it so easy. Next to treason, arson was Rome's worst capital crime, and Olympius had sealed his fate when he was caught. Hence the reason for the show of justice at the Temple of Saturn, which itself had been rebuilt after a deadly fire.

As her litter reached the temple, Coelia heard Teo's shouted instruction—*Deponite!*—and her lectica set down. A large crowd had already clustered around the base of the stairs to watch the execution from below, but Coelia followed a soldier up the stairs to an exclusive witness section reserved for those who had either suffered at Olympius's hands or simply paid extra for the thrill of watching his execution up close. Brogos was there, looking subdued, his arms crossed and his three dogs sitting obediently at his feet. Lucilla was also there, her posture rigid but resigned. Coelia sat beside her.

"I did not think you would want to see this, Mother," said Coelia. "He's going to be—"

"I know, and he's fortunate they let him choose the method," Lucilla interrupted. "He should've been fed to the beasts in the arena."

That was true enough. *Damnatio ad bestias* was the preferred execution method for arsonists. Not only was it an effective use of resources—the beasts had to eat—but it was also a spectacular deterrent against a particularly abhorrent crime, one that often sent those it didn't kill into abject poverty. Under the reign of Emperor Nero centuries earlier, arsonists had set the stables at the Circus Maximus ablaze. The infamous fire had started by burning the city's prize racehorses alive and hadn't stopped until it had done the same to countless men, women and children, leaving Rome a smoldering ruin. The arsonists had been fed to the beasts, and Nero assassinated shortly thereafter, though not for punishing the criminals—he had Rome's full support for that—or even for his own immorality. Ultimately, Nero had fallen out of favor for the tax increases he had approved to rebuild the city in the fire's aftermath. After all, the only thing as bad as burning to death was being taxed to death.

Without any show of ceremony, General Arbogastes emerged from the temple's sanctum and strode onto the platform. Behind him followed a magistrate and two soldiers, each of whom gripped one of the condemned man's arms to guide him—not *quite* pulling, but close—to the center of the platform. Olympius looked as dejected, as hopeless, as any man Coelia had ever seen. His tunica was torn, and because he wore no loincloth, his genitals were half exposed. Like the rest of him, they looked bruised and beaten, though nothing was as disturbing as the crusty gash on the back of his head from where a vigile had struck him unconscious with the blunt end of an axe blade. The somber crowd grew even more so as a soldier dropped a low, blackened block of wood in front of Olympius. It landed on the marble with an ominous *clunk*.

The stage of execution needed only one more player—the executioner. But Arbogastes had reserved the starring role for himself. Coelia suspected it was an attempt to make amends with Brogos, to apologize in some way for not prompting Eugenius to spare Deimos, but she knew it wouldn't work. Brogos now resented the general as much as she did. Still, it was Olympius who was truly to blame, and his death would bring some sense of justice. Arbo marched toward Olympius and kicked his legs from behind, sending him to his knees directly in front of the chopping block. The soldier who had positioned the block passed an executioner's long-bladed axe to the general.

The magistrate spoke to the crowd. "On the charge of *incendium* with malice, Senator Olympius has been found guilty, his deliberate act of arson resulting in the destruction of half a city block of insulae in the Subura region and the loss of eight lives. His sentence will now be carried out on behalf of the Senate and people of Rome."

Arbo gripped the long handle of the executioner's axe in both hands. "Pray to whatever miserable god breathed life into you," he said to Olympius.

Olympius's shoulders began to shake. At first, it looked like fearful sobbing, but then he flashed a cynical smile and those pointed eye teeth and chortled with a relinquishing sort of laughter.

"How the fuck would I know who that is?" he asked. He spat out a mouthful of blood and stared at the chopping block.

Coelia could not imagine what was going through his mind. What did a person think about at the moment of death? Was he regretting his actions? Was he hastily deciding which god to pray to? Was he thinking about trying to make a run for it or professing his innocence?

Olympius leaned forward, placing his neck on the chopping block. Coelia knew him well enough to know why. He wouldn't give Arbo the satisfaction of forcing him onto it. As his hands reached out to grip the sides of the block, he shifted his eyes upward—and met eyes with Lucilla.

Oh no, thought Coelia. She turned to Lucilla. "Mother, don't look at him."

But it was too late. Lucilla and Olympius held eyes for too long, to the point that Olympius's hard veneer began to crack. He took his neck off the block.

"Any last words, citizen?" asked Arbo.

Olympius stood on his knees. His eyes drifted over the crowded Forum below, then returned to the closer witness sections, searching the faces of those around him—including Coelia's—looking for a way to save himself. In a brilliant flash of self-preservation, he found it.

"*Si dea clemens est, vir melior ero,*" he called out.

If Coelia hated him before, what she felt for him in that moment transformed into something far greater, more intense, an indescribable contempt that rushed through her veins and made her skull throb from the pressure of it.

He isn't praying for divine clemency, she thought. *He is threatening me.*

Clemens. That was the name of the animal handler in the amphitheater, the man Olympius had paid to release the lions. It was the same man who had later extorted Olympius for more money, coin that Coelia had partly provided to silence him.

She could read the threat in Olympius's eyes, and she knew the words he would speak before the axe came down: *The Vestalis Maxima conspired with me to release the lions from the amphitheater! She used funds from the Vestal Order to pay off our extortionists!*

It was only half true, of course. But a half-truth as awful as this one was just as damning as a full truth. Coelia's thoughts flew to her statue—it would be carted out of the Forum by sundown if the pontiffs or senators heard a whisper of a rumor.

Ignoring Olympius's plea, Arbo nodded abruptly to the soldier who had given him the axe. The soldier grabbed Olympius by the hair and tried to force his neck back onto the chopping block, but this time, the senator fought back.

The soldier leaned over. "Don't resist," he whispered into Olympius's ear. "You'll just make it worse for yourself."

Olympius shook his head free of the soldier's grip and locked his eyes on Coelia. "I have something to—"

Coelia stood. "By the authority invested in me by the College of Pontiffs, the Senate and the people of Rome, I pardon Senator Olympius."

A shockwave moved through the witness section, quickly flowing down the stairs to strike the larger gathering in the Forum. Arbo turned to the magistrate for guidance, but he looked just as dumbfounded as the rest of the crowd, all of whom knew how much the high priestess now detested her business partner. Half of Rome had seen her weep in the stadium at Deimos's death and at Brogos's guilt-ridden grief. The magistrate hurried over to speak with her.

"High Priestess, are you certain that—"

"It is within my power as a Vestal Virgin of Rome to pardon this man, and I do so," she said. Turning to address those gathered below in the Forum, she compelled her mind to stay a beat ahead of her words. "Our first Caesar brought a spirit of clemency to Rome by forgiving his enemies," she declared. "He believed the weight of mercy was greater than the weight of revenge. His spirit of temperance and his desire for concord are still spoken of to this day. By pardoning Senator Olympius today, it is my hope as your Vestalis Maxima that we Romans abide by these virtues. I sacrifice my own vengeance to Concordia and Clementia for the good of our city and its people."

Slowly, the soft mumblings of surprise and the hard words of opposition coalesced into an emotional chorus of admiration. Death was easy in Rome. Life was hard, but it was valuable, and their priestess knew that. They began to bless her name.

It was the sound of salvation to Olympius. He looked at the chopping block one last time and then gazed out into the Forum, as if for the first time noticing the soaring pediments of temples, the gleaming marble of columns with their gilded capitals that shone in the sun, the splendid flocks of birds that swam through the blue sea of the sky above, seeing it all, seeing the whole world, through the eyes of a man reborn.

But one man's rebirth was another man's betrayal. Coelia looked at Brogos—he was standing now, fists clenched, accusatory eyes on her. She moved to speak with him, but he turned away and quickly descended the steps into the Forum, the black dogs following closely behind as he disappeared into the crowd.

CHAPTER XXXVI

The moon was still out when the Senate convened not in the Curia, but at the Temple of Mars Ultor in the Forum of Augustus. The senators had arrived from all parts of the city, having stumbled from their bedchambers to their chariots in tunicas instead of togas, hair hastily combed, minds assuming the worst. Only the most veteran senators among them had experienced the alarm of a midnight emergency session before, and their grim expressions did nothing to reassure those who hadn't. After all, an urgent assembly at the temple of the war god could only mean one thing, and General Arbogastes's announcement confirmed it:

Theodosius has named his young son Honorius the emperor of the west. He has declared Eugenius an illegal emperor, and his army is advancing. The Gates of Janus are open, brothers, and we are at war.

The news wasn't entirely unexpected, and yet like all bad news—especially that which was delivered at night—it still felt that way, and it left Arbo with a sickening feeling in the pit of his stomach. Despite the countless letters that had traveled the road from Rome to Constantinople and back again, from his hands to Stilicho's and back again, he had known it was just a matter of time, for he and Stilicho weren't the only ones sending letters. The bishops had sent their own letters to both Eugenius and Theodosius, chastising the emperors for their permissiveness with Rome's pagans. There was only one god, and the Romans had no right to behave otherwise.

Arbo moved through one of the colonnades that flanked the forum, answering a barrage of questions from stone-faced senators and magistrates. Proceeding to the opposite colonnade, he finalized the orders of his tribunes, centurions and other key soldiers. There was no time to waste. They would all ride out tonight, by the light of the moon, to join Eugenius's army in Mediolanum. Arbogastes had to wonder when he would next see the sun rise in Rome.

The last of his orders given, the pensive general left the company of his soldiers and ascended the wide staircase of the temple. The great doors were open, and soldiers were filing in and out of the sanctum. Arbo acknowledged all of them as he entered the sacred space to pray to Mars before departing. The temple was dominated by a colossal statue of Mars in full armor, spear and shield in hand, the war god bordered by a statue of Venus on one side and the divine Julius Caesar on the other. They had stood there since the time of Augustus, when the emperor had built the temple to commemorate his victory over Brutus and the other assassins of Julius Caesar. The weapons of Rome's mightiest rulers and warriors were displayed within niches in the marble walls—the sword of Julius Caesar, the shield of Agrippa, the helmet of Vespasian and an ancient *balteus* that, legend had it, was worn by Scipio Africanus when he defeated Hannibal.

Seeing the contemplative general enter the temple, the high priest of Mars waited by the doors until the last of the soldiers already inside finished their prayers and exited. As they did, he closed the doors behind them, granting Arbo some reflective solitude in the temple. The general walked slowly to the far end of the cella, his eyes fixed on the larger-than-life face of Mars. Moving his red soldier's cloak aside, he knelt and looked up into the god's face, seeing his fearsome visage vitalized by the flames of the sacrificial tripods that stood all around.

"Heavenly father of Rome," he said. "Watch over my men. Protect them from the wounds and horrors of battle. Bring them home victorious, so they may return to the arms of their parents, wives and children as heroes."

The high priest appeared before him, holding a golden bowl in one hand. He dipped his fingers in the bowl and withdrew them, coated in blood, before covering the general's cheeks and forehead in red. The liquid was still warm from the blood of the sacrificial bull.

"*Mars Pater,*" the priest prayed, "*despice et fave huic militi.*" He poured the remaining blood over the feet of the war god's statue. "*Sic semper tyrranis,*" he said to Arbo, and left the general to contemplate both the god and the war in peace.

But then, Arbo felt another presence and looked up to see Coelia standing beside him. She seemed startled by his blood-covered face, but knelt beside him and lifted the edge of her palla to wipe his cheeks and forehead clean. Whatever had transpired between them in the past needed to remain there right now. He was Rome's last hope, and it was her duty to embolden him however she could.

"You are one of the greatest generals the empire has ever known," she said. "You fight for the same Rome that Agrippa fought for, though your cause is even more noble."

The force of her words made Arbo's eyes moisten. He took one of her hands and kissed the back of it. "If I am victorious," he said, "I will stable my war horses in the basilica of Mediolanum and conscript its clergymen into the army."

"They will make poor soldiers."

"Someone needs to wash the pots after breakfast."

Coelia felt Arbo's fingers tighten around her hand. He had been a soldier since childhood, but despite his skill for it, had always seemed ill-suited to the discipline. She knew that he carried each swing of the sword, each death and each trauma, with him every day, whether it was peacetime or war. She had a sudden image of him on his rooftop by the Tiber, tossing grain down to his pigeons. That is the only life he had ever wanted.

"I will pray every day for your safe return," she said. "Every day your name will be spoken in Rome."

He brushed a thumb over the back of her hand, his thoughts turning from the future to the past. "I am sorry for deceiving you."

Coelia gently withdrew her hand. "You have larger concerns than a soured romance, General."

"I would give anything to go back to that day. Not just to make things right with you. I think about Victor every day. The regret follows me everywhere, like a shadow."

"What's done is done."

"It's not my only regret. Tell Brogos that I'm sorry."

"I will try," said Coelia, "but he hasn't spoken to me since the day I pardoned Olympius."

"When I return, I will make it right," he professed. "All of it." Venturing further, he added, "Perhaps then, you and I can speak again. *Potius sero quam numquam.*"

Coelia allowed herself to study his face. His fair hair and beard now had streaks of gray, and there were deep lines around his light-colored eyes. She and Arbo had aged together, or if not together, at least at the same time.

"Yes," she said. "We will speak again."

He nodded. Maybe she meant it or maybe she was just unwilling to be cruel before he departed. He chose to believe the former. "Will you remain at the temple while I'm gone?"

"I will. That is my duty." The Vestal coffers had been replenished in full, but the College of Pontiffs and the Senate preferred constancy in the priesthoods during times of war. Domitia would have to wait a little longer to wear the veil of the high priestess.

"If I can, I will send you a message," said Arbo. "Meanwhile, we will both do our duty."

Coelia stood. "*Dei tibi faveant, miles,*" she said.

"*Item tibi, Sacerdos,*" he replied.

Coelia wrapped her blood-stained white palla around her shoulders and turned away from Arbo, quickly crossing the marble floor of the sanctum and stepping outside into the night, noting with melancholy that there was still no hue of sunrise against the black sky.

CHAPTER XXXVII

There were only two things that Gaius truly hated in life. The first was taxes and the second was his father-in-law. In a miserable conflation of bad timing and bad luck, he was presently dealing with both, for no sooner had the *publicanus* from Rome left with half his season's profits—a third of which Gaius saw the corrupt bastard slip into his own purse—than his father-in-law had galloped to his front door and tossed him the reins of his horse, entering Gaius's modest farmhouse without even scraping the mud off the bottom of his sandals. The visit had started at a low point and gone downhill from there.

"*My back is sore,*" complained the cantankerous old man. So Gaius had offered his good bed, and he and his wife had slept squished together on a straw mattress on the triclinium floor.

"*This garum is cheap,*" the old man whined, so Gaius had sent his son to the market with money they didn't have to purchase more expensive sauce.

"*My grandchildren are disobedient,*" the old man reproached, so Gaius had beaten them on the spot.

"*There is an awful draft in this room,*" the old man quibbled, so Gaius had spent an entire day patching holes that did not exist, just to shut the graybeard up.

"*You know I can't stomach goat meat,*" the old man griped, so Gaius had fed the goat to the dog and put on his boots for the trek through the pouring rain to the sheep barn. As he trudged through the muck, fighting against the suction of the sticky mud with each step, he reached a paddock and opened the gate, closing it behind him as several goats gathered around, bleating for treats he hadn't brought.

Reaching the sheep barn, he swore under his breath to find the wooden door ajar. No doubt his father-in-law had left it open after making his rounds through the farm, taking smug note as he always did of any squeaking hinges or wobbling fence posts so that he could point them out to Gaius, and everyone else, in the middle of supper. Huffing in frustration, he put his hand on the barn door, noticing but not paying any heed to the strange smudge of color—it looked like gold paint, though he had nothing so fancy—on the doorframe. Passing over the threshold, he stepped out of the wet mud and onto the dry straw of the barn floor.

Except that it wasn't straw. It was wool—piles of it, bloodstained and mixed with chunks of meat—and it covered every inch of the barn floor. Gaius looked around in despair. The dismembered bodies of ten or more sheep lay scattered among the bloody wool, while a group of twitching, quiet lambs huddled in the far left corner of the barn before a stack of bundled green hay. Gaius would not have thought that animals could be traumatized by the observance of carnage, but the look in their eyes changed his mind.

"Bloody wolves," he grumbled. "More likely, the neighbor's damn dogs... I'll chop their heads off the next time—"

The growl rose as if from the depths of Hades, ominous and spine-chilling. As Gaius watched in wondrous fear, the maned head of golden lion rose from behind the stack of green hay, like a monster lazily waking from an afternoon nap. The beast looked at him and licked its bloody muzzle. And then, most amazing of all, lowered its head and went back to sleep.

Gaius took a slow, breathless step backward into the wet mud and pushed the barn door, praying it would close in silence. As he did, the hatred that he had always felt for his father-in-law blossomed into the sweetest, purest, most loyal love that Gaius imagined one man could feel for another. The delightful old man had already oiled the squeaky hinges of the barn door, and they closed without a sound.

CHAPTER XXXVIII

For almost a month, Rome had been as silent as a tomb. On the ides of September, the news arrived that the decisive battle between the armies of Theodosius and Eugenius had been fought near the Frigidus River. Seven days later, this day, the victors galloped through the gates of Rome and arrived in the Eternal City. Their triumphant march proceeded directly to the Roman Forum and the Rostra where, in front of stunned senators, officials, and citizens, they raised the head of Eugenius on a spike.

As Coelia neared the Rostra and the macabre display upon it—the emperor's head had been mounted in the enemy's camp before traveling to Rome and was already rotten—she had the unmistakable sense that she was moving through a conquered city.

A military horn sounded, and Commander Constantius strode to the edge of the Rostra, looking down on the people of Rome. Although he was General Stilicho's second in command, the conceit in his mannerisms seemed at odds with the soldierly brand of pragmatic diplomacy that Stilicho had inherited from the likes of Bauto and Arbogastes.

"By order of His Highness, Imperator Theodosius Augustus," he declared, "I hereby inform the subjects of Rome that the army of the usurper Eugenius has been defeated on the eastern border of Italy. With my own eyes, subjects, I saw how the righteousness of our true emperor Theodosius was rewarded on the battlefield! For the savior sent winds of such force that the weapons of the heathens were torn from their hands, and they perished, defenseless!" He paused, expecting a cheer, but receiving none from this particular crowd, continued. "Subjects of Rome, your emperor wishes to celebrate his victory with you. Therefore, in preparation for the arrival of His Highness in Rome, oaths of loyalty will be sworn in the Senate and in all public offices and military units without delay." Preferring to end on a note of authority, Constantius descended the platform, leaving Eugenius's gaping mouth to say anything he had forgotten. He disappeared into a group of his soldiers.

Coelia tried not to falter at the stricken expression on the faces of Domitia and Proculeia. "Go back to the temple," she said.

They left with their guards, and Coelia scoured the somber crowd for Symmachus, finally spotting him as he emerged from the Senate House with a man she guessed by his eastern fashion was an administrator of Theodosius. No doubt he had been sent ahead to consult with the important senator before the emperor's arrival. Symmachus glanced up at the sight on the Rostra, but looked away immediately, his expression unreadable. Seeing the Vestal advance, and anticipating her question, he took her aside.

"General Arbogastes escaped capture," he said. "No one knows where he is."

"Might he be regrouping somewhere? Gathering more men?"

"General Stilicho enlisted the forces of the Visigoth leader Alaric," said Symmachus. "That means he had no shortage of disposable soldiers to send into senseless slaughter against Arbogastes. It is unlikely our side can recover enough numbers. There is nothing we can do for now" — he jutted his chin at the Rostra — "but endure this performance." He sighed. "Stilicho will be coming to Rome with Theodosius. We remain on good terms. I will learn more from him." He patted her on the arm. "I must attend to business. Go home. Be patient."

Be patient, Coelia brooded. *Was more aggravating advice ever given?*

Seeing no alternative but to take it, she began to walk along the colonnade of the Basilica Aemilia, back toward the House of the Vestals, as Teo followed a few paces behind. She hadn't gone far before a figure leaning against a column, his back to her, made her slow her step.

"Brogos?" she asked cautiously.

The gladiator spun around. Seeing it was her, he pushed himself off the column and began to march away. Coelia sprinted to catch up to him, tugging on the back of his tunica.

"Let go," said Brogos. "You'll make a fool of yourself."

"I am so bloody beyond caring about that. Stop and talk to me."

He stopped and swatted her hand away, then slumped against an archway in the basilica. "What do you want?"

"What do you think I want? I want to explain."

"What's to explain? I saw it myself. Your mother broke down in tears for that prick, and you saved him."

"My mother cursed Olympius after what he did to you and Deimos. And yes, she cried when the axe was raised over his neck, but she never asked me to intercede." She cocked her head. "*Si dea clemens est, vir melior ero.* That's what Olympius shouted. That didn't seem strange to you, coming from him? Clemens. Where have you heard that name before?"

Brogos narrowed his eyes. "Oh."

"I can't let what I did—another of my mistakes—bring scandal to the Vestal Order, especially not now." She looked into the Forum, her gaze going straight to the head of Eugenius. "Or maybe I wasn't thinking about the Order. Maybe I just didn't want to find my own head on the chopping block. When it comes down to it, I'm just as solipsistic as anyone else."

"As what?"

"As solip—as selfish. I'm sorry about what you had to do to Deimos. I tried to stop it. I called out to Arbo..." she broke off. She hadn't told Brogos that before. He already felt betrayed by the general's inaction. This revelation wouldn't help. She tried to cover the wound quickly. "I saw Arbo the night he left for the war. He wanted me to tell you that he was sorry."

Brogos scoffed. "He can go fuck himself." Seeing the conflict on her face, feeling it himself, he relented. He had already lost too many people he cared about. He stepped toward Coelia and put his arm around her shoulder. "Yet he is in my prayers," he said, his anger abating. "Arbo will send word to you when he can."

"You mean *if* he can."

"Yes," Brogos said sadly. "That is what I meant."

There were only two men in the world that Coelia trusted to escort her in confidence to the villa of Agrippa—Teo and Brogos—but she wasn't willing to endanger either of them. If she was caught traveling to the home of the traitor General Arbogastes, she would find herself accused of the same crime, and it wouldn't be the first time. The same accusation would be leveled against them. So she had left her carriage, left her lectica, left her guard and her gladiator behind. Without telling anyone where she was going, she had wrapped an unadorned blue cloak around her shoulders, pulled the hood over her head and weaved through the streets, alone and on foot, like a common criminal trying to evade capture.

Reaching the Tiber, she crossed the Bridge of Agrippa and continued along the road that ran through the stone pines until the gleaming marble columns of the home's semicircular portico came into view. She tried not to think about the first time she had walked this now pristine path... back then, it had been forgotten and consumed by weeds, and it was all she could do to avoid stepping on an army of slugs on the chipped stone. Continuing on, her eyes and ears alert, she found what she had expected— Arbo's slaves and staff had abandoned the property. They would not risk being interrogated by Theodosius's men. She knew that she was taking a risk, but Brogos's assertion that Arbo would send word when he could had planted a thought that wouldn't wither.

She pressed on, relieved to see no signs that Theodosius's soldiers had yet descended upon the place. Indeed, as she approached Arbo's stable, topped by the equestrian statues of the Dioscuri that Victor had given the general in better days, she was met by the restless squeals of stabled horses. It must have been days since they had been fed. The Vestal released them from their stalls. They snorted as they stomped by her, off to graze, though like her, aware that change had swept into their lives. Proceeding to the rear of the stable and the spiral staircase that led to the roof, Coelia ascended until she reached the city of dovecotes on top of the stable.

Like the horses, Arbo's pigeons called out for care and freedom. There weren't as many of them as in days gone by—the general's hobby had fallen by the wayside since his appointment as magister militum—and Coelia instantly spotted one uncaged bird sleeping contentedly in an open columbarium. She picked it up, eliciting a soft coo from its feathery throat. As she had both hoped and dreaded, it carried a weathered message on its right leg. Cradling the pigeon in her arm, she removed the small piece of papyrus, set the bird back in its niche and unfurled the note. A bloody fingerprint obscured the ink, but the words were still legible:

They keep advancing, without the burden of principle, and will never stop. Think only of yourself. Take what you can and leave. No one could have done more.

Coelia brushed her thumb over Arbo's bloody fingerprint. There was no way in this moment, standing on this rooftop, that she could know how she truly felt. The emotions were too cloudy, too conflicting. All except for regret. She felt that with merciless clarity. She should have said more to him that night in the Temple of Mars Ultor. Something more intimate.

Curling the little paper that held the general's last words, she tucked it into her *strophium* and moved among the dovecotes, opening each one in turn. The pigeons burst out like feathered cyclones. Some flew to the trireme-shaped water basin, while others landed on the roof of the stable to impatiently await their food. Coelia emptied the grain bins.

"Eat your fill," she said to them. "And then fly away."

CHAPTER XXXIX

Years earlier, six lions had escaped from the amphitheater in Rome. Two had been captured and killed before they could get very far, but four had fled onto the streets and eventually into the countryside. The beasts had quickly become things of legend—the Gilded Lions of Rome. The first of the at-large four was hunted down in the catacombs of Rome. The second died on the Aqua Marcia. The third drowned in a bath complex in Ostia. The fourth—well, people had given up hope of ever seeing its capture. *It is a ghost,* mothers and fathers told their children when they wanted to spook them. *So come home before dark!* But truth be told, it was the parents who were still spooked, who still looked over their shoulder when they turned down a quiet street or walked in the woods.

So when the news broke that the last Gilded Lion of Rome had been caught, people temporarily set aside their differences, worries and griefs—the head of Eugenius was still rotting on the Rostra, and the suicide of General Arbogastes had been con-firmed—and rushed to the amphitheater to watch the legendary beast meet its deserved fate. Not only was it a much-needed cause for celebration, it would provide glorious entertainment for the visiting Emperor Theodosius and his powerful General Stilicho. For better or for worse, Rome would have to make their peace with them, and it was up to senators like Symmachus—who had kept good relations with Theodosius, even as he had tacitly supported Eugenius—to make it so. The sage senator had also issued judicious advice to Coelia. *Carry on as normal. Remain gracious.*

For her part, Coelia hadn't been to the amphitheater since Brogos had been forced to kill Deimos with his bare hands. That gloomy memory was bad enough, but the mournful image of Arbo wandering alone for days in the forest before finally taking his own life meant she was in no hurry to watch Theodosius and Stilicho parade onto the Imperial Box as victors, too close for comfort to the Vestals' Box. But she had a duty to uphold, and that meant taking Symmachus's advice to attend.

Indeed, it seemed like all of Rome had chosen to attend, and the arena staff had gone to quick and great lengths to ensure the beast hunt would live up to the hype. Coelia regarded the hundreds of gold and red banners that hung throughout the sprawling oval of the stadium, each one bearing the likeness and name of a Gilded Lion: Umbra, Rapax, Lucens, Nox. Vendors moved through the stands selling lion trinkets and lion-shaped cakes. The jovial anticipation of so many people only deepened Coelia's melancholy. She turned her focus to the pregame performance in the arena—a comedic pantomime of hunters variously hunting, and being hunted by, four giant lion puppets—and accepted a fresh strawberry from Domitia, chewing absently.

"Daughter, oh daughter!" waved Lucilla.

Coelia forced her lips into a smile and waved at her bejeweled mother and her companion—Olympius, grinning wryly—as the couple entered the nearby Imperial Box to take their seats in the senatorial section.

Coelia leaned toward Domitia. "Leave it to Olympius to emerge from the chaos like a rising star," she said.

Domitia popped a strawberry into her mouth and spoke as she chewed. "The man is a prophet."

She wasn't wrong. It was as if Olympius had predicted the future, for no sooner had he stepped away from the executioner's block than he had pounced on the opportunity to ingratiate himself to Theodosius in the most ingenious of ways: by sending the newly appointed child-emperor Honorius a chunk of wood… wood that, according to the enterprising locals in Jerusalem, was a piece of the table at which Christ had last supped with his apostles. It was eye-rolling sycophancy, but it had kept him—and his bride-to-be, Lucilla—in Imperial favor.

A trumpet blared. Looking as arrogant as he had on the Rostra, Commander Constantius entered the Imperial Box and extended his arms to the tens of thousands of spectators seated in the amphitheater.

"All hear this! Behold your lord and emperor, His Highness Theodosius Augustus! Behold his victorious general, Flavius Stilicho!"

Theodosius strode to the balustrade of the Imperial balcony to acknowledge his subjects, taking silent but bitter note of the half-hearted cheer that emanated from the full stadium. He turned to Stilicho, nodding for the general to similarly greet the crowd, but the triumphant soldier had triumphed over so many seated around him that the half-hearted cheer dwindled to a quarter. For Stilicho, it was sufficient and perhaps better than he had expected. As the emperor reclined on his golden throne, Stilicho held out an arm for his wife, Serena.

"Come sit, darling."

Dressed in the eastern fashion that she preferred, Serena took his arm. "To think," she said excitedly, "that you and I were both here when the Gilded Lions escaped." She sat beside her husband as he offered diplomatic smiles to the surrounding senators and magistrates. "They are fortunate you are so good to them," she stated.

"I still have strong friendships in Rome," he replied, nodding respectfully to Symmachus who sat nearby. "If I am to act as Honorius's regent until he comes of age, I will have to rely on them."

Serena noticed Olympius. "You have enemies, too." She sniffed, amused. "Look, he is still with the Vestal's mother. The world is full of wonders."

"Indeed it is," said Stilicho. His thoughts jumped from Olympius, to Lucilla, to Coelia, and he looked into the Vestals' Box, directly at her.

Coelia had not seen him in years, but other than a nasty burn scar on his cheek that looked to be recent—he must have suffered it in battle against Arbo—he appeared unchanged, still possessed of the good looks that had helped him win Serena's hand. Coelia held his gaze, civil but unsmiling. That was as close as she could get to Symmachus's call for graciousness.

What is he thinking? she wondered.

Stilicho knew of Arbo's feelings for her and likely knew of their one-time plans to marry. Perhaps he blamed her for inciting Arbo to fight the war that had killed him, or perhaps he wondered whether she blamed him for the general's death. Regardless, he looked away, turning his attention toward the arena as the master of ceremonies took to the floor.

Exuberant on an ordinary game day, the master of ceremonies was positively giddy on this special occasion. He met the capacity crowd's eager cheers and foot stomping with outstretched arms and an extra spring in his step, adjusting the faux lion's mane around his neck as he cleared his throat to speak.

"Romans! Long ago, in another land, the citizens of Nemea lived in terror of a monstrous lion, a murderous man-eating beast made invincible by golden fur that no weapon could pierce! It was only by the club of Hercules that the Nemean lion was slain!" He waited for the rise of clamorous foot stomping to fall before continuing. "Romans! We too have been terrorized and torn apart by shades of that legendary creature! The Gilded Lions of Rome!" Delayed by a maniacal outburst, he again waited for it to settle before proceeding. "These shining beasts stalked and devoured us for too long! But today, dear Romans, the ludi of gladiators are pleased to bring you, and our holy emperor Theodosius

Augustus, justice—arena justice!—as the last Gilded Lion of Rome faces the club of Roman Hercules!"

The master of ceremonies departed to the sound of rollicking cheers—not for him, but for the celebrity gladiator Brogos who charged onto the sand of the arena floor dressed like the heroic Hercules, a heavy lion skin draped over his broad shoulders. In one hand, he wielded a massive club and, in the other, gripped a golden length of coiled rope. Raising both weapons in the air, he roared madly at the impassioned crowd, as if he were a wild lion himself. And then, it was the moment they had all been waiting for. In the middle of the stadium, hoisted up from below by the workers in the hypogeum, the last Gilded Lion of Rome rose to the surface world amid the sound and fury of thunderous applause.

Which promptly ceased.

This was no monster. It was barely a beast. Emaciated from years of wandering and from age, the old lion named Nox crouched unmoving in the sand, its sunken eyes surveying its inscrutably foreign surroundings in abject terror, its thin skin twitching in fear over bony ribs. Its sparse mane, like the rest of it, had been freshly doused in shimmering gold paint by the animal handlers, though the effect only shone more light on the creature's pathetic condition.

Coelia felt her melancholy return in full force as she studied the animal. The scar on its muzzle... this was the same lion that she and Arbo had run for their lives from in the stadium years ago. How far they had both come, she and this beast, only to end up in the same place.

Domitia set the strawberry in her fingers back in its bowl, her appetite suddenly gone. "The thing is as ancient as Rome," she said.

As the crowd continued to react to the sight, Brogos approached the animal, club at the ready, prepared for the beast to attack. It didn't. Instead, it lowered its head and let out a faint echo of what at one time must have had been a vicious, sky-splitting roar.

"*Futuo*," Brogos muttered to himself. As he got closer, he kicked a spray of sand in the animal's face, hoping to provoke a response, but again, nothing. The lion was long past putting up a fight. Brogos had the distinct impression he'd be putting the thing out of his misery more than exacting any revenge upon it.

The gladiator studied the encircling crowd. Their uncertain expressions, their hesitation, the way one person shouted "Kill the bastard!" only to be swatted by his neighbor, suggested they felt the same ambivalence that he did. He glanced up at Olympius—despite it all, the prick was still the boss—looking for direction, but the senator only shrugged in a way that said *Might as well go through with it.*

So he did. He raised his club and brought it down hard on the lion's head. The animal fell onto its side, tongue hanging out, giant paws twitching in the sand, as if it were reliving a hunt from its younger, stronger, mightier days.

Stepping around the back of the animal, Brogos dropped his club and unfurled his rope. He wrapped it around the lion's neck once, twice, and pulled. The lion did not fight back, but only closed its eyes, blocking out the sight of the slack-jawed creatures surrounding it and—Coelia hoped—picturing itself racing in freedom across the great plains of Africa.

CHAPTER XL

"I was a colossal bore when I married your father, but I was fifteen and he sixteen, and he was not interested in philosophy. But as I marry for the second time, I have acquired the nature of the philosopher—I stay up all night thinking about things, and I am growing a beard—while at the same time I have lost all the features of being fifteen." Lucilla stared at herself in the looking glass in the dressing chamber of the House of the Vestals, running her fingers over her orange wedding veil and tucking in a stray lock of her long hair. She was lucky she still had any hair to tuck in, such were the number of grays she had ordered the cosmetician to pluck out. "What would your father say if he knew I was marrying again at my age, and to a man like Olympius?"

"He would fly into a rage of jealousy and tear the branches off all the trees in Elysium," replied Coelia. "Then he would slowly haunt Olympius to madness and suicide."

Lucilla smiled. "That does make me feel better. Thank you, daughter." She turned to Coelia. "Let's go to the Temple of Jupiter and make an offering before the ceremony. We have time." She spoke to the other Vestals in the dressing room. "You don't mind if my daughter and I go alone, do you?"

"Of course not, Lady Lucilla," said Domitia. "We need to dress for your party anyway. I can't wait. We are in need of a reason to celebrate these days." She kissed Lucilla on the cheek. "*Pulchra es*," she flattered. "Senator Olympius will be dazzled."

Mother and daughter left the dressing room and the home of the Vestals, exiting onto the street where a fine lectica awaited the chief Vestal and her mother, the bride-to-be. It was still early, and many buildings in the Forum were closed for the Epulum Jovis.

"It is so quiet," said Lucilla. "I can hear the morning birds."

The sound of a bell rang out, followed by a rise of conversation and laughter, and the two women looked up in the direction of the Altar of Juno on the Capitoline where a small group had already gathered to witness the imminent union of Lucilla and Olympius. Uncharacteristically, Lucilla had chosen to have a humble ceremony at the altar—Juno being the goddess of marriage—officiated by Symmachus as Pontifex Maximus and attended by only a handful of close friends. The reception, however, was quintessential Lucilla. Her wealthy friend Lady Aurelia, whose taste for the extravagant matched Lucilla's, was hosting the social event of the year at her garden estate on the Esquiline Hill. It was a venue that rivaled the Gardens of Maecenas. As for the guest list, it was quicker to name those in Rome who were not attending. Olympius might have back-stabbed half of Rome, but Lucilla didn't have an enemy in the world. Coelia was relieved that her mother's expenditures were now his to bear.

They slipped into the lectica together, Coelia noting that someone had tucked peacock feathers into the stitching. A reference to Juno, the feathers were a sweet touch, and she would have to remember to thank whomever had done it. The *lecticarii* lifted the vehicle, and the women sat back in comfort as the orange-canopied transport moved like a small but striking sunrise through the Forum. Reaching the marble ramp of the Capitoline

Hill, it proceeded up and past the gilded monuments and shrines on top, toward the most magnificent temple of all—the Temple of Jupiter Optimus Maximus—where the two women wished to make an offering before continuing to the nearby altar for the wedding ceremony.

The porters set the vehicle down at the base of the temple's grand marble staircase, and the Vestal and her mother stepped out next to a lively fire that snapped and crackled on a massive marble altar. In days gone by, a sheep or a ram would have been sacrificed at this altar and its meat consumed in the subsequent banquet to Jupiter. These days, pagans placed ram-shaped cakes in the altar fire and prayed it was sufficient. Coelia led her mother up the steps, toward the fluted gold-capped columns and three sets of golden doors that led to the adjacent cellas of the holy triad—Jupiter in the center, flanked by his daughter Minerva and his wife Juno. High above, the soaring pediment was decorated with elaborate relief sculptures and crowned by painted statues of the gods so realistically rendered that one might fear they would step down at any moment to crush it all underfoot.

Statius, the high priest of Jupiter, greeted them before the tall bronze doors that led to the central cella. He smiled cordially at Coelia. "*Salve*, High Priestess."

"*Salve, Sacerdos.*"

He shook his head at the sight of Lucilla's wedding veil. "A sad day for the men of Rome."

"Statius, you dog," said Lucilla.

"My wife and I are looking forward to your reception at Lady Aurelia's tonight," he said, just as another wedding bell, this one louder, and a burst of laughter sounded from the Altar of Juno. The wedding guests were signalling the bride to stop dawdling and to make her grand appearance. The priest grinned and opened one of the doors for the women to pass. "May the heavenly father bless your wedding."

"He had better," quipped Lucilla. She held up a denarius. "Or this will be the last silver your temple gets from my purse."

The two women entered the sanctum to stand in the presence of Jupiter, god of gods. A colossal statue of the sky god seated on a throne—a thunderbolt in one hand and a scepter in the other—dominated the space, and as Coelia marveled at the bearded visage of the shining father, she felt the same awe that she always did when she entered this temple. While the cella was faced with every color and variety of known marble, the designers had made their masterstrokes in purple and gold, thereby crafting a startling phenomenon: Whenever a worshipper blinked, purple and gold lingered behind the closed lids, as if flashes of Jove's lightning were entering the soul. The religiosity of the effect was intensified by the snapping flames of an altar fire, the sound of which reverberated in the cella like thunder strikes. Lucilla approached the fire and handed the coin to Coelia, watching as her daughter placed the token offering on top of the marble altar.

Coelia tapped a finger on the altar, thinking. "I hope the Albanum wine I ordered arrives at Lady Aurelia's before the reception tonight."

"Stop worrying, Coelia."

"I'm trying."

Lucilla put her arm around her daughter's waist. "I don't care about the damn Albanum wine. All I want is to see my daughter smile for a day. For a night." She looked at Coelia. "It has been a horrible couple of months," she said, "but the important thing is that you've kept your looks through it all." When Coelia smirked, Lucilla squeezed her affectionately. "If you cannot give me a proper smile, then give me a promise that you will come with us to Cumae."

"I promise," said Coelia, "but there always seems to be something in the way. When Domitia saw Eugenius's head on the Rostra, she changed her mind about wanting to serve as high priestess. Now I have to train Proculeia."

"Then do it quickly," urged Lucilla. "I want to see the sea breeze blow through your hair before it's as gray as mine. Now let's go marry me off, blushing maiden that I am, before I succumb to the fear of being ravished on my wedding night and run away."

"Gods," Coelia sputtered.

They turned to leave the peaceful grandeur of the sanctum, but as Coelia tried to push open one of the golden doors, she met resistance. She pushed harder. This time, the door opened, though Statius was standing almost too close for them to slip out.

"Sacerdos," said Coelia. "You're in the way."

"Oh..." he said distractedly.

The resistance eased, though only slightly, and Coelia looked at Lucilla—*what in the world?*—pushing harder until the women could exit. They did, immediately noticing that the sounds of wedding bells and laughter that had followed them into the temple were gone. A strange, almost eerie silence had descended on the Capitoline.

Coelia studied the priest. His face was contorted in confusion as he moved to look out over the Roman Forum below. Slowly, he turned around and put his hands on Coelia's shoulders, dispensing with protocol as he guided her back toward the sanctum. "I think you should go back inside the temple," he said. "Something is happening."

The Vestal pushed his hands away. Distracted by whatever was going on below, Statius didn't press the matter, but ran down the steps—Coelia and Lucilla close behind—and hurried along the marble pathway until all three of them had a relatively unobstructed view of what was transpiring in the Forum.

Below, a swarm of soldiers moved through the streets of the Forum like army ants.

Coelia gasped. "Are we being invaded?"

"Yes and no," Statius replied, his voice husky. "Those are Theodosius's men. From Constantinople."

"What are they doing?" asked Lucilla.

An angry shout caught their attention, and they all looked down at the Temple of Concordia to see a young priest falling down the tall staircase, a bucket of water tumbling down after him to drench his robes. Coelia knew him well: Sextus, the son of a popular centurion, obviously assaulted while on his way to wash the holy items inside the sanctum. He pushed himself to his knees and shook his fist at someone at the top of the steps, though from her vantage point, Coelia could not see who.

Another shout, this one from the Temple of Saturn. This time, Coelia could see it all play out. A group of six or seven soldiers stormed into the sanctum and emerged moments later, unceremoniously dragging two priests behind them. They tossed the sacerdotes onto the landing of the staircase. While two soldiers brandished their swords to keep the protesting priests at bay, another two struggled to secure the temple's doors with heavy iron bars.

Another cry of surprise and alarm, another howl of rage and objection, this time from the opposite direction. Coelia's stomach sank as she turned to look at the Temple of Antoninus and Faustina. On the landing atop the steps, a pair of soldiers was similarly locking the doors of the sanctum with impregnable iron bars as the priests shouted curses into the morning air.

Statius's words were barely a whisper. "It is happening... they are closing the temples."

A deep voice called out. "*Lucilla!*"

It was Olympius. Dressed for his wedding in a traditional *toga virilis*, his wrists encircled with gold cuffs, he reached Lucilla's side and grabbed her by the hand.

"What is happening?" she asked him.

"You can see what's happening," he snapped. "Theodosius has ordered all the temples closed." Still clutching Lucilla's hand, he looked at Coelia. "Come with us," he said. "There's nothing you can do. Think only of yourself."

The words echoed those in Arbo's dying message to her. Coelia's chest tightened, and she curled her fingers into fists, hastening farther along the path until she had a clear view of what was happening at—

"*No!*" she shrieked.

In the distance below, no fewer than twenty soldiers had amassed in front of the doors of the Temple of Vesta. More were on their way, coming from all directions like moths drawn to a flame, overturning the firebowls that burned in porticos and along the street as they closed in. Coelia bolted off before any-one—her mother, Olympius or Statius—could stop her. She ran down the marble ramp of the Capitoline, past a line of soldiers heading up to the Temple of Jupiter. Behind her, she heard voices rise into the air.

Olympius argued with Lucilla: "I don't care, woman! We're go-ing home *now!*"

Statius called out to other priests: "Gather the relics! They'll be here in moments!"

A soldier's voice boomed: "By Imperial Edict of Emperor The-odosius, it is hereby ordered that this temple be closed and secured under iron!"

Reaching the bottom of the marble ramp, Coelia ran past the temples of Concordia and Saturn and along the Via Sacra, notic-ing that despite the footfalls of the soldiers, the shouts of the priests and the clangs of iron bars slamming down to lock the temple doors—the sound of each latching rang out like a metallic thunderclap in the air—the Forum was quieter than usual for this time of day. Being the morning of the banquet to Jupiter, the Sen-ate and most offices were closed, leaving the soldiers to fulfill Theodosius's edict without excessive witnesses or opposition, and against a dreamlike placidity that belied the magnitude of the assault. Lifting the bottom of her dress to run faster, Coelia raced along the empty arcade of the Basilica Julia and under the Arch of Augustus, finally reaching the Temple of Vesta.

The sacrilege that was unfolding before her eyes sapped her strength and tightened her throat in grief-stricken rage. Two sol-diers were swinging a battering ram at the bronze double-doors of the temple. The Vestals on watch, Terentia and Sergia, had pre-sumably locked the doors from the inside. Outside, Domitia and Proculeia were on their knees, pleading with the commanding sol-dier to make his men stop. It was like every nightmare Coelia had ever had, materializing instead of dissolving, in the morning light.

"Coelia!" Domitia cried out. "They're going to extinguish the fire!"

Forcing her legs to keep moving until she reached the commanding officer, Coelia clasped her hands in front of her. "I am the high priestess of this temple," she said, breathless. "I ask—"

The officer held out a scroll to her. "Step back."

Coelia took the scroll, but didn't bother to break the Imperial seal. She knew what it authorized these soldiers to do. "I ask only that I be permitted to perform the rites of extinguishment."

"Rites of extinguishment," scoffed the officer. "I won't say it again—step back."

A sickening crunch of metal and wood sounded out, and Coelia looked to the doors of the temple just as they burst open, revealing Terentia and Sergia inside the circular sanctum, both women standing in front of the sacred hearthfire as if their slight bodies could shield it from the force of the soldiers.

"*Exstinguite!*" Coelia shouted to the Vestals.

Terentia lunged for a nearby amphora of wine, but felt a painful impact as one of the soldiers struck her hard, sending her to her knees on the tile floor. Sergia tried to reach the amphora next, but a soldier shoved her aside.

The sight of the men laying their hands on her sisters, the sight of them violating the goddess's sacred temple and the contempt on their faces as they neared her divine flames—it all roused in Coelia a sorrow that she had never before felt. Not when her mother had told her of her father's death, not when she had watched Brogos make his killing strike against Deimos, not when she had read the blood-stained message from Arbo alone on his rooftop as his pigeons softly cooed around her.

The damaged bronze doors of the temple creaked on their hinges, slowly gravitating toward each other to settle in a crookedly closed position that blocked Coelia's view of the inner sanctum, like torn curtains obscuring the tragic scene playing out within. She tried to slip past the commanding officer, but he grabbed her arm to restrain her.

"Settle down, lady," he grumbled. "We have our orders."

Coelia's eyes moved from the shuttered doors of the temple, up the columns, to the domed roof. The sound of crashing marble sounded from within the sanctum, and she heard Terentia and Sergia shriek in horror. As Coelia watched, her sorrow expanding with every heartbeat, the healthy plumes of smoke emanating from the oculus swayed strangely and began to thin.

"Aeneas, Son of Heaven," she whispered. "Keep watch."

Another heartbeat, and the smoke disappeared altogether. Rome's guardian flame, Vesta's sacred fire, which had burned in its temple for over a thousand years, was extinguished.

✳   ✳   ✳

"That is enough," Symmachus said to the officer who still held Coelia's arm. "Release her."

The soldier let go of the high priestess. Meanwhile, his two subordinates kicked open the broken doors of the temple from within and all but tossed Terentia and Sergia down the steps. Sergia turned at the last moment, trying to pry something away from one of the soldiers—it was the Palladium—but he yanked it away. As the two Vestals joined Coelia, the pair of soldiers remained on the small landing as a third approached with a heavy iron bar. It took effort, but between the three of them, they managed to pull the damaged doors together and lock them.

Coelia turned away from the surreal sight of the temple's locked doors and looked at her sister Vestals. Terentia and Sergia were red-eyed and panting from the physical struggle inside the sanctum, while Domitia and Proculeia wore expressions of disbelief.

"Where is Florina?" asked Coelia. "I thought she was on duty."

"She panicked and ran off," Terentia replied.

The high priestess lifted her chin. She would not allow the soldiers to see any further weakness in the Order. "The goddess sees your strength," she said, her tone underlining her instruction to maintain a dignified front. "Come with me."

As the priests from the nearby temples converged on the scene, gasping and falling into prayer at the calamitous extinguishment of Vesta's fire, Coelia led the other priestesses toward the portico of the House of the Vestals. Their usual guards were missing, though the sight of a helmet, two daggers and Teo's cloak lying haphazardly on the blood-spotted pathway suggested that they hadn't left without a fight. Coelia pulled one of the doors open, and they all slipped inside, rushing into the courtyard.

Now beyond the view of the soldiers, Terentia's false composure crumbled. "We could not stop it!" she cried. "They dumped wine on the flames and then..." she broke off, sobbing.

"And then one of them pushed over the altar," finished Sergia. "They walked right through the ashes."

By now, the other Vestals and novices had woken from sleep. Drawn by the commotion, and still wearing their nightdresses, they hastened into the courtyard with bare feet. They had barely arrived when Rufinia pointed toward the peristyle.

"You!" she exclaimed. "You cannot come in here!"

They all turned. Emerging from the peristyle and flowing into the courtyard like murky floodwaters through an open gate, a company of brown-robed clerics and Imperial officials—all men—entered the cloistered House of the Vestals. Some looked at the priestesses, but most looked past them entirely, gawking at the fineries of the multistoried house. They spread out nosily, some wandering into Coelia's office, others heading toward the baths or triclinium, and still others ascending the marble staircase that led to the Vestals' private apartments. One lingered by the decorative pool of fish, dipping his fingers into the water.

"Don't touch my fish!" yelled the novice Tertia. She turned and looked up at Coelia, panic in her eyes. "Tell him not to touch my fish!"

The man heard her, but kept his fingers in the pool, clinging to his moment of power. Finally, he curled his wet finger at Coelia, bidding her to approach him.

"What a bloody—" began Galeria, but Coelia silenced her.

The high priestess spoke from where she stood. "I am the custodian of this residence, and you are trespassing," she said. "This is the cloistered house of the Vestal Virgins."

"I know who you are," the man replied. "This house is state property. It's now under the jurisdiction of Bishop Siricius and will serve as the residence of his court." He shifted his eyes to the scroll that Coelia still clutched in one hand. "It's all there." He flicked the water off his fingertips. "The others can leave," he said to Coelia, "but you are ordered to stay for questioning." He walked off, eyeing the statues of the Vestals in the peristyle and disappearing into the dining room.

A shouted obscenity followed by a burst of laughter made the women look up to the upper level of the house. Ptolema was standing outside the open door to Coelia's apartment, berating an official who had emerged from the high priestess's private quarters. The sight of his smile, the knowledge that he had seen and touched things that were hers alone, made Coelia's skin crawl.

"Have you no decency?" railed the slave. "These are the rooms of the virgins!"

Sergia had remained remarkably steady to this point, but now the tears burst forth. "Why do they hate us so much?" she asked.

Proculeia was more pragmatic. "Our assets..."

Coelia glanced at the priestesses. At least she could give them this much. "The night that Arbogastes left for the war," she said hushedly, "I sent the deeds to our personal estates and the money in the coffers to Laurentum. Everything is in safekeeping there." She gestured to the terrified novices. "Take them to their parents," she instructed. "And then go home to your families. They will be worried."

"What do they want to question you about?" asked Domitia.

Coelia pulled the veil off her head. Between Stilicho and Ambrosius—one thought her a traitor, the other a whore—it could be anything. "I don't know," said Coelia. "I will write when it is safe. Now go." She kissed each of her sisters on the cheek. "*Valde vos amo.*"

The high priestess watched them go, only little Tertia looking back worriedly at her fish before being urged ahead by Domitia. The huddle of women and girls hastened past the unfamiliar faces of the guards at the doors, leaving their home with only the clothes on their backs, and leaving Coelia to stand alone in the courtyard as the intruding men rummaged through the priestess's sacred residence, satisfying their salacious curiosity of the private lives of the Vestal Virgins.

Exploiting their interest in the more intimate spaces of the house, Coelia moved cautiously toward the kitchen. Out of the corner of her eye, she saw Ptolema descend the stairs to follow her into the kitchen, the room still hot and fragrant with the smell of morning bread. Though the oven fire was almost out, its flames were sufficient to consume the Imperial scroll that Coelia tossed inside, while Ptolema lit the thick wick of a beeswax candle.

Coelia paused, listening. "Are they coming?"

Ptolema shook her head. "The bastards are too busy going through your undergarments."

Together, the high priestess and the slave moved deeper into the kitchen, slipping behind a curtain to enter the pantry. Coelia ran her hand along the brick wall until her fingers landed on an indent. She pushed it and a small square door swung open. Taking the candle from Ptolema, she squeezed through the opening, running a hand over the floor in the dim light until she found the recessed handle concealed in the tile. She pulled it upward, lifting the floor tile to expose the black void below. Peering into it, she compelled her eyes to adjust until she could discern the outline of the ladder that extended downward.

Sticking her head back through the little doorway, she looked up at Ptolema. "Come on."

"I am too old to be fleeing through escape tunnels," said Ptolema. "My cracking joints would draw too much attention." She gripped the little door. "They don't care about me. It's you who must go." She pulled the door closed, speaking as she disappeared behind it. "Get to the Tiber. Quickly."

Knowing it was pointless to argue and dangerous to delay, Coelia spun around on her knees and descended the first few rungs of the ladder, leaning her chest against it for balance as she reached up over her head to try and close the hatch. Ptolema was right. If she could get away, if she could follow the tunnel to the sewer line and then all the way to the Cloaca Maxima where it emptied into the Tiber, Domitia would have a boat waiting for her. She pulled harder on the hatch, the effort knocking the candle out of her other hand. It hit the dirt floor of the tunnel with a soft thud, snuffing out the flame. Everything went black, but there was nothing to be done about it. She would have to make her way in the dark.

"*Futuo,*" she whispered, and reached up with both hands to pull the stubborn hatch closed.

A hard, fast force from above yanked the hatch open again, nearly ripping Coelia's arms out of their sockets as she clung to it from below.

"I've got her!" shouted a soldier.

Coelia felt hands tighten painfully around both of her wrists as the soldier lifted her out of the hole, scraping the flesh of her legs against the rungs of the ladder and the jagged tile that encircled the mouth of the tunnel. He dragged her back through the little doorway and into the pantry.

"Get your hands off me!" Coelia yelled, and squirmed out of the man's grip.

The soldier stepped back slightly and extended a hand to help her stand. She swatted it away and stood to face him, a recognition slowly dawning on her. She knew this man. He had for a short time been posted at the Temple of Vesta. In her distress, she struggled to remember his name.

"Lucius," she finally said. "What are you doing? Help me!"

"I have a family, High Priestess," he said. "I am sorry, but I cannot."

✳   ✳   ✳

They led her into her office like a prisoner. An official wearing a thick beige tunica was already sitting behind her desk, his arm swiping the piles of scrolls scattered across its ivory surface into a waste basket. She had the sense he had waited until that very moment to do it. He nodded curtly to a subordinate, and the man carried the basket away.

"Sit down," the official said to Coelia. He scratched his head of short, curly hair with a stylus from her desk, and as the Vestal sat in the chair opposite him, began to write something on a fresh piece of papyrus. He spoke without looking at her. "Your order has been formally disbanded," he said. "Any personal belongings of the previous occupants of this residence will be collected, and you will be notified of where to collect them. All other items on and in this property—that includes this house, the temple and the Regia—belong to the state and are to be administered by me." He set down the stylus and looked at her. "That includes any items of monetary value, any slaves, and anything of historical significance. I am sure there is no shortage of wonders hidden within the architecture. A secret tunnel under the kitchen floor, for example. You people are like little squirrels, stuffing your valuables in hiding spots. It will make this period of transition easier for all of us if you disclose them willingly."

"There are no additional tunnels that I am aware of," said Coelia.

"The *penetralia*," said the official, referring to the rumored secret Vestal vaults where Rome's most ancient relics were kept. "You will show my men where they are."

As Coelia absorbed the man's aggression, as she regarded his arrogance, the prolonged state of shock that had gripped her since the moment she had stepped out of Jupiter's sanctum that morning withered into a strange fatigue. A defiant state of indifference. What could he do to her that he hadn't already done? Imprison her? Torture her? If that is what the goddess needed of her, if that's what it took to maintain the dignity of her office as Vestalis Maxima, she would endure it. It was all she had left, and it was certainly better than giving this petty tyrant what he wanted.

"From what I understand," she replied, "your churches have more than enough relics of their own. "In fact, whenever their numbers suffer, they seem to unearth another one. Why would you need Rome's ancient relics?" She knew the answer, of course. *Tinder and trophies.* The most dangerous relics—the ones that could rekindle worship of the immortal gods—would be burned to ash or melted down. The rest would be displayed as spoils of war.

"Where is the Palladium?"

"You should know," said Coelia. "One of your vandals ripped it from the goddess's sanctum."

The man twisted around in his chair to pick something off the floor. Turning back to Coelia, he set the statuette on the desk. "A decoy," he said. "Where is the real one?"

"I have heard it rumored that it is buried under the emperor's palace in Constantinople."

The official slammed his hands on the desk and stood.

"Stand down," said a voice. It was Stilicho, entering the office with Symmachus. The general jabbed his thumb toward the door, and the fuming official stepped away from Coelia's desk, brushing by her as he exited the office.

"I would like to free our senior house slave, Ptolema," Coelia said, not sure which of the two men she should speak to. "She is old and will not serve men."

It was Symmachus who replied. "I will have her manumitted and provided with an honorarium."

"She has her own money," replied Coelia. "She just needs the papers." She looked up at Symmachus. "Did you know this was going to happen?"

Stilicho leaned against Coelia's desk and crossed his arms. "The senator did not know," he said. "The order to close the temples and extinguish the fire was carried out prematurely by my commander, Constantius. He will be reprimanded for it." The general looked at Symmachus. "I had planned to wait until after the epulum. I wanted it to be done respectfully, by your own priests." The sound of rummaging, of male laughter, drifted into the office, and Stilicho turned back to Coelia. "You will remain under house arrest in your *domus* on the Esquiline Hill for now. It is for your own safety as much as anything else."

"And the other priestesses?" she asked.

"They are Roman citizens and noblewomen," he replied. "Providing they do not perform any pagan rituals or prayers, they have the protection of law."

"And if they are seen lighting a candle? If they are seen tossing a crust of bread into a fire? Or purchasing incense in the market?"

"It is better that they are not seen doing any of those things," said Stilicho, "if you want my honest opinion." He pushed himself away from the desk. "I will have a carriage take you home."

Stilicho exited the office, leaving Symmachus and Coelia alone.

"It would be best to go quickly," said the senator.

Coelia gripped the arms of the chair. "This has been my home for nearly forty years," she said. "There is something of me in every corner. How can I walk out with empty hands?"

"Walk out with me," he replied somberly.

His eyes were downcast when Coelia looked at him. She had been so focused on her own shock and grief that she had not thought about what the day had done to him. No one had tried harder, for longer, or in more ways to preserve Romulus's vision and the freedom of his people. Her thoughts flew back to the day that Claudia had taken her into the Regia, reprimanding her for disrespecting the senator.

"*Symmachus and those like him,*" Claudia had said, "*they have protected us in ways that you will never know. All they ask in return is that we respect them and uphold the dignity of our service.*"

"I have not always been gracious to you," said Coelia. "I am sorry."

She stood, and together they walked out of the office and along the peristyle filled with statues of Vestal Virgins. She glanced at the pretty pools, pink rose bushes and marble pathway, trying to divert the flood of memories that came rushing back—racing Domitia around the pool as children, picking the roses while the gardeners wagged their fingers, watching Ptolema chastise Brogos for letting his dogs muddy the pathway. How many priestesses had made and left their memories in the goddess's beautiful house?

The guards opened the chestnut doors, and she and Symmachus walked out together, passing through the portico and turning toward the Arch of Augustus. On the other side, a horse-drawn carriage and two guards awaited her. The emblems of the Vestal Order were still on the gilded vehicle, though Coelia knew she would be the last Vestal Virgin to travel with the dignity of the sacred symbols.

She looked up at the Capitoline. Word of the fatal Imperial edict had spread, and the sacred hilltop was now overrun. Men mounted frantic, disjointed efforts to defend the temples while women prayed before the shrines, begging for them to be spared, but nothing could stop the inevitable. The soldiers batted their way through it all, executing their orders with ruthless purpose, slamming iron bars onto the temple doors and stripping the shrines of their idols. Below, soldiers continued to run through the streets of the Forum to fulfill the same orders, and beyond the walls of the Roman Forum, the shouts and metallic thunderclaps that sounded from the Imperial Fora lent an even greater sense of devastation to it all, as if the entire world was being torn apart from the inside out.

Coelia walked past her marble statue without looking at it. She walked past the iron-barred doors of the Temple of Vesta, though she could not stop herself from looking at those. How many days, weeks, months and years had she spent in that circular sanctum? How many times had she stood around the sacred fire with her sisters, feeling Vesta's warmth on her face, hearing the goddess's voice in her ears, and watching her breath rise up through the oculus to dissolve into a bright blue sky or a pitch black one? She thought of the last watch she had performed in the temple—it had been a month earlier, with Proculeia. If only she had known it would be the last time, she would have clung to every moment instead of just letting them pass.

To thy hands Troy entrusts her holy things and household gods,
And Vesta's ever-bright, undying fire.

Rome had entrusted Vesta's ever-bright fire to her hands, and she had let it die.

She reached the carriage and nodded farewell to Symmachus before stepping inside and closing the curtain behind her.

CHAPTER XLI

During his recent visit to Rome to celebrate his victory over the usurper Eugenius and the traitor Arbogastes, Emperor Theodosius had seen for himself that the bishops were right. The open and persevering worship of the heathen gods in the Eternal City had become intolerable. He had therefore summoned the senators of Rome to the Curia and all but pleaded with them to abandon their superstitions and idols for the good of a unified empire. But he was only met with obstinance. If it weren't a sacrilege, he might almost say that he admired their conviction. Yet seeing it so closely—the way they squared their shoulders, the way they looked at their gods, the way they petitioned, relentlessly, for religious freedom—had cemented the truth of it for Theodosius. He had come to accept that it didn't matter how many laws he passed or how many men he sent into exile or how many wars he won or how many heads he put on spikes. The old gods were in every stone and flower, in every sunbeam and rainfall, in every cup of wine and every crackle of fire in Rome. Until darkness fell upon every temple in the city, those who worshipped the old gods would always be drawn to their light.

Yet there were hundreds of temples in Rome, hundreds of shrines, and untold thousands of monuments and statues in gold, bronze, ivory and marble. There were so many pagan structures that it simply wasn't feasible to close, remove or dismantle everything, and so Rome's new administrators—carefully chosen by Theodosius before departing Rome for Constantinople—had to make some practical decisions. Some temples and facilities—like the Temple of Antoninus and the House of the Vestals—could be converted to Christian or other official use. The Temple of Concordia had been reopened strictly as a museum, for example, though many would be forbidden from visiting it. That included the Vestalis Maxima Coelia Concordia. It also included the other Vestal priestesses, all of whom, in fact, were forbidden from visiting any pagan temple. That measure, and the potential for false accusations, had seen their families send them out of the city and into the safety of their countryside estates. The priestesses were also prohibited from discussing their religion or assembling: Theodosius could not risk giving them the opportunity to regroup or rally sympathizers.

But neither could Theodosius risk ignoring the advice of General Stilicho. He had given Stilicho top command of the military as magister militum and made him regent over the young Honorius—unaware of Stilicho's hatred for the dullard, of course—and knew that the general's roots in Rome went deeper than his own. Regarded as a moderate who cared more about protecting Rome's borders than persecuting its people, the general truly understood the city and had the friendships to prove it.

That is why Theodosius had conceded to Stilicho's request to keep one temple open for pagan worship. Located on the Palatine Hill, and therefore out of the sight and reach of the vast majority of Romans, it allowed the city's pagan senators and elite to feel a fragment of the familiar, albeit under guard. The rules were simple: Pray in silence, do not speak to anyone while you are there, do not leave an offering, and do not start an altar fire.

After a week of house arrest on the Esquiline, Coelia's daily letters to Symmachus and his subsequent petitions to Stilicho had succeeded in their purpose, and she had been granted permission to visit the open temple. Although her Vestal privileges had been revoked and she was no longer able to command a carpentum, she was allowed to travel in an undistinguished lectica. She had done so alone and quietly, not thinking much of anything as the porters navigated the curves and slopes of the streets that led to and up the Palatine. They set the vehicle down on the platform below the Temple of Magna Mater, and Coelia opened the curtain. One of the soldiers who had been posted to her home helped her step out. The man was unfriendly but not uncivil, though his coolness made her long for the easy companionship of Teo or Brogos. She had no idea where the former was, though she knew the latter was still close by. Only the day before, she had heard his foul-mouthed altercation with the guards outside her home as he was denied access to see her.

Coelia hadn't known what to expect upon her arrival at the temple complex on the western slope of the Palatine, but she found it peaceful enough despite the large number of worshippers roaming the opulent grounds or visiting the temple, some heading up the staircase to enter the sanctum and others on their way out. The mood was subdued, and Coelia felt their eyes on her as she ascended the staircase. She heard their whispered voices, too.

"*Pray for us, High Priestess.*"

"*Cave atque salva es, Sacerdos.*"

As she crested the top step, she felt the abraded skin on her thighs pull—she hadn't fully healed from being yanked out of the tunnel—and it was a relief to reach the landing. She stopped before the statue of the great mother seated on a throne, lions at her feet, and said a brief prayer before proceeding through the columned portico and into the sanctum. Another statue of the enthroned goddess stood just inside, this one made of wood, but just as colorful and spectacular. Every spring, it was taken from the temple and carried through the streets of Rome in a great celebratory parade. People played music and sang, tossed flowers onto the street and handed free toys to children. Coelia doubted she would ever see that again in her lifetime.

The mood inside the temple was more repressed than outside, owing to the guards posted throughout. Some watched worshippers with keen eyes, actively monitoring for a transgression. Others looked the other way, giving tacit permission for worshippers to do as they pleased. Coelia strode by them toward her destination: a shrine to Vesta, the huge marble alcove of which housed statues of the fire goddess and her mother, Ops. Reaching the shrine, she was saddened but not surprised to find the altar fire extinguished. At least the statues were unchanged, though. Ops in particular was as opulent as always. Her head was crowned with flowers, and she cradled a cornucopia like a swaddled infant. Rich jewels accented the marble: emerald earrings dangled from Ops's ears, while a golden necklace studded with pearls and carnelian stones hung around her neck.

Coelia knelt before the statue of Vesta. On the other side of the sanctum, a guard began to walk toward her, but stopped when his young colleague shook his head.

"She's not doing any harm," said the younger man. "Leave her alone."

Holding her palms up in prayer, Coelia gazed into the face of the goddess. "Mother Vesta," she said. "Forgive the hands that failed your sacred fire. Recall the piety that your immaculate priestesses have shown in Rome, Tivoli and Bovillae, in the cities and provinces of the empire, in Alba Longa and in Troy, and in the names of cities and places lost to time. Know that your flame burns eternal in the hearts of your exiled priestesses. Vesta, enter the flames that burn in the household hearths of your faithful. Protect them as they honor you, even in silence. I have nothing to offer, holy virgin, except the duty I have already performed in your name."

A cacophony of voices resonated within the temple, shattering the sanctity of the space and abutting the priestess's prayer with vulgarity. The young soldier peered around a corner and then hurried to Coelia's side.

"You'd better go," he warned her.

He offered her a hand—how old she must have appeared to the youth—and she took it, rising to her feet, though not before the source of the voices appeared before the alcove. It was Serena, accompanied by an escort of three guards, the most handsome of which she was glibly chatting with. As the wife of Rome's top man, she was dressed as a self-styled empress, complete with a purple dress and gold diadem. Spotting Coelia, she furrowed her brow.

"Lady Coelia," she said. "It must be so hard for you to be here." Having already said what she came to say to the goddess, and having nothing to say to Serena, the priestess turned to go. Embarrassed by the slight, Serena blocked her path and spoke to one of the guards stationed in the sanctum. "What was she doing in here?"

"Just praying," said the younger guard.

The older one, keen to make a good impression, bowed before Serena. "My lady," he said. "I did hear her praying aloud."

Serena looked at Coelia. "I could have you arrested." Still, the Vestal said nothing. The noblewoman studied her, thinking. She could order Coelia's arrest, but then Stilicho would only face backlash from the pagans and release her... and he would be livid with Serena for stirring things up. An idea came to her, and she turned to the statues of Vesta and Ops.

"I have toured several of the heathen temples now," she said, "and I am always appalled by how much finery drapes the necks of the more whorish idols." Approaching the more bejeweled of the two statues, she removed the gold necklace from Ops and placed it around her own neck. She straightened the gold chain tauntingly.

"You will never be the empress of Rome," said Coelia. "I know it, and so does the goddess you steal trinkets from. You can commit any sacrilege that amuses you, but you only shame yourself, Serena."

"How *dare* you speak to me like that!" shouted Serena. "I will have my uncle raze this temple to the ground!" She turned to her guards. "Throw her outside!"

Serena's guards clamped their hands around Coelia's arms like vices and began to drag her along the marble floor of the temple, past the other worshippers, as Serena followed behind, her anger venting as cruel laughter. Seized with the indignity of it, Coelia tried to get her feet under her and resist, but it was useless. Reaching the portico, she again tried to stand, but—shockingly—felt the unyielding momentum of the guards' strength as they threw her out the temple doors and onto the landing of the high staircase, no different than a beggar being thrown out of a shop and into the street. She landed hard on her hands and knees, feeling the skin on her palms peel away. It left a streak of blood on the white marble. Reeling from the assault, Coelia stared in disbelief at her bloody hands. Were these the same hands that, only weeks ago, had been entrusted with the oldest and most sacred duty in Rome? With nothing left to fight with but the certainty that the gods were real, Coelia turned to them for vengeance.

Still on her knees, she looked up at Serena and began to shout. "I call upon the divine children of Ops to avenge the sacrilege against their great mother! Juno and Ceres, curse this woman's marriage bed and afflict her children with barrenness! Neptune and Pluto, plague her sleep with nightmares and reduce her husband to ruin! Jupiter, deliver the justice she deserves!" The Vestal wiped her bloody hands in her dress, and kept her final words private. *Vesta, let them all run from the flames.*

Slowly, Serena approached until she was standing above the priestess. She might have had slight regard for Coelia's superstitions, but a curse... that was something else. She took the pendant around her neck in her fingers and toyed with it until her affected aloofness returned. Leaning over, she whispered something into the ear of the handsome guard.

Trying to summon whatever dignity was left to her, Coelia had just begun to rise on unsteady legs when she felt a steely force against her side and realized with a sinking despair that the guard had pushed her. She teetered on the very edge of the landing for an awkward, humiliating moment before tipping over and tumbling down the marble steps, her flailing body making uncontrolled impacts with the hard stone—first an elbow, then a knee, then her head, then the other elbow. Serena's renewed laughter followed, step by step.

Coelia landed on her back at the bottom of the staircase. Her veil had been torn off in the fall, and her tunica was up around her waist. Ignoring the throbbing pain that shot through her limbs, ignoring the blood that seeped from her palms, ignoring her aching knees—and the worry that they would not support her—she kicked out her legs and struggled to lower the hem of her dress.

"High Priestess, let me help," said a voice. It was Statius, the high priest of Jupiter. He rushed to her side.

"Step back!" Serena shouted from the landing above. "Don't you know it is forbidden to touch a Vestal? Lay a hand on her, and I'll have you beaten to death in front of your mother!"

Coelia waved Statius away. Twisting and turning on the ground, she finally managed to pull down her blood-streaked white dress, covering her bare legs and praying that no one had seen her underclothes. She heard weeping and turned to see Statius's wife—herself a priestess of Ceres—kneeling on the ground nearby, crying into her hands. Statius moved to his wife's side and knelt down, wrapping his arms around her.

It took several more mortifying efforts to roll onto her stomach and make it onto her swollen knees, and then to her feet, but at last Coelia managed. She hobbled back to the unembellished lectica and opened the curtain, stepping inside. She pulled the heavy fabric closed behind her as quickly as she could, desperate to disappear into the darkness, to retreat into oblivion, where she could fall apart in peace.

FIFTEEN YEARS LATER

CHAPTER XLII

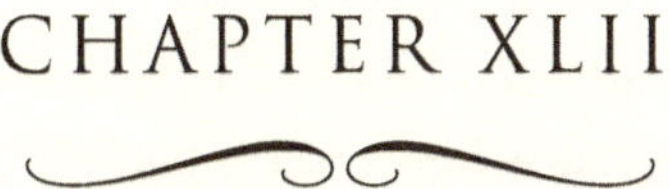

Just outside of Cumae (five days by horse south of Rome)

If she looked out to sea, the world shed its form and faded into nothing more substantial than the color blue, as though the sky and water had been painted with the same brushstroke. Even her little wooden boat was blue, and as the smooth underside thumped gently against the mildest of waves, Coelia peered over the edge to see something sleek and secretive swimming under the surface. She often rowed out to this distance, far enough from shore to see the villa that she had lived in as a child. She had initially planned to purchase it back from the current owner, but after Victor's assassination and the investigations that followed, the man had balked at selling the property to a friend of the fallen emperor. She had therefore settled for a villa farther along the shore. Ultimately, it had been for the best. There was something pure about creating a new life instead of trying to live in the past.

She reached for the oars and began to row back to land, feeling a skim of cool water at her bare feet—there was a crack or hole somewhere—and listening to the swishing of the water against the blades as they lazily propelled the boat along. As she neared the shore, she stroked harder, giving the boat the momentum it needed to softly ram the sandy beach that fronted her seaside villa. She stepped out of the boat and into the clear blue water, letting the bottom of her emerald-green tunica soak up the sea water as she pulled the small craft onto shore. She could have fastened the boat to the dock, but after falling into the water once in the attempt—Brogos hadn't stopped laughing for an entire afternoon—she preferred this approach.

Although one of her sandals was where she had left it, one of the feral dogs that Brogos insisted on feeding had scampered off with the other, and it took her a while to locate it in a flower bed. The animal had chewed the strap, though not tragically, so she fastened both sandals and trekked to the gate of her property where the town's messengers left her mail from Rome. A single scroll was there. It bore the Imperial seal of the emperor Honorius, though it was not from him, but rather from Olympius. He had managed to snake his way into becoming a key minister in the young emperor's court, and he always used the Imperial seal when he wrote to Coelia. It was the only way he could ensure his correspondence to her remained private.

She broke the seal and read. The letter was full of Olympius's usual profanity-laden grievances about the general Stilicho and his commander Constantius, followed by a long-winded recital of the senatorial debates surrounding monies due to the king of the Visigoths, Alaric. Alaric had lost thousands of men fighting the late Theodosius's war against Eugenius, and still hadn't been paid. Not only were increasing numbers of allies-turned-enemies of Rome rallying around him, but his demands for payment were seguing into threats... or some such thing. Coelia skimmed over the politics—she had left that world behind long ago—and reached the bottom of the letter. Here, too, was the expected: an emotional account of how Olympius had seen the soul of Lucilla in the flame of a torchbearer during a Mithraic ritual. Coelia rolled up the papyrus. Olympius and her mother had been married for twelve years, and Lucilla's death three years earlier had devastated him. His ongoing grief had led him to join those in Rome who secretly practiced the mysteries of Mithras. It was only when praying in a subterranean shrine of Mithras, he said, that he was able to commune with her.

Drawn by the scent of spiced chicken, Coelia strolled back to the house and headed directly to the kitchen where Brogos was already carving up supper. She sat on a stool on the other side of the counter, passing him the scroll. He took it and tossed it into the oven fire before handing her a plate of steaming meat. She dug in without ceremony, while he threw the scraps out the open window to the dogs and joined her.

"It's good, this," she said.

"One of the older hens, too," he replied. "It's all in the seasoning and a slow roast. I don't just dump salt in the pan and then wander off until it burns, like you do."

"I learned to cook late in life," said Coelia. She washed a mouthful of chicken down with a swallow of wine. "When I was on the water, I thought I saw soldiers coming to the house."

Brogos licked his oily fingers and nodded. "You did, but they weren't the usuals. They were from the port. Wanted to know if we'd seen any signs of pirate ships."

Coelia scoffed. "You'd think the fleet would know before us."

"You'd fucking think."

Outside the window, the dogs fell into a yapping frenzy—the warning kind—and the two friends exchanged looks of concern.

"Did you lock the gate after the soldiers left?" asked Coelia.

"I can't remember. Maybe not."

Brogos set down his handful of chicken meat and left the kitchen to investigate. Even after all these years, neither of them had completely lost their fear of unexpected visitors. Coelia hurried behind the counter to peer out the window, watching Brogos raise a civil but standoffish wave to an approaching figure—a woman in a turquoise colored cloak, the hood of which was over her head. One of the churchwomen from town, perhaps, coming to proselytize to the fallen Vestal. Coelia couldn't hear what she and Brogos were saying to each other, but he gestured for her to remove her hood. She did, and he drew back in surprise before both of them began to walk toward the open window, looking in at Coelia. It took Coelia a moment. After all, it had been over twenty years, and the face was from another time, another place. Another life entirely.

"Antonia?" she asked through the window.

The woman smiled. "Either I have aged so poorly that you don't recognize me, or so well that you're in shock."

"Ha," said Coelia. She quickly rounded the counter and rushed out of the house to meet Antonia's open arms with her own.

"Your hair is so long," commented Antonia.

"And as silver as a new denarius," said Coelia, as the friends faced each other.

"Nonsense, it is still brown," replied Antonia. She twirled a lock of her own hair around a finger—brown strands, though like Coelia's, now streaked with silver. "We are neither young nor old," she said. "Our lives hang in the balance."

Coelia cast Antonia a curious look. "Honestly, I never expected to see you again. I'm surprised you even knew where to find me. What brings you to Cumae?"

"I wanted to see an old friend."

"Ah, well, come in," said Coelia. "I have some delicious hibiscus tea. We'll drink like the pharaohs."

Antonia followed Coelia inside, noting the upscale home's fine furnishings and frescos, the walls dominated by marine blues and pretty paintings of starfish and seahorses. Yet as Coelia led her into the kitchen and continued behind the counter to gather the ingredients for the hot infusion, Antonia looked back at Brogos in curiosity.

"Is it just the two of you here? No servants?"

"Just the two of us," confirmed Coelia.

Antonia nodded, trying to hide her surprise as Coelia prepared the beverage herself, adding hot water and honey and stirring it all up before handing Antonia and Brogos their cups.

Brogos accepted his and headed toward the door. "I have repairs in the stable," he said, finding an excuse to leave the two women alone. Before he left, he cast Coelia a warning look. *Be careful. Don't trust anyone.*

Antonia caught his parting message. Sitting on the dining couch, she lifted her legs and sat curled up as Coelia sat beside her in a similar position.

"Very nice," said Antonia, taking a sip of the hot drink.

Coelia smiled. "You look like the city mouse visiting the country mouse, wondering how she possibly manages to survive."

Antonia patted the rich fabric on the dining couch. "There is still some city in you." She lowered her eyes. "It must have been awful for you, Coelia," she said. "These last years."

"These last years have been anything but awful," replied Coelia. "The first years... well, those were harder."

"I wanted to come sooner. I wanted to write."

"You were wise not to. Neither was safe." Coelia swirled the tea in her cup. "I assume you are still in Rome?"

"I am," said Antonia. "I have been fortunate. I left the Order years before the temples were closed, plus my cousin married into the family of Bishop Siricius. They're good people, and have always shielded me."

"So you got out just in time," said Coelia. "Unscathed." She shook her head. "I didn't mean it like that. I'm happy for you."

"I have always blamed myself..."

"Now who speaks nonsense," said Coelia. "None of us were to blame." After a thoughtful beat, she added, "Claudia risked coming to see me a few years ago. I thought she looked good. She told me that Proculeia and Terentia had moved to Greece. Domitia moved somewhere up north." Coelia sensed a slight quaver in her voice as she spoke Domitia's name. Even after all these years, she missed her old best friend as keenly as ever. "Have you seen Claudia recently?"

"She passed two years ago, Coelia," said Antonia.

Coelia's fingers tightened around the cup. "Oh. I didn't know that."

"There were rumors it was you who had died," said Antonia. When Coelia only shrugged indifferently, Antonia turned to lighter news. "Rufinia is still in Rome. She married into the Flavii and has two boys. I see her now and then at the market. We're still under official orders not to speak to each other, but her boys ferry messages back and forth. They are quite handsome."

"Is that wise?" asked Coelia. "What if they are caught?"

"It's not like it was," said Antonia. "After the edict to disband the Order, we were all watched fairly closely. But I haven't been questioned about anything in six or seven years."

"Me neither," said Coelia, "but soldiers still come by. They like to remind me that I'm not permitted to visit the temples in town, as if I could forget."

"Have you entered the cave of the Sibyl?" asked Antonia, referring to the underground caverns in Cumae where the prophetess had kept the famous Sibylline Books.

"No, I'm forbidden from doing that as well," said Coelia. "I don't really care anymore."

"Liar."

Coelia set her cup on the floor. "Why exactly did you want to see me, Antonia?"

"Stilicho burned the Sibylline Books the day before I left Rome," Antonia replied. "Do you know why?"

"I assume for the same reason they've burned every other scrap of papyrus about the gods," said Coelia.

"No. It had nothing to do with religion. It was paranoia. His wife's paranoia. Serena knows that you live in Cumae. Her husband has more enemies every day, and she feared you were helping them use the words of the Oracle to curse him. She has become obsessed with curses since you—"

Coelia stood. "Olympius has written to me about this rubbish," she said. "I don't want to hear it."

Antonia stood to face her. "With Alaric issuing demands and threats outside the city walls, and with the emperor's cronies sabotaging each other inside, Rome is floundering. Alaric has already blockaded some grain shipments, and now we're under rations. You know the panic that instills in people. Everyone is saying there hasn't been a threat like this since Brennus. People are desperate and afraid. They seek the goddess's protection."

Coelia tensed. "You're risking both of our lives with such talk."

"Rome has been dying since the very moment the sacred fire was extinguished," pressed Antonia. "The ancient prophecy— that Rome will die when Vesta's flame goes out—is coming true."

"Perhaps," said Coelia. "Or perhaps it is not that simple. All those years ago, when I was accused of treason for consulting the Oracle in Praeneste, I never told anyone what the prophetess said to me."

"Ptolema told you not to," replied Antonia. "And she knew the ways of the Oracle."

"Well, I'm going to tell you now," said Coelia. "She told me that a nation extinguishes many flames before its fire finally dies." She sighed. "Rome has been killing itself for decades. Corruption, oppression, division. This crisis was inevitable, ancient prophecy or not."

"No one can fault you for losing your faith," said Antonia, "not after what you've been through."

"I haven't lost my faith. I just honor the goddess in my own way now."

"You are still Vestalis Maxima."

"Of an outlawed priesthood."

Antonia was undeterred. "There are many of us. We meet in secret, but our numbers grow every day," she said. "Traditionalists and the newly converted. I heard what you did at the Temple of Concordia during the famine years ago. You could do it again."

"Antonia, I don't—"

"The temple fire was extinguished by profane hands, without the rites. You are the only one who can—"

"Antonia, I just don't want to," Coelia interrupted. "Please understand. I lost years of my life worrying about Ambrosius, constantly enduring his insults. I worried about the coffers, I worried about famine, I worried about bloody lions roaming the streets. I lost Victor and Arbo, and I saw Eugenius's head on a spike. I worried every day and every night, I prayed and offered to all the gods, but it made no difference. Men still broke through the temple doors and extinguished the flame, they still rampaged through our home like drooling satyrs. Our time is past." She put her hands on her hips. "I like it here. Brogos and I have a good life. I have a few friends, and Brogos has half the women in town wrapped around his finger. We have fresh food and the sea is peaceful. I have no desire whatsoever to thrust my hands back into the wildfire that is Rome."

"It is your duty."

"I was forbidden from doing my duty fifteen years ago." Coelia rubbed her eyes. "I am sorry you came all this way just to hear no," she said. "I have no servants to escort you back to town, and I don't tell Brogos what to do. You will have to walk back by yourself."

"I have a carriage waiting on the road."

"Of course you do."

A tense moment followed, but Antonia broke it. She put her arms around Coelia and spoke softly into her ear. "I have lived with the shame of leaving the goddess every day of my life for over twenty years." She pulled back and brushed away a tear. "No one knows me in Cumae. Perhaps I will go to the acropolis and pray at the shrine of Vesta."

"They removed that shrine when I arrived," said Coelia. "They are very thorough, sister. Take my advice. Find a house by the sea, and stop trying to live in the past."

CHAPTER XLIII

Rome

General Stilicho didn't spend a lot of time in his residence on the Palatine Hill. Although it was one of the finest homes in all of Rome—it was, after all, the former palace of the emperor Domitian—he often chose to sleep at his residence in the Campus Martius. It was just easier that way. Except for those days that the Senate was in session, he was in the Campus Martius from before sunrise to after sunset anyway, attending to his various duties as magister militum. Yet there was one thing that was always guaranteed to ensure an overnight stay on the Palatine, and that was the chief housemaid's discreet memorandum that a new female servant had come into the home's employ. Stilicho insisted on greeting every new female staff member personally. It was a greeting that sometimes took place in the staff bathhouse or even the kitchen, but most usually took place between the sheets of the small bed assigned to the fresh-faced newcomer.

Physically spent from coupling with the new servant, Stilicho rolled out of the squeaky little bed and dressed wordlessly, his mind already turning to the day's senatorial business. Whatever last remnants of pleasure he felt ebbed away at the thought of walking into the quarrelsome chamber, and especially of having to face that prick Olympius and his constant connivances. He left the girl, and the servants' quarters, without looking back.

Once he was gone, the servant—her name was Leah, not that Stilicho had asked—pushed off the covers and swung her legs out of her tiny bed, reaching down to retrieve her clothes. Carrying them in a bunch to the wash basin in the corner, she sponged off his perspiration and cleaned herself before dressing and heading out into the corridor. Two older servants were on their knees, washing the tile floor. They looked up at the young woman, her long auburn locks a tangled mess, and exchanged knowing smiles.

"I see you have been initiated into the house of Stilicho," said one.

"How was it?" the other one asked.

Leah leaned against the wall. "Boisterous."

The two women laughed, and the younger one nodded. "Ah, I remember my initiation," she said. "It was ten years ago. Of course, he hasn't given me a second look since."

"Then I must've had something you didn't," taunted the older servant. "Because he initiated me twice."

This time, all three women laughed.

"Where are you from, my dear?" the younger servant asked Leah.

"Syria."

"That sounds interesting."

"No place is interesting when you grow up there," replied Leah. She peered down the corridor, in the direction that Stilicho had gone. "Does his wife know about his initiations?"

The two house servants sat back on their heels, squeezing the water from their sopping rags into the bucket. They eyed each other, as if deciding how much to tell the new girl.

"His wife knows," said the older servant.

"Oh, come on," prompted Leah. "There's a story there. Tell me."

"It's a sad story," said the younger servant. "Poor Lady Serena. It isn't bad enough that her husband is possessed by Priapus—

really, the man is insatiable—but her older daughter died last year."

"Really?"

"Her name was Maria. She was married to Honorius, and I must say, sharp in all the ways that the emperor is dull."

"How did she die?"

The older servant piped up. "That is where things get interesting. She just died in her sleep one night. No one knows why for certain, but—"

"—but she was barren," the younger interrupted. "The physicians said that she probably died from one too many fertility concoctions that her mother gave her. The rumor in the palace is that Lady Serena used to slip all kinds of things into her daughter's food and drink, and even mix it into her ointments."

"That's awful," said Leah.

"And then there's the curse..." baited the older servant.

"A curse?" asked Leah. "Oh, tell me."

The older servant reached up to take Leah's hand, pulling her to the floor so she could whisper the gossip. "Years ago, just after the pagan temples were closed, Lady Serena pushed the head priestess of Vesta down the steps of a temple on the Palatine, and—"

"—and the Vestal cursed her," the younger servant broke in. "From what I've been told, it was a pretty thorough curse, too. Faithless husband. Barren child. Bad dreams."

"Does she have bad dreams?"

"Oh, all the time," said the younger servant. "Every night, she dreams that her youngest child, her daughter Thermantia, is found dead in the bath. The same dream, every night. And not only does she have bad dreams, but she sees things... ghosts. Spirits."

"And she's not the only one who's seen them," said the older. "A lot of us have."

Leah sniggered. "You aren't serious."

The younger servant gave the lower part of the wall a half-hearted wipe and turned back to Leah. "Once," she began, "I was walking by the master's bedchamber—he wasn't home, but Lady Serena was in bed—when I heard the most dreadful sound coming from behind the door. It sounded like a hundred mice squealing at once, but strangely so... like they were underwater. I tell you, it made my blood run cold. But I couldn't help myself, I had to see what it was. So I opened the door, just a crack, and peeked inside. It was dark, and it took a few moments for my eyes to adjust, but then I saw it. Lady Serena was sitting straight up in bed, staring at something by her feet. And there, just at the foot of the bed" — the servant pointed in the air for emphasis — "was the ghastliest thing I've seen in my whole life. A little man, but with a shrunken horse head instead of a man's head." She swallowed, recalling the sight. "And then the most disturbing thing of all happened. Lady Serena opened her mouth and started screaming, but her screams were all muffled and muted, like she was underwater."

"What did you do?" asked Leah.

"I closed the door and ran for my life," said the younger servant. "And to this day, I do everything I can to avoid going into the master's bedchamber."

Leah sucked in her breath, feeling her skin prickle. "That is terrifying."

The older servant looked into the bucket of water. "This is too dirty," she said. "My dear, go get two tired ladies a fresh bucket, would you?"

"Sure," said Leah. She lifted the bucket and shuffled down the corridor, still shivering from the story.

When she was out of sight, the older servant whipped her rag at the younger. "You are the devil," she said, and they laughed together.

The young emperor Honorius sat on his throne in the packed Senate House, jabbing an angry finger at Senator Junius, who had the floor. "Alaric demands another thousand pounds of gold?" he asked. "I'll give him iron up the ass before I give him another ounce of gold!"

"*Hear, hear!*" exclaimed an indignant body of senators.

Stilicho rose from his seat and strode to the center of the senatorial chamber, his hard gaze landing on the loudest cheerers—Olympius and Lampadius—before softening into diplomacy and turning to Honorius. "Highness, Alaric is a lodestone. Every barbarian soldier that Rome has wronged rushes to his side, salivating at the thought of laying siege to our city. With the legions as depleted as they are, we cannot—"

Olympius stood. "The depleted legions," he ruminated cynically. "Our soldiers didn't disappear through sorcery. They weren't swept away by the wind. They died or buggered off under General Stilicho's command as magister militum. So this assembly must ask itself—should we persist in stupidity by letting the man who brought us to the brink push us over it?" He met eyes with the emperor, a private message moving between them.

Stilicho saw it and tensed. Olympius had long been Honorius's biggest sycophant, but always behind the scenes. This boldness was something new. So too was Honorius's quickness to side with Olympius instead of accepting the recommendations of his former regent. Since Maria's death, Stilicho had steadily lost influence over the long-faced dullard. Now, the rate of that decline had increased. As he perused the faces that surrounded him in the Senate, he wished Symmachus were still alive. Rome would never be in this position if he were here to talk sense into both the assembly and the young emperor.

"Peace always comes at a cost," said Stilicho. "Right now, for the security of the city, it is time to pay our debts. These grain blockades must end. We all know what is happening in the streets."

Senator Lampadius stood. "So Rome should cower to barbarians for a few loaves of bread? You do not offer peace, Stilicho, you suggest servitude!"

The general glared at the senator, his eyes issuing a warning, and Lampadius sat down. There was a fine line between challenging the magister militum and courting retribution.

Stilicho turned to Honorius. "Highness, I suggest that we deliver the gold as requested. That will allow us to—"

"You can give the king of the beasts some silver," said Honorius. "Preferably from your wife's jewelry closet."

A few senators chuckled.

Stilicho rounded on them. "It is Alaric who should be laughing," he rebuked. "We bicker and backstab our countrymen, while he rallies our enemies around him and grows stronger."

Honorius stood. "I am hungry," he said, "and sick of your nattering."

Bristling at the young emperor's arrogant indifference—it was almost as profound as his incompetence—Stilicho stepped back as Honorius brushed by him and stomped out of the senatorial chamber without even waiting for the session to be formally closed. Around him, the senators continued to debate and argue. Finally, the session drew to a close, and the strident orations settled into a mangle of disparate conversations.

Stilicho marched out of the Senate House and into the fresh air, spotting his son Eucherius. He was standing by the *Lacus Curtius*, chatting with Valerius—one of Stilicho's commanders— and a number of footsoldiers. Although Eucherius had grown up with Honorius and the two had enjoyed the same advantages, the gap that had existed between them in childhood had only widened in adulthood. And it wasn't just Eucherius's superior abilities. His virtues shone next to Honorius's, whose primary concerns seemed to be eating and fornicating.

Eucherius looked up at his father, the young man's expression as keen and alert as ever. In that instant, the insufferable injustice of it all—Honorius's ineptness, Alaric's demands, the Senate's infighting and Olympius's ceaseless scheming—boiled over in Stilicho's veins.

"I'll give Alaric his fucking gold," he growled. He turned toward the Capitoline Hill, shouting to his men over his shoulder.

"Me sequimini!"

Valerius and his footsoldiers fell into line behind him. Drawn by the angry command, so too did many of the senators discoursing in front of the Senate House. By the time Stilicho reached the base of the Capitoline, no fewer than thirty men were following him. By the time he ascended the steps and crossed the hilltop to reach the Temple of Jupiter—his determined march picking up more people en route—it was no fewer than fifty.

Breathing heavy at his father's side as he struggled to match his pace, Eucherius's voice was apprehensive. "Father, what are you doing?"

"They need a show of power," replied Stilicho. "I can't lose my grip."

As the procession arrived at Jupiter's great golden doors, Stilicho signalled to a group of workmen who, by all appearances, had just descended from the temple's roof on ladders, their tools slung over their shoulders in leather bags.

The foreman rushed over to Stilicho. Glancing nervously at the large gathering and privately wishing he'd taken an early lunch, he bowed to the general. "Sir," he said. "How can I help you?"

Grabbing the sleeve of the foreman's tunica, Stilicho dragged the man right up to the doors of the temple. "I want you to peel the gold off these doors," he commanded. "Now."

The foreman—a pagan—balked. "General... "

Reaching into the man's workbag, Stilicho gripped the protruding handle of a small hatchet and withdrew it. He tapped one of the doors with the blade. "The gold comes off these doors," he said, and then pointed the blade at the foreman, "or the head comes off these shoulders."

"Eum audivistis," the foreman barked to his workers.

At once, the workmen all set to hammering, chiseling and peeling the gold from the sacred doors.

A loud cry of protest sounded from the pagan senators as they exchanged looks of disbelief. When would the insults end?

Junius, one of Stilicho's staunchest supporters in the Senate, stormed over to the general's side. His face blazed with anger.

"General, this is too far! There are other ways!"

But Stilicho wasn't listening. His gaze was now fixed on what was happening behind Junius: A group of men—Honorius, accompanied by Olympius and four well-armed guards—was quickly approaching. At the sight of them, Stilicho's hatred for the Imperial imbecile and his smuggest lackey returned in full force. Something had to be done.

Stilicho glanced at Valerius and his footsoldiers. "Are you with me?"

"We are with you," replied Valerius. He nodded curtly to the other soldiers, and they all put their hands on the hilts of their swords.

Junius stepped toward Stilicho. "General..." he said, his tone urging for calm.

Stilicho raised the hatchet in his hand. "Move away, my friend."

As the gravity of the coming confrontation dawned on those gathered, a few of the more fragile souls in the crowd slunk off, leaving the bold and the curious to gather more tightly around. Their voices fell to whispers as the emperor arrived on the scene.

"I said no gold!" shouted Honorius. He strode to Stilicho, fists clenched, and screamed into the general's face. "I won't be mastered by barbarians, whether it's Alaric or you!"

Assessing the situation—the danger—better than his master, Olympius shrunk back.

"Highness," said Olympius. "Let us all return to the Senate House." He flicked his eyes between Honorius's armed but somewhat coiffed guards and Stilicho's war-hardened footsoldiers, hoping the emperor would take his meaning—*It isn't safe... we need to leave and get more men.*

"Return to the Senate?" asked Honorius. "It is the Senate that causes all the trouble!"

Certain of nothing but the need for calm, Eucherius positioned himself between his father and the emperor he had grown up with. "Highness," he said, his voice placating. "Come take lunch with a friend."

Honorius redirected his shouts from Stilicho to Eucherius. "A *friend?* Do you take me for a fool? You have wanted my crown for years! You are no friend to me!"

Olympius swallowed hard. Honorius's scrawny neck was getting closer to Stilicho's blade with every word he spoke, though the emperor was too obtuse to realize it. Worse, the idiot was taking Olympius with him.

"Enough of this," said Stilicho. He looked at Valerius and opened his mouth to give the order to assassinate.

But before he could, the foreman emitted a cry of terror. "*Jupiter Pater, parce mihi!*"

The workers who had been stripping the gold from the doors stumbled back in fright as the reason for the foreman's outburst was revealed to all. There, below the gold plates, inscribed in the ancient wood, were words that caused a tremulous silence to envelop the sacred hilltop:

This gold is reserved for a ruinous ruler.

One of the workmen put his hands on his head. "Another curse!" He looked aghast at Stilicho. "First his wife, and now him!"

Shouldering his way through the stunned and murmuring crowd, Olympius reached the doors to inspect the inscription. The letters were deep and black, as if they had been burned into the wood instead of carved, albeit with flawless precision. An idea came to him.

"Romans," he shouted. "This can only be the work of Apollo!" He pointed to Stilicho. "The general burned the Sibylline Books inside this temple, but the Oracle's words flew out of the flames. Here they are, foretelling his treachery!"

The bewildered silence on the hilltop held for a moment, but was soon shattered by an explosion of discordant voices. A few called for calm and reason, but most descended into a panicked condemnation of the general. Stilicho's previous alliances with Alaric, his ambition, his military missteps and reliance on

Germanic troops... were those not the signs of a ruinous ruler? The burning of the Sibylline Books and the charred inscription were too much of a coincidence. With the barbarians at the gates of the city, perhaps the Oracle was warning them to maintain the status quo of Honorius's leadership, inept as it was.

Faltering at the unnerving appearance of the inscription and the stomach-sinking reversal in the current of power, Stilicho turned to his commander and footsoldiers. The doubt on their faces drained the blood from his. He was losing them.

"Hold fast," he said to Valerius, inwardly cursing himself for sending his most trusted men, men like Constantius and Sarus, away from Rome to suppress revolts in other areas of the empire.

Olympius forced his way through the crowd—everyone was now jostling to see the inscription for themselves—and made it back to Honorius's side. He spoke into the emperor's ear.

"Strike while you can," he said. "If he has the chance to regroup, you are a dead man."

Honorius nodded curtly to his chief guard, and the man pushed his way to Valerius. "You are now under my command," he declared. "General Stilicho is relieved of duty."

"Yes, sir," said Valerius.

Stilicho turned to his son. "*Run!*"

But it was too late. Eucherius was already being forced to his knees by two of the emperor's guards. Stilicho's legs were ready to bolt, but he held himself in place. If they were doomed, he would not leave Eucherius to face death alone. The general did not resist as the emperor's guards pushed him to his knees beside his son.

"Honorius," said Stilicho, dispensing with honorifics. "Your father entrusted me with your life. Think how I have protected you over the years."

"*Protected*, you say?" challenged Olympius. He turned to Honorius. "Highness, this man was about to take a hatchet to your skull!"

"Send me into exile," said Stilicho, the first hue of a plea coloring his words. "Eucherius and me. Send us to—"

"Exile is a half measure," replied Honorius. "That's what you always told me."

Now, Stilicho's voice broke. "Eucherius is no threat to you!"

Eucherius cried out. "*Neither* of us are threats to you!" he exclaimed. "Honorius, have mercy!"

Honorius stood before the two kneeling men. He had spent most of his life trying to ignore the pitiful looks and whispered comparisons: *Look how much stronger Eucherius is than Honorius! Look how much handsomer! See how much better he rides a horse! See how much better he writes in Greek!* He had spent most of his life under Stilicho's regency and protection, but as he looked at the general now, he could see clearly the contempt that Stilicho had spent years trying to hide. Olympius was right. He was a wolf in sheep's clothing.

The emperor nodded to his guards. "Do it."

Hushed and expectant, the crowd closed in to witness the tectonic executions. Even those senators who had supported Stilicho for years waited and watched, some soured by the general's sacrilege and shaken by the inscription, others not believing a single word of it, but nonetheless subdued by the force of Honorius's sudden imperiousness.

Stilicho sensed a darkness fall over him. He looked at the ground to see the shadow of a long sword being raised in the air. "Son, he said. "Do not be—"

Eucherius shrieked in horror as the blade took off his father's head.

"No!" The young man looked up at the emperor, his eyes desperate and begging. "Honorius, I don't want to die!" He tried to fight, to make it to his feet, but hands held him down.

"Stay still, son," said the executioner, the blade of his sword smeared with Stilicho's blood. "You don't want me to miss."

Olympius peered through the crowd, catching sight of Stilicho's head. It had rolled along the smooth marble, but had come to rest against the stack of gold plates from the doors of Jupiter's temple. He heard a collective gasp of revulsion, and a moment later, the father's head was joined by the son's. A few women began to cry. Olympius spoke into the emperor's ear.

"You can sleep soundly tonight, Highness," he said, thinking only about how peaceful his own slumber would be.

CHAPTER XLIV

Cumae

"Let's go that way," Coelia said to her friend Fausta as they wandered past a vendor selling salted fish. "There's a shoemaker I like over there."

"Oh, yes," nodded Fausta, following Coelia's direction. "He does good work."

Although the marketplace next to the Cumaean amphitheater was always busier than usual on theater days like this, the congestion and the crowds were evidence of something else—the influx of new vendors arriving from Rome. Since Honorius's execution of his magister militum Stilicho, things in the Caput Mundi had gone from bad to worse. Stilicho had been the only person capable of managing Alaric, and in his absence, the king of the Visigoths had grown even more powerful, placing more demands on the Senate and issuing more threats. His repeated sieges had forced the city to increase grain and oil rationing, and the fear of an all-out invasion grew greater by the day. Those who could leave the city were doing so.

Reaching the shoemaker's stall, Coelia perused his selection of sandals, wishing she had visited him before today. Her chewed sandals poked out embarrassingly from the bottom of the pretty orange tunica she had chosen to wear to the theater.

The shopkeeper looked down at her sandals and raised an eyebrow. "The dogs again, Domina?" he asked.

"Yes, the damn things," she complained, unfastening a small cloth purse from her belt. "And one of them just had a litter of pups, too."

The prospect of ongoing work made the vendor smile. "Well, don't forget that 'Saro's Sandals' uses the best leather in Cumae," he said, stepping aside to reveal his shop's new colorful sign. "All these shops from Rome use rotten cat skin, I'm sure of it. Very poor quality."

"I won't forget," said Coelia. She pointed to a pair of sandals. "I'll take those ones."

Opening her purse, she dipped a finger inside and withdrew a denarius. The vendor held out his hand, but she hesitated.

It had been a while since one of these *denarii*—it bore the image of her ancestor Gaius Coelius Caldus—had passed through her fingers. A high-ranking official and avid Republican who had served alongside Cicero, Gaius's visage had been captured in silver coinage centuries before hers had been sculpted in marble statuary. Coelia studied his face, looking for a resemblance: the straight nose and large eyes, the resolute expression. She saw the same large eyes when she looked in her mirror. She turned the coin over. On the reverse was a depiction of the Epulum Jovis, the ritual that her family had financed up until Theodosius's last edict.

"Domina, do you want a different pair?" asked the vendor.

"No, these are fine." She placed the coin in his palm, hoping to leave thoughts of Rome—and Antonia's recent visit—with him. "Keep the remainder."

"*Gratias ago*, my lady." He again glanced down at her feet— somewhat judgmentally, it struck Coelia—and gestured to a curtained area in the back of his stall. "Why don't I help you put your new ones on now?"

"All right," Coelia agreed.

The vendor led her behind the curtain, directing her to sit on a stool as he removed her old sandals. "These are worn, but still useful," he said. "I will replace the chewed strap and have my boy run them to your house tomorrow."

"Thank you."

Fitted with her new sandals, Coelia rejoined Fausta and together they strolled through the market until the sound of drumrolls began to summon spectators to the amphitheater. Heeding the summons, the friends entered the open-air venue to find it already three-quarters full. Fausta led them to their seats. Though Coelia's former status as a Vestal had made her something of a celebrity within Cumae's pagan circles, it was Fausta who afforded them prestige seating. Her late husband had been one of the theater's greatest benefactors.

"What play are they performing?" Fausta asked.

"*Annales*," Coelia replied.

"Oh. Who wrote that?"

"Ennius."

"How long is it?" asked Fausta.

"Not long," Coelia lied. "We'll be eating sweets on your terrace before you know it." She felt a pinch of pain from her left ankle and bent down to readjust the strap on her new sandal. "Maybe I should've kept my old ones on for now," she said. Sitting back up, something caught her eye—something around the neck of a woman taking her seat two rows ahead of them, farther down the curve of the stands.

Fausta noticed her friend's curious stare. "What is it?"

Coelia pointed to the woman. "Do you know her? The one in the yellow dress."

"That's Lady Tiberia. She's from Mediolanum, but her son has a villa here. His wife just had a baby."

Coelia stood. "I need to speak with her."

"Now? Can't you wait until after the show?"

"The show is four hours long," divulged Coelia, ignoring Fausta's groan of despair. "I can't wait."

Fausta sighed, but stood. "I'll introduce you."

Brushing by the other spectators and apologizing along the way, the two women reached Lady Tiberia. She greeted Fausta with open arms and a pleasant peck on the cheek.

"Lady Fausta, it has been too long," said Tiberia, speaking in that way—loud, attention-seeking—that so many patricians from larger centers did. Her eyes moved to Fausta's companion as she awaited an introduction, taken aback by the intensity with which the woman was staring at her necklace.

"Lady Coelia," said Fausta, "this is Lady Tiberia. Her daughter-in-law just had her first child, and I am told she is—"

"Your medallion," said Coelia. She raised an arm toward it. "May I?"

"Why yes, I suppose..."

Coelia took the gold medallion in her fingers and turned it over. There, on the back, was the inscription she knew she would see:

MCVIII AUC

One thousand one hundred and eight years from the founding of the city. It was the year she had been initiated into the Vestal Order. There was no question. This was the same medallion that Emperor Julian had gifted to her.

"It's a very lovely piece," said Coelia. "May I ask where you acquired it?"

"My father bought it for me," Tiberia replied. "From a jeweller in Rome, I think. Why do you ask?"

"I have seen something similar before." Coelia took a last look at the large pendant—a central carnelian stone encircled by pearls, representing the sacred fire and its priestesses—and smiled warmly at Tiberia. "Thank you for indulging me."

"You're most welcome. I am flattered."

After another quick round of pleasantries—and a hasty farewell as someone shouted "*Oh, go sit down!*"—Fausta led Coelia back to their seats. As they settled in and the actors took to the stage floor, Fausta looked at her friend and leaned affectionately against her arm. She knew exactly what had happened... back then, and just now.

Concurrent with the temple closures years earlier, the Vestals had been evicted from their customary home without warning and with half-hearted assurances that their personal belongings would be returned to them. Yet when it came to anything of value, especially jewelry, only one piece out of fifty had made it back to its owner, and even then only bronze. It was common knowledge that anything silver or gold had been sold to jewelers for profit, melted down or simply kept. More than one churchman's mistress roamed the streets wearing a pendant or bracelet that once belonged to a Vestal Virgin.

"Do you want me to ask for it back?" asked Fausta. "Tiberia is pagan. She would be mortified if she knew where it came from."

Coelia shook her head. She wasn't sure if it was the spirit of the Cumaean Sibyl at work or just a coincidence, but between Gaius's denarius and Julian's medallion, she had no choice but to accept a troublesome truth. You can't live in the past, but you can't always leave it behind, either. She turned to Fausta and smiled.

"I've seen this show before, and you despise the theater," she said. "Let's go sit on your terrace and eat sweets all night. I'm leaving for Rome in the morning, and we might not see each other for a while."

CHAPTER XLV

Outside of Ravenna (seven days north of Rome by horse)

Alaric would only meet before dawn, when the sky seemed darkest and the wind strongest, leaving the two emissaries from Rome with no choice but to huddle in the miserable camp tent and await his arrival. Not only was the tent devoid of the warmth and light of a fire, it was as porous as a sieve and the gusting wind that slipped through the worn fabric was forceful enough to blow back the hair of the lead envoy, an already sour man named Elgius.

"There are two things I hate above all," Elgius grumbled as he pulled his heavy woolen cloak tighter around his body. "Early mornings and the cold. I am doubly assaulted."

His co-envoy spoke through chattering teeth. "I cannot feel my toes."

A teenaged Goth dressed in a light sleeveless tunica and thin pants entered the tent as if impervious to the weather, lighting two torches in anticipation of Alaric's arrival. The two older Romans exchanged quick glances—this was embarrassing—and Elgius stood.

"When will your king be coming?" he demanded.

"His king is here," replied Alaric as he strolled into the military tent. Like the teenager, he was dressed in only light pants and a short tunica, his bare arms not even prickling against the frigid air. He snickered at the sight of the two shivering men and looked at the young soldier. "Your mother is a camp cook, no? Go fetch a couple of her shawls for our Roman guests."

The boy laughed. "At once, sir," he said.

Alaric sat on a low stool in the center of the tent, waiting for Elgius to sit back down. He did, noting that the king of the Visigoths hadn't even bothered to bring guards with him. He was making a point: *Romans are no threat to me.* Elgius wished he felt that way about the Visigoths, but with Alaric's imposing frame and icy eyes, the most he could do was hope Alaric would assume the extra tremble in his voice was due to the predawn chill.

"My gold," said Alaric. "You did not bring it with you."

"Emperor Honorius has refused your demands."

"I have control of the Tiber and your grain shipments," said Alaric, amused by the envoys' feigned indifference. "Not another loaf of bread will rise in Rome until I say so."

Elgius raised his voice. "Emperor Honorius—"

"—will have fled Rome by the time you return," stated Alaric. "He will be safe in his palace dining on flamingo tongues and red mullets, while the rest of you are eating your children's dogs."

Elgius tensed. It had already come to that, and much worse, in many regions of the city. "This blockade of the Tiber must end," he said. "It is not in the interests of equity."

"Equity," Alaric said bitterly. "When has the empire ever been equitable with me?" He sat up straight, the stool creaking under his weight. "I gave Theodosius my army, and he sent thousands of my men—twice what was necessary—straight to the front lines against Arbogastes, just to cull my ranks. And now Honorius looks the other way as the families of Goth soldiers, those same men settled by Rome, are slaughtered like vermin by Romans in the countryside." He stood and kicked the stool away. It hit a wooden crate and splintered. "Tell your emperor that I have rebuilt my army with the legions of soldiers he has betrayed, men now left with only one feeling in their hearts—hatred for Rome." He raised his chin. "Let us forgo weights and measurements, envoy. If I am not given every piece of gold there is in Rome, right down to the wire in every rich man's mouth, I will unleash my men in your streets and let them take it for themselves."

"Romans were born for war," Elgius said defiantly. "Every father and son in the city is prepared to—"

"The Romans you speak of are no more," said Alaric. "Your men are cowards and your sons have grown soft. So unless you're going to send your women into the streets to beat us with their kitchen pots, you can begin collecting my gold. Your city will not shine like it used to, but at least you will have your lives." He strode to the tent's exit, chuckling to see the boy waiting just outside with a pair of women's shawls, one a faded orange and the other dull yellow. He took them and tossed them at the envoys. "Keep warm, mighty Romans," he added, and left.

CHAPTER XLVI

Rome

The guards stationed at the Porta Praenestina had asked Coelia and Brogos the same question twice: "Are you sure you want to come *in* to Rome?"

As the city continued to atrophy under Alaric's grain blockades and fret at the prospect of invasion, the guards had intensified their inspections at the gates. Nonetheless, Coelia had only to flash the deed to her Roman home and she and Brogos were permitted to enter, though not oblivious to the different reactions of the guards as the former high priestess passed in her small horse-drawn carriage. Some scowled and others smiled, but they all looked a bit amazed, and as the carriage pulled away, she and Brogos could hear the gossip already spreading.

I have every right to be here, Coelia reminded herself. *I was never exiled. I am still a Roman citizen with property to care for.*

The pair traveled unspeaking along the streets of the Esquiline Hill, toward the stable closest to Coelia's house. As they did, they noted the predominance of homes that had been fortified with iron bars and thick wooden boards, an ominous background to the privately hired and well-armed watchmen that patrolled the neighborhood. Arriving at the stable, Brogos drove the horses up to the attending stableman—Coelia didn't know him, but it had been fifteen years—and they both stepped down from the carriage. The stableman took the reins. After inspecting Coelia's deed, his standoffishness segued into an eager welcome.

"High Priestess," he said, revealing himself a pagan. "I am surprised to see you in Rome. I thought you lived down in Campania."

"I do, sir," she replied. "I have only come to check on my home."

"Oh, I know the one," he said. "The house of the chief Vestal. It is becoming famous on the Esquiline." He leaned in conspiratorially. "Everyone in Rome is talking about the curse you cast on General Stilicho's wife, Lady Serena. They say it is all coming to pass. They say the general and his son met their end because of it, and that Serena spends her days in prayer trying to lift the curse. They say—"

"I have heard what they say," said Coelia. Olympius's last letter had included a joyfully descriptive account of Stilicho's execution, followed by his own assertions that her curse was—as the stableman had said—coming to pass.

The stableman patted Coelia's white spotted horse on the neck as he spoke. "Ah, well, regardless, you should know that Miss Penelope takes excellent care of your house. She is far more pleasant than your previous caretaker. I don't mean to speak ill of the dead, but that Miss Ptolema was a tyrant. Used to do surprise inspections here at the stable, and if your horses' stalls weren't freshly picked, heads would roll. Then again, with what we're up against, we could probably use her."

"The streets are quieter than I expected," said Brogos.

"Don't let that fool you," replied the stableman. "It's every man for himself right now."

"I'll remember that," said Brogos. He rubbed the horse's muzzle. "Be good, Nereus."

As he and Coelia turned to walk the rest of the way, the stableman raised a hand to delay them. "High Priestess," he said. "May I have a blessing? It has been a long time."

Coelia hesitated, glancing around. But the man's head was lowered, and she would not deny one of Vesta's faithful. "It has been a long time for me, too, sir," she said. She put her hand on top of his head, feeling prickly pieces of straw that she suspected never quite washed out of his hair. "*Virgo te et familiam tuam custodiat.*"

He looked up. "Thank you, Priestess." He patted the horse again. "I will take good care of him for you. Everyone knows Oracio spoils all the beasts in his stable. I treat each one like Pegasus, entrusted to me by Jove. No need to worry."

"Thank you, Oracio," said Brogos.

Leaving the horse and carriage with the stableman, Coelia and Brogos traveled the rest of the way on foot, Brogos's hand never leaving the hilt of the dagger that hung from his belt. As with the other homes in the area, they arrived at Coelia's to find that it too had been reinforced with iron and wood. Unlike the other houses, however, fresh flowers and trinkets had been placed along the high wall that enclosed the property. They were considering the significance of this when a trio of watchmen noticed them loitering at the locked door and approached.

"Leave whatever junk you want and move along," said one of the watchmen.

"This is my house," replied Coelia.

The watchman did a poor job of disguising his surprise and an even worse job of hiding his disdain. He blew his whistle in three short increments, though close enough to Coelia's ear to make Brogos bristle in anger.

"Any violations of the law will be reported," he said. He gestured to the gifts lining the home's wall. "You're lucky we let this shit go."

The clang of iron unlocking sounded from behind the door—someone within the house, summoned by the whistle. A few moments later, the door opened to reveal a woman in her late twenties, her curly hair ending at her shoulders and her tunica doing nothing to hide the gauntness of her frame. Still, the woman's resemblance to her great aunt, Ptolema, was obvious.

"Are you Penelope?" asked Coelia. When the woman nodded, Coelia put her hand to her chest. "I am Coelia Concordia."

The woman gasped. "Priestess," she said. She opened the door wider. "What are you doing here?" She caught herself—this was the Vestal's house, after all. "I mean, what are you doing here *now*? The city isn't safe."

"So we've heard," said Coelia.

"Come in, come in. I have taken good care of your home. You will see."

As Brogos secured the door behind them, Coelia followed Penelope inside the house, taking it all in: the marble impluvium in the atrium, the frescoed walls, the bright furnishings... it all came back to her, forgotten for fifteen years, but now instantly as familiar as ever. Other than the absence of her lararium and the household gods—the authorities had removed those when she was put under house arrest years earlier—the house looked unchanged. It seemed like not a cushion was out of place.

"You learned your housekeeping from your great aunt," said Coelia.

"Thank you for letting me stay here after she passed," replied Penelope.

"Ptolema spoke highly of you," said Coelia. "And she never spoke highly of anyone." Penelope laughed, an act that exacerbated the boniness of her otherwise youthful face. Coelia frowned. "Has the money I sent been enough to sustain you? You're not going hungry?"

"The money has been sufficient," said Penelope, "but the rations haven't. They get worse every day." She managed a smile. "But I flirt with the stableman, and he sometimes brings by some of the oats designated for the war horses." She perked up. "You saw the flowers outside, along the wall? People put them there every day, hoping you will return. I leave them until they wilt, and then I burn them in the hearth."

"I see. You have done a fine job, Penelope." She gestured to her companion. "This is Brogos."

"*Salve*," Penelope said to him.

Sighing, Coelia began to unpin her cloak. "It was a long trip. I am going to take a bath."

"I can prepare it for you," said Penelope, "but it may take some time. I've been boiling water from the cistern." She fidgeted. "Priestess, now that you are home, would you like me to... I mean, I don't really have anywhere else to go."

"This has been your home more than it has been mine," Coelia affirmed. "You can live here for the rest of your life, if it pleases you." Her thoughts turned to her true home in Rome. They lingered there as she pictured the pink flowers that used to grow in the courtyard and the orange fish that once swam in the decorative pool. She refastened her cloak. "And never mind the bath," she added. "It can wait."

Coelia had seen dead bodies before. Her father's body had been the first, followed by more than she could remember in the amphitheater. She had seen Eugenius's head on a spike. She had seen her mother's body. But what she had never seen, not until now, were dead bodies lying in the streets of Rome, casualties not of age or slaughter, but of starvation. The wealthier residents of the Esquiline might have been resourceful enough to ward off the worst of the consequences of Alaric's grain blockades and the panicked violence it wrought on the streets, but the vast majority of Romans were wholly vulnerable and very hungry.

Brogos trailed two steps behind her, an alert and protective shadow as she navigated down what used to be a busy street of modest but reputable vendors. Now, only a few shabby stalls stood, tended to by predatory sellers whose eyes moved over her and Brogos, searching for anything they could steal.

"*Abi!*" Brogos shouted at a skinny young man who stepped toward Coelia. He didn't look evil. He looked desperate. "You'll die for nothing, boy."

Coelia wanted to say something to the boy, to offer some kind of blessing or comfort, but she could not risk it. The act would draw attention, and she wanted to reach the Forum incognito.

Turning down another city street, Coelia's hand instinctively moved to cover her mouth and nose. The shockingly rank smell of rotting corpses hung thickly in the air, and bodies lay scattered on the streets. There were more of them here, and her throat tightened at the sight of a dead young woman curled up in a doorway, her arms wrapped around an unmoving swaddled infant. A dead child of no more than two years of age lay sprawled out an arm's length away, still clutching his mother's *tunica*.

Coelia turned down another street, and then another, moving ever deeper into hell, until she came upon a scene that made her certain she had arrived. A sickly thin middle-aged man was sawing off the leg of a dead woman while an emaciated teenaged girl, presumably his daughter, stood above him with a bucket. Coelia stopped in her tracks, and the man looked up at her, his brief expression of shame fading to conviction. He didn't care what anyone thought. He would feed his family. Someone coughed and Coelia glanced around, suddenly aware that this father wasn't the only one cannibalizing the dead. There were two or three others, maybe more—she had to look away—all sawing and hacking at the corpses as swarms of black flies buzzed around them. She heard Brogos gag behind her.

"*Futuo*," he said and spat on the ground. "Keep moving."

They turned down another street, this one mercifully empty of both the living and the dead.

As Coelia moved through the apocalyptic streets of Rome, reacquainting herself with a city now demoralized and on the brink of invasion, she realized a species of invasion had already occurred during her long absence. Crosses were now affixed not just to the top of pagan temples, but to the monuments as well, those trophies won by Rome's pagan Caesars, the symbols of their hard-won victories arrogated by bishops so bloated they couldn't fasten a cuirass if their lives depended on it.

Finally arriving at the Roman Forum, Coelia did her best to appear aloof as she waited at the gates to gain entry. Thankfully, her upscale but not extravagant attire, combined with the presence of a personal bodyguard, was sufficient to see her waved through without inspection—a relief, since it was still illegal for her to be here—and she started along the Via Sacra, her eyes scrutinizing her surroundings for signs of change.

It was everywhere and nowhere. The bronze tiles that used to shine atop the massive Temple of Venus and Roma were stripped bare, and the colorful statues of the goddesses that used to adorn the temple complex were gone. Yet the elaborate flower gardens looked completely unchanged, the bees that buzzed around no different than the bees of fifteen years ago. She kept walking along the basilica until she reached the Temple of Romulus, her chest tightening in an emotional clutch of anger and grief to see the tall cross affixed to the top.

Continuing on, she neared the area sacred to Vesta, taking note of the space where her statue had once stood. Olympius had mentioned in a letter years earlier that the priests of the religious college had hidden it on the Esquiline Hill shortly after the temples had been closed. As for the whereabouts of the Vestal statues that used to line the courtyard of the priestesses' residence, no one knew for sure. Yet according to one of the clerics Olympius was friendly with, they had been piled in a rubbish heap somewhere in the Forum. Coelia sloughed off that image and braced herself for what she would see next.

The goddess's white marble temple came into view at the same time that the mournful sound of a Christian hymn being sung within floated through the air. The domed roof of the temple was lifeless, devoid of Vesta's breath since the sacred fire had been extinguished. From what Coelia could tell, the oculus had been closed and—she could hardly force herself to look at it—a tall cross had been screwed to the spot. The circular sanctum seemed to droop under the weight of it, defeated and desecrated.

Don't cry, Coelia told herself. But it was no use. Seeing the temple in this state of defilement was like seeing Vesta herself stripped naked in the streets, exposed to the leering eyes of those who hated her—feared her—the most. Her head throbbed in a helpless outrage that manifested in a sudden burst of tears: The work of emperors like Theodosius and bishops like Ambrosius had outlived them. Brogos appeared at her shoulder.

"Coelia," he said. "You've seen what you came to see. Let's go home."

"Home?" asked Coelia.

She turned toward the House of the Vestals, walking toward it with faltering steps. The flowers that had lined the Via Sacra in front of the house were gone, as were the marble pedestals that once held bronze fire bowls. Also gone were the chestnut doors with their intricately carved rosettes, the portico now dominated by two plain wooden doors. Coelia was staring at these, weeping uncontrollably now, when one of the doors opened from within and a man in a long brown robe exited the house.

Quickly, Brogos moved in front of her and put his arm around her shoulder, shielding her face. "Now, now, dear," he said soothingly. "I said I was sorry. Let's not fight." The man passed by the domestic quarrel with indifference. Once he was out of sight, Brogos took Coelia by the hand. "We're leaving," he said firmly.

She didn't resist as he pulled her back the way they had come. He was right. She had seen what she had come to see, and she couldn't stomach the sight of it for one moment longer.

Coelia and Brogos had barely spoken during their walk home from the Forum to the Esquiline Hill. Brogos had initially tried to strike up a conversation, but it had only prompted an embittered tirade from Coelia, one that had lasted at least three city blocks. Rather than risk another, he had refrained from speaking to her again and instead left her to her silent fuming. Yet as her house came into view in the distance, her anger and tears returned in full watery force.

"I have returned to Rome for nothing," she wept to herself, to Brogos, to the banished gods. "The city I knew is gone."

"Gods almighty," groaned a voice behind her. "I'm glad your mother never whined like that."

Gasping in surprise—neither she nor Brogos had seen anyone approach—Coelia spun around to find herself staring at a changed, but nonetheless familiar, face. He was older, and the slicked-back black hair had gone grayer, but otherwise Olympius had lost none of his acerbity.

"Olympius," she said. "How long have you been following us?"

"Long enough to know that this one" — he raised an unimpressed eyebrow at Brogos — "needs to pull his head out of his ass and pay better attention to what's going on around him."

"Snakes are often hard to see in the grass," said Brogos.

Olympius grinned and tongued one of his viper-like teeth, his eyes shifting to scrutinize Coelia. Despite sending countless letters to her home in Cumae to keep her apprised of events in Rome, he hadn't seen her in person since Lucilla's death three years earlier. The grin melted away. "You're starting to look like her," he said.

His plaintive tone matched her own disconsolate mood, and she gestured to her nearby home. "Let's go inside. Perhaps there is some wine in the pantry."

"We don't have time right now," said Olympius. "We need to go."

"Where?"

"To the gardens at Praetextatus's villa," he replied. "That is where we meet. Everyone's been gathered since midmorning waiting for our guest of honor." He glanced around. "We need to leave before we're followed." He shot a critical glare at Brogos and started walking. "Can't be too careful."

"Olympius, wait," said Coelia. She shuffled ahead and put her hand on his chest, stopping him in mid-stride. "I have seen what is happening on the streets."

"And?"

"And I've seen what has become of the temples in the Forum. Including Vesta's temple."

Olympius shook his head impatiently. "No, I meant *and* what is your point?"

Coelia dropped her arms to her side, surrendering to the hopelessness of it. "It is too far gone. They've won."

"They've won," muttered Olympius. "You're too old to speak like a child." He moved past her. "Let's go."

"I am not going anywhere except back to Cumae."

Olympius stopped. Slowly, he turned to face her. "So you've just now discovered that life is unjust?" he asked. "You've just now come to realize that, in this brave new world of ours, the most corrupt among us have come out on top? You are an educated woman, Coelia. You are a student of history and philosophy. It should come as no surprise to you that the most corrupt fuckers always have a way of coming out on top. How do you think I made my fortune? But everybody falls eventually." He turned back around and kept walking, his voice rising. "Now come on. I have to piss, and I can't hold it like I used to."

Acquiescing, Coelia followed, though stubbornly remaining a few steps behind. The villa and expansive gardens of her late friends Praetextatus and Paulina were still owned by the couple's children and were located close to her own home on the Esquiline, making the trip mercifully short. Even better, they hadn't seen anyone following them. That would likely change soon. The guards at the city gates and the impudent watchman she had encountered at her home would report her return to the authorities, if they hadn't already.

They arrived at the villa of Praetextatus and were admitted onto the property by a trio of expectant guards who looked only slightly peeved when Olympius emptied his bladder against the estate's high walls. Breathing a sigh of relief, he continued to lead Coelia and Brogos toward the estate's manicured gardens via a smooth cobblestone path that wound its way through a large orchard, terminating at the border of a treed grove that looked as thick as any wild forest. The journey didn't end there, though, and he entered the trees with his companions in tow, the light diminishing under the canopy of high leafy branches.

"How much farther?" asked Brogos.

Olympius didn't answer him, but led them deeper into the grove, proceeding along a thin dirt path that was criss-crossed with raised tree roots until they arrived at what looked to be the entrance to an underground cavern. Coelia was not entirely surprised. As soon as they had entered the grove, she had suspected Olympius was leading them to a *Mithraeum*, a subterranean temple to the god Mithras. Like Olympius, Praetextatus had been a senior initiate into the rites of Mithras and must have spent many hours here in communion with the god.

It was dim but not dark inside the cavern, and Olympius entered first. Coelia followed closely behind, entering the rectangular sanctum to see perhaps fifty people within. Some chatted and drank as they reclined on the long benches that lined the chamber, while others stood in clusters as they mingled in the rather small space. She had never been inside a Mithraeum before, and stepping into the underground temple was like stepping beyond the curtain of the night sky to enter a temple of the cosmos. The vaulted ceiling was inscribed with stars, while the walls were decorated with colorful relief carvings of the signs of the Zodiac and the constellations. More relief carvings—Sol Invictus and Luna, god of the sun and goddess of the moon—were engraved in marble behind a row of altars, and the mosaic floor depicted a scattering of constellations. At the front of the cavern, a statue of Mithras slaying Taurus the bull was illuminated by torchlight, the scene symbolizing the strength of the spirit to overcome adversity and to enter the eternal cycle of life, death and rebirth.

The faces inside turned to look at the Vestal, just as Olympius spoke.

"Next time, someone else can go," he said. "I waited outside her house for half the day."

"Coelia!" The voice was Antonia's. She scrambled off the bench she had been reclining on and embraced Coelia, kissing her on the cheek.

As others gathered around, Coelia recognized many of the faces that greeted her. The respected senator Junius—his white hair now thinning—and the younger Nicomachus were there, the latter being the son of the former prefect Virius Nicomachus who had committed suicide along with Arbo after Eugenius's defeat. A number of other illustrious senators, magistrates, aristocrats and former priests, along with their smiling wives and the former priestesses of Ceres, were there as well.

"There are many more than what you see," said Senator Junius, "but we dare not meet in greater numbers than this."

Coelia nodded, feeling her face flush with the awful awareness that she was putting not just herself, but all of them, in danger. It was illegal, upon penalty of destitution or death, for pagans to meet in secret or to even discuss their religion, never mind practice it. And no one was a greater tinderbox to the authorities than Rome's returning Vestalis Maxima, a figure that could spark precisely the kind of pagan resurgence they were once again struggling to snuff out. And yet, the faces of those around her were hopeful, proud and full of conviction. She felt the same rise of sadness and anger that had seized her in the Forum, the same disbelief that so often gripped her. How had it come to this? Here were men and women from some of the greatest families of Rome, ancient families who had been stewards of the city for centuries, now reduced to meeting underground, risking their very lives to speak freely in their own country.

"What can I do?" Coelia asked Junius.

The senator directed her to sit on a bench, his words coming quickly. They had already been gathered much longer than was prudent.

"Our plan is twofold," he said. "First, we will try to return your status to you in some official, but not thoroughly religious, capacity. The Senate has dispatched repeated envoys to Alaric, but each one has only made matters worse. I will make a motion to send you into Alaric's camp as an envoy of peace, according to the old customs. If you are successful, you will amass considerable political influence, which can segue into religious stature."

Nicomachus stood beside Junius. "If we cannot get the motion through the Senate," he said, "we will have no choice but to be direct. We will move that you, as Vestalis Maxima, relight Vesta's fire in the temple. We will also petition for a public sacrifice to be made at the Temple of Jupiter on the Capitoline."

"Bishop Innocentius will never permit such actions," said Coelia, referencing Rome's new top clergyman. "Especially not the relighting of the goddess's flame. He will let the whole city burn before he lets Vesta's fire burn."

"I am not so sure," countered Junius. "With respect, High Priestess, you have not been in Rome these past years. We are living a prophecy that is as old as the city itself. We are seeing it come true with our own eyes. Without Vesta's guardian flame, Rome will fall. And this bishop, he is not strictly like the others."

Coelia regarded those around her, but directed her words at Antonia. "I understand how much it hurts," she said. "I also long to feel the goddess's presence inside her temple. But from what I saw today, the Rome that we in this chamber once knew, that our ancestors knew, has already fallen."

"My father would upbraid you for such talk."

Everyone turned to look at the man who had just entered the Mithraeum. Coelia's eyes narrowed as she tried to place him, though it was his resonant voice—so much like his father's—that helped her put a name to the face. It was Memmius Symmachus.

"Your father lived his final years in fear," said Coelia.

"And yet never turned away from his duty to the gods," replied Memmius. He looked over his shoulder as a woman carrying a small white terracotta oil lamp stepped out from behind him.

The woman's face was easier to place than Memmius's had been, even though the scattering of freckles that had covered her cheeks as a girl had faded slightly over the years.

Coelia stood. "Florina?"

The former Vestal priestess held out the oil lamp. "Quick thinking and tunnels," she said. "You once told me that is how Vesta's fire came to Rome from Troy."

Coelia accepted the oil lamp, instantly feeling the vessel's warmth against her palms. She stared into the vibrant orange flame. "It can't be... "

"Terentia and Sergia were inside the temple," said Florina. "They had just asked me to take embers from the sacred fire and light the firebowls by the portico of our house. But as soon as I stepped out, I heard a strange clanging. That's when I saw the soldiers locking the temples."

"We thought you panicked and ran," said Coelia.

"I did," said Florina. "I ran into the house with the embers."

"And escaped through the tunnel in the kitchen," surmised Coelia. She set the oil lamp on the altar of Mithras. The dimness of the space made the flame shine even more vibrantly. "Where...?"

"First, at my parents' villa in Cures," said Florina. "After I married, I took embers to my husband's estate in Veii. A thousand times, I wanted to write and tell you that the temple's flame still burned, that my family and I were caring for it in our hearthfire, but I was too scared. It was only when I heard rumors of what Antonia and the others were doing in Rome that I wrote to Senator Symmachus."

Coelia knelt before the altar and the single orange flame that burned on top. The true fire of Vesta. The unextinguished flame from the temple, still moving, still flickering, as though not a day had passed. "*Vesta Mater, sacerdotis tui memento,*" she whispered.

Antonia and Florina knelt beside her, the three women clasping hands.

"The sacred flame has come home," said Antonia. She looked at Coelia. "Just like you."

CHAPTER XLVII

Since the executions of her husband and son, Serena rarely admitted visitors to her palatial home on the Palatine Hill. When she wasn't in prayer with Sister Marcia, the head of the Christian women's monastery at the church of Laurentius, she was writing letters to Honorius, pleading with him to provide her with enough Imperial soldiers to safely transport her, and her daughter Thermantia, out of Rome. If they were captured by Alaric's men, they would be killed, or worse. But the emperor refused. It was better for Rome that they stayed, he said. It would only cause panic if they fled, he said. Of course, he had fled long ago... but that was different.

And now things were worse. *She* had returned to Rome.

As Serena knelt at her bedside in prayer and clutched a crucifix, she sensed a presence behind her and turned to see the auburn-haired servant Leah bringing in fresh linen. As she always did when she entered Serena's bedchamber, the servant moved quickly and nervously, surveying the room with misgiving. Serena knew why.

"I have seen no spirits today," she said to the servant, her voice grave. "I did see one in the latrine, though. That is why I only use a chamberpot now. It is over there. You can take it away and bring me a clean one."

"Yes, Domina," Leah replied. She crossed the room to collect the chamberpot, turning up her nose to see that Serena hadn't even bothered to place the lid on top after using it. She secured the lid and carried it back across the room, the contents inside sloshing against the sides from her quick stride.

"Wait," said Serena. "Come and pray with me."

Leah set the chamberpot on the floor and moved slowly toward the bed, hoping Serena would notice her reluctance and release her. But it was not to be. She knelt at Serena's side and clasped her hands together, saying nothing as her mistress pressed her face against the bed and whispered frantic prayers into the mattress.

"Shall I go fetch the sister for you?" asked Leah.

"They meet in secret, you know," said Serena, her voice full of revelation as she turned to Leah.

"Who does, Domina?"

"The heathens. They conspire and practice magic. I could have them killed" — she laughed humorlessly — "but there are so many that Alaric would have no one left to kill once he invades." She rested her head against the edge of the mattress.

"Shall I go and get the sister for you?" Leah asked again. "She can pray with you."

"The sister has been useless," Serena replied. "Her prayers have done nothing to lift the curse." She turned to the servant, suddenly suspicious. "Are you not a Christian?"

Leah hesitated, but answered honestly. "I am not, Domina. But I do not meet with anyone or practice magic. I obey the law."

Serena sat back on her heels. "Do you know about curses? How to remove them?"

"No, my lady," said Leah. "You would have to consult a hierophant or a priestess of Proserpina. They guard the secrets very closely. If they didn't, curses would be pointless."

"There was a priestess of Proserpina in Cumae," said Serena. "I had her brought to Rome, but she refused to help me, even under torture."

Leah tensed, partly in anger, but mostly in fear. "Perhaps she will change her mind," she said.

"She died in the Carcer," said Serena. She put her hands on her face and emitted a long cry before turning back to Leah. "Are you sure that you don't know *anything* about how to lift a curse?"

There was something about the way she asked the question—with an edge of *I'll find out one way or another*—that made Leah's heartbeat quicken. She had to think of something, fast.

"Salt," said Leah. "You need to drink salt water." She forced a glint of concern into her eyes. "Drink it three times during the day, and then mix it with charcoal and drink it twice during the night. That will remove the curse."

At once, Serena's tearful eyes shone with hope. She clutched the bedsheets and pulled herself to her feet, ignoring the protests of her cramped leg muscles. "Go and get me some salt and water," she ordered. "You will prepare it and stay with me."

Leah stood. "As you wish, my lady."

The servant strode out of Serena's bedchamber and continued down the corridors of the palace, making her way directly to her small servant's room where she lifted the thin mattress and grabbed the purse of coins underneath. Heading back, she crossed the courtyard and peristyle, finally exiting the house.

She had just enough coin to pay for passage out of Rome. It was risky, but it was the only way. For although Leah was no hierophant, no priestess, no oracle, she needed none of those talents to predict her own certain death if she stayed in the presence of the cursed Lady Serena for one more day.

CHAPTER XLVIII

Senator Perses stood in the center of the senatorial chamber, facing off against Olympius. "You've spent years kissing Honorius's ass, and how does he repay your sycophancy?" challenged Perses. "He abandons you to Rome's fate, just like the rest of us. Our citizens starve and eat each other like rats in the sewer, while he runs off to hide under the overflowing dining tables of his palace in Ravenna. Some emperor! His cowardice is so absolute that he refuses to part with even a single soldier to defend Rome!"

"Take your mad rants to Stilicho's tombstone," Olympius rebuffed. "He might as well have marched Alaric to the high walls of Rome himself!"

"Stilicho's body is long rotted," Perses replied. "Stop digging him up to take the blame!"

Exasperated, Senator Pompeianus stood. "What good can this antipathy do?" he asked. "We must focus on the barbarians!"

Another senator, Attalus, rose. "I will ride out to meet with Alaric," he said. "He will—"

The Senate erupted in jeers. Though Attalus had at one time been Alaric's voice and would-be puppet in the Senate, he had fallen out of favor with the fractious Visigoth. Peace seemed more impossible than ever.

"We have exhausted all options," said Lampadius. "Bishop Innocentius has said that to save our—"

"Who cares what the bishop says?" cried Perses. "When has he ever missed a meal? Meanwhile, Alaric has reduced Romans to cannibals!"

Senator Junius rose, directing his speech to the Senate as a whole. "All the more reason for the members of this assembly to come together as men," he said. "As Romans. We must put our differences aside and think only of our city. I do not believe that we have exhausted all options."

"Why dance around it?" asked Senator Pompeianus. "We have all heard the news. Coelia Concordia has returned to Rome."

"It is a sign," said Junius. "No one can deny it."

Pompeianus faced him squarely. "What do you propose?"

"When our fledgling city faced its first crisis under Romulus," said Junius, "when the Sabines invaded and nearly defeated us in our own streets, it was the king's wife who brokered a peace. After that, and throughout our history, the Vestal Virgins were trained as emissaries and trusted as envoys of peace. I move that we send High Priestess Coelia Concordia into the enemy's camp, to Alaric's own feet, to petition for peace."

Lampadius scoffed. "A woman?"

"A Vestal Virgin," said Junius.

A pensive silence fell in the assembly, broken after several long moments by Pompeianus. One of the most devout Christian senators in Rome, his words took everyone by surprise.

"I second the motion," he said.

Lampadius extended his arms, his jaw dropping in incredulity. "*Insania!*"

"What did the last emissaries accomplish," posited Pompeianus, "other than beating their chests in front of Alaric and provoking him even more? Why squander a chance for peace? We must do all we can to spare our wives and daughters the horrors of invasion."

"I am not oblivious to the risks we face," said Lampadius. Turning to Perses, he added, "Neither is the bishop. Who has tried harder to broker a peace between Alaric and Honorius? You have no right to speak against him."

"Then allow me," said Pompeianus. "Innocentius has been ineffective. And I challenge you, brother—what bishop can truly be trusted to put the needs of the common people before his own or the church's? It is the women of our faith who brave the streets to share their own meager rations with the hungry. It is ordinary Christians who observe the spirit of the Lord and open their humble doors to the poor. The gilded gates of the *patriarchium* have always remained locked. But we are senators of Rome. Our highest duty is to govern for the good of the people."

Lampadius's face grew redder. "The Roman senator is no model of altruism," he said. "And feeding the poor is one thing, but there is no place for women at this level of diplomacy. Those who persist in worshipping idols and false gods—yes, nearly every man in this chamber, some more openly than others—are only exploiting Alaric's siege to revive their dying superstitions!"

"Superstitions are no threat to the Almighty," asserted Pompeianus. "And it is the Lord himself who gave women their softer nature. I say that we have sent enough braggarts to incite an enemy of greater force. It is not a sacrilege to fall back on a customary practice during a time of extreme crisis."

Lampadius shook an accusatory fist in the air and rounded on his pagan colleagues. "I know why you want to send the priestess to Alaric. You want Rome to worship her as a savior! But there is only one savior, and I assure you that any illegal rituals and any conversions will be reported to—"

"Romans are *eating* each other in the streets, Lampadius!" exclaimed Perses. "Is that not sufficient reason for you to set aside your pride and incessant persecutions? You once opposed such tyranny, sir!"

Olympius stood and addressed the chamber. "Let us take a vote," he said. "A simple show of hands, since in case we've all momentarily forgotten, time is of the fucking essence right now." He exhaled. "All in favor of sending Coelia Concordia to Alaric, make it known."

Eighty out of a hundred hands went up.

Lampadius seethed. "This is a religious matter," he said. "It is for the bishop to decide."

"How is it a religious matter?" asked Perses. "This is a senatorial decision."

"*Everything* is a religious matter," replied Lampadius.

"Then take it to the bloody bishop," said Olympius. "Providing he has the balls to unlock the gilded gates of his palace long enough to let you through."

"Those rogue sons of bitches," growled General Constantius as he paced the length of his military tent in the Campus Martius. "I'd like to lock the doors of the Senate and burn every one of those pricks alive."

"What did they do now?" asked his subordinate, a soldier named Sarus.

Constantius chewed his lip in irritation. "They asked Innocentius if they could send—get this—Coelia Concordia as a peace envoy to Alaric."

Sarus poured himself a cup of wine and downed it in two swallows. "You know what the problem is, don't you? Stilicho was too friendly with them. He let them away with far too much. They still think that Rome is theirs to manage."

"Yes, I know," said Constantius. "I must've told Stilicho a hundred times to kill Olympius before he acted first, but he wouldn't do it. He didn't want the Senate to think he was a tyrant. The mistake cost him his life." He stopped pacing. "It cost Rome their best defense, too. Honorius wants me in Hispania to deal with the mess there. I issue more commands from the road than from the battlefield." *Not that anyone appreciates it*, he thought. *They will never see me as Stilicho's equal.* "You will stay in Rome to carry out my orders."

"Yes, sir," said Sarus.

Constantius moved to the table at the front of the tent and tore a wedge of bread off a round loaf. It was dry, but better than what most people in the city were eating. He chewed, his thoughts ruminating on the growing pagan resurgence in Rome. From what he had learned from his spies, it was being led by some of the most respected people in the city, men and women who had formed a secret council of sorts to advance their cause. While it wasn't welcome news, it did confirm his long-held suspicion that most of the heathens had never truly renounced their false gods, but had only pretended to.

That wasn't the worst part, though. The worst part was that some panicked Christians were turning to the superstitions of the past. Some were even calling for the pagan temples to be reopened and, since the chief Vestal's return to Rome, for the ancient fire to be relit. It had to be stopped. The Senate and the people of Rome had for too long put the ancient priesthood of women on a pedestal. *The brides of Rome, the daughters of Rome, the guardians of Rome.* Their time was over, and it was past time they accepted that.

Vita pergit. Life goes on. It was an oft-repeated sentiment at the music-filled banquet hosted by Antonia's cousin, a perpetually—some would say insufferably—optimistic woman by the name of Prisca. Yes, there might be barbarians prowling outside the walls of Rome, but wasn't there always some kind of wolf at the door? If one wanted to be happy, didn't one need to accept the ever-present potential for imminent disaster, and yet find a way to keep living?

"*Carpe diem,*" Prisca quoted to her pagan friends, celebrating the words of the poet Horace, before proclaiming the words of the scriptures to her Christian friends: "*Let us eat, drink and be merry!*" Although raised pagan, she had converted to Christianity upon marrying into the family of the former bishop Siricius. Whether the conversion was authentic or not was anyone's guess, though frankly, most people didn't care enough to guess. Everyone was welcome in her opulent home on the Caelian Hill, and those who frequented it tended to have the same attitude. That included Senator Pompeianus, the man whom Antonia was currently chatting with. For although he was a staunch Christian and not sympathetic to the pagan cause, Pompeianus would not let religion stand in the way of doing what was right for Rome. Indeed, he had recently demonstrated as much by voting in favor of sending Coelia to act as a peace envoy to Alaric. His support, his friendship, was worth nourishing. That was Antonia's task.

Antonia nudged his arm and pointed at one of the several food tables in the courtyard.

"It's been a while since I've seen that much fresh bread," she said.

"You must try the cook's special," said Pompeianus, leading her across the courtyard. "He stuffs the bread with goat cheese, walnuts and olives. I had it the last time I was here."

They strolled to the table and indulged while they could. Alaric had not lifted his blockades, but after the Senate had managed to scrounge up another few thousand pounds of gold, he had allowed a number of grain shipments to enter the city. Some of the gold had come from the personal assets of the senators, but most had come from whatever was left in the pagan temples.

Antonia was swallowing another mouthful of rich bread—it was delicious—when Prisca joined them, reaching past Pompeianus to take a wedge of bread for herself. She took a bite and groaned in delight, making Antonia and the senator laugh.

"The things we took for granted," Pompeianus reflected. "Like fresh bread." He waved his bread in the air as he spoke. "The news out of Ravenna is that Honorius has renewed negotiations with Alaric."

Prisca brushed breadcrumbs off her tunica and smiled. "That sounds very promising!"

"Promising is too far," Pompeianus qualified. "But at least there is some hope." Noticing his wife waving him over to join her companions, he smiled at Antonia and Prisca. "Excuse me, ladies."

Sensing something at her feet, Antonia stepped back and glanced under the food table. Prisca's eight-year-old great nephew was there, sitting cross-legged and playing quietly with his toys. Antonia squatted down to face him.

"Ancus," she said. "What are you doing under there?"

He looked at her and smiled, holding up one of the toys: a small figurine of a golden lion. Three more just like it lay scattered around him. "My tutor gave these to me. He said they used to be famous because they escaped from the arena."

"They did," said Antonia. "I remember it very well."

The boy grew serious. "You do?"

"Of course."

"Tell me about it."

Antonia picked up one of the toy lions. "Well, there were six that escaped, but two didn't make it far. The other four roamed the streets and countryside for ages." She shifted onto her knees to speak more comfortably. "It was very scary," she said dramatically, "because you never knew where they were. You might be minding your own business at the market or playing with your friends in the street and" — she attacked his arm with the toy lion, and he giggled — "the next thing you know, you're dinner!"

"Did they have names?"

"Oh, yes. There was Umbra, Rapax, Lucens and Nox," she said, tapping each toy lion in turn. "Did your tutor not tell you their names?"

"He said he couldn't remember."

Antonia nodded, though the comment made her feel suddenly quite melancholic. The Gilded Lions of Rome had been household names for years, but now it had been years since she had heard anyone speak of them. How easy it was to forget the greatest of things, and in less than a generation.

"Now that you know their names, you can teach your tutor something," said Antonia.

"He will not like that," said Ancus. He tilted his head questioningly. "Only one of the lions was captured alive, right? Which one?"

"Only Nox. He was killed in the arena."

"Did you get to watch?"

"No, I didn't want to. I found it a bit sad, to be honest." Antonia smiled. "It was scary, but I kind of liked knowing that they were out there, prowling the streets. It was exciting. Everybody was talking about them."

"I'll bet Nox put up a good fight," said Ancus. "I'll bet he nearly killed the gladiator."

"From what I heard, he was a lion to the last roar." No point telling the boy the truth. It just wasn't a good ending.

"Do you remember how—"

The boy dropped the toy in his grip as a man's hands grabbed him from the other side of the table, pulling him out from underneath. The abruptness of the act caught Antonia off guard, and she pushed herself to her feet, realizing that the music and conversation around her had stopped. Instantly sensing danger, she turned around to look at what everyone else was already looking at. Four soldiers had entered the courtyard and were standing by a column in the peristyle.

Prisca's cheery disposition segued into indignation as she stomped over to them. "What could *possibly* justify this intrusion?" she asked.

"Lady Prisca," said one of the soldiers. "We have an order of arrest."

Prisca drew back. "For who?"

"For Lady Antonia Secunda."

Struck by a wave of dizziness, Antonia swayed on her feet. She felt a hand on her arm and turned to find Pompeianus at her side, supporting her.

"Stay calm," he said.

"Let me understand this," Prisca said curtly to the soldier. "Criminals are looting every empty home in Rome, we don't have enough guards to defend the gates—we all know about the breach at the Porta Naevia—and you are dispatched to a dinner party to arrest a noblewoman for committing the capital offense of... what? Eating goat cheese bread?"

The soldier who had spoken before did so again, this time addressing the gathering. "Which of you is Lady Antonia Secunda?"

Pompeianus leaned closer to Antonia. "You will have to speak with them," he said. "I will come with you." After escorting her across the garden to where the soldiers stood, he held out a demanding hand. "Let me read the order."

The senior soldier slapped a scroll into his palm and waited as the senator reviewed the document. "You can see it's all there," he said. "She is charged with heresy, sorcery and seditious conspiracy."

Pompeianus glanced at Antonia, his posture slumping at the sight of her blanched face. He turned back to the soldier. "Who has issued the—"

The soldier snatched the scroll from the senator's hand, his eyes moving from Pompeianus to survey the larger gathering of guests. "The accused has not been acting alone," he declared.

It was enough to achieve his purpose. Pompeianus took a step back. So did Prisca. In the courtyard, husbands put their arms around their wives, ushering them to safer corners of the garden. Others took no chances and simply headed for the exit, leaving without taking the time to thank their hostess.

Knowing she had no other option—she could not plead with them, overpower them or outrun them—Antonia merely focused on staying upright and conscious as the soldier's fingers tightened around her arm. The world was still spinning around her as he led her out of the courtyard and toward... well, she didn't know toward what just yet.

CHAPTER XLIX

The Senate's request to send the former Vestalis Maxima Coelia Concordia to Alaric to broker for peace—or to beg for mercy at his feet, if that's what it took—had been denied. Constantius had pulled rank and come up with a better idea: He would send his senior officer, Sarus, to act as an emissary of peace. Sarus had an even better idea: Instead of following his orders to negotiate for peace, he would launch a spontaneous attempt on Alaric's life. As it turned, out, Alaric had the best idea of all: He would send a lookalike into the military tent to meet with Sarus before entering himself.

The sum effect of all these better ideas was that Sarus was dead and Alaric was alive, though outraged at the assassination attempt and outright refusing to receive further envoys. The blockades were back. The threat of an imminent invasion was back. The starvation, the panic, the despair, the fear, were all back. And that is why Coelia's decision to walk through the perilous streets of Rome in the dead of night, with only a very jumpy Brogos for protection, was possibly the worst idea she had ever had in her life. Nonetheless, she arrived at her destination—the checkpoint at the foot of the Palatine—safely, living proof that fortune often favors the foolish.

Or perhaps not the foolish, she thought. *Just the desperate.*

Despite Antonia's well-connected Christian family pleading for her release, despite influential Christian senators like Pompeianus requesting a pardon, despite Bishop Innocentius himself calling for compassion and conciliation, General Constantius— the most powerful voice in Rome since Stilicho's death—had refused to relent. He had even denied Antonia the comfort of house arrest, the usual method of confining an upper-class Roman, and had instead kept her imprisoned in the notoriously harsh Carcer. The only hope now was to appeal directly to Honorius. Yet with everything else going on in Rome, Coelia knew there was only one person who might be persuaded to petition the emperor on Antonia's behalf.

The pair of guards at the checkpoint were young—all experienced soldiers had been sent to guard the various gates of the city—and while one of them did an adequate job of feigning nonchalance at the unexpected midnight appearance of the curse-invoking Vestal, the other didn't even try to hide his trepidation. After running up and then back down the Palatine, he took off his helmet and spoke respectfully to her, a slight tremor in his breathless voice.

"Priestess," he said. "I am to escort you."

"Thank you," said Coelia. She looked at Brogos. "Wait here."

The young guard led her up the torch-lined street without speaking, but that didn't mean the journey was a quiet one. The sounds of mayhem—shouting, banging, calling—from the streets and suburbs beyond the Palatine Hill floated upward from the city below to hang in the air above their heads. Finally arriving at the Palace of Domitian, Coelia noted the sparse guard at the grand portico. They noted her, too, keeping their eyes glued to her in curiosity as she passed through the doors.

The guard led her into a lavish atrium lit by two fireplaces and rows of large oil lamps. The lararium that once held statues of the household gods now held a statue of Christ's mother, and the death masks of the emperor's ancestors—including the emperor Vespasian—that once graced the wall above the lararium were gone. Coelia moved to stand directly beside the more lively of the two fires. And then she waited.

Serena entered the atrium wearing a white tunica, her long hair down and freshly brushed. The color of her dress had been a quick but instigative choice. She was well aware that Coelia was prohibited from wearing white. It was an order specific to the former chief Vestal, though like all pagans, she was also subject to the general law that forbade people from wearing pagan symbols of any kind. Yet if Serena thought the white dress would perturb her unscheduled guest, she was mistaken. In fact, the sight of the priestess who had cursed her made her own heart skip a beat.

For Coelia's choice of attire had been a deliberately incendiary one as well. In contrast to Serena's white dress, Coelia wore a fitted black tunica, cinched at the waist with a belt in the style of a black snake, the smooth obsidian stones that dotted its length reflecting the flames of the nearby fire. Her hair was pulled back into a bun, and the only color on her person was the simple braided red-and-white wool bracelet around her wrist, a testament to the red-and-white wool ribbons the Vestal Virgins wore under their ceremonial veils.

Coelia regarded Serena for a contemplative moment. The woman's round face had maintained an aura of youth despite a scattering of fine lines, and looking at her transported Coelia back to that day fifteen years ago—the day Serena had lifted the golden necklace from the statue of Ops and placed it around her own neck. The pain of tumbling down the marble steps of the temple, the humiliation of landing at the bottom with her body exposed, returned... but Coelia would not succumb to her hatred, not with Antonia's life hanging in the balance. Indeed, much seemed to hang in the balance at present. For Antonia wasn't the only dissenter who had been arrested for meeting in the secret caverns of Mithras. Others had, too, and someone—no doubt under torture—had revealed that the true fire of Vesta, an unextinguished flame from her temple in the Forum, still burned in a secret location in Rome.

Soldiers had immediately been dispatched to extinguish the hearthfires of every priestess or novice who had ever served at the temple. That had included Coelia's hearthfire on the Esquiline. Yet the true flame, the temple flame, was still safe, still burning in a hideout in Rome where Florina continued to care for it. The woman had risked as much as anyone, having left her husband and children in Veii to bring the flame back home.

"The emperor Domitian was assassinated in this house," said Coelia, a dark tone in her voice. "He was betrayed by those closest to him. It happened just a few years after he buried the Vestalis Maxima Cornelia alive in the Evil Field."

Serena lifted her chin. She would not concede the advantage so easily. "What do you want?" she asked.

"Lady Antonia, a former priestess of the Vestal Order, has been condemned to death. General Constantius has refused all appeals for mercy."

"And you want me to ask Honorius to pardon her," guessed Serena. "A strange request, since he is the same man who executed my husband and my son."

"Nonetheless, you are still family to him," said Coelia. "He may yet listen to you."

Serena's eyes landed on the red-and-white wool bracelet on Coelia's wrist. "I know what that is. I could have you arrested for that. And for much worse."

"The day I am arrested is the day you bury your last child," said Coelia. "It doesn't matter where you've hidden her. I will call upon the *Venti* to curse the air she breathes, and she will fall."

Serena inhaled a sharp breath and took an involuntary step back. "Do not hurt my daughter," she entreated. "She has done nothing to you! You have spared her until now, why—"

"I never spared her," said Coelia. "I only saved her for later use."

"It is not easy to get messages out of Rome. The city is under siege."

"You'll find a way, Serena."

There was no point arguing with the black-clad priestess, so Serena said nothing as Coelia abruptly turned and left, stepping out of the atrium to be reabsorbed back into the night that had delivered her.

Serena's thoughts turned to her daughter, Thermantia. The young woman was as clever and noble as her now dead siblings Maria and Eucherius had been, and she was all that Serena had left in the world. She pictured Thermantia's face, that kind but wry smile, and heard her gentle voice in her ears: *Mother, come sit with me and listen to the nightingales.*

That voice gave way to another.

It doesn't matter where you've hidden her.

The truth was, Serena didn't know where Thermantia was hidden. After Honorius had refused to grant her and her daughter an Imperial escort out of the besieged city, she had resorted to hiring a trio of mercenary Goth soldiers to smuggle Thermantia out, hoping that her own continued presence in Rome would be enough to appease the emperor. The mercenaries had been a crude lot—not a mouthful of teeth between them—but that was good. It would make it easier for them to blend into the barbarian landscape outside the city walls.

Serena remembered the morning they had departed. She had asked where they would take Thermantia, but the gruffest of the bunch had said it was better that she didn't know:

If Alaric invades and you're tortured, you'll give up her location. Best for both of you if you don't know.

But the not knowing had proven unbearable. Not knowing where Thermantia was, not knowing what she was being fed, not knowing whether the mercenaries would respect her honor or violate her every night, not knowing whether they would stay loyal or ransom her for their own profit. And now, not knowing whether the Vestal would poison the very air she breathed.

Serena thought about kneeling before Mary to pray, but decided that could wait and headed instead toward the tablinum. She needed to write to Honorius and plead for the life of a Vestal Virgin.

CHAPTER L

As tens of thousands of Visigoth soldiers began to marshal and encamp outside the high walls of Rome, so close that the smell of their roasting venison brought tears to the eyes of the starving Romans inside, so inescapable that the sound of their terrifying laughter and clashing swords quickened the pulse of the besieged citizens within, Constantius found himself faced with yet another intolerable crisis. Throughout the city, statues of the gods were being dragged back inside their sanctums. Pagan shrines were being reclaimed on street corners, people again openly praying to Jupiter and Juno, Mars and Venus, Roma and Minerva. Altar fires were being relit, and people were talking about the one altar fire—the most important fire of all—that still needed to be rekindled. Vesta's fire. Yes, all of this was illegal and people were afraid of the consequences, but at the moment, it seemed like Alaric was their biggest worry, not the law.

Constantius knew that all of this had to change. Rome had to stop panicking, stop turning away from the one true God the moment their faith was tested, stop letting Alaric invade their minds before he had invaded the city. They had to fear the law. He had therefore already written to Honorius encouraging the emperor to proceed with his expanded anti-pagan laws. These included laws that would punish not just those who honored the old gods, but also those who didn't report or condemn their pagan neighbors, friends or family. Christian apostates would similarly be penalized with property confiscation or execution. The old gods might refuse to die, but those who continued to honor them were mortal enough.

But the law on papyrus and the law in action were two different things. That is why Constantius had today ordered the gates of the normally fortified Roman Forum to be opened wide. He wanted as many people as possible to witness what was about to happen on the Rostra. Unfortunately, he couldn't be there to witness it. He couldn't leave Hispania. Neither could his commander Sarus be there, since the idiot had gone as rogue as the Senate itself. But he could still get Rome to behave itself.

Coelia, however, would be there to witness it. She had spent the morning in silent prayer at her home on the Esquiline Hill, repeating the same petition to the goddess:

"*Vesta Mater, viam Sacerdotis Antoniae inlustra.*"

And then she had dressed in a red tunica—she was told that was what Antonia would be wearing—and walked through the streets of Rome with Brogos, sensing his protectiveness intensify as they arrived at the packed Roman Forum and stepped into the maelstrom of wretchedness therein.

Coelia had known about the starvation. She had seen it for herself on the streets, and she knew it had only worsened. Once, the worst anyone could imagine was a desperate father cannibalizing dead bodies. Now, they heard of hopeless mothers killing their infants to feed their older children. But what Coelia had not seen, not until now, was the disease. As people ran or shuffled by her, as they bumped into or brushed against her, she recoiled in self-preservation from the rashes, the pustules, the weeping eyes and noses, and the smell. After all, Alaric hadn't just blocked food and supplies from entering the city, he had cut off much of Rome's fresh water supply by commandeering the aqueducts. The fountains and springs within the city had quickly become polluted, the public latrines could not be flushed into the sewer, and the public baths were closed altogether. Thirst, filth and sickness had now compounded Rome's hunger pangs.

These afflictions had also undermined Constantius's plan to use the public execution of the heathen Lady Antonia as a reminder for Romans to obey the law. For once the gates of the Roman Forum were opened to the sick, starving, thirsty and afraid, it became apparent that Romans didn't care about a woman being executed. Many had seen worse things in the street outside their own windows. What they *did* care about was the rumor that the warehouses in the Forum still held grain. What they *did* care about was the Spring of Juturna in the Forum, which still held clean, healing water. What they *did* care about was the valuables that still remained in the Forum's basilicas, shops and magisterial offices, riches that might be enough to purchase mercy from Alaric's marauding soldiers when they came banging at the door.

Coelia wound her way through the throng as men, women and children foraged within the buildings and structures of the Forum, indifferent to the shouted announcement that summoned them to the Rostra to witness the impending execution. She arrived at the Rostra just in time to see a cluster of soldiers leading Antonia up the steps of the grand platform. The four burly armed soldiers dwarfed her slight frame, though Coelia didn't know if the show of excessive force was deliberate or not. Either way, it made her heart sink. She looked around, but couldn't see any of Antonia's friends in the crowd. If they were there, they were keeping a low profile. She couldn't blame them.

But she couldn't let Antonia be alone, either. Ignoring Brogos's pleas for caution—for all they knew, there was an order for her arrest as well—Coelia pushed forward to the space directly in front of the Rostra and looked up at Antonia. Her bare arms were shivering, and her legs trembled so violently they shook the fabric of the long red tunica that her condemners had dressed her in. Only a few steps away sat the chopping block. Antonia stared at the low black mass as though it were the only thing of substance in the world.

An official in a blue tunica ascended the Rostra to stand beside her. He read from a scroll. "On the charges of heresy, sorcery and seditious conspiracy, Lady Antonia Secunda has been found guilty and sentenced to death according to the laws of Rome and of His Highness Flavius Honorius. Her sentence will now be carried out on the authority of the emperor and on behalf of the people of Rome." He looked into the square before the Rostra, wondering whether it was worth issuing a stern condemnation of her under-ground network of co-conspirators. He decided it wasn't. No one was really listening. They were too busy scurrying along the arcades of the basilicas, seeing which doors were unlocked. He ceded his position to a black-robed executioner and descended the platform.

"Antonia!" Coelia called out. "I am here!"

Her body and senses petrified with fear, Antonia did not hear, but only continued to gape at the chopping block. One of the sol-diers urged her to step forward toward the object of her macabre fascination, but when she remained fixed to the spot, he and an-other soldier each took one of her arms and dragged her the short distance. They pushed her down onto her knees before the black block. She did not resist. The stark terror of her plight had reduced her to an empty, unresponsive husk.

Brogos looked sympathetically at Coelia. "Fuck," he mum-bled. "Don't watch."

"Antonia!" Coelia called out again. This time, Antonia's eyes met hers. "Do you remember when we were novices? When we would make speeches on the Rostra after the Forum closed?" Coelia forced—with all her might, *forced*—levity into her voice. "You used to pretend you were Empress Livia! Such a snob!"

A spark of life, of memory, lit Antonia's eyes. The sides of her mouth curled upward into a shade of a smile as, somewhere in her mind, she retreated to another time.

The executioner grabbed a handful of Antonia's long hair and pushed her head down, placing her neck in the groove of the chopping block. "*Seda, mulier*," he said. He raised the blade of his sword, lining it up with the back of the woman's neck.

"We are just playing on the Rostra," Coelia shouted. "That is all, Antonia!"

The blade came down and Antonia's head fell with a thump onto the Rostra, the cold metal ending her life only steps away from her childhood home, from the goddess's home, and from the temple where she had guarded the sacred flame for the city that had betrayed her.

Barely anyone noticed.

CHAPTER LI

Even the most skeptical or stubborn citizen could not avoid the truth of it. Rome had broken the pax deorum, its crucial concord with its ancient gods and goddesses. It had extinguished its guardian flame. Its people had abandoned the customs of their ancestors, those rites and traditions that had sustained the city through the centuries and given the Roman people the solidarity they needed to conquer the world. Now, as Alaric's massive army of Visigoths attacked the various gates of Rome, as his battering rams shook the ramparts and the conquerors faced being the conquered, the people prayed they were not too late to make it all right again.

Accordingly, Senator Pompeianus had been chosen as the best candidate to bring an astonishing twofold petition to Bishop Innocentius, one that would have been unthinkable even a year earlier. First, the Senate and the people of Rome wanted official permission for the priests, led by Memmius Symmachus, to perform the ancient sacrificial rites at the Temple of Jupiter on the Capitoline Hill. Second, they wanted permission for the Vestalis Maxima Coelia Concordia to relight Vesta's sacred fire in her temple.

Pompeianus had spent most of the morning at the bishop's palace discussing the petition, the meeting ending only when Innocentius's sanctioned Gothic guard arrived to usher him safely out of the besieged city. The bishop's many letters to Honorius, imploring him to either make peace with Alaric or send more soldiers to defend Rome, had proven fruitless. He would have to brave passage to Ravenna and plead with the emperor in person, providing there was something left to plead for by the time he arrived.

As Innocentius headed north out of Rome, Pompeianus headed to the Roman Forum and the Senate House to deliver the bishop's decision to the anxious assembly. The senators had been gathered since dawn for this emergency session, and though almost every seat in the chamber was full, the familiar clangorous debates were absent, giving way to an apprehensive hum of whispered conversations that resonated within the high marble walls. Every man present felt a rush of relief when Pompeianus finally arrived to share Innocentius's answer. Yes or no, it was better than not knowing.

Coelia arrived in the Forum to find the doors of the Senate House closed and the assembly still in session. She also found that she wasn't the only one waiting to hear the news. Half of Rome—the half that still had the energy to traverse the city—had also gathered in the Forum, hoping to hear that the gods would soon be coming to their rescue. Many wore the pagan symbols they had previously hidden away under the floorboards or in the rafters: a silver pendant of Minerva here, a golden cuff engraved with the spear of Mars there, a wedding ring inscribed with the faces of Jupiter and Juno, or a seal ring with the figure of Vesta. There hadn't been so many signs of the gods in the Forum in years.

Coelia pulled the hood of her cloak over her head to hide her face while Brogos stayed at her side, completing the charade that they were just another anonymous couple in the hopeful crowd. She wasn't afraid of being arrested at this point—every soldier, guard, sentry and vigil had been ordered to the walls to defend the city—but she didn't want to be mobbed by those seeking a blessing. If the Senate doors opened and the answer was yes, she didn't have a moment to lose. She would march straight to the goddess's temple—*it was so close!*—and fling open the doors to start undoing whatever damage had been done. The sanctum and altar would have to be repaired, the oculus would have to be reopened, and the religious implements would have to be retrieved in order to properly return the goddess's true flame to her temple.

And yet the moment the doors of the Senate opened and she saw Olympius's crestfallen face, Coelia knew that none of it would come to pass. His tired eyes moved over the crowd as he searched for her. Spotting Brogos, he led them toward a shaded spot alongside the Curia as, meanwhile, Senators Junius and Pompeianus proceeded to the Rostra to address the larger gathering.

Coelia lowered the hood of her cloak. "The bishop said no," she assumed.

"Actually, he said yes," said Olympius. "At least at first." Suddenly looking even more fatigued, he leaned against the exterior wall of the Senate House. "You'll fucking love this. Apparently, Innocentius agreed to it all. The sacrifice on the Capitoline, the rekindling of the sacred fire, whatever we wanted to do, he was ready to allow it. Pompeianus said he was willing to try anything if it might spare the lives of Romans."

"So what happened?" asked Coelia.

"Sister Marcia showed up," Olympius replied. "Someone told her the bishop was talking to a delegate from the Senate, and she probably guessed why."

Deflated, Coelia stepped toward the wall and leaned against it, facing Olympius. "*Futuo,*" she said.

"You've got that right," concurred Olympius. "According to Pompeianus, she lost her mind. Started lecturing Innocentius about how the temple prostitutes were seducing their Christian flock, how the chief demoness—that's you, in case you're wondering—could never be allowed to relight a hellfire in the heart of Peter's city. Her big flourish was insinuating that she'd write to

Constantius about it, and we all know how he'd react." He rubbed his eyes, trying not to think about Antonia. He had admired her dedication to their shared cause and, despite himself, had come to care for her. "Anyway," he continued, "after the sister left, Innocentius offered Pompeianus a compromise. He said we could perform the rites, but not in public."

"I'm assuming the Senate voted against that," said Coelia.

Olympius nodded. "The sacrificial rites must be performed on the Capitoline Hill under the open sky or there's no point," he said. "The gods won't see otherwise." He rubbed his face harder, leaving blotches of red on his cheeks. "I can't believe it."

But Coelia could. As the head of the Christian women's monastery, Sister Marcia would do anything to efface the Vestal Virgins. *Perhaps I have had it wrong all these years*, thought Coelia. *Perhaps the blame does not lie with the bishops, but with women so eager to subjugate themselves and their sisters.* None of it could happen without their determination to spread contempt for the great goddesses and destroy millennia of tradition that had dignified the role of women in the temples. How galling, and how sad. How easy it would have been to step forward, as Coelia had tried to do by reforming the Vestal Order, instead of backward. Like the pit in the Evil Field, there was only fear and darkness there.

A collective cry of disappointment sounded from the Rostra where Senators Junius and Pompeianus had just finished delivering the devastating news to the crowd. The rites would not be performed. The gods were not coming. The sacred hearth would stay unlit. The three companions by the Senate House stood unspeaking for some time.

"It is my fault," said Coelia. "I should have fought harder."

No, the fault is mine, thought Olympius. He closed his eyes against a wave of regret. Turning the weak-minded Honorius against Stilicho had been the worst mistake of his life. His successor Constantius had none of Stilicho's military acumen, none of his moral conviction and none of his religious tolerance. Stilicho would never have executed Antonia, and if he thought the sacred rites might have saved Rome, he would have dragged the bull to the altar himself. Mad shouts from the direction of the Palatine Hill—the disappointment in the Forum had mounted to rage and panic—broke through Olympius's remorse. They needed to get out of the city.

Brogos was thinking the same thing. "I have arranged for horses," he revealed. "Two of them."

Olympius regarded him with surprise. Most of the donkeys and horses in the city—other than the war horses—had been slaughtered for meat long ago. "How did you manage to keep two horses out of the pot all this time?" he asked.

"The stableman on the Esquiline," said Brogos. He turned to Coelia. "He has kept them in hiding for us. Once Alaric breaches the gates, we'll wait for the first rush of invasion to pass and then—"

"Fuck that," said Olympius. "I say we open the gates for the bastard in exchange for our lives. Oh, don't look at me like that, Coelia. It's just a matter of time."

By now, the anger in the Forum had grown fiercer, the aggrieved crowd proliferating and amassing before the temples of Saturn and Concordia.

"We're about three breaths away from an all-out riot," said Brogos. "Let's get back to the Esquiline while we still can. Cover your head, Coelia."

She did, positioning herself between the two men as the trio left the relative peace of their shaded spot alongside the Curia to venture onto the Via Sacra and into the disarray. They hadn't gone far when they stopped in unison, all three of them seeing the same thing at once. A man in a short tunica and pants was dragging Serena by the hair, while the mob closed in all around. Shouts rang out.

"We must break the curse! Kill her!"

"Avenge the goddess! Strangle her!"

"She conspires with Alaric! Execute her!"

Shrieking in protest, Serena clawed at the man's hands as he lugged her along, her body trailing behind him like a twisting sack of grain. She kicked her legs furiously and cried out for help, but no one came to her aid. Too many in the mob had felt helpless and oppressed for too long, and the feeling had started long before Alaric showed up. Their need to act, to reclaim a sense of power, to feel a moment of vengeance, was unyielding.

As Coelia watched from under the hood of her cloak, the mob hauled Serena to the statue of Mercury that stood by the staircase of the Temple of Concordia. Someone tossed a length of rope into the fray and hands found it, working together to bind her body to the statue. The rope wrapped around her again, snaking up her body, crushing her breasts and finally finding its resting place—her neck. The same neck that had once so goadingly sported the golden necklace from the statue of Ops.

Coelia had watched Serena die a thousand times in her mind, fantasizing about how it would happen and how long it would take. In reality, it took longer than she would have thought. Perhaps the strangler was weak, or perhaps he was trying to prolong her suffering to satisfy the crowd, but either way, Serena struggled against the garrote and gaped for breath for an almost disturbing length of time. At last, she succumbed, and her head fell to the side.

Whether victim of a Vestal's curse or just circumstance, Serena's death evoked no sympathy from Coelia. Even if she could forgive the woman for her sacrilege and the humiliation, she could never forgive her for failing to secure Antonia's pardon. Nonetheless, there was still something hollow about the resolution... a lingering bitterness brought about by the realization that Serena had been betrayed by Rome as much as Coelia had been.

"Alaric has entered the city!"

The bellow of alarm came from the Capitoline Hill, and all heads looked up to see a frantic young man with a blood-stained tunica standing by the Temple of Jupiter.

"From what gate?" someone shouted up to him.

"The Salarian!" the young man replied. *"Run for your lives!"*

CHAPTER LII

Eight hundred years earlier, a Gallic chieftain named Brennus had breached the high walls of Rome and sacked the Eternal City for the first time in its history. As his men ran wild through the streets, committing every atrocity the human mind could conceive of, some of the senators of the great Roman Republic came to the aid of the Vestal Virgins, helping them flee the city with the relics and embers of Vesta's sacred fire. Those senators that remained stood outside the Curia in defiance, dressed in their togas—that symbol of civilized men—determined to meet their deaths with dignity in the Roman Forum. Once Brennus had taken control of the city, his army held all of Rome hostage, starving its people and forcing them to strip the gold from their temples to buy their own lives. For a while, it had seemed like things were hopeless and that Brennus was invincible.

But then word of the city's invasion and Brennus's iniquity reached the ears of an exiled Roman general by the name of Marcus Furius Camillus. Gathering legions and momentum along the way, Camillus had swept into Rome with a force and fury worthy of his great name, he and his men cutting through Brennus's army like scythes. After they had slain the last Gallic soldier, Camillus dragged Brennus to the piles of Roman gold he had stolen and cut off his head. The city was saved, the sacred fire returned to its hearth, and Roman fathers had yet another legendary tale of Roman bravery to pass down to their sons.

But as Alaric's army invaded a very different Rome, there would be no returning hero, no brave legions, no unified city or republic to come to its own rescue. The emperor of the Western Empire wasn't even in Rome, but in the new capital of Ravenna, playing with his favorite chickens. As Coelia ran for her life through the streets of her fallen city, choking on smoke and ducking into porticos to avoid being trampled by the incoming hordes of mounted Goths and the multitudes of Romans running for their own lives, she remembered what the stableman on the Esquiline had told Brogos the first day they had arrived back in Rome: *It's every man for himself.* She felt that instinct—get out of the city, whatever it takes!—but she fought against it.

After taking a moment's shelter in an archway along the Septa Julia to catch her breath, Coelia stepped back into the chaos and ran along the Via Flaminia, flanked by Brogos and Olympius. They hadn't made it more than fifty strides before yet another horde of invading Goths on horseback—their dented helmets shining in the sun, and their mouths open in a war cry—galloped by, lighting anything combustible on fire with their blazing torches. One of them ignited a wooden laundry cart. It burned slowly for a moment, but then a gust of wind caught it and it went up with a *whoosh*, billowing into another black cloud of smoke for Coelia to choke on. She coughed and kept running.

Olympius shouted over the panicked clamor. "We're running in the wrong fucking direction!"

"We have to get Florina!" Coelia shouted back.

Olympius hacked up a mouthful of blackened sputum and spat it out. "Why did you tell her to go to the *ustrinum*?" he demanded. "Of all the places to meet, it's the—"

Coelia squandered a precious moment of progress to stop and

shout back at him. "Because I didn't know they'd enter through the bloody Salarian Gate! I'm not the fucking Oracle, Olympius!" She pointed into the current of running bodies. "Leave if you want!"

Olympius clenched his jaw. He might have, if he didn't think Lucilla would haunt him.

Brogos took Coelia by the wrist and pulled her along. "We need to keep moving!"

Of all the places to meet...

Coelia knew that Olympius was right about that much. But days earlier, when she and Florina had decided upon where the latter should go if the city fell, the ustrinum at the Mausoleum of the Augustus in the Campus Martius seemed like a reasonable choice. Not only was the site of the Imperial funerary pyre close to the private residence that was hiding Florina, but the crematory's caretaker was pagan and had agreed to shelter her there, inside the enclosure if need be, until help arrived. On top of that, the breaches at the Porta Naevia and other gates of the city had suggested the invasion would start elsewhere.

Someone must have opened the gates from the inside, thought Coelia. *Another betrayal.*

Or just desperation. As eager as Alaric and his men were to get into the city, many Romans were just as eager to get out.

They careened past the Pantheon, but by the time they reached the Ara Pacis, the current of people rushing in the opposite direction—away from the waves of invaders streaming into the city—had grown so thick and fast that their progress became even more onerous. Coelia looked up at the towering multilayered Mausoleum of Augustus that dominated the skyline ahead. The colossal bronze statue of Augustus seemed to be suspended in the sky, the emperor's arm raised in command of legions long dead.

Suddenly, a trumpet blared—a foreign trumpet—and Coelia felt Brogos's fingers tighten around her wrist. As if called into being by the blare of the Gothic trumpet, a massive troop of barbarian footsoldiers appeared on the street before them. Like those on horseback, they shouted war cries into the air, their eyes gleaming with exhilaration, not a trace of fear in their aspects. They were taking an undefended city—the abandoned heart of the empire—and they knew it. Invading Rome, sacking the Eternal City, was as much a symbolic victory as a military one.

The force of Brogos's grip yanked Coelia downward. "Get down!" he ordered her. "Lower your head."

As she, Brogos and Olympius knelt on the street, Coelia's forehead nearly touching the cool stone of the pavement, the Gothic soldiers ran by, viciously swinging their swords at any man, woman or child too proud or simply too dazed not to have prostrated themselves before them. Shrieks of shock and agony rang out. Though Coelia did not dare raise her head, she could hear Romans collapsing around her, their dead or wounded bodies slumping to the ground—*thump, thump, thump.*

The earth-shaking footfalls of the passing soldiers lasted impossibly long. *There are thousands of them*, thought Coelia. She turned her head without raising it and shouted at Brogos. "Where are they all going?"

He looked at her, small stones embedded in his forehead from the street. "The Forum," he said. "They will loot as much as they can from the public buildings and basilicas first, and then they will... " his voice trailed off. He needed to get her out of Rome before what they would do next.

As the mass of footsoldiers finally passed and a small break in the fierce incursion presented itself, the trio stood and rushed ahead until they reached the ustrinum, located adjacent to the great mausoleum.

Coelia called out. "Florina!"

Either oblivious to the danger or mired in enough panic to dispense with caution, the young woman ran out of the crematory's enclosure. Yet at the sound of a trumpet blare and the sudden appearance of fifty or more mounted Goths bursting out of a black cloud of smoke, galloping full-speed toward the mausoleum, she clutched the terracotta vessel she held to her chest and ducked behind the thick trunk of a black poplar. Coelia, Brogos and Olympius did the same, each diving for the small slants of shade—woefully desperate shelters—offered by the grove of trees around the ustrinum. Still, it was enough to save them as the single-minded Goths continued hurtling toward their destination.

Olympius studied the Goths, his eyes narrowing. "That..." he struggled for breath. "That is Alaric himself," he said. "The one with the gold cuirass."

From behind the screen of shade, the Vestal watched as Alaric and his men dismounted their horses. Two of the mausoleum's caretakers were on their knees before the entrance, by all appearances having already unlocked the doors for the invaders. The Goths poured into the monument. The sounds that issued forth—their crude laughter mingled with the noise of destruction—went on for a contemptibly long time. Alaric reemerged first. In his hands was the golden funerary urn of Augustus.

The king of the Visigoths lifted the urn over his head and, with all his might, smashed it onto the ground. The lid of the urn flew off, and a cloud of ash billowed up. As his men surrounded him, congratulating him and roaring with laughter, Alaric picked up the urn and dumped the ashes of Rome's first emperor onto the ground. The wind picked them up, and they blew away.

"*Sacerdos virginalis tua flet, Caesar,*" whispered Coelia. She turned to Florina, noting the white terracotta vessel in her hands. Molded into the shape of a round hut and ventilated by a single hole in the domed lid, it held whatever hope was left inside her.

"They are strong embers," said Florina. "Coals are best for a journey."

The four shrunk behind the tree trunks as Alaric and his men climbed back on their horses, shouted something in a foreign language, and charged away in the direction of the Forum. Coelia did not let herself think about what they would do when they got there. Her only concern now was getting the embers of the sacred hearthfire back to the Esquiline, and then out of Rome. Keeping the goddess's true fire burning was still her sworn duty as a Vestal.

Though the efforts of so many to restore it to its temple hearth had failed, if she and Florina could survive this day, so might the eternal flame.

Racing, trudging, weaving and pushing their way through the infernal streets of Rome was a dark odyssey that only grew more dismal as the invasion spread. The fires set by the Goths sent roaring orange flames reaching into the sky, while plumes of choking black smoke hung heavily in the air. The shouts of the terrorized and the wounded were everywhere. They called out to their spouses, parents or children, they called out to their neighbors for help, they even called out to the Goths for mercy.

As Coelia and her companions rushed past another blazing insula, a young mother carrying her infant escaped the flames and ran into the street. A Goth with bloody bare arms spotted the silver bracelet on the woman's wrist and grabbed her, knocking the infant out of her arms. Had the young mother known the silver would have bought her child's life, she would have given it willingly. But she didn't know, and instead of submitting, she fought against him, struggling to reach her child. The Goth had enough and picked up the infant by one leg, hurling it back into the flames before knocking the woman unconscious. He ripped the bracelet from her wrist and moved on.

At long last, Coelia and her fleeing companions reached the streets of the Esquiline Hill. Yet if they had held out any lingering hope that the wealthier districts would somehow be insulated from the carnage, it was dashed by the sight of a frantic father throwing gold coins at the feet of the smiling Goth who was dragging his teenaged daughter toward a prison cart full of captive young women.

"Christ in heaven, have mercy!" the father pleaded as he emptied the gold purse on the street. "Take it all! Take it all!"

His wife ran out of the house, piles of silk dresses in her arms.

"Take them!" she shrieked. She ran past her husband, dropping the dresses and clawing at the Goth.

The invader scooped her up in his free arm and tossed both mother and daughter into the cart. At that, a young man bolted from his hiding spot behind a dry fountain.

"Mother!" he cried, running toward the cart.

Another Goth stabbed him in the side of the neck, and he collapsed to the ground.

"No!" The man of the house rushed to his son's side. As blood continued to pulse out of the young man's neck, he placed his palms over the fatal wound, trying but failing to tamp the bleeding. His wife and daughter shrieked from inside the prison cart as it began to roll toward the next estate. "Be strong!" the man called out to them. "I will find you!"

Coelia's heart sank—she knew the family. Fellow residents of the Esquiline, she had met them several times at functions held in the hilltop's famous gardens. The last time she had seen them, the couple was showing off their new baby girl, presumably the same young woman now imprisoned in the cart with the other daughters of the Esquiline.

Olympius saw Coelia's resolve fading and cast her a severe look. "There isn't a fucking thing you can do about it," he said, "unless you want to get in the cart with them. Keep moving."

She did, though moving forward brought no reprieve. Just up ahead, a pair of Goths were restraining an old man by the arms while a third waved the flame of a torch before the man's face, scalding his skin and setting his hair on fire. The soldier with the torch laughed and patted the flames out.

"I told you!" the man screeched. "I have given you everything! There is no more, I swear to the gods!"

Brogos, who was leading the way, pointed to the right. "This way." Ducking to avoid low-hanging branches, he led them into a small orchard of peach trees. It was precious cover.

"I need to rest," said Olympius. The oldest among them, his face was dripping with sweat, and the muscles in his legs were trembling from the strain of their journey.

"This is a shortcut to the stables," replied Brogos. "You can rest once I've pushed your ass up onto a horse."

Olympius drew in a wheezing breath, and Coelia glanced at Brogos. "Let him catch his breath," she said, panting. She turned to Florina. "How are the coals?"

Florina knelt on the leafy ground and removed the domed lid of the terracotta vessel. Taking a dry branch from the ground, she stoked the coals and nodded. "Still strong."

They set off again, treading carefully over the roots and fallen branches in the orchard until they emerged on the other side, only steps away from the stable. The stableman Oracio was standing out front, gripping an axe with white knuckles. His eyes darted here and there in anticipation of an attack by the invaders. It was a small miracle that he had kept his word by meeting them at the stable instead of running off to hide, and they shared a moment of relief.

A look of relief crossed Oracio's face, too, upon spotting the Vestal and her companions rushing toward him. It faded almost immediately as they all heard the direful sound of approaching footfalls and clinking armor.

"They're coming!" he said. "Hurry, you can hide back here."

Frantically, he led the two women to a high stack of debris—a pile of fence posts, with shattered terracotta *amphorae* all around—next to the door of the stable and all but shoved them behind it. He scurried back to stand beside Brogos and Olympius, the three of them dreading the arrival of the men that were rounding the treed grove. Yet as the figures came into view, the relief returned. These were Roman soldiers, not Goths.

Arriving at the stable, the stockier of the two muscly soldiers pointed at Oracio. "*Tu!*" he said. "Are there any horses here?"

Oracio shook his head apologetically. "This stable is empty, *legionarie*. The army took my last two mares months ago."

"Then what are you three doing here?" asked the soldier.

"We were going to hide here, sir," said Oracio.

The second soldier, who was bleeding from his left shin, threw up his thick arms in exasperation and glowered at his colleague. "I told you all the horses were gone!"

"You never know," replied his companion. He turned back to the Romans. "Stay safe, citizens."

"Stay safe, *legionarii*," said Oracio.

The soldiers turned to go, but the taller of the two hesitated. With brows furrowed in suspicion, he turned back around to stare more inquisitively at one of the stableman's companions. "Senator Olympius?"

"What of it, boy?" demanded Olympius.

The soldier nodded slowly, processing his discovery. "I'm told that you commanded legions in the north," he said. "So you weren't always a backstabbing politician."

A tense silence hung for only a moment before collapsing into sudden violence. The two soldiers charged toward Olympius, the squatter one knocking the senator to his knees and quickly wrapping a well-muscled arm around his neck. The soldier with the bleeding leg withdrew his dagger and pointed it at Brogos and Oracio. The stableman retreated at the burst of brutality, but Brogos stood his ground.

"Standing orders of General Constantius," the wounded soldier said to Brogos. "Do not interfere."

Brogos's thoughts tumbled over each other. He had no particular desire to help Olympius—he deserved whatever he had coming to him, for Deimos's death as much as Stilicho's downfall—but Coelia had softened to the man over the years. If she revealed herself to try and save him, the soldiers' blades would turn to her. Exhausted as Brogos was, it would be hard to fight off two soldiers in their prime, even if one was injured.

"Legionarie," he said, his voice infused with desperate diplomacy. "We are all Romans here." He gestured down the street, in the direction of a roaring conflagration and a swell of screaming cries for mercy. "Listen to what is happening!"

"We know what is happening," the soldier retorted. "And it's this prick's fault." Turning back to the restrained Olympius, he brought the blade of his dagger to the side of his head—and sliced off Olympius's right ear. He tossed the flap to the ground. Olympius howled in pain, but the soldier hollered over him. "That's for whispering your fucking poison into the emperor's ear!"

The stockier soldier released Olympius, and the senator's hand flew to the gaping wound on the side of his head. He pressed his palm against the spot where his ear used to be, but the feeling was too grotesque and the blood too slippery, so he simply bent over and grimaced. The soldier who had cut him sheathed his bloody dagger and, as if a thought had just occurred to him, spun around to spy the stack of fence posts that was shielding Coelia and Florina. Olympius felt a hammer of panic. If Constantius had ordered Antonia's death and his own, it was possible that he had ordered Coelia's death, too.

As the soldier took a step toward the pile of fence posts, the bleeding old man at his feet sprang up and struck him on the side of the head, moving with the speed and strength of a man twenty years younger. Had the soldier truly known Olympius—unpredictable at best and lethal when cornered—he would not have turned his back on him, even if a whole cohort were present. Stunned by the force of the impact, he stumbled away to regain his bearings.

His colleague swore in surprise and advanced on Olympius, though he too felt the senator's reserve of power as Olympius raised his arms to deflect the soldier's strike, grabbing his arm and sending the thickset man to the ground. The soldier landed with a winded grunt.

"*Porcus tu*," said Olympius, gasping for breath. "Your centurion should hide your fucking rations once in a while."

The soldier swore again and struggled to get his feet under him, but Olympius knew he couldn't let him gain any ground. He was losing too much blood from his ear, and he could feel his strength draining away with it. Careful to avoid the soldier's grasping hands, he kicked him squarely in the face, feeling the cartilage in his nose collapse. Leaving him to mutter obscenities in agony, Olympius turned to see Brogos and the other soldier wrestling for a dagger. He felt a stream of blood from his wound trickle down to pool at the side of his mouth, wiped his lips, and dove forward to help Brogos fight off the larger soldier.

Olympius heard the stableman's warning — "*Look out! He's coming!*" — a moment too late. The stocky soldier was back on his feet, gripping a heavy fence post in his hands.

His anger and his pain driving him to more brutality that was strictly necessary to get the job done, the soldier swung the fence post directly at the back of Olympius's skull. The crushing blow sent a spray of blood flying into the air. Olympius dropped to his knees. The soldier swung again, and Olympius's body fell on its side. The soldier swung again. And again.

He would have kept swinging, too, had the stableman not roused his courage, retrieved his pitchfork, and impaled him from behind, pushing hard to force the rusty prongs through the soldier's thick back and out his chest. The soldier's body collapsed on top of Olympius's. Distracted by his colleague's implausible fate, the larger soldier wavered just enough for Brogos to gain the advantage. Taking hold of the dagger's hilt, he sunk the blade into the bottom of the soldier's jaw, pushing it upward to pierce his brain. He fell to the ground.

His chest heaving for breath, Brogos stumbled toward the fallen Olympius. He pulled the corpse of the smaller soldier off the senator's body. What he saw below made him cry out. "Fuck!"

"Olympius…"

Depleted of energy, Brogos turned to find Coelia standing behind him, blinking in disbelief at Olympius's remains. Florina had an arm around the older woman, though she herself could not bear to look.

"Coelia…" said Brogos. He reached out to take her arm and lead her off, but she pushed both him and Florina away.

The Vestal stared at Olympius's body. Fragments of his skull and teeth, wet with blood and tissue, were scattered around his collapsed head. His lifeless limbs lay at impossible angles, and the fingers of his left hand were twitching, as if the intractable senator still refused to give up. *How my mother would weep to see him like this*, thought Coelia. Somewhere behind her, she heard the sound of squeaking hinges as the stable doors opened.

"Come on," said Oracio. "We need to get the horses out."

Coelia remained where she was as Brogos and Florina followed Oracio inside the stable—only to find rows of empty stalls within.

It was all too much for Brogos. The riot in the Forum, the fires and executions on the street, the near-brush with Alaric himself, the young women being taken into captivity, the fight with the soldiers, the sight of Olympius's mangled skull... had he witnessed every form of human cruelty and suffering, and labored to keep Coelia alive through all of it, only to be duped by a madman's delusions of grandeur?

"Gods help me!" he yelled. "You're a fucking lunatic!"

"Lunatic, you say?" challenged Oracio.

He hastened to the back wall of the stable, hurriedly tossing aside the rakes and shovels that leaned against it. And then, as if by magic, he opened the wall and made two horses appear behind it—one of them was Coelia's horse, Nereus—both animals prepared for the road and contently chewing oats.

Brogos shot the stableman a look of awe. *He must've been a Vestal in another life*, he thought. For if he had learned anything by befriending a Vestal, it was that the priestesses had a peculiar affinity for hiding valuable things in just the right places. His body suddenly recharged with hope, he patted Nereus's white spotted neck before inspecting the other horse. A beautiful brown mare, she looked even better fed than Nereus. With this advantage, if they were fast—and lucky—they might actually make it out of the city.

Still standing by Olympius's body, Coelia heard the *clip clop* of horse hooves and turned to see Brogos and Oracio leading the horses out of the stable, her spirits brightening slightly at the sight of Nereus. Florina slipped out from behind the horses and darted up to her. The terracotta vessel that held the temple's sacred embers was still in her grip.

"My husband owns vineyards that stretch from Veii to the coast," she said. "I will take the coals to our estate in Caere. It should be safe enough to keep the flame there, and the port is close by if I want to go farther."

"I planned to take some coals with me," said Coelia. "I prepared a special vessel at my house, but the Esquiline is too dangerous now. We can't risk going back."

But I can improvise, she thought. Wiping her eyes, she pulled Florina back to the pile of debris that had sheltered them, searching the ground until she found something that could work—a cracked but intact terracotta amphora. The inside smelled slightly of wine, but otherwise it was clean enough. Understanding her purpose, Florina pulled the lid off the vessel that held the sacred embers and tipped it, sending three black-and-red coals tumbling into the new receptacle. Coelia stuffed a handful of dry grass down the neck of the amphora. It would be enough to house the goddess's glow for now.

They returned to the horses to find Brogos and Oracio doing a final check of each animal's riding gear. By now, the thunderous footfalls and raucous cries of the Goths were alarmingly close. The invading horde may have looked chaotic, but they had a remarkable ability to pillage and plunder with sequential precision. Taking the terracotta vessels out of the women's hands, Brogos secured each one in the leather satchel that hung from each horse.

"Coelia, you and I will ride Nereus," he directed. "Florina, you will take the mare. We'll leave the city together through the Porta Praenestina, and then we'll go our separate ways."

Coelia put her hand on Brogos's arm. "No. You go with Florina."

"Fuck that," he said. "The mare is healthy and will be fast. Once we get out of the city, she can make her own way. She knows the roads."

"Brogos," Coelia said sternly. "I have not given you a proper order in decades, not since the day you and your dogs first followed me into the house with your muddy feet. Don't make me start now. Please, go with Florina."

Brogos's expression fell. "Coelia. I don't want to."

The Vestal took one of his hands and kissed the back of it. "My dearest friend," she said. "I am begging you to keep this woman, this flame, and this man" — she touched his chest — "alive."

Brogos knew that she would argue until she had her way, and he knew that none of them had the time for it. He relented. "Be bloody careful on the roads. They'll be packed with Goths and opportunists heading to Rome. And when they're done here, you can bet they'll head south to Campania. I'll get Florina to safety, and then I'll come home."

"All right," said Coelia.

He wrapped his arms around her, squeezing too tightly. "If something happens, you know what to do. *Te amo*, Patrona."

"*Teo amo*," replied Coelia. After offering Oracio a quick blessing and her gratitude, she embraced Florina. "When you are safe enough to again wake those sleeping embers, remember what I taught you about Vesta's earliest days."

"I understand," said Florina.

Seeing the dolor on the former Vestal's face, Coelia straightened. "If we are indeed the last, sister, we have served the goddess well enough. No one could have done more. The rest is up to the Fates." She kissed Florina on the cheek. "I will pray for you and your family. *Cura ut valeas, Sacerdos.*"

"Be safe, High Priestess," Florina replied. "*Laus Vestae.*"

Coelia reached for the reins and, with Brogos's help, mounted Nereus. Eager only for the open road and oblivious to its dangers, the animal whinnied impatiently. Brogos mounted the mare and then pulled Florina up after him.

And then, with Brogos leading the way, they galloped away from the stable on the Esquiline, through the fiery streets and toward the Porta Praenestina. Bursting out of the open gates, they rode away from Romulus's fallen city, none of them having the heart to look back, all of them choosing to remember the Eternal City, the Caput Mundi, the city of the gods, the way it once was.

CHAPTER LIII

Between the silver in her hair and the stiffness in Nereus's gait, between her dirty tunica and the worn leather satchel that hung from her horse, Coelia didn't look like a woman worth taking the time to stop or steal from. That kept her alive as she rode south, dodging the bands of barbarians who were still heading to Rome to make their fortune by stealing someone else's. Once she reached the Via Appia and put more distance between herself and Rome, the stream of marauders thinned out, and her greatest struggle became keeping Nereus on the road and away from the fresh grasses that grew alongside it. When they reached an empty stretch of road, she gave in and dismounted so that he could eat and she could care for the coals in the terracotta amphora.

For four days, she rode along the Via Appia, counting the stone pines that lined the road, forgetting what number she had reached, and starting over. She could have counted the tombstones along the way, but that seemed too dreary, so she stuck with the trees. Now and then, she came across a shrine to Mercury or Diana and stopped to pray, disregarding the scars of desecration and repair on the small altars. The sky was vivid blue, free of clouds but full of birds, and the sun radiated with a perfect late August balance of light and heat.

Unbelievably—and it did seem unbelievable to her—she passed travelers who had no idea of what was happening in Rome. Even when she told them, most seemed only mildly interested. *"We keep to ourselves,"* they said. *"There's always some crisis happening, nothing we can do about it. It'll pass."* At first, the indifference had struck her as cruel, but as the humble travelers selflessly shared their bread with her, some even offering her coin they obviously could not afford to part with, she changed her mind about that.

Although Oracio had stuffed a few coins into the leather satchel, more than enough to pay for an overnight stay in a tavern or resort, Coelia's fear of patrols from Rome made her hesitant to risk it. She had instead led Nereus into the trees and slept on the forest floor for three nights in a row. Other than the ants that chewed at her ankles, it wasn't that bad. In fact, sitting amongst the greenery was peaceful. There was plenty of sustenance to keep the coals glowing, and the flowing streams she stumbled upon were fresher and more invigorating than any fountain in Rome. Struck with a sudden burst of courage, one kindled by the freedom of her solitude, she had even disrobed and lain naked on the smooth stones of one stream, letting the water cascade over her body.

I am no longer a priestess, she mused. *I have become a river nymph.*

Continuing along the Via Appia, she arrived in the town of Formia and passed the spot along the road where Cicero had been assassinated on the orders of Marc Antony. Although the site was marked with an impressive monument, Coelia was more moved by the fresh flowers that people who cared about such things had left on the roadside. The town was full of tourists who had come to watch some big performance in the theater, so Coelia used the anonymity of the crowd to finally pay for a night's stay and a good meal in a modest resort. It was only when she was mounting Nereus the following morning that she heard the first tone of alarm in the voices of her fellow travelers. News of what had happened—was still happening—in Rome was spreading, and people were finally starting to accept that, this time, it really was different.

As she left the Via Appia for the Via Domitiana, the stone pines gave way to towering cypress and even more expansive villas. Riding by some of the biggest fig trees she had ever seen—she certainly didn't remember them on her way to Rome—she plucked her fill and ate until her stomach ached. She spent the night by a babbling brook surrounded by pink wildflowers, giving herself the freedom to cry herself to sleep as she remembered the pink roses in the courtyard of the House of the Vestals. Her dreams were filled with the faces and voices of her past—Claudia and Domitia, Victor and Arbo, Symmachus and Lucilla—every forgotten feature pulled to the front of her memory. She was still crying when she woke up.

The sun was just starting to set on yet another clear blue-sky day when the familiarity of home prompted Nereus to pick up his pace until they reached Coelia's seaside villa just outside of Cumae. The gate was closed but not locked, so she opened it and walked Nereus through. He shook his head, and she quickly stripped him of his riding gear and the leather satchel, letting him run off to do as he pleased. The feral dogs yipped in excitement at their return—and the prospect of an easy meal, no doubt—and sniffed at her, looking around for Brogos. Not finding him, they ran back to torment Nereus.

She entered her domus to find it unchanged. Even the cup she had left on the kitchen counter was still there, though the water inside had evaporated. Pulling off her sandals, she headed for the brick hearth. As he always did, Brogos had left dry grasses and branches nearby for easy kindling. She arranged them just so in the hearth, and then used a set of small iron tongs to retrieve the glowing coals from the terracotta amphora, placing them one at a time on the tinder. Leaning close, she whispered a prayer to Vesta over the coals, her breath coaxing them to glow hotter and redder until a swirl of smoke formed and a flame ignited. She added more branches and the fire grew stronger, thick orange flames swaying over the wood and sending embers snapping into the air.

It had been a long time since Coelia had seen the goddess's visage or heard her voice with such clarity. She stared into the moving flames—the last to have burned inside Vesta's temple—and felt herself slip into a peaceful communion.

Yet even as the warmth of the fire soothed her, she remembered something she had to do, something that couldn't wait. Reaching into the leather satchel, she retrieved a coin and the handful of teeth she had plucked from the dirt around Olympius's head. She set the teeth—two were those pointed eye teeth she had seen the man flash so many times—in the fire and placed the coin on top. Payment for Charon to ferry Olympius across the River Styx. Now he could finally join her mother in the afterlife.

And now Coelia could finally rest for a moment... she was so tired. After all her labors to bring the sacred embers home, surely the prayers and offerings could wait just a little while longer. She shuffled to the couch and rested her head on a marine blue cushion.

Arf! Arf!

Jolted awake, she opened her eyes—she didn't remember drifting off—and looked at the fire. It was still burning, though more subdued, and the room had grown dark with the night. She added a piece of wood to the flames and rubbed her eyes.

Arf! Grrr....

The dogs were barking at something. Probably a deer, and hopefully not a skunk. She began walking toward the front door, but something changed her mind. Pivoting, she headed into the kitchen and leaned over the counter, unfastening one of the wooden window shutters and pushing it open just a crack. It was enough to see it, though: the reflection of the moon in the metal blade of a sword. Ducking to the side, she tried to get a better look, but it was as dark outside her house as inside. Straining to listen, she heard it: the whispered strategizing of men.

"There's a servant's entrance at the back."

"Why bother? There's a bloody window right here."

"Remember our orders—nothing fancy. Kill her the moment you see her."

Strangely, the midnight appearance of the assassins triggered no sense of panic in Coelia. Instead, she only felt a sense of... certainty? No, that wasn't quite right. It was more like... resignation. Yes, that was it. There was only one thing to do now.

Tiptoeing back to the hearthfire, she reached into the flames to grasp the still-cool end of the kindling she had just added, holding the burning end out like a torch. She touched the flame to the cushions of her couch and chair, and then began to move methodically through her house like she were an invading barbarian, starting everything she could on fire: the tapestries on the walls, the furniture, the carpets that lined the floors, the linens on her bed, the dresses in her wardrobe. As the heat and crackles of the flames grew, as the dark house filled with smoke, Coelia stumbled her way to the front door. She opened it and slipped into the night.

The soldiers were still gathered outside the kitchen window, though the unmistakable sound of fire and the sight of smoke rising from the house had stoked anxious confusion. Their hushed strategizing had escalated into shouted arguments about what to do. Should they enter the burning house and look for her? Should they just report to Constantius that they killed her or that she burned to death? By the time one of them had the sense to suggest that maybe, just maybe, the Vestal had started the fire as a ruse and was actually escaping, it was too late. Coelia had already reached the shoreline.

As the soldiers ran around the blazing house in search of her, she soundlessly slipped her little wooden boat into the water and climbed inside with bare feet, pushing away from shore with one of the oars and then placing both into the oarlocks. She rowed quietly, careful not to knock the oars against the sides of the boat or disturb the water more than was necessary. Silently, she propelled herself to safety, the distance and the night sky shielding her from the men's view.

When she was too far out to be seen, she stopped rowing and just watched. The sight of Vesta's fire raging wildly on the shore was mesmerizing. The vibrant orange flames stretched into the black sky above, but also stretched out below, reflecting off the surface of the black water as if it, too, were on fire. Even as the boat continued to drift, she could feel the heat from the flames radiating outward, as if the warmth itself was pushing her farther away.

She thought of Florina, thought of her spreading the goddess's true flame from hearthfire to candle to oil lamp, keeping it alive and ever-expanding in the private homes of Vesta's faithful. That is where the goddess had always burned the brightest. That is how she had burned in the beginning, ages before the first temple was built. After all these centuries, that is how she would burn again.

That was beautiful enough, yet Coelia Concordia knew that only a Vestal Virgin could know the beauty of beholding the Eternal Flame as it burned in its bronze firebowl within the Aedes Vestae. Only a Vestal Virgin could know the beauty of witnessing the gray wisps of smoke twist upward to slip out the oculus in the domed roof and return to the heavens. Only a Vestal Virgin could know the beauty of hearing the snaps of the flames and the whispered prayers of her sister priestesses resonating within the marble walls of the sanctum. As the last Vestalis Maxima to have led those prayers, she was truly blessed.

As the inferno continued to illuminate the sky above and the sea below, Coelia noticed for the first time how her little boat sat just slightly lower in the water than it used to. That was to be expected, though. She had packed the space under the false floor of the vessel with so many gold coins that she didn't know how she would spend them all. But she would worry about that when she got to Egypt. She and Brogos would climb a pyramid, look down over the world, and decide then.

She felt a flutter in her stomach, a soft sense of excitement rising inside her, the feeling getting stronger the farther she drifted away from the shore. It hadn't happened when or how she had expected—what in life ever did?—but her duty to the Vestal Order was finally over. Now, her future was her own. That was the promise that Vesta made to her faithful priestesses. It was a pact she had made and kept for over a thousand years in Rome, a city that had broken its own pact with the glowing goddess, and would be darker for it. But that was all behind Coelia now. So she gripped the oars and rowed away from the fiery shore, leaving the past but not forgetting it, to begin anew. If the goddess could do it, so could she.

FINIS

APPENDIX

Illustration of Coelia Concordia statue from the Justi Lipsi de Vesta Vestalibus Syntagma. Public Domain image.

About this Illustration

In the late 16th century, a statue was excavated on the Esquiline Hill in Rome. It was found without its head or arms. The base was found with it, allowing it to be identified as the statue of Coelia Concordia, Vestalis Maxima of Rome. Fortunately, a contemporary illustration was done, giving us a fairly accurate idea of what it looked like at the time of discovery. It isn't shown here, but a smaller accompanying illustration does show the presence of the Vestal's vittae on the back side.

I incorporated this statue and medallion (more on the medallion soon) into the novel's storyline. I surmised, as others have, that the high priestess most likely held a patera. The statue itself was found on the property of Senator Praetextatus and his wife Paulina on the Esquiline, and the inscription on the base tells its own true story, which I weaved into the novel as well. The inscription reveals the statue is dedicated to the great Coelia Concordia, Vestalis Maxima, by Fabia Paulina, on account of the chief Vestal's chastity and holiness in the worship of the divine. It states that Paulina dedicated the statue because the Vestal had previously paid for a statue of Paulina's husband, Vettius Praetextatus.

You may remember in the novel that Coelia and the Vestal Order commission a statue of Praetextatus in gratitude for his friendship and support of the Order. You may also remember that Symmachus disapproves of this. This is a true anecdote—Symmachus didn't want her to commission a statue of a man, but she did it anyway—and one that I relied upon in my depiction of this important woman. I found this unconventionality and personal agency very appealing in a prominent female figure, especially considering the larger backdrop of the times. By openly defying one of the most powerful male senators and priests in Rome, perhaps this chief Vestal was sending a message. Perhaps it was her way of showcasing the difference between the Vestal Virgins and the Christian virgins (early nuns). Perhaps it was her way of advancing the Vestal Order, or trying to find a way for it to survive in a changing world. Perhaps it was just her personality.

Regardless, by allowing herself to subsequently be the subject of a bejeweled and rather shapely statue made of fine marble, this Vestalis Maxima certainly recognized the stature of her position and was proud of it. No doubt she was well aware of how detractors like Ambrosius spoke of the Vestal Virgins, and both her actions and her statue suggest that she was not the type to simply shrink into the shadows in the face of conflict or criticism, whether it was from an ally or an enemy.

Again, all of this was in mind when I fleshed out Coelia's character. Whether it was her choice of business venture, her personal relationships, her efforts to reform the Vestal Order, her Vestal's curse—a true event according to the historian Zosimus, and the poetically just end of Serena—or her eleventh hour attempts to relight the sacred fire in the temple, she is a woman determined to represent the goddess and live life on her own terms, to the very end. (As an aside, it is worth noting that there are no objective accounts of any Vestal Virgin converting to Christianity, including Coelia Concordia.)

The actual statue of Coelia Concordia—the one depicted in the illustration—is extant; however, it is has been significantly reworked into a Muse. A head has been added, as well as arms and implements (a flute and a mask). The statue has long been in the care of the Colonna Gallery in Rome, and that gallery has very graciously provided me with a number of excellent photographs. You can see them on my author site at **AllThingsVesta.com**.

Unfortunately, the base of the statue has been lost—or if not lost, at least tucked away well enough that I have been unable to track it down!

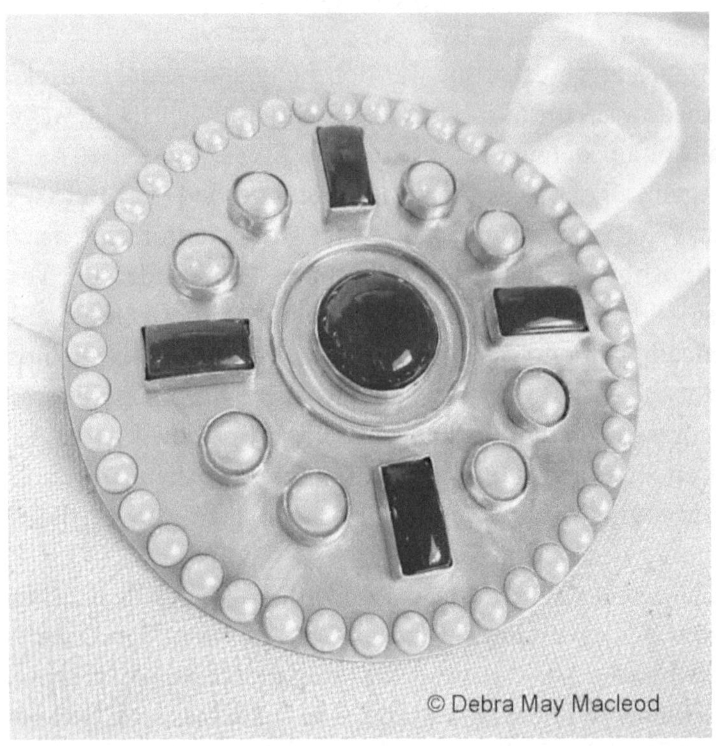

About this Photograph:

This is a photograph of a reproduction medallion I commissioned a jeweler to make, based on the appearance of the large medallion on the illustrated statue of Coelia Concordia in the *Justi Lipsi de Vesta et Vestalibus Syntagma*. The illustration suggests that an arrangement of jewels was inset into the medallion in the so-called pagan cross formation. It is believed that Vestals wore this pagan cross around their neck in the same way that Catholic nuns came to wear the Christian cross.

As in the novel, I imagined a gold piece inlaid with garnets or carnelian stones (representing the sacred fire) and pearls (representing the priestesses and purity). This red and white color scheme would be consistent with the red and white infula worn by a Vestal Virgin. Large disc brooches or pendants of this nature were often worn by important or wealthy people, and the *Virgo Vestalis Maxima* of Rome would certainly fall into that category.

About this Photograph:

This is a photograph of an ancient Roman coin in my collection. It is a denarius of the Republican period, minted in Rome. It shows the head of Gaius Caldus Coelius. This is the gens that Coelia Concordia belonged to. It is the coin I had in mind when I was writing the scene where Coelia purchases new sandals at the market in Cumae.

The reverse of this coin depicts the Epulum Jovis. Other coins of this gens variously show Sol, Roma, or Victory driving a chariot.

I invite you to visit my author site to see many more images that bring to life the people, events and elements depicted in this novel. You'll also find a wealth of fascinating content—a gallery, books, videos and much more—on ancient Rome, Vesta, and the remarkable Vestal Virgins.

AllThingsVesta.com

DRAMATIS PERSONAE AND OTHER NOTABLES

(indicates a real-life historical figure)*

Abigail A Roman noblewoman; friend of Helena; associate of the charlatan Aulus

Agrippa* *Referenced only* (died 12 BCE) Marcus Vipsanius Agrippa; a famous general and personal friend of Augustus

Alaric* The leader / king of the Visigoths

Alexander* *Referenced only* (died 323 BCE) Alexander the Great; a king of Macedon (in Greece) and perhaps the most famous and successful military commander in Western history. His legacy helped shape Western culture, and he was revered by Rome's emperors. He founded many cities, including the eponymous Alexandria in Egypt. Both Julius Caesar and Augustus visited the tomb of Alexander in Egypt, though the tomb's current whereabouts are unknown.

Ambrosius* A bishop of Mediolanum (modern day Milan); a prominent proponent of Christianity who worked to expand the church's influence in secular matters; an opponent of Arian Christianity and paganism; a critic of the Vestal Virgins; he is considered a father of the early church

Ancus Prisca's great nephew

Andragathius* The Master of Cavalry for Magnus Maximus

Anthea A young Roman noblewoman; daughter of Perses and Helena

Antinous A male prostitute at baths in Ostia

Antonia Secunda A Vestal Virgin

Antoninus Pius* *Referenced only* (died 161 CE) A Roman emperor

Arbogastes* (Arbo) A Roman general / magister militum of Frankish origin

Attalus* A Roman senator

Augustus* *Referenced only* (died 14 CE) Gaius Julius Caesar Augustus; also known as Octavian; first emperor of Rome; adopted son of Julius Caesar; founder of the Julio-Claudian dynasty

Aulus A religious charlatan; associate of Abigail

Bauto* *Referenced only* A Romanized Frank general

Brennus* *Referenced only* A Gallic chieftain whose forces sacked Rome in the late 4th century BCE

Brogos A Roman guard; celebrity gladiator

Catus A celebrity gladiator

Celunno An assassin

Cicero* *Referenced only* (assassinated 43 BCE) Marcus Tullius Cicero; celebrated Roman statesman, lawyer and writer

Claudia* A Vestalis Maxima

Clemens The lead animal trainer in the amphitheater

Cleopatra* *Referenced only* (committed suicide 30 BCE) A famous queen of Egypt who married Marc Antony and went to war against Rome

Coelia Concordia* A Vestal Virgin; the last Vestalis Maxima of the Roman Empire (died early 5th century CE)

Constantine* *Referenced only* (died 337 CE) First Roman emperor to personally convert to Christianity; proclaimed an edict for religious freedom (the so-called Edict of Milan)

Constantius* A Roman general who rose to power under the emperor Honorius (and who briefly became co-emperor—

Constantius III—of the Western empire, with Honorius, after the events of this novel)

Constantius II* *Referenced only* A Roman emperor (died 361 CE) who was succeeded by Julian

Cornelia* *Referenced only* A Vestalis Maxima during the time of the Flavian dynasty (1st century CE)

Damascus* A bishop of Rome

Deimos A celebrity gladiator

Delilah A prostitute favored by Valentinian

Diocletian* *Referenced only* (died 316 CE) A Roman emperor

Domitia A Vestal Virgin

Elgius A Roman envoy

Eucherius* The son of Stilicho and Serena

Eugenius* A Roman administrator; Roman emperor

Fausta A noblewoman; friend of Coelia Concordia

Florina A Vestal novice; Vestal Virgin

Gabinus A tomb painter in the catacombs

Gaius A farmer

Gaius Caldus Coelius* *Referenced only* Ancestor of Coelia Concordia who lived during the time of the Roman Republic

Galeria A Vestal novice; Vestal Virgin

Gnaeus A Roman vendor

Gratian* A Roman emperor

Hadrian* *Referenced only* (died 138 CE) A Roman emperor

Hannibal* *Referenced only* (died 181 BCE) A general of Carthage who fought against Rome

Helena Roman noblewoman; mother of Anthea; wife of Perses

Homer* *Referenced only* (c. 8th century BCE) A celebrated Greek poet, author of the *Iliad* and the *Odyssey*

Honorius* The son of Theodosius; Roman emperor

Innocentius* A bishop of Rome

Julia Domna* *Referenced only* (died 217 CE) The wife of Septimius Severus; empress of Rome

Julian* *Referenced only* (died 363 CE) Flavius Claudius Julianus; A Roman emperor who converted from Christianity to paganism / Hellenism; the last openly pagan emperor

Julius Caesar* *Referenced only* (assassinated 44 BCE) A famous general and dictator of Rome in the late republic

Junius A Roman senator

Kaunos A lanista / gladiator trainer

Laeta* The wife of Emperor Gratian

Lampadius* A Roman senator

Leah A servant in the house of Stilicho

Livia Drusilla* *Referenced only* (died 29 CE) Wife of Augustus and empress of Rome; mother of the emperor Tiberius

Livy* *Referenced only* (died 17 CE) A celebrated Roman historian who wrote *Ab Urbe Condita* (From the Founding of the City)

Lucilla Coelia A Roman noblewoman; mother of Coelia Concordia

Magnus Maximus* A Roman emperor; father of Victor

Manta An assassin

Marc Antony* *Referenced only* (committed suicide 30 BCE) A famous Roman general who married Cleopatra and went to war against Rome

Marcella* *Referenced only* A Christian widow who adopted asceticism; her palatial home on the Aventine became a focal point of Christian charity and pursuits; she opposed heretics and was a respected Bible scholar who was careful to defer to male scriptural authority

Marcus A weapons and armor purveyor

Marcus Aurelius* *Referenced only* (died 180 CE) A Roman emperor and Stoic philosopher; author of *Meditations*

Marcus Furius Camillus* *Referenced only* (died c. 365 BCE) A Roman statesman and officer who purportedly saved Rome when it was sacked by the Gauls in the 4th century BCE

Maria* *Referenced only* The elder daughter of Stilicho and Serena; wife of Honorius

Memmius Symmachus* A Roman nobleman; son of Symmachus

Nero* *Referenced only* (committed suicide 68 CE) The last Roman emperor of the Julio-Claudian dynasty

Nicomachus* Virius Nicomachus, the elder; a Roman senator; his son, also named Nicomachus

Occia* *Referenced only* (died 19 CE) A Vestal Virgin / Vestalis Maxima during the late republic and early empire who served the Order for over 50 years. (This priestess is the central character in my book trilogy *The Vesta Shadows: Brides of Rome (book 1), To Be Wolves (book 2), Empire of Iron (book 3)*).

Octavian* *Referenced only* (Gaius Octavius) The birth name of Rome's first emperor, Augustus

Olympius* A Roman senator and aristocrat

Oracio A stableman on the Esquiline Hill

Ovid* *Referenced only* (died c. 18 CE) A celebrated Roman poet who lived during the time of Augustus, and who wrote the *Metamorphoses*. He also wrote love poetry.

Paulina* Aconia Fabia Paulina; Roman aristocrat and priestess; wife of Praetextatus

Penelope A housekeeper on the Esquiline Hill; niece of Ptolema

Perses* A Roman senator; husband of Helena; father of Anthea

Peter* *Referenced only* An apostle of Jesus Christ and an important leader in the early church

Phobos A celebrity gladiator

Pliny* *Referenced only* (died 79 CE in Stabiae when Mount Vesuvius erupted) Pliny the Elder; Roman author and naval commander; author of the encyclopedic work *Naturalis Historia* (Natural History)

Pompeianus* A Roman senator

Praetextatus* Vettius Agorius Praetextatus; a Roman senator and priest; husband of Paulina

Primigenia* *Referenced only* A Vestal Virgin from Bovillae who left the Order to follow a lover

Prisca A Roman noblewoman on the Caelian Hill; kinswoman to Antonia

Priscus* *Referenced only* A famous gladiator

Proculeia A Vestal Virgin

Ptolema A slave in the House of the Vestals

Publius Mallius A guard at the luxury resort in Baiae

Richomeres* *Referenced only* An officer of Frankish origin in the army of Theodosius

Rufinia A Vestal novice; Vestal Virgin

Sarus* A soldier under the command of Stilicho

Scipio Africanus* *Referenced only* (died 183 BCE) A Roman general who defeated the Carthaginian general Hannibal

Septimius Severus* *Referenced only* (died 211 CE) A Roman emperor; founder of the Severan a.k.a. Septimian dynasty

Serena* A niece of Theodosius; wife of Stilicho

Sergia A Vestal novice; Vestal Virgin

Siricius* A bishop of Rome

Sister Marcia The head of a Christian women's monastery

Statius The high priest of Jupiter

Stilicho* Flavius Stilicho; Roman general

Suetonius* *Referenced only* (died c. 122 CE) Roman historian and author of *The Twelve Caesars*, a compendium of the biographies of twelve Caesars, from Julius Caesar to Domitian

Sulla* *Referenced only* (died 78 BCE) A Roman general and politician

Symmachus* Quintus Aurelius Symmachus; a celebrated Roman statesman and senator; Pontifex Maximus

Teo A guard of Coelia Concordia

Terentia A Vestal Virgin

Tertia A Vestal novice

Theodosius* A Roman emperor who, in 380 CE, made Nicene Christianity the official religion of the Roman Empire (via the Edict of Thessalonica), branding other faiths "heresy" and authorizing their punishment

Thermantia* *Referenced only* The younger daughter of Stilicho and Serena

Tiberius Caesar* *Referenced only* (died 37 CE) The second emperor of Rome; adopted heir of Augustus

Titus* *Referenced only* (died 81 CE) A Roman emperor; a son of Vespasian

Trajan* *Referenced only* (died 117 CE) A Roman emperor; considered one of the "good emperors" of the Nerva-Antonine dynasty. He oversaw many building projects and supported social care programs in Rome. An accomplished soldier and statesman, it was during his rule that the Roman Empire reached its largest size.

Uros An assassin

Valentinian* A Roman emperor

Valerius A soldier under the command of Stilicho

Vercingetorix* *Referenced only* (executed by Julius Caesar in 46 BCE) A Gallic king who fought against Rome

Verus* *Referenced only* A famous gladiator

Vespasian* *Referenced only* (died 79 CE) A Roman emperor; founder of the Flavian dynasty; credited with building the Flavian amphitheater (the Colosseum)

Victor* A son of Magnus Maximus; a Roman emperor

Virgil* *Referenced only* (19 BCE) A celebrated poet in the time of Augustus; author of the epic *Aeneid*

GODS, GODDESS AND BEINGS OF LEGEND OR MYTH

Achilles A great Greek warrior and hero of the Trojan War; central figure in Homer's *Iliad*

Aeneas A Trojan prince and hero who escaped burning Troy; ancestor of Rome's founder, Romulus

Ajax A great Greek warrior who fought in the Trojan War

Altar of Victory An altar with a golden statue of the goddess Victory; established in the Roman Senate House by Octavian in 29 BCE after his victory over Marc Antony and Cleopatra

Apollo The Greek and Roman god of several forces, including the sun, the arts, prophecy and healing

Ascanius The son of Aeneas; founder of Alba Longa

Asclepius The Greco-Roman god of medicine

Athena The Greek goddess of wisdom and war; her Roman equivalent is Minerva

Bacchus The Roman god of wine; his Greek equivalent is Dionysus

Bona Dea A Roman goddess associated with fertility, healing and protection

Castor One of the Dioscuri a.k.a. Gemini; twin brother of Pollux; celebrated for great horsemanship

Cerberus The three-headed hound that guards the entrance to Hades / the underworld

Ceres The Roman goddess of grain; her Greek equivalent is Demeter

Cetus A giant sea monster

Charon The "ferryman" of the underworld who carries the souls of the deceased across the river Styx, to the land of the dead

Charybdis A giant sea monster that, along with Scylla, endangers the lives of sailors trying to pass through a narrow strait of water

Concordia The Roman goddess of harmony and agreement

Consus A Roman god, possibly of Sabine origin, who protected the health of grain and crops

Cumaean Sibyl A prophetess and priestess who lived in the city of Cumae; she sold the Sibylline Books to the last king of Rome

Cupid The son of Venus; god of desire and attraction; his Greek equivalent is Eros

Cyclopes Giant one-eyed creatures from Homer's *Odyssey*

Diana The Roman goddess of wildlife, nature and the hunt; her Greek equivalent is Artemis

Dioscuri Twin brothers who assisted shipwrecked sailors; known for great horsemanship; a.k.a. the Gemini

Fates Three sisters who represented destiny or the "thread of life." They were responsible for ensuring humans, and all beings, fulfilled the destinies assigned to them. Their names were *Nona* (Greek *Clotho)* who spun the thread of life, *Decima* (Greek *Lachesis*) who measured its length, and *Morta* (Greek *Atropos*) who cut the thread. As powerful as the gods (more powerful in some traditions), they also enforced the destiny of deities. Their decisions were usually final, although Jupiter / Zeus as the king of the gods—and their father—could sometimes appeal to them. The Fates are also called the Parcae, and in Greek, the Moirai.

Fortuna The Roman goddess of luck and fortune

Furies Greco-Roman goddesses concerned with exacting revenge on the guilty

Hades The underworld; also the name of the Greek god of the underworld; the Greek equivalent of Pluto

Harpocrates A god of confidentiality

Hector A Trojan prince and great warrior in Homer's *Iliad*

Hecuba The queen of Troy; wife of King Priam

Hercules A demigod hero with great strength; famous for adventures and his twelve labors; known as Heracles in Greek

Hestia Greek equivalent of Vesta; goddess of the home and the hearthfire; one of the twelve Olympian gods

Hygieia A goddess of health, healing and hygiene

Io A Greek princess and mortal lover of Zeus who was turned into a heifer

Isis A central and very ancient Egyptian goddess; a divine mother

Janus Roman god of new beginnings, doorways and transitions; depicted with two faces, one looking back and one looking forward

Juno Roman queen of the gods; goddess of the state and women; wife of Jupiter; her Greek equivalent is Hera

Jupiter Roman king of the gods; god of the sky and thunder; most important god in the Roman pantheon; also called Jove; his Greek equivalent is Zeus

Juturna Roman goddess of fountains and healing waters

Luna Roman goddess of the moon

Lupa The she-wolf that nursed the twin infant sons of Mars and Rhea Silvia—Romulus and Remus—after finding them floating in a basket along the Tiber River

Magna Mater The "great mother" goddess; her Greek equivalent is Cybele; associated with the Sibylline Oracle

Mars Roman god of war; divine father of Romulus and Remus, with Rhea Silvia; his Greek equivalent is Ares

Mercury Roman god of messages, finances and travel; his Greek equivalent is Hermes

Minerva Roman goddess of wisdom and war; her Greek equivalent is Athena

Mithras A Roman god first appearing in the 1st century CE; a very popular but mysterious pagan religion associated with underground worship and the cosmos

Nemean Lion A giant lion with impenetrable golden skin; slain by Hercules as one of his twelve labors

Neptune Roman god of the sea; creator of the horse; his Greek equivalent is Poseidon

Numa The second king of Rome (after Romulus) who is credited with formalizing many of the Roman priesthoods

Nymphs Female spirits that inhabit natural places (e.g. bodies of water, meadows, trees)

Odysseus The hero of Homer's epic poem, the *Odyssey*; Greek king of Ithica who spent ten years trying to return home after the Trojan War

Orbona A Roman guardian goddess of children

Ops The Roman "goddess of plenty," associated with crops and abundance, and likely of Sabine origin; mother (with Saturn) of Vesta, Jupiter, Juno, Ceres, Neptune, and Pluto; her Greek equivalent is Rhea

Panacea A Greek goddess of healing remedies

Paris A Trojan prince whose love affair with the beautiful Helen of Sparta sparked the Trojan War

Pegasus A beautiful white stallion with wings

Penelope Queen of Ithica and wife of Odysseus

Pertunda The Roman goddess of the act of sex

Philoctetes A Greek hero of the Trojan War, celebrated for his archery skills

Pluto Roman god of the underworld; his Greek counterpart is Hades

Pollux One of the Dioscuri a.k.a. Gemini; twin brother of Castor; celebrated for great horsemanship

Priam The king of Troy; killed by the son of Achilles during the sack of Troy

Prometheus A Titan (pre-Olympian god) who gifted fire to humanity; the god who created humanity out of clay

Proserpina Roman goddess of spring and the underworld; daughter of Ceres; wife of Pluto (the Greek Hades); her Greek equivalent is Persephone

Quirinus A god of the Roman state; the god that Romulus becomes after he dies and ascends to the heavens; one of the three gods in the ancient Capitoline Triad (along with Mars and Jupiter)

Remus One of the twin sons of the Vestal priestess Rhea Silvia and the war god Mars; brother of Rome's founder, Romulus; slain by Romulus

Rhea Silvia A princess in the Silvian dynasty (founded by Ascanius) of Alba Longa; priestess of Vesta; mother of the twins Romulus and Remus, who were fathered by the war god Mars. (Rhea Silvia is the central character in my novel *Rhea Silvia*, which is book 1 in *The First Vestals of Rome* trilogy.)

River Styx A river in the underworld that separates the world of the living from the world of the dead

Roma A great female goddess who personified the city and state of Rome

Romulus The founder of Rome; one of the twin sons of the Vestal priestess Rhea Silvia and the war god Mars; twin brother of Remus

Saturn Roman god of time, generations, prosperity and liberation; father (with Ops) of Vesta, Jupiter, Juno, Ceres, Neptune, and Pluto; his Greek equivalent is Cronus

Satyr Greek mythical creatures known for their wild passions; they often had goat-like features; similar to the Roman faun

Scylla A frightening monster that, along with Charybdis, endangers the lives of sailors trying to pass through a narrow strait of water

Shades The spirit of a deceased person

Sibyl The name of an oracle or prophetess; famous sibyls include the Delphic Sibyl, precursor of the Pythia (the Oracles of Delphi) and the Cumaean Sibyl (who sold the Sibylline books to the last king of Rome)

Silvian kings The kings of Alba Longa who comprised the Silvian dynasty; descendants of Ascanius (son of Aeneas). It is this dynasty that Rhea Silvia, and her twin sons Romulus and Remus, belonged to.

Sirens Female mermaid-like creatures with beautiful voices, famous for tempting Odysseus and his shipmates

Sol The Roman god of the sun; his Greek equivalent is Helios

Triton A Greek god of the sea; son of Poseidon

Uranus Greek elemental god of the sky; husband of Gaia (Earth), with whom he fathered the Titans (who preceded the twelve Olympian gods)

Venti Roman gods of the four winds (north, south, east and west)

Venus The Roman goddess of love and beauty; her Greek equivalent is Aphrodite

Vesta The Roman goddess of the home and (domestic and state) hearthfire; symbolized by an eternal fire; her Greek equivalent is Hestia

Victory The Roman winged goddess of victory; her Greek equivalent is Nike

Vulcan Roman god of fire and the forge; the inventor of metalworking; his Greek equivalent is Hephaestus

Zagreus The divine son of Hades and Persephone

GLOSSARY OF OTHER TERMS AND PLACES

Abi! Get lost!

Ad nauseam To the point of nausea; reference to something that has been done or repeated so often as to make one ill

Adiuva me, obsecro! Help me, I beg you!

Aedes Vestae The dwelling of Vesta—that is, the temple or sanctuary of Vesta

Ager Vaticanus The ancient Vatican field, perhaps first associated with an Etruscan settlement called Vaticum; ancient burial site of Romans

Agrigento An ancient and important city of Greek origin in modern-day Sicily; location of various grand temples to the gods

Alba Longa An ancient city, located southeast of Rome, founded by Ascanius (son of Aeneas); the mother city of Rome; birthplace of Rhea Silvia and her twin sons (by Mars) Romulus and Remus. There was an active Vestal Order in Alba Longa (inscriptions include VIRGINES VESTALES ALBANAE) that likely moved to the town of Bovillae after the destruction of Alba Longa.

Amphitheater Originally referred to as the Flavian Amphitheater (it was the Flavian emperors who built it), this is today's famous Colosseum. The name "colosseum" comes from the Latin *colossus,* in reference to the colossal statue of Nero, and later Sol, that stood nearby.

Amphora (plural *amphorae)* Storage jars, generally with a neck that is narrower than the body; some were finely painted

Annales Latin epic poem (only fragments survive) covering the early history of Rome, written by the Roman poet Ennius

Aqua Marcia One of various aqueducts that supplied fresh water to Rome

Aquila The Eagle; the symbol of Rome

Ara Pacis (*Augustae*) Altar of Augustan Peace; commissioned by the Senate to honor Augustus; the Vestal Virgins are depicted on this monument

Arbor felix An oak tree on the Capitoline believed to be sacred to Jupiter

Asses (singular *as*) A standard low-value Roman coin, originally bronze and later copper

Attat! A Latin expression of wonder, fear or surprise

Augur A special priest who looks for signs from the gods via the flight of birds or other sky events (e.g. lightning strikes)

Auguraculum An open-sky *templum* (temple) on the Capitoline Hill (specifically, on the Arx) where augurs practiced augury

Augusta Treverorum The City of Augustus in the Land of the Treveri; modern day Trier, Germany

Augustus The name of Rome's first emperor; also a title used by subsequent emperors

Ave A word of greeting or farewell; the "hail" in "Hail, Caesar!"

Aventine Hill One of the Seven Hills of Rome; this is the hill that Remus preferred to the Palatine when he and Romulus were debating where to found their city

Baiae Famous luxury resort town in ancient Rome; located south of Rome, on the bay of Naples

Balteus A belt worn by a legionary soldier, from which he could carry a sword

Basilica Aemelia Large civic basilica in the Roman Forum, near the Senate House

Basilica Julia Large basilica in the Roman Forum, opposite the Basilica Aemelia, used for official business

Basilica of Constantine A basilica in the Roman Forum, sometimes called the Basilica Nova, but most commonly called by its original name, the Basilica of Maxentius

Bene vale A farewell parting that means "be well" or "be healthy"

Bonam noctem Good night

Bovillae Ancient Latin town that was a colony of Alba Longa; there was a Vestal Order in Bovillae, likely moving there after the destruction of Alba Longa in the 7th century BCE

Caelian Hill One of the Seven Hills of Rome; the residents of Alba Longa were settled here after their city was destroyed by Rome

Caesar Julius Caesar; also a title used by later emperors

Campus Martius The Field of Mars; a large region that held military training facilities and various important monuments including the Pantheon, the Mausoleum of Augustus and the Ara Pacis, among other religious and civic structures

Campus Sceleratus The Evil Field; location of an underground vault near the Colline Gate where Vestals convicted of breaking their vows would be interred alive

Capitoline Hill One of the Seven Hills of Rome; location of some of the most important temples and shrines in the city, including the Temple of Jupiter Optimus Maximus and the Temple of Juno; situated between the Roman Forum and the Campus Martius

Capitoline Triad The name of the three most significant deities worshipped on the Capitoline Hill—Jupiter, Juno and Minerva

Captio The ceremony or ritual where a girl was taken as a novice Vestal

Capua City to the south of Rome, in the region of Campania; a prosperous city famous for its gladiators

Caput Mundi A Latin phrase that means "head of the world"—that is, Rome

Carcer An infamous building where prisoners were kept

Carpe diem An expression meaning "seize the day," taken from the work of the Roman poet Horace

Carpentum A two-wheeled horse-drawn carriage reserved for the transport of privileged people

Caudex A common slur meaning blockhead or moron

Cave atque salva es, Sacerdos Beware and be safe, Priestess

Cella The inner part of a temple where an image or statue of the god was kept

Cerberus, ausculta! Cerberus, listen!

Circus Maximus A large outdoor stadium in ancient Rome used for chariot races, public games, gladiator matches and more

Cloaca Maxima The "great sewer" that emptied into the Tiber River

Collegium Pontificum The College of Pontiffs; a body that included the highest ranking priests of Roman religion, including the Vestal Virgins

Columbaria (singular, *columbarium*) Latin word for dovecote, a structure that houses pigeons

Comitium The original open-air assembly space of ancient Rome, created by Romulus; this is where the Senate House would eventually be built

Constantinople A "new Rome" built by Emperor Constantine on the site of the older city of Byzantium (current day Istanbul, Turkey)

Crimen incesti The charge made against a Vestal believed to have broken her vow

Cumae A prosperous city south of Rome, home of the Cumaean Sibyl

Cura ut valeas, Sacerdos Take care and be well, Priestess

Cures A town of ancient Sabine origin, located northeast of Rome; the birthplace of Rome's second king, Numa Pompilius

Curia The Senate House in the Roman Forum

Cursus publicus The "post office" service of the Roman Empire, though typically used for official purposes only

Curule chair A wooden chair in the Senate House, used by those who held the power of imperium (that is, the emperor)

Damnatio ad bestias A punishment where the condemned was killed by animals

Damnatio memoriae An act that sought to erase a person from memory, typically by removing their name from public monuments or documents, or removing their statues

Dei tibi faveant, miles May the gods favor you, soldier

Dei, date mihi vires Gods, give me strength

Dei, mihi miseremini Gods, have mercy on me

Denarius (plural *denarii*) A very common Roman silver coin worth four *sestertii*

Deponite! Set down!

Dii Consentes The twelve major deities of ancient Roman religion, comprised of six gods and six goddesses: Jupiter, Mars, Mercury, Neptune, Vulcan, Apollo, Juno, Minerva, Vesta, Ceres, Diana and Venus

Divine Augustus, fida sacerdos tua Imperii tui renovatam flammam tibi fert Divine Augustus, your faithful priestess brings to you the renewed flame of your empire

Domina / Domine The title a slave or servant would use to address their female / male owner

Domus the Latin word for house or home

Domus Augusti The House of Augustus

Domus Tiberiana The House of Tiberius

Dum spiro, spero While I breathe, I hope

Edict of Constantine (Edict of Mediolanum / Milan) An agreement made in 313 CE calling for the benevolent treatment of Christians and a policy of religious freedom for all people

Eleusinian rites The secretive rites performed in Eleusis (ancient Greece) which involved the goddesses Demeter (Roman Ceres) and Persephone (Roman Proserpina); one of the most important, respected and enduring religious rites of ancient Greece and Rome. Although little is known, the rites involved a symbolic rebirth and attested to the eternity of life. It is said that those who participated lost their fear of death.

Elysium Also known as the Elysian Fields; the afterlife; a land of eternal spring

Epulum Jovis A feast to Jupiter and the gods

Esquiline Hill One of the Seven Hills of Rome; famously home to Augustus's friend and close advisor, Maecenas, whose estate boasted elaborate gardens and other structures

Etruscan The Etruscan people lived in a region called Etruria, north of Rome (modern day Tuscany). Their ancient civilization of city-states was strikingly rich in culture, art and learning, and greatly influenced Rome, which ultimately conquered it. The famous bronze Capitoline Wolf (now located in the Capitoline Museums) is attributed to the Etruscans of the 5th century BCE.

Eum audivistis You heard him

Evil Field In Latin, the *Campus Scleratus*. This is the underground vault, near the Colline Gate, where Vestals found guilty of breaking their vows of chastity were interred alive. A convicted priestess would be made to descend a ladder into the pit, and a bit of bread and water would be lowered down to her. This is because, strictly speaking, it was a sacrilege to "kill" a priestess of Vesta. One can only imagine the horror of such a fate. Did the condemned priestess pray for rescue? Did she accept her fate? Did more empathetic priests perhaps send down poison or something that might more quickly end her suffering? We will never know. What we do know, however, is that some priestesses were falsely accused and convicted as scapegoats for the failures of others. In other cases, priestesses were likely guilty of breaking their vows. Regardless, in the long history of the Vestal Order, this severe punishment was a rarity. We must remember that many Romans knew these women since they were novice girls, and there was likely much opposition to such treatment. On top of that, a Vestal priestess lived a life of luxury and respect, and always had the option of retiring from the Order as a still youngish (mid to late 30's) wealthy woman. The risk of breaking her vows may simply not have been worth it for her (or for her potential lover, who would also face ruin and/or execution).

Ex Africa semper aliquid novi There is always something new out of Africa; an expression drawn from Pliny's *Natural History*

Exstinguite! Extinguish!

Fasces An ancient symbol of Roman authority, carried by a lictor when accompanying a magistrate or Vestal Virgin; a smooth bundle of sticks with a protruding axe blade. While the meaning of this symbol is somewhat cloudy, it may have originally reflected the authority to inflict capital punishment (via a beating with the sticks, and then beheading with the axe). Since touching a Vestal was a crime, having the Vestals accompanied by the fasces-carrying lictors may have served as a reminder to the public to keep their distance. Perhaps this symbol even reflected the primacy of supplying wood for Vesta's eternal fire.

Ficus Ruminalis An ancient fig tree located close to the area where the infant twins Romulus and Remus were found

Flamines Maiores The major priests who performed the rites of Jupiter, Mars and Quirinus

Foederatus A "barbarian" (e.g. Frank, Vandal, Visigoth) soldier who fought for Rome under treaty

Forum (specifically, the Roman Forum) The original public square of ancient Rome, located in the valley between the Palatine Hill and the Capitoline Hill. Arguably one of the most significant locations in the history of the Western world, since it is from this place that many of our laws, cultural and religious ideas, etc., sprang forth and spread.

Forum Boarium The large cattle market located by the Tiber River

Futuo An expletive, essentially meaning "fuck"

Gaul The term used by the ancient Romans to describe modern day Northern Italy, Switzerland, France, Belgium, the Netherlands and Germany

Gladius (plural *gladii*) A sword used by Roman soldiers and gladiators

Gratiae deis Thank the gods

Gratias tibi ago / Gratias ago Thank you

Hierophant A priest or priestess who brings people into the presence of the divine; one who interprets sacred mysteries

Horrea Galbae Large warehouses by the Aventine Hill that stored grain, olive oil and more

Ides The middle (the 13th or 15th) of any given month; the notorious "Ides of March" (when Julius Caesar was assassinated) is March 15th

Ignis Fire

Ignis inexstinctus The inextinguishable fire

Imperator Emperor; before that, the title given to the individual who held the legal power of imperium (sweeping military and political authority)

Imperial fora As opposed to the original Roman Forum, the Imperial fora were public squares that included the Forum of (Julius) Caesar, the Forum of Augustus, the Forum of Vespasian, the Forum of Nerva and the large Forum of Trajan

Imperium A type of authority, legally obtained, that bestowed a senator, general or other important citizen with significant powers

Impluvium A pool that captured rainwater as it fell through the open-sky atrium of a Roman house

Infula The red and white wool headband that Vestals wore under their veil

Item tibi, Sacerdos And you, Priestess

Iuppiter Jove or Jupiter

Jupiter Pater, parce mihi! Father Jupiter, spare me!

Kalends The first day of any given month

Lacus Curtius A mysterious monument—possibly a former ancient lake or abyss—in the Roman Forum, associated with various legendary stories

Lanista A gladiator trainer

Laus Vestae Praise Vesta

Lavinium A port city south of Rome where, legend has it, Aeneas landed in Italy

Lectica (plural *lecticae*) A couch-like vehicle for transport, typically only used by the elite, and carried by porters or *lecticarii*

Lecticarii (singular *lecticarius*) Porters / litter-bearers who carried important people in *lecticae*

Legionarie (*plural legionarii*) A soldier in the Roman legions

Leo est! It's a lion!

Libation A liquid offering to a god or goddess. The Vestals offered wine, oil and milk to Vesta

Libet A way to say "It is my honor"

Lictor A special official or guard that accompanied important people and that carried the fasces

Ludi Public games such as beast hunts, gladiator matches, races, typically held in the Flavian Amphitheater (the Colosseum) or the Circus Maximus

Ludus Magnus A large gladiatorial training school in Rome, located close to the amphitheater and connected via an underground tunnel

Lugdunum A Roman city in Gaul (modern day Lyon, France)

Lupa in fabula An expression meaning "The wolf in the story." If we are speaking about someone and that person suddenly shows up, they are the "wolf" in the story. This is similar to "Speak of the devil."

Magister equitum Master of the Cavalry; a commander that served a dictator or other powerful figure

Magister militum High-ranking military command used from the reign of Constantine onward

Mare nostrum Our sea: This is what the ancient Romans called the Mediterranean Sea

Mars Pater, despice et fave huic militia Father Mars, look down and favor this soldier

Mars Pater, miserere Father Mars, have mercy

Mater Mother

MCVIII AUC One thousand one hundred and eight years from the founding of the city. Before the dating practice of using BC (Before Christ) / AD (Anno Domini) or BCE (Before the Common Era) / CE (Common Era) was invented, ancient Romans indicated the year by one of two means. First, they could state who the consuls were during that year. Second, they could count the year from the founding date of Rome (753 BCE). Here, the MCVIII is the Roman numeral for 1108, while the AUC stands for Ab Urbe Condita (in Latin, this means "from the founding of the city"). So this is 1108 years from 753 BCE, which gives us the year 355 CE – the year that, in the novel, Coelia Concordia is initiated into the Vestal Order.

Me sequimini! Follow me!

Mediolanum Modern day Milan; it is from here that Constantine issued the so-called Edict of Milan which called for religious freedom for all people within the Roman Empire

Mehercule! By Hercules!

Mentula An ancient Roman way to say "dickhead" or "prick"

Meretrix Prostitute

Mithraeum A temple used by those who worshipped Mithras, sometimes a natural cave and sometimes a building resembling a cave

Mola salsa A special salted-flour mixture made by the Vestal Virgins and used in various capacities, including sacrificial rites

Murmillo A common type of gladiator who wore a helmet, arm guard, leg protection and a belt, and carried a gladius

Naturalis Historia *Natural History*. Essentially an early encyclopedia, the scope of which includes the entire natural world and life itself. It was written by Pliny the Elder (who died in 79 CE during the eruption of Vesuvius), and remains one of the most ambitious and influential works from antiquity.

Nunc et semper Now and always

O dei, cur? Oh gods, why?

Oleum ex albis ulivis est This is oil from white olives

Omnes All of them

Oracle An oracle is a priestess, or sometimes a priest, trained in receiving and interpreting prophecies / messages from the gods

Ordinem sustinete! Keep order!

Ostia The port city of ancient Rome

Palatine Hill One of the Seven Hills of Rome, and the one upon which Romulus first founded the city of Rome. It was home to the Imperial palaces and other structures, including a library and various temples. There was a shrine to Vesta that was situated close to the House of Augustus on the Palatine. From the top of the Palatine, one can look down directly onto the temple of Vesta and the House of the Vestals, a proximity that emphasized the Vestals' duty to care for the empire's hearthfire.

Palatium Magnum The great palace of Constantinople

Palla A long shawl-like piece of clothing, often very colorful and beautiful, though pure white for a Vestal Virgin. A woman could pull this over her head (e.g. to show respect when honoring the gods or when attending a formal function or location).

Palladium A wooden statue of Pallas Athena (Minerva to the Romans) that the Trojan hero Aeneas saved from the burning city; one of the greatest protective relics of Rome, entrusted to the care of the Vestal Virgins

Panis candidus An expensive type of white bread

Pantheon The word pantheon means "of all the gods," and honoring the gods was likely the original purpose of this great domed temple first imagined by Agrippa, with the large rotunda symbolizing the heavens.

Patriarchium The residence of the early bishops of Rome, located on the Caelian Hill

Papyrus A type of paper originally made in Egypt

Patella A small bowl or dish

Pater Father

Patrician The term used to denote a Roman who belonged to the aristocracy or who came from a very noble lineage

Patrona / Patrone The title a person would use to address their female / male employer; the equivalent of "boss"

Pax deorum This translates to "peace of the gods" and refers to the "pact" between the Roman people and her gods. As long as humans maintained this pact through proper worship, the gods would protect them.

Penetralia Hidden spaces where important holy items or relics were stored

Plebeian The term used to denote non-patrician Romans. Plebeians could be commoners or they could be from respected families—though not patrician families—that were quite wealthy and influential: Coelia Concordia seems to have belonged to this latter class of plebeians. A person's status as a patrician or plebeian was hereditary.

Poetovio The location, in modern day Slovenia, where the army of the (eastern) emperor Theodosius defeated the army of the (western) emperor Magnus Maximus

Pons Fabricius The Latin word *pons* means bridge, so this is the Fabrician Bridge. It extends halfway across the Tiber River, from the Campus Martius to the Tiber Island.

Pontifex Maximus The great or supreme priest in the College of Priests. It was the most powerful religious position. From the time of Augustus, it was a position held by the emperor, but this fell out of practice with the rise of the Christian emperors. The word *pontifex* is suggestive of the word *pons*, and it may be that the term originally referred to a priest acting as a bridge between mortals and the gods, due to his knowledge of the sacred rites.

Porcus tu You're a pig

Porta Praenestina An eastern gate of Rome in the Aurelian Walls

Posca A lower quality wine

Potius sero quam numquam Better late than never; a sentiment taken from Livy's *Ab Urbe Condita*

Praeneste A luxury town that rivaled Baiae. The location of a large religious complex that included a Temple of Fortuna and an oracle.

Prodigiosus Amazing

Provocator A common type of gladiator that initially resembled a soldier. He wore arm protection, a helmet with visor and a breastplate. They typically carried a shield and a gladius.

Pulchra es You look beautiful

Pulvinar The temple-like seating structure alongside the Circus Maximus from which the higher classes and important people could watch the games or races in luxury

Quirinal Hill One of the Seven Hills of Rome. Legend has it that, before it fell under the sway of Rome, it was the location of a village of Sabines who worshipped the god Quirinus.

Regia The original home of the kings of Rome, later used as the office of the Pontifex Maximus and the Religious College

Relatio A "relatio" is any motion or matter that is put before an authority, such as a Senate or an emperor. In this novel, it is used to identify the specific relatio that Symmachus and the Roman Senate put before the emperor Valentinian concerning the Altar of Victory and the funding of the Vestal Virgins. The short excerpt of the relatio included in this novel – "We see the same stars..." – was borrowed from a 1917 thesis paper and translation by one Katherine Tener Randall (University of Illinois).

Religio illicita An illegal / illegitimate religion

Res Gestae (*Divi Augusti*) Meaning "things done," this is essentially the autobiography of Augustus in which he outlines his political life, victories and benefactions. It was originally inscribed on bronze pillars on the Mausoleum of Augustus. Today, you can see it inscribed on the outside wall of the Ara Pacis Museum in Rome.

Retiarius A common type of gladiator who fought with a trident and weighted net, and wore little armor

Rostra The famous speaker's platform in the Roman Forum, so-named for the parts of conquered ships that decorated it. In addition to untold speeches, decrees and events of historical importance delivered from, or witness upon, this platform, it was from here that Marc Antony delivered his famous funeral oration for Julius Caesar.

S SAC COELIA CONCORDIA Holy Priestess Coelia Concordia

Sabines An ancient tribe of people that neighbored early Rome; they lived in the region called Sabinum

Sabine women A group of women from Sabinum who were abducted during the early years of Rome and taken as wives. When their kinsmen entered Rome to rescue them and began to battle the Romans, it was the Sabine women—now wives and mothers to Romans—who brokered a lasting peace between Rome and the Sabine people.

Sacerdos / Sacerdotes Priest or priestess / Priests or priestesses

Sacerdos virginalis tua flet, Caesar Your virgin priestess weeps, Caesar

Sacerdotem Vestalem, quae sacra faciat... ita te, Amata, capio Words taken from the rite of Captio, when the Pontifex Maximus initiated a new novice into the Vestal Order. They read along the lines of, "Thus I take you, beloved one, to be a Vestal priestess who performs the sacred rites..."

Salarian Gate A gate in the Aurelian Walls of Rome, through which Alaric and his forces invaded the city of Rome in 410 CE

Salve A greeting; hello: if spoken to more than one person, it is *Salvete*

Sancta Diana, ei miserere Holy Diana, show him mercy

Sanctum A sacred place, such as inside a temple

Seda, mulier Stay down, woman

Septa Julia A rectangular complex in the Campus Martius used for various purposes at different times (e.g. a voting place, a meeting space, a marketplace)

Seres The name the ancient Romans gave to the Chinese, whom they credited with making fine silk

Sestertius (plural *sestertii*) A large ancient Roman coin worth four *asses* (and worth less than the smaller *denarius*)

Si dea clemens est, vir melior ero If the goddess is merciful, I will be a better man

Sibylline Books The books purchased from a Cumaean Sibyl by the last king of Rome (Lucius Tarquinius Superbus c. 6th century BCE), which contained oracular guidance the Romans could consult, through the priests, during times of crisis

Sic semper tyrranis Thus always to tyrants; a sentiment expressing the desire, and inevitably, of overthrowing a tyrant or tyrannical force

Sicilia Modern day Sicily

SILVA • VIA SACRA T CONCORDIAE This is what is written on the note attached to Arbo's pigeon. It means that Silva (the name of the bird) was released from the Temple of Concordia on the Via Sacra (this refers to the temple in the city of Agrigento, not Rome).

Simpulum A ladle-like sacred implement used to offer libations to a deity

Sine missione Without mercy; a gladiator match that was fought "to the death"

SPQR *Senatus Populesque Romanus* – the Senate and the People of Rome

Stipendium castitas The stipend that Vestal Virgins received from the Roman state

Stola A traditional dress worn by married Roman women and Vestal Virgins

Stylus (plural *styli*) An ancient writing tool

Suffibulum The formal headdress / short veil of a Vestal Virgin

Taberna The Latin word for shop

Tablinum The equivalent of a home office in a Roman domus

Tabularium Located on the slope of the Capitoline Hill facing the Roman Forum, the Tabularium held the official records and many state documents of ancient Rome. The Temple of Concordia was in front of this building.

Tarpeian Rock An infamous execution site on the south side of the Capitoline Hill. It was a high cliff from which criminals were thrown to their death. It was named after the Vestal Virgin Tarpeia, who lived during the time of Romulus, and was said to have betrayed Rome by opening the gates of the city to the Sabine army. (Tarpeia is the central character in my novel *Tarpeia*, which is book 2 in *The First Vestals of Rome* trilogy.)

Te amo I love you

Temple of Jupiter *Optimus Maximus* The Temple of Jupiter "Best and Greatest" located on the Capitoline Hill

Temple of Mars *Ultor* The Temple of Mars "the Avenger" located in the Forum of Augustus

Tessera A piece of stamped clay that served as a ticket to attend the amphitheater, and which included the spectator's specific seat location within the stadium

Tiber River A river in Rome associated with great history and legend, including the founding mythology of Rome. It was on the banks of the Tiber that the infant sons of Rhea Silvia (by Mars), Romulus and Remus, were found in a basket and nursed by a she-wolf.

Tivoli An affluent town north-east of Rome which had (and still has) a Temple of Vesta. It is also the location of the emperor's Hadrian's luxury villa.

Toga virilis The traditional white toga worn by adult Roman men

Trajan's Column A freestanding column with a spiral relief that depicts Trajan's war with, and victory over, the Dacians

Triclinium The dining room in a Roman domus, typically decorated with couches (the Romans typically reclined while dining) and frescoed walls

Triumph A great ceremonial procession into Rome, typically awarded to a victorious general by the Senate. The triumph followed a traditional route and included religious and political elements, often displaying the spoils of war or even captives. Cleopatra committed suicide to spare herself the indignity of being paraded through the streets of Rome in Caesar Octavian's triumph after the battle of Actium (the battle where he and Agrippa defeated Antony and Cleopatra).

Trojan War A famous decade-long war between the Greeks and the city of Troy. It begins when Helen of Sparta engages in a love affair with Paris of Troy, compelling her husband (Menelaus, king of Sparta) and his brother (Agamemnon, king of Mycenae) to wage war with Troy—she is thus "the face that launched a thousand (war) ships." Unable to break through the walls of Troy, the war only ends when the Greek soldier Odysseus has the idea of leaving a giant wooden horse outside the gates of the city. Thinking the Greeks have left, the Trojans pull the horse inside their gates. When they do, Greek soldiers file out of its belly to burn the city to the ground, kill its men and take its women captive. As the city falls, the Trojan hero Aeneas escapes—and it is his descendant, Romulus, who ultimately founds Rome. The Trojan War is the subject, in various ways, of countless works of literature and art, including Homer's *Iliad* and the *Odyssey*, Virgil's *Aeneid* and Euripides's *The Trojan Women*.

Troy Also called Ilion. Home of the Trojans, this is a very ancient city of legend and reality. Its ruins are believed to be located near modern day Hisarlik, Turkey.

Tu! You!

Tunica A versatile piece of clothing worn by both women and men, of varying lengths (knee to ankle), quality and decoration. Simple tunicas could be worn under a toga or a dress (stola), but finer tunicas could also be worn as outer garments.

Twelve Tables The first formal laws of Rome, written in the mid-5th century BCE

Ustrinum A place where cremations were carried out via a funeral pyre

Valde vos amo I love you very much

Vale A parting sentiment; farewell; if spoken to more than one person, it is *Valvete*

Vasculum A vessel

Veii A city of Etruscan origin, located northwest of Rome

Venator A hunter

Venus Verticordia An aspect of the goddess Venus meaning "Venus, who changes hearts"

Vesta Aeterna Eternal Vesta

Vesta Felix Lucky / fortunate / happy Vesta

Vesta Mater, sacerdotis tui memento Mother Vesta, remember your priestess

Vesta Mater, tuam altissimam sacerdotem me accipe Mother Vesta, accept me as your high priestess

Vesta Mater, viam Sacerdotis Antoniae inlustra Mother Vesta, light the path of your priestess Antonia

Vesta Sancta Holy Vesta

Vestal Virgin A priestess of the goddess Vesta, tasked with keeping the eternal fire of Vesta going in the temple

Vestalia The festival that honored Vesta, held June 7th to 15th. This was the only time during the year that Roman women (other than the priestesses) could enter the sanctum to leaving offerings.

Vesuvius Mount Vesuvius is the volcano that erupted in 79 CE and destroyed the cities of Pompeii, Herculaneum and Stabiae (it was on the shore of Stabiae that Pliny the Elder met his end)

Via Appia The Appian Way, one of the most significant and celebrated roads of ancient Rome

Via Sacra The Sacred Way, the road that led from the Capitoline Hill, passed through the Roman Forum and by its various temples and structures, to the area of the amphitheater (Colosseum)

Vigiles The watchmen and firemen of ancient Rome

Vinalia An ancient Roman wine festival

Virgo te et familiam tuam custodiat May the virgin protect you and your family

Virgo Vestalis (plural *Virgo Vestales*) Vestal Virgin

(Virgo) Vestalis Maxima The "great" or high priestess of the Vestal Order

Vittae The wool ribbons that hung down over a Vestal's shoulders; part of the infula

VVM COELIA CONCORDIA Virgo Vestalis Maxima Coelia Concordia

XII scripta A Roman board game

OTHER NOVELS BY
DEBRA MAY MACLEOD

THE FIRST VESTALS OF ROME TRILOGY

Book 1: Rhea Silvia
Book 2: Tarpeia
Book 3: Amata

Set in the 8th century BCE, *The First Vestals of Rome* is an action-packed trilogy that dramatizes the sensational, often perilous lives of three legendary women who gave rise to Rome's powerful order of Vestal Virgins. All of them central to the life of Romulus, these tectonic women were fated to shape the history of the Eternal City as much as any Caesar who came after them.

THE VESTA SHADOWS TRILOGY

Book 1: Brides of Rome: A Novel of the Vestal Virgins
Book 2: To Be Wolves: A Novel of the Vestal Virgins
Book 3: Empire of Iron: A Novel of the Vestal Virgins

The Vesta Shadows trilogy spans decades, from 45 BCE to 14 CE. Amidst civil war, the fall of the Republic and the rise of the Roman Empire, Vestal priestess Pomponia Occia finds herself swept up in the intrigue, violence and bedroom politics of Rome's elite. Faced with the dangers and dilemmas that come from living inside Caesar's inner circle, Pomponia must be willing to sacrifice everything to protect the Vestal Order...